USA Today bestsell...
romance was first sti...
Roberts years ago. ...
eighteen...ish. Publish... her
days writing sizzling ... heart, a touch of
humour and snark. She is wife to Superman – or his
non-Kryptonian equivalent – and mother to the most
awesome kids ever. They live in perfect, sometimes
domestically-challenged bliss in the southern US.

Michelle Smart is a *Publishers Weekly* bestselling
author with a slight-to-severe coffee addiction. A book
worm since birth, Michelle can usually be found
hiding behind a paperback, or if it's an author she
really loves, a hardback. Michelle lives in rural
Northamptonshire in England with her husband and
two young Smarties. When not reading or pretending
to do the housework she loves nothing more than
creating worlds of her own. Preferably with lots of
coffee on tap. Visit michelle-smart.com

Melanie Milburne read her first Mills & Boon at age
seventeen in between studying for her final exams.
After completing a Masters Degree in Education she
decided to write a novel and thus her career as a
romance author was born. Melanie is an ambassador
for the Australian Childhood Foundation and is a keen
dog lover and trainer and enjoys long walks in the
Tasmanian bush. In 2015 Melanie won the HOLT
Medallion, a prestigious award honouring outstanding
literary talent.

Enemies to Lovers

Enemies to Lovers:
Love, Honour and Betray

NAIMA SIMONE

MICHELLE SMART

MELANIE MILBURNE

MILLS & BOON

First Published in Great Britain 2022
By Mills & Boon, an imprint of HarperCollins*Publishers,* Ltd
1 London Bridge Street, London, SE1 9GF

www.harpercollins.co.uk

HarperCollins*Publishers*
1st Floor, Watermarque Building,
Ringsend Road, Dublin 4, Ireland

ENEMIES TO LOVERS: LOVE, HONOUR AND BETRAY © Harlequin
Enterprises ULC.

Black Tie Billionaire © 2019 Naima Simone
A Bride at His Bidding © 2018 Michelle Smart
Engaged to Her Ravensdale Enemy © 2016 Melanie Milburne

ISBN: 978-0-263-30488-6

MIX
Paper from
responsible sources
FSC™ C007454

This book is produced from independently certified FSC™ paper
to ensure responsible forest management.

For more information visit: www.harpercollins.co.uk/green

Printed and Bound in Spain using 100% Renewable electricity at
CPI Black Print, Barcelona

BLACK TIE BILLIONAIRE

NAIMA SIMONE

To Gary. 143.

One

She was beautiful.

Gideon Knight tuned out the man speaking to him as he studied the petite woman weaving a path through the crowded ballroom. Even wearing the white shirt, black bow tie and dark pants of the waitstaff, she stood out like the brightest jewel among the hundreds of guests at the Du Sable City Gala, the annual event of the Chicago social season, rendering those around her to mere cubic zirconia.

How was it that only *he* noticed the elegant length of her neck, the straight line of her back that tapered at the waist and flowed out in a gentle, sensual swell of hips? How did the other people in the room not ogle the particular way the light from the crystal chandeliers hit her bronze skin, causing it to gleam? How did they not stop and study the graceful stride that wouldn't have been out of place on the most exclusive catwalk?

Had he said beautiful? He meant exquisite.

And he hadn't even seen her face.

Yet.

"Excuse me." Gideon abruptly interrupted the prattling of the older gentleman, not bothering with a polite explanation for walking away.

The other man's surprised sputtering should've dredged up a semblance of regret, especially since Gideon's mother had hammered better manners into him. But just ten years ago this gentleman wouldn't have deigned to acknowledge Gideon's existence. Then he'd been just another penniless, dream-filled, University of Chicago business student. He hadn't been *the* Gideon Knight, cofounder and CEO of KayCee Corp, one of the hottest and most successful start-up companies to hit the market in the last five years. Now that he was a multibillionaire, this businessman, and people of his tax bracket and social sphere, damn near scraped their chins on the floor with all the bowing and kowtowing they directed Gideon's way.

Money and power had that peculiar effect.

Usually, he could dredge up more patience, but he despised events like this high society benefit gala. One thing he'd learned in his grueling battle to breach the inner sanctum zealously guarded by the obscenely wealthy one percent was that a good portion of business deals were landed at dinner tables, country club golf courses and social events like the Du Sable City Gala. So even though attending ranked only slightly higher than shopping with his sister or vacationing in one of Dante's nine levels of hell, he attended.

But for the first time that he could remember, he was distracted from networking. And again, for the first time, he welcomed the disruption.

He wound his way through the tuxedoed and gowned throng, pretending not to hear when his name was called, and uttering a "Pardon me" when more persistent individuals tried to halt him with a touch to his arm. Many articles written about him had mentioned his laser-sharp focus, and at this moment, it was trained on a certain server with black hair swept into a low knot at the back of her head, a body created for the sweetest sin and skin that had his fingertips itching with the need to touch…to caress.

That need—the unprecedented urgency of it—should've been a warning to proceed with caution. And if he'd paused, he might've analyzed why the impulse to approach her, to look into her face, raked at him like a tiger's sharp claws. He might've retreated, or placed distance between him and her. Discipline, control, focus—they were the daily refrains of his life, the blocks upon which he'd built his business, his success. That this unknown woman already threatened all three by just being in the room… Not even his ex-fiancée had stirred this kind of attraction in him. Which only underscored why he should walk away. It boded nothing good.

Yet he followed her with the determination of a predator stalking its unsuspecting prey.

How cliché, but damn, how true. Because every instinct in him growled to capture, cover, take…bite.

She would be his tonight.

As the strength and certainty of the thought echoed inside him, he neared her. Close enough to glimpse the delicate line of her jaw and the vulnerable nape of her neck. To inhale the heady, sensual musk that contained notes of roses, and warmer hints of cedarwood and amber…or maybe almond.

Tonight's mission would be to discover which one.

For yet another time this evening, he murmured, "Excuse me." But in this instance, he wasn't trying to escape someone. No, he wanted to snare her. Keep her.

At least for the next few hours.

Look at me. Turn around and look at me.

The plea rebounded off his skull, and the seconds seemed to slow as she shifted, lifting her head and meeting his gaze.

His gut clenched, desire slamming into him so hard he braced himself against the impact. But it still left him reeling. Left his body tense, hard.

A long fringe of black hair swept over her forehead and dark-rimmed glasses perched on her nose, but neither could hide the strong, regal lines of her face, the sharp cheekbones, the chocolate eyes or the lush siren's call of her mouth.

Damn, that mouth.

He dragged his fascinated gaze away from it with a strength that deserved a gold medal. But nothing, not even God Himself, could cleanse his mind of the acts those curves elicited. Acts that left him throbbing and greedy.

"Did you need a glass of champagne?" she asked, lowering her eyes to the tray she held.

No, keep your eyes on me.

The order rolled up his throat and hovered on his tongue, but he locked it down. Damn, with just a few words uttered in a silk-and-midnight voice, he'd devolved into a caveman.

Once more, a warning to walk away clanged inside him, but—like moments earlier—he ignored it. Nothing else mattered at the moment. Nothing but having that sex-and-sin voice stroke his ears. Having those hands slip under his clothes to caress his skin. And those oval-shaped eyes fixed on him.

"What's your name?" He delivered a question of his own, answering hers by picking up a glass flute full of pale wine.

If he hadn't been studying her so closely, he might've missed the slight stiffening of her shoulders, the minute hesitation before, head still bowed, she said, "I need to continue…"

She shifted away from him, preparing to escape into the crowd.

"Wait." He lifted his arm, instinct guiding him to grasp her elbow to prevent her departure. But at the last moment, he lowered his arm back to his side.

As much as he wanted to discover how she felt under his hand, he refused to touch her without her permission. Rich assholes accosting the waitstaff was as old a story as a boss chasing his secretary around the desk. Even though his palm itched with the lack of contact, he slid his free hand into his front pocket.

The aborted motion seemed to grab her attention. She raised her head, a frown drawing her eyebrows together.

"Gideon Knight," he said, offering her his name. "You have my name. Can I have yours?"

Again, that beat of hesitation. Then, with a small shake of her head, she murmured, "Camille."

"Camille," he repeated, savoring it as if it were one of the rich chocolate desserts that would follow the dinner course. "It's a lovely name. And it fits you."

Her eyes widened, an emotion he would've labeled panic flaring in their depths before she lowered her lashes, hiding her gaze from him. Again. "Thank you, Mr. Knight. If—"

"Gideon," he corrected. "For you, it's Gideon."

Her full lips firmed into a line seconds before she met his stare with one glinting in anger. How insane did it make him that he found the signs of her temper captivating...and sexy as hell?

"No offense, *Mr. Knight*—"

"In my experience, when someone starts a sentence with 'no offense,' they intend to offend," he drawled.

Once more he saw that flicker of anger, and an exhilaration that was usually reserved for fierce business negotiations surged in his chest. The exhilaration meant he was engaging with a worthy opponent.

"I'm going out on a limb and assuming your ego can take the hit," she shot back. Then, as if she realized what she'd snapped—and who she'd snapped at—she winced, briefly squeezing her eyes shut. "I apologize—"

"Oh, don't disappoint me now by turning meek, Camille," he purred, arching an eyebrow.

In a distant corner of his mind, he marveled at who he'd become in this moment. Flirting, teasing, god-damn *purring*—they weren't him. His mouth either didn't know this information or didn't care. "I assure you, I can take it," he added.

Take whatever she wanted to give him, whether it was her gaze, her conversation or more. And God, he hungered for the *more*. Greedy bastard that he was, he'd claim whatever she chose to dole out.

"Mr. Knight," she began, defiance clipping his name, "I don't know if approaching the staff and toying with them is one of your usual forms of entertainment. But since you've invited me not to be *meek*, let me tell you this might be a game to you, but the wait-staff aren't toys to alleviate your boredom. This is a livelihood for workers who depend on a paycheck and not getting fired for fraternizing with the guests."

Shock vibrated through him like a plucked chord on his favorite Martin D-45 acoustic guitar.

Shock and…delight.

Other than his mother and family, no one had the balls to speak to him like she had, much less reprimand him. Excitement—something he hadn't experienced in so long he couldn't remember the last occurrence—tripped and stumbled down his spine.

"I don't play games," he said. "They're a waste of

time. Why be coy when being honest achieves the goal faster?"

"And what's your goal here, Mr. Knight?" she challenged, not hiding her sneer.

If she understood how his pulse jumped and his body throbbed every time she stated "Mr. Knight" with a haughtiness worthy of royalty, she would probably swear a vow of silence.

"Cop a feel in a dark hallway? A little slap and tickle in a broom closet?" she asked.

"I'm too old to cop a feel. And I don't 'slap and tickle' either, whatever that is. I fuck."

Her head jerked back at his blunt statement, her eyes widening behind the dark frames. Even with the din of chatter and laughter flowing around them, he caught her sharp gasp.

A voice sounding suspiciously like that of Gray Chandler, his business partner and best friend—his only friend—hissed a curse at him. How many times had Gray warned him to temper his brusque, straightforward manner? Well, to be more accurate, his friend described Gideon as tactless. Pretty words weren't his forte; honesty was. Normally, he didn't regret his abruptness. Like he'd told her, he didn't indulge in games. But in this moment, he almost regretted it.

Especially if she walked away from him.

"Is that why you stopped me? To proposition me?" She dropped her gaze to the champagne glass in his hand, and with just that glance let him know she didn't buy his pretense of wanting the wine. He shrugged, setting it behind him on one of the high tables scattered around the ballroom.

"Why single me out?" she continued. "Because I'm so beautiful you couldn't help yourself?" she mocked. "Or because I'm a server, and you're a guest in a position of power? What happens if I say no? Will I suddenly find myself relieved of my job?"

Disgust and the first flicker of anger wormed its way through his veins. "Do I want to spend a night with you? Inside you? Yes," he stated, and again her eyes flared wide at his frankness before narrowing. "I told you, I don't lie. I don't play games. But if you decline, then no, you would still have a check and employment at the end of the evening. I don't need to blackmail women into my bed, Camille. Besides, a willing woman, a woman who wants my hands on her body, who pleads for what she knows I can give her, is far more arousing, more pleasurable. And any man worth his dick would value that over a woman who's coerced or forced into handing over something that should be offered or surrendered of her own free will."

She silently studied him, the fire fading from her stare, but something else flicked in those dark eyes. And that "something" had him easing a step closer, yet stopping short of invading her personal space.

"To answer your other question," he murmured. "Why did I single you out? Your first guess was correct. Because you are so beautiful I couldn't help following you around this over-the-top ballroom filled with people who possess more money than sense. The women here can't outshine you. They're like peacocks, spreading their plumage, desperate to be noticed, and here you are among them, like the moon. Bright, alone, above it all and eclipsing every one of them. What I don't understand is how no one else noticed before me. Why every man in this place isn't standing behind me in a line just for the chance to be near you."

Silence swelled around them like a bubble, muting the din of the gala. His words seemed to echo in the cocoon, and he marveled at them. Hadn't he sworn he didn't do pretty words? Yet it had been him talking about peacocks and moons.

What was she doing to him?

Even as the question echoed in his mind, her head tilted back and she stared at him, her lovely eyes darker…hotter. In that moment, he'd stand under a damn balcony and serenade her if she continued looking at him like that. He curled his fingers into his palm, reminding himself with the pain that he couldn't touch her. Still, the only sound that reached his ears was the quick, soft pants breaking on her pretty lips.

As ridiculous as it seemed, he swore each breath slid under his clothes, swept over his skin. He ached to have each moist puff dampen his shoulders, his chest as her fingernails twisted in his hair, dug into his muscles, clinging to him as he drove them both to the point of carnal madness.

The growl prowled up his throat and out of him before he could contain it.

"I—I need to go," she whispered, already shifting back and away from him. "I—" She didn't finish the thought, but turned and waded into the crowd, distancing herself from him.

He didn't follow; she hadn't said no, but she hadn't said yes, either. And though he'd caught the desire in her gaze—his stomach still ached from the gut punch of it—she had to come to him.

Or ask him to come for her.

Rooted where she'd left him, he tracked her movements.

Saw the moment she cleared the mass of people and strode in the direction of the double doors where more tray-bearing staff emerged and exited.

Saw when she paused, palm pressed to one of the panels.

Saw when she glanced over her shoulder in his direction.

Even across the distance of the ballroom, the electric shock of that look whipped through him, sizzled in his veins. Moments later, she disappeared from view. Didn't matter; his feet were already moving in her direction.

That glance, that look. It'd sealed her fate.

Sealed it for both of them.

Two

Shay Camille Neal pushed through the doors leading into the huge, industrial kitchen that wouldn't have been out of place in a Michelin-star restaurant. With a world-famous chef renowned for his temper as well as his magic with food, a sous chef and army of station and line cooks bustling around the stainless steel countertops and range stoves, the area hummed with activity.

Under ordinary circumstances, she would've been enthralled, attempting to soak up whatever knowledge she could from the professionals attending. But the current circumstances were as far from ordinary as chicken nuggets were from coq au vin.

First, as a member of one of the oldest, wealthiest and most influential families in Chicago, she usually attended the Du Sable City Gala as a guest, not a server.

But when her best friend, Bridgette, called her earlier in the afternoon sounding like a foghorn had replaced her voice box, Shay had agreed to take Bridgette's place as a member of the catering staff. Though her friend owned and ran a fledgling food truck business, she still helped mitigate expenses and pay her personal bills with jobs on the side. The position with this particular catering company was one of her regulars, and Bridgette couldn't afford to lose the gig.

Shay had planned on skipping the gala, anyway. Facing a night at home with another binge of *House of Cards* on Netflix versus actually working in the periphery of a famous chef, the choice had been a no-brainer. Besides, Bridgette had assured Shay that most of her duties as an assistant to the line cooks would keep her in the kitchen.

Still, she'd donned a wig, dark brown contacts and glasses, as well as Bridgette's uniform. Because while she'd decided to skip out on the social event of the season, her older brother, Trevor, and his fiancée, Madison Reus—Senator Julian Reus's only daughter—were attending. Trevor already didn't approve of Shay's friendship with Bridgette. If he caught Shay doing anything less-than-becoming of the Neal name, especially because of her best friend, he would lose it. And Shay was pretty certain he would consider prepping vegetables and serving champagne cardinal sins.

In her defense, though, when the catering supervisor shoved a tray of sparkly wine at her and ordered her to make the rounds of the ballroom, she couldn't exactly say no.

Still, everything should've been fine—would've been fine—if not for one Gideon Knight.

Smoky desire coiled in her belly. She set the almost empty tray on one of the stations and pressed a fist to her navel. Not that the futile gesture extinguished the glowing embers.

Swallowing a groan, she strode toward the back of the kitchen and the employee break room. Shutting the door behind her, she entered the bathroom and twisted the faucets, thrusting her palms under the gushing water. Her quick version of a cold shower. Shaking her head at her foolishness, she finished washing her hands, but afterward, instead of returning to the kitchen, she stood in front of the mirror, staring at her reflection. But it wasn't her image she saw.

It was Gideon Knight.

They're like peacocks, spreading their plumage, desperate to be noticed, and here you are among them, like the moon. Bright, alone, above it all and eclipsing every one of them.

She exhaled slowly, the words spoken in that all-things-secret-and-sinful voice echoing in her head. In her chest. And lower. With any other man, she would've waved off the compliment as insincere flattery that tended to roll off men's tongues when they came across the heiress to one of the largest financial management conglomerates in the country. The compliments meant nothing, like dandelion fluff on a breeze. No substance and changing with the wind.

But not with Gideon Knight.

There had been a ring of truth in the blunt observation. As if his description of her wasn't an opinion but fact. She'd just met him, but she couldn't shake the sense that he didn't dole out flowery compliments often. As he'd stated so flatly, he didn't play games.

She believed him. But it only deepened her confusion over why he'd approached her of all people. To most of the attendees in the ballroom, she'd been invisible, inconsequential. Just another staff member there to serve them.

But not to him.

Even in a room full of Chicago's wealthiest and most glamorous people, he stood out. In the way a sleek, silent shark would stand out in a pool of clown fish.

God, she was officially losing it. And she laid the blame squarely at the feet of Gideon Knight.

Because, really, how could any woman stare into those midnight eyes and not forget everything but how she could willingly drown in them, even as he submerged her in a pleasure as dark and stunning as his gaze?

As soon as the illicit thought entered her head an image of him crouched over her, all that midnight-black hair loose from its knot and flowing over his shoulders, tumbling around them, flashed through her mind. Her heart thumped against her chest, and she exhaled an unsteady breath, that flame of unwanted desire dancing low in her belly again. With a mental shove, she thrust the hot image out of her mind, but the vision of how he'd looked just moments ago, when she turned for one last glance, refused to be evicted as easily.

His tailor, whoever he or she was, must've been in love with Gideon because his tuxedo traced his powerful but lean frame. From the wide shoulders and chest that tapered to a slim waist and down to long, muscular legs, he was the picture of urbane elegance and wealth. Strength. Beauty.

Imperial.

The word leaped into her head, and though she wanted to scoff at the description, she couldn't. It fit. With the beautiful eyes, the sharp slant of cheekbones, the arrogant nose, the wide, sensual, almost cruel curve of his mouth and the rock-hard jut of his jaw, he reminded her of a long-ago king from a mysterious Asian country, standing on a wall, an unseen wind teasing his long black hair as he surveyed the land he ruled. Hard, shrewd, somehow removed from the masses.

He would've been completely intimidating if not for the incongruity of all that hair pulled into a knot at the back of his head. Someone so polished, so sophisticated, so rigid in his appearance wearing a...man bun.

It was the rebellious flouting of the unspoken, constricting rules that governed their social realm that had stirred a curiosity she couldn't erase. Even now.

You're being ridiculous.

Shaking her head, she emitted a sound of self-directed disgust and yanked a brown paper towel from the dispensary. She quickly dried her hands, tossed the now damp towel in the trash and strode from the bathroom. With at least another three hours of work ahead of her, she couldn't afford to remain hiding back here any longer. More prep work awaited her, as dinner hadn't even been served yet—

The door to the break room swung open, and she barely managed to stifle her startled gasp.

The tall, imposing figure of Gideon Knight filled the doorway.

Her heart lodged in her throat. What the hell was he doing back here? But only seconds passed before the answer whispered through her skull.

You.

Denial, swift and firm, rose within her. But it couldn't extinguish the kindling of desire and traitorous, *foolish* hope.

"What are you doing here?" she demanded, swiping her already-dry palms down the sides of her pants. And when his gaze took in the nervous gesture, she cursed herself for betraying her agitation to this man.

"Looking for you."

Excitement fluttered in her before she could smother the reaction. Crossing her arms over her chest, she frowned. Fought the instinctive urge to retreat from the intense, sexual magnetism that seemed to pour off him and vibrate in the room.

"Well, I need to return to work." She pretended to glance down at the slim, gold-faced watch on her wrist. "So, if you'll excuse me…"

An emotion crossed his face, but was there and gone before she could decipher it. Probably irritation at being told no. "I wanted to apol—"

But the rest of his explanation snapped off as the room plummeted into darkness.

Three

A cry slipped out of Shay, panic clawing at her throat.

The deep, thick dark pressed down on her chest like a weight, cutting off her breath.

What was going on? What happened? Why...?

"Camille." The sound of that calm voice carrying an undercurrent of steel snapped her out of the dizzying fall into hysteria. Hands wrapped around both her upper arms, the grip firm, steadying. His voice and his touch grounded her, although her pulse continued to thud and echo in her head like a hammer. "Easy." One of his hands slid up her arm, over her shoulder and slipped around the back of her neck. Squeezed. "Stay with me. Breathe."

She closed her eyes, as if that could block out the utter lack of light. Still, she latched on to him—his voice, his fresh yet earthy scent of wind and sandal-wood, the solid density of the forearms she'd at some point clutched. Seconds, minutes—hell, it felt like hours—passed while she focused on calming her racing heart, on breathing. And soon, the sense of being buried alive started to lift.

His hold on her arm and neck never eased.

As the initial bite of panic slowly unhinged its jaws, the weight of his touch—the security and comforting effect of it—penetrated her fear.

"—I'm sorry." Embarrassed, she heard a wobbly chuckle escape her. Belatedly, she loosened her grip on him and dropped her arms. "God, I don't... I'm not even afraid of the dark," she whispered.

"You have nothing to apologize for," he reassured her.

His hands abandoned her neck and arm, but one located and clasped her fingers. In the next instant, a pale blue glow appeared. A cell phone. The illumination barely pushed back the inky thickness surrounding them, but it highlighted his face, and relief weakened her knees. Only moments ago, she'd wanted to get as far away from him as possible. And now her eyes stung with gratefulness for his serene presence. For not being alone.

"I need to go see if I can find out what's going on. Here." Holding the cell out in front of him, he carefully guided her to the couch against the far wall. Still holding her hand, he lowered her to the cushion. "Will you be all right? I have to take my cell with me to try and either get a call or text out. I promise to return in a few minutes."

"Of course." She nodded, injecting a vein of steel into her voice. God, she was stronger than this. "I'll be fine here."

In the cell's minimal light, she caught his steady, measuring stare. "Good," he said after a few moments, returning her nod. "I'll be right back."

He disappeared, returning her to the dark. She focused on maintaining even breathing, reminding herself she hadn't been catapulted into a deep pit where terrifying, malformed things lurked, eager for the chance to take a bite out of her. She really shouldn't have watched Stephen King's *It* last night...

"Camille."

She jerked her head up, and once more that rush of relief washed over her as Gideon and his beautiful light appeared in front of her again.

"Hey," she said, unable to prevent the emotion from flooding her voice. "Were you able to find out anything?" Please let it be something fixable and short-lived, like the owner of this mansion had forgotten to pay his power bill.

"Blackout," he explained, tone grim, and her heart plummeted toward her stomach. "I wasn't able to get a call out, but I was able to send and receive a couple of texts to a contact on the police force. It's city-wide. They're advising people to remain where they are, which," he continued, his full lips flattening for a brief second, "won't be an issue with us. I overheard security speaking to the chef and his staff. The tech guru who owns this overcompensating monstrosity of a home installed a so-called cutting-edge security system. And with the blackout, it's malfunctioned. We're all locked in for the foreseeable future."

She expelled a pent-up breath, pinching the bridge of her nose. Where was Trevor? Were he and Madison okay? What about Bridgette? Sick and in the dark? More than ever, Shay cursed leaving her phone in her car. Bridgette had warned her that her supervisor frowned on the staff having cells on them, so she'd stashed hers in her glove compartment, but now...

"We're going to be fine, Camille," Gideon said, his rough silk voice dragging her away from her worried thoughts. "Most likely, the blackout will only last several hours, and hopefully the boy genius will have his system worked out by them," he finished drily.

In spite of the anxiety over her brother and friend that still inundated her, she snorted. "Boy genius?"

Gideon arched a black eyebrow. "Have you seen him? He can't be more than twenty-three. I swear, I can still smell the milk on his breath."

This time she snickered, belatedly palming her mouth to contain her amusement. "So you're what? The ripe old age of thirty? Thirty-three? And if you're here as a guest, then that means you must be at least wealthy or connected enough to have been invited. Which makes you what, Mr. Knight?" she asked, narrowing her eyes. "An idle man living off his family name and money? Or a successful businessman in his own right?"

She didn't know him, but he struck her as the latter.

There was nothing about him that screamed idle. No, the sharklike intelligence that gleamed from his dark eyes belonged to a man who forged his own path, not one satisfied with walking the one others had paved for him.

He didn't immediately reply, but treated her to another of his intense gazes. He seemed to peer beneath skin and bone to the soul. To her secrets. With effort, she didn't shirk away from his scrutiny, instead notching her chin up and meeting his eyes without flinching.

Something glinted in his gaze, and the faint light from his phone tricked her into believing it might be admiration.

"I own and run a start-up that provides privately held companies with their equity needs. I suppose you can say we've been successful."

The vague and carefully constructed answer didn't stop recognition from rocking her. Start-up? As in KayCee Corp start-up? He couldn't possibly be *the* Gideon Knight, founder of the corporation that had taken the financial world by storm five years ago? If so, he was either exceedingly modest or being cagey with information.

Because KayCee Corp had been more than "successful." The electronic platform serviced major businesses, helping them track their shares with its top-of-the-line, unrivaled software. They'd recently announced their intentions to branch out and work with companies that were rolling out their initial public offerings. Though Trevor tried to keep Shay securely ensconced in the Social Development branch of

RemingtonNeal Inc., their family business, she knew of KayCee Corp. Knew that Trevor desperately longed to acquire it.

Her wig, contacts and glasses concealed her true identity, but she still lifted her fingers to her cheek as if Gideon could see beneath the camouflage. Her throat tightened. Now would be a good time to come clean about who he sat with in the dark. But something held her back. Something, hell… She could identify it even without him searching her soul.

In that ballroom, Gideon Knight had gazed upon her with fascination, admiration…hunger. And he'd had no idea she was Shay Neal, heiress to a global financial empire. Not that she was an ugly duckling in a lake full of swans, but she bore no illusions. Her money, social status and connections were often just as much, if not more, of an allure than her appearance.

But not for him.

Even now, his dark stare roamed her face, lingering on her eyes before drifting over her cheekbones, her jaw, her mouth. Though it belied reason, she swore she could feel his gaze stroke over her skin. An illicit, mysterious, desire-stoking caress.

And here, in the isolated depths of this mansion, she wanted more.

Even if just for a little while.

The cloak of anonymity bestowed her with a gift of boldness—of freedom—she didn't ordinarily possess.

"I wonder what's going through your head right now?" he murmured, drawing her from her thoughts. "And would you honestly tell me?"

That would be a no. "Careful, Mr. Knight," she
drawled, tone dry. "You're beginning to sound a little
too Edward Cullen-ish for my comfort."

"Last time I checked, I didn't sparkle in the sunlight
or age out at eighteen years old. Although I do admit
to a little biting. And liking it."

A blast of heat barreled through her, warring with
surprise over his recognition of her *Twilight* reference.
Curling her fingers into her palms, she willed the searing desire to abate, but it continued to burn a path
along her veins.

"Still blunt, I see," she said, and no way could he
miss the hoarseness rasping her voice. "You weren't
lying when you claimed not to play games."

"Am I making you uncomfortable, Camille?" he
asked, his head cocking to the side. His eyes narrowed
on her, as if searching out the answer for himself.

She should say yes. Should order him to keep his
straight-no-chaser compliments and need-stirring
comments to himself.

Instead, she matched his head tilt. "And if I said
you were?"

"Then I'd go out there in that kitchen and drag one
of those chefs in here so you wouldn't be. Is that what
you want?"

She shook her head, the denial almost immediate.
"No," she said, although wisdom argued she should
have him invite the whole crew into this small room.
Protect her from herself. The self that couldn't help
wondering if those stark angles softened with plea-

sure. Wondering if that hard-looking mouth became more pliable.

Wondering if that icy shield of control shattered under desire's flame?

A shiver danced over her skin. Waltzed along her nerve endings.

She was the moth dancing too close to those flames.

"What do you want?" he pressed, the deep timbre of his voice dipping lower.

He didn't move, didn't inch closer to her on the couch. But God, all that intensity crowded her, rubbed over her, slipped inside her. He wasn't a coy or playful man; he grasped the wealth of possibilities that question carried. And he offered her the choice of not addressing them…or taking all of them.

A lifetime of playing by the rules slowly unraveled beneath his heated stare. His question vibrated between them, a gauntlet thrown down. A red flag waved.

"Too many things to possibly number in the space of a blackout," she finally replied. Truth. And evasion. "But I'm fine with you here with me." She paused, and with her heart tapping an unsteady rhythm against her chest, added, "Only you."

A fierce approval and satisfaction flashed like diamonds in his eyes. "Good," he said, those same emotions reflected in the one word. "Because now we don't have to share this with anyone else." Reaching down, he picked up a plate and set it on the cushion between them. A grin curved her lips at the sight of the braised lamb, roasted vegetable medley and risotto piled on the fine china.

"Now, that's lovely," he murmured, his gaze not on the dinner but on her face.

She ducked her head, wishing the strands of the wig weren't tied back in a bun so they could hide the red stain creeping up her neck and flooding her face.

"You're certainly resourceful," she said, reaching for an asparagus tip. "Or sneaky."

His soft snort echoed between them. "I've been accused of both before. And both are just words. Whatever works to achieve my goal."

"Yes, I clearly remember your goal for this evening. You didn't mince words out there earlier. I guess you've achieved your aim. Spending the night with me."

Why had she brought up that conversation? What had possessed her to remind him of his claim to be with her—*inside* her? To see that glint of hunger again? To tempt him? God, she was flirting with danger. And doing so with a rashness that bordered on recklessness.

"Do you really want to dive into that discussion right now, Camille?" The question—a tease, a taunt—set her pulse off on a rapid tattoo.

Yes.

No.

"Not on an empty stomach," she whispered, retreating. From the faint quirk of his lips—the first hint of a smile she'd glimpsed on his austere face—he caught her withdrawal. "And you wouldn't happen to be hiding a bottle of wine over there, would you?"

The quirk deepened, and her heart stuttered. Actually skipped a couple beats at the beauty of that half smile. Jesus, he would be absolutely devastating if he ever truly let go. Her fingertips itched with the urge to trace those sensual lips. To curb the need, she brought her hands to her pants, intent on rubbing them down her thighs. But stopped herself, recalling they were damp from the food she'd just eaten.

"Take this." He reached inside his jacket and offered her a small white handkerchief.

Startled, she accepted it, again struck with how perceptive he seemed to be.

"Thank you," she murmured.

For the next half hour, they dined on the pilfered food, and as stellar and flavorful as the cuisine was, it didn't steal her attention like the man across from her. He...fascinated her. And after they finished, when he asked her if she would be fine with him turning off the phone's light to conserve the battery, she okayed it without hesitation.

Though he was basically a stranger to her, he emanated safety. Comfort. As if he would release all that barely leashed mercilessness on her behalf instead of against her. Maybe that made her fanciful, too. But in the dark, she could afford it.

Perhaps the blackness affected him in a similar fashion, because he opened up to her—well, as much as someone as controlled as Gideon Knight probably did. They spoke of mundane things. Hobbies. Worst dates. The best way to spend a perfect, lazy afternoon. All so simple, but she hung on every word. Enjoyed it. Enjoyed him.

Enjoyed the lack of sight that peeled away barriers.

Reveled in the desire that thrummed just below the surface like a drum keeping time, marching them forward to…what? She didn't know. And for the first time in longer than she could remember, she didn't weigh the effect of every word, the consequence of every action on the Neal family name.

Here, with him, she was just…Camille.

"We'll never see each other again once the lights come back on," she said. And it was true. They'd never see each other as Camille and Gideon, even if they happened to cross paths in the future. Because then, she would once more be Shay Neal of the Chicago Neals. "That almost makes me…sad," she confessed, then scoffed, shaking her head, though he couldn't see the gesture. "Ridiculous, right?"

"Why?" he asked. "Honesty is never silly. It's too rare to be ridiculous."

A twinge of guilt pinged inside her chest. She was being dishonest about the most basic thing—her identity. "Because fantasies are for teenage girls, not for grown women who know better."

"And what do you believe you know, Camille?"

She turned toward him, toward the temptation of his voice. "That if not for a citywide blackout, a man like you wouldn't be with me…" She paused. "Talking."

"I don't know if I should be more offended that you're belittling me or yourself with that statement." A whisper of sound and then fingers—questing, gentle, but so damn sure—stroked across her jaw, her temple, the strangely callused tips abrading her skin. What did a man like him do to earn that hardened skin that spoke of hard labor, not crunching numbers? "Yes, I do. It annoys me more that you would demean yourself. A woman like you," he murmured. "Beautiful. Intelligent. Bold. Confident. What man wouldn't want to spend time with you? Only one too blind or stupid to see who stands right before his eyes. Read any financial blog or journal, Camille. I'm not a stupid man."

She snorted, trying to mask the flame licking at her from the inside out. Cover the yearning his words caused deep within her. "How did you manage to compliment yourself and reprimand me at the same time?"

But he ignored her attempt to inject levity into the thick, pulsing atmosphere. No, instead, he swept another caress over her skin. This time, brushing a barely there touch to the curve of her bottom lip. She trembled. And God, he had to sense it, to feel it. Because he repeated it.

"I don't date," he informed her, and the frankness of the statement caught her off guard. Almost made her forget the long fingers still cradling her jaw.

Almost.

"Excuse me?" she breathed.

"I don't date," he repeated. "I know something, too, Camille. Relationships, commitments—they're lies we tell ourselves so we can justify using each other. Sex. Need. Passion—they're honest. The body can't lie. Lust is the great equalizer regardless of social status, race or tax bracket. So no, I rescind my earlier statement. If not for this blackout, it's very possible we wouldn't have passed these last couple of hours talking. But I don't care if we were in a ballroom or a boardroom, I would've noticed you. I would've wanted you. I would've done everything in my power to convince you to trust me with your body, your pleasure."

Oh damn.

She couldn't breathe. Couldn't move. Suspended by the hunger swamping her.

"Your turn, moonbeam," he said, his hand falling away from her face. And she immediately missed his touch, that firm grasp. Because he couldn't see her, she lifted her fingers to the skin that continued to tingle. "Tell me again what you know."

Moonbeam. The endearment reminded her of their conversation in the ballroom. Her brain argued that the word had nothing to do with love or sweetness and everything to do with hunger and darkness, and yet she jolted at the coiling in her lower belly.

"I know you're telling me you haven't changed your mind about wanting to spend the night with me. Inside me," she added, on a soft, almost hushed rush of breath.

"And have you changed yours?"

From the moment you called me your moon.

The truth reverberated against her skull, but she clenched her jaw, preventing it from escaping. Her defenses had started crumbling long before he'd come looking for her.

Did this make her a cliché? He wasn't the first

man to profess he wanted her, but he was the first she longed to touch with a need that unnerved her. She'd never yearned for a man's hands on her body as much as she longed for Gideon Knight's big, elegant, long-fingered ones stroking over her breasts. Or gripping her hips, holding her steady for a deep, hot possession that had her sex spasming in anticipation...in preparation.

She exhaled a breath. Right, he still waited for her answer, and she suspected he wouldn't make a move, wouldn't feather another of those caresses over her until she gave it to him.

"Yes," she confessed, her heart thudding heavily against her rib cage.

"About what, Camille?" he pressed, relentless. "What have you decided? What do you want?"

He wasn't granting her a reprieve; he was making her say it. Making her lay herself bare.

Her sense of self-preservation launched a last-ditch effort to save her from who she'd become in the dark. Who she'd become in that ballroom. But desire crushed it, and she willingly surrendered to the irresistible lure of freedom...of him.

"You," she whispered. "I've decided on you."

She slid across the small space separating them and located his face. A soft groan rolled up her throat, and she didn't even try and trap it. Not when she curved her hand around the strong jut of his jaw, the faintest bristles of what would become a five o'clock shadow abrading her palm. Unable to stop, she stroked the pad of her thumb over the mouth she had been craving since she first noticed him.

Strong teeth sank into the flesh of her thumb, not hurting her but exerting enough pressure that she gasped. Then whimpered.

How had she gone twenty-five years without being aware that spot connected to her sex? That it would make her thighs clench on an ache so sweet, it maddened her?

Another gasp broke free of her, this one of surprise, as his fingers closed around her arms and abruptly dragged her to her feet. She swayed, but he didn't release her until she steadied. Then the sudden flare of light from his cell phone startled her again. After the dark, the pale glow seemed almost too bright. She blinked, glancing from the screen to the shadows it cast over Gideon's face.

"Why…" She waved toward the phone. "What about saving the battery?"

He shook his head, his features sharper, appearing to be hewn from flint. Except for those glittering, almost fevered eyes. *Oh wow…* Such intensity and…and greed there. It stirred her own hunger, stoking the fire inside her until she burned with it.

"I don't give a damn. I need to see you," he growled, shrugging out of his jacket and tossing it to the floor. Still controlled, but the movement carried an edge. And it thrilled her. "Take off your shirt, Camille. Show me what you've decided I can have."

With trembling fingers, she reached for the buttons of her white shirt. It required several attempts, but she managed to open it, and with his black gaze fixed on her, slipped it off. Warm air kissed her bared shoulders, the tops of her breasts and stomach.

A part of her argued that she should feel at least a modicum of modesty, and maybe Shay would. But not Camille.

As crazy as it seemed, here, with Gideon, she had become a different person. The flip side of the same coin. Normally reserved, bound by expectations and family. But now... uninhibited, free to indulge in her own selfish desires.

"Gorgeous," he rasped. "So fucking gorgeous. Come here." He beckoned.

His almost growled compliment stole more of her breath.

"Your turn," she ordered, remaining in place, although her fingers already prickled to stroke the skin and muscle hidden beneath the thin veneer of civility presented by his tuxedo. "Show me what you promised me I can take."

His fingers tightened around the edges of his shirt, and for a moment, she feared—hoped—he would just rip it off. But once more, that control reemerged, and he removed his cuff links, tossing them carelessly on top of his jacket. Then, button by button, he revealed himself to her.

She stared at the male animal before her. Miles and miles of smooth flesh stretched taut over tight muscle and tendon. Wide shoulders, a deep chest. Narrowed waist. A corrugated ladder of abs. A thin, silky line of hair started just above a shadowed navel and traveled below, disappearing into the waistband of his suit pants. And darker swirls and shapes she couldn't make out spread over the left side of his ribs, emphasizing the hint of wildness, of fierceness he couldn't quite conceal.

Perfection.

He was utter perfection.

This time, he didn't need to demand she come to him. Shay covered the distance on her own, arms already extended. With a hum of pleasure, she settled her palms on him, smoothed them up to his shoulders, pushing the shirt down his arms. Then she returned to her exploration. Scraping her nails over small, flat nipples, mapping the thin network of veins under his skin, following the path of hair that started midchest. Dragging her fingertips down the delineated ridge of muscles covering his stomach. Tracing the black lines of his tattoo, wishing she could aim more light on it so she could decipher its shape.

He stood still, letting her tour him without interference, though he fairly hummed with intensity, with barely leashed power.

"Are you finished yet?" he growled, and she tilted her head back to meet his hooded gaze, her fingers settling on the band of his pants.

"Not even close," she breathed. "Kiss me."

Someone with his extraordinary sense of restraint most likely didn't take or obey orders from anyone. But with a flash in those eyes, he gripped the bun at the back of her head and tugged. She gave only a brief thought to the security of the wig before her neck arched. The next breath she took was his.

Her groan was ragged and so needy it should've embarrassed her. Maybe it would tomorrow in the harsh light of day. But tonight, with his tongue twisting and tangling with hers, she couldn't care. Not when he tasted like everything delicious but forbidden—chocolate-flavored wine, New York cheesecake, impropriety and wickedness. Not when he nipped at her bottom lip, then sucked it, soothing and enhancing the sting before returning to devour her mouth. As if she, too, was something he knew he shouldn't have but couldn't resist.

He lifted his head, taking that lovely mouth with him, and she cried out in disappointment. But he shushed her with hard, stinging kisses to the corner of her lips, along the line of her jaw, down her chin and neck…over the tops of her breasts. In seconds, he stripped her of her bra, baring her to him. His big hands lifted, cupping her, molding her to him. To his pleasure. And hers.

She grasped his shoulders, clung to him, her ability to think, to move, to breathe a thing of the past as he lowered his head to her flesh. All she could do was stand there with increasingly wobbly knees and receive each lick, suckle and draw of those sensual lips and tongue. And enjoy them.

Unable not to touch the lure of his hair, she swept her fingers over his head, tunneling them under the knot containing the midnight strands. Eager to see him undone, she briefly wrestled with the thick locks, freeing the tie restraining them. The rough silk fell over her wrists, cool and dense, sliding through her fingers.

"Oh," she whispered, at a loss for words as the strands tumbled around his sharp cheekbones and strong jaw. They should've softened his features—should have. Instead, they only emphasized the stark planes of his face and his visceral sexuality.

"God, you're beautiful." The praise exited her mouth without her permission, but she couldn't regret the words. Not when they were the truth.

Pulling his mouth away from her breasts, he dragged a hot, wet path up her chest, her throat, until he recaptured her mouth. This kiss was hotter, wilder, as if the tether on his control had frayed, and suddenly, her one purpose was to see it snap completely.

With a small whimper, she trailed her hand over his shoulder, chest and torso, not stopping until she cupped his rigid length through his pants.

Damn. She shivered, both need and feminine anxiety tumbling in her belly and lower. He more than filled her palm. Reflexively, she squeezed his erection. God, he was so thick, hard…big.

A rumble emanated from his chest, and his larger hand covered hers, pressing her closer, clasping him tighter. His hips bucked against her palm in demand, and she gladly obeyed. Even as his mouth ravaged hers, she stroked him, loving the growl that rolled out of him. Wanting more.

Impatient, Shay attacked the clasp of his pants, jerking them open and tugging down the zipper in a haste that would later strike her as unseemly. But right now, she didn't give a damn. Nothing mattered but his bare, pulsing flesh in her hand. Touching him.

But just as she reached for him, an implacable grip circled her wrist, stilling her frantic movements.

"Not yet, moonbeam." He lifted one of her arms and placed an openmouthed kiss to the center of her palm, the resulting feeling radiating straight to her damp, quivering sex. With a quick crush of his lips to hers, he swiftly divested her of her remaining clothes and shoes, leaving her trembling and naked before him, except for the decidedly *un*sexy plain, black panties.

A burst of self-consciousness flared inside her chest, and she fought not to edge backward, away from the weak glow of the cell phone's light. But as if he'd read her intentions, Gideon cupped her hip, preempting any movement she might've made to hide.

"When a man stands before beauty like yours, there's only one position he's supposed to be in," he murmured. Slowly, he lowered himself to his knees, tipping his head back to continue to meet her gaze. "You deserve to be worshipped." He swept his lips across her stomach. "And pleasured." Another sweep, but over the top of her sex. Heat coiled tight, and her core clenched at the tantalizing caress. "Give me permission to give you that."

It might've emerged as an order, but he wouldn't continue without her go-ahead. She somehow knew that.

"Yes," she breathed, tunneling her fingers through his hair. Holding on tight.

With a deliberate pace that had her internally

screaming, he drew her underwear down her legs and helped her step free of them. Big, elegant hands brushed up her calves and thighs, and once more she wondered at the calluses adding a hint of roughness to the caress. But then she ceased thinking at all.

"Gideon," she cried out, fisting his hair, trying to pull him away or tug him closer—she didn't know. Couldn't decide. Not when pleasure unlike anything she'd ever experienced struck her with great bolts of lightning. Jesus, his lips, his tongue... They were voracious. Feasting on her, leaving no part of her unexplored, untouched. Long, luxurious swirls, decadent and wicked laps and sucks... He drove her insane with pleasure.

Just as he'd promised. Just as he'd assured her she deserved.

He spread her wider, hooking her leg over one of his wide shoulders, granting himself easier access. Like a ravenous beast, he growled against her sensitive, wet sex, and the vibration shoved her closer to the edge of release.

"You're so fucking sweet," he rasped, nuzzling her. "So fucking sweet and pure. A man could get addicted to you. But you have more to give me, don't you, baby? I'm a greedy bastard, and I want it all." He uttered the last words almost as if to himself, and with one palm molded to her behind, he dragged the other up the inside of her spread thighs.

Then he was filling her. Two fingers plunged inside her, and like a match struck to dry kindling, she sparked, flared, exploded into flames. Dimly, she caught his rough encouragement of "That's it, baby. That's it." She loosened a hand from his hair and clapped it over her lips, muffling her cries as she came against his mouth, her hips rolling and jerking.

Raw, dirty ecstasy, stripped to its barest essentials. That's who she'd become in this moment as he lapped up every evidence of her desire from her flesh, from the insides of her thighs.

"Please," she begged, weakly pushing his head away as he circled her with tender but relentless strokes. "I can't."

"That's nothing but a challenge to me, moonbeam," he rumbled, standing, his mouth damp. But when he lowered his head and took her lips in a torrid kiss that replicated how he'd just consumed her, she didn't back away from the flavor of herself on his lips and tongue. No, she opened wider to him, turned on so bright it ached.

Palming the back of her thighs, he hiked her in the air. On reflex she wound her legs around his waist. He crossed to the couch, and with each bump of her swollen, sensitive core against his stomach, that recently satiated heat flickered back to life, and she moaned with each caress.

Her back met the cushions, and Gideon towered over her, half his face cast in shadow. That obsidian gaze never left hers as he removed a thin wallet from his pants pocket and withdrew a condom. He tossed it down, next to her feet, and then she watched, enraptured, as he stripped off his clothes. Her breath snagged in her throat. *Jesus.* He'd been stunning in a perfectly tailored tuxedo. But naked, the trappings torn away, all that thick, midnight hair falling around his face and broad shoulders… He was *magnificent*. Long legs, powerful thighs… Good God, she'd felt him, but *seeing* him… Like the rest of him, his erection was proud, beautiful. Perfect.

As if of their own volition, her arms lifted, beckoning him to her. He tore open the foil square and sheathed himself then came to her, moving the cell phone to the floor next to them. His hard body covered hers, and a sigh escaped her at the contact. For a second, she couldn't smother the sense of never having felt so cherished, so protected.

"Ready, moonbeam?" he murmured, raising off her slightly. Grasping her hand in his, he brought it between their bodies. As he'd done earlier, he wrapped her fingers around his thick length. "Show me," he ordered, planting his palms on either side of her head, granting her control.

Even if she harbored the smallest seed of doubt about this illicit encounter in the dark—which she didn't—his gesture would've eradicated it. Her chest tightened, her heart thudding against her rib cage. But her hand was steady as she guided him to her entrance. Shifting her palm to his taut behind, she pushed as she lifted her hips, taking him inside. Fully. Widening her thighs, she didn't stop until he was buried within her.

She gasped, a ripple rocking her body. God, he was *everywhere*. Over her, around her, inside her. So deep inside her. The weight and length of him stretched her, burned her, and she flexed against him, her flesh struggling to accommodate the sweet invasion.

His eyes closed, and he bowed his head, pressing his forehead to hers, his breath pulsing over her lips. Tension vibrated through him, strained the muscles in his arms, stilled his large frame. Long moments later, he lifted his head, and the effort to hold back was etched onto his features.

"Gideon," she whispered, waiting until he lifted his ridiculously dense lashes to meet her eyes. "Let go."

As if those two words sliced through the last threads of his restraint, he groaned and lost it.

On the tail of another of those sexy snarls, he dragged his erection free, lighting up nerve endings like an airport runway, before snapping his hips and thrusting back inside her. Driving her breath from her lungs and a wail of pleasure from her throat.

Oh God. She wasn't going to survive this.

Pleasure inundated her as he plunged into her body. Over and over, relentlessly. He hooked an arm under her leg, tugging it higher and impossibly wider. With a choked cry, she wrapped her arms around his neck, holding on, a willing sacrifice to his possession. He rode her, wild and untethered, giving her no quarter. Not that she asked for any. She loved it. Every roll of his hips, every slap of flesh against flesh, every rake of his teeth over her shoulder.

In his arms, under his body, she transformed into a sexual creature who lived, breathed for him, for the ecstasy only he could give.

Electric pulses crackled down her back, sizzling

at the base of her spine. Every thrust intensified the sensation. When he slid a hand between them and rubbed her, an avalanche of pleasure rushed toward her, burying her, stealing her consciousness. But not before Gideon stiffened above her, his deep, tortured groan echoing in her ear, rumbling against her chest.

"Camille," he whispered, and it sounded like a benediction, a prayer.

And as she tightened her arms around him before sinking under, she foolishly wished to be his answer.

Four

Gideon frowned, reaching out to shut off his alarm. Drowsiness still clung to him, a warm lassitude weighing down his muscles, and he wanted to savor it instead of drive it away. But that damn alarm.

"Damn it," he grumbled, but instead of hitting the digital clock on his bedside table, he slapped air. No table. No clock. Hell, no bed.

He sat up, groaning at the pull of muscle in his lower back. Tunneling his fingers through his hair, he dragged it back from his face, scanning the small room with a television, a long table against the far wall, a short row of gray metal lockers and the couch he was sprawled on.

The blackout.

Camille.

As if her name released a floodgate, the memories

from the previous night poured forward. Serving Camille dinner. Talking with her. Kissing her. Being inside her. In response, his body stirred, hardening as image after image of her twisting and arching beneath him, taking him, flashed across his mind's screen like an HD movie.

He whipped around, scanning the room with new eyes, searching for any sign of her. But only his clothes and the empty dinner plates littered the floor. No Camille.

Adrenaline streaked through his veins, and he snatched his pants from the floor, dragging them on. She couldn't have gotten far. Weak morning light trickled into the room through the high window, so it still had to be pretty early. And with the house still locked down...

No, not locked down. For the first time, the low drone of the small refrigerator in the far corner reached his ears. Power had returned, which meant the blackout had ended. Still, how much of a head start could she have? He had to find her.

Just as he swept his shirt off the floor a Queen song erupted into the stifling room. It'd been this that he'd initially mistaken for his alarm, but it was his mom's special ringtone. He strode the few steps required to recover the phone from beside the couch, arching his eyebrows in surprise that it still had power.

Only 3 percent, he noted, swiping a thumb across the screen.

"Hey, Mom," he said in greeting, fastening buttons as he spoke. "I have very little battery left, so I can't talk long. But I'm okay—"

"Gideon," she said, and her solemn tone cut him off.

Anxiety and the first spike of fear speared his chest. He'd come to associate that particular note with one thing. And as she murmured, "It's Olivia," his guess proved correct.

Closing his eyes, he straightened his shoulders, bracing himself. "What happened?"

"She's in the hospital. I had to take her in last night." Her sigh echoed in his ear; the weariness and worry tore at him. "Gideon." She paused. "She saw the news about Trevor Neal's engagement."

A familiar anger awakened in his chest, stretching to life.

"I'm on my way."

Gideon exited his sister's private room on the behavioral health floor of Mercy Hospital & Medical Center, quietly shutting the door behind him.

Behavioral health. Fancy words for psychiatric ward.

Scrubbing a hand down his face, he strode through the hall to the waiting area where his mother and her parents perched on chairs. The three of them zeroed in on him as soon as he entered the small space with the connected seating and mounted television. God, it reeked of sadness and exhaustion. The same emotions etched in his mother's and grandparents' faces.

"How is she?" his mom asked, rising.

Frustration, grief and anger choked him, and for a moment he couldn't speak. Instead he gathered his mother in his arms and hugged her close. Ai Knight had been his rock—his family's rock—since his dad died when Gideon was nine years old. Though his grandparents were here now, that hadn't always been the case. When she'd married Gideon's father, they'd disowned her. As immigrants from Kaiping who'd settled in Canada in the 1960s, they'd wanted their only daughter to marry a Chinese man from the "Four Counties," not a Caucasian from Chicago. But Ai had, and after she'd moved to the US with him, she and her parents hadn't spoken for almost ten years. But since then they'd reconciled, and his grandparents had even moved to Chicago to be closer to Ai and their grandchildren. Which Gideon was thankful for, since his father had been a foster child, and so his mother's parents were the only extended family he and his sister had.

"Gideon?" his mother prompted.

Sighing, he released her. God, he hated seeing her here in this room, the gravity of her daughter's illness weighing down her delicate but strong shoulders.

"Sleeping. They have her heavily sedated at the moment," he replied. Which wasn't much of an answer.

"How long will she be here?" his grandmother inquired, stretching her arm out and clasping her daughter's hand.

"I'm not sure, Po Po," he said, using the Taishanese term for maternal grandmother. His grandfather—his gung gung—remained silent, but settled a hand on his wife's thin knee. "The doctor said definitely the next seventy-two hours. Maybe more."

They remained there, silent but connected through physical touch. After several moments, he squeezed his mom's shoulder. "Can I talk to you out in the hall?"

She nodded, following him out of the waiting

room—and out of earshot of his grandparents. They might be a tight family, but there were some things even they didn't know, and Gideon preferred to keep it that way when it came to his younger sister.

"What happened?" he demanded, softening the hard tone of his question by enfolding her hand in his.

"Since the announcement of Trevor's engagement, I've tried my best to keep her protected from the news. Even going on her computer and phone and blocking those society sites. But I knew that was only prolonging the inevitable. And last night, she found out. I heard her sobbing all the way from downstairs, Gideon," she whispered, the dark eyes she'd bequeathed to him liquid with tears. "I ran to her room and found her curled up in a ball on the floor of her bedroom, crying uncontrollably. Unable to stop. I was afraid. So I called the ambulance."

He ground his teeth together, an ache flaring along his jaw as he struggled to imprison the blistering stream of curses that would not only offend his mother but would be pointless.

Nothing he said could ease his sister's anguish. And no amount of release could extinguish his hatred toward Trevor Neal, the bastard responsible for shattering the kind, loving, fragile woman who'd given him her heart. A heart Trevor had trampled, then tossed aside like trash.

It'd been a year ago, but to Olivia, Trevor's betrayal might as well as have been yesterday. She'd kept her love affair with the CEO of RemingtonNeal, Inc. from Gideon, because he and Trevor had no love lost between them; they'd been rivals and enemies for years. Gideon had never hidden his hatred toward the other man.

Which explained why Trevor had targeted her in the first place.

He'd romanced Olivia, manipulated her into falling in love with him, making promises of a future together. Then, out of the blue, he'd cruelly dumped her. But that hadn't been the worst of it. Olivia had been pregnant with his child. Trevor hadn't cared. He'd even ordered her to get an abortion, which she'd refused. But in the end, it hadn't mattered. She'd miscarried, and the loss had sunk her into a depression that had begun to lift only a couple months ago. Seeking to protect her from any further hurt, Gideon and his mother had kept the information about the engagement to themselves.

But now this had happened.

"I'm sorry." His mother interrupted his thoughts by cupping his cheek. "I know this has to be difficult for you, too. This whole engagement thing. How're you doing?"

He covered her hand with his and then pressed a kiss to her palm before lowering it. Schooling his features, he submerged the jagged knife of pain and humiliation beneath a sheet of ice. "I'm fine, Mom. I'm not the one who needs your worry today."

She didn't immediately reply, studying him. "I'm a mother. I have enough concern to spread around evenly," she said, and amusement whispered through him. "She was your fiancée, Gideon," she pointed out, as if he didn't know. "Cheating on you was hurtful enough, but this? And with him of all people?" She shook her head. "There's no way you can possibly be 'fine.'"

"Let it go, Mom," he murmured, sliding his hands into the front pockets of his pants and slightly turning away from her incisive gaze. "I have."

Lies.

He would never forget Madison Reus's betrayal. Or forgive it. Not when the man she'd cheated with had been Trevor.

The other man had made it his mission to bring Gideon down a peg. And this latest stunt—pursuing Madison, fucking her and now marrying her— had been a direct hit. Anger at his enemy and his ex swelled within him. Both were selfish, narcissistic and uncaring of who they destroyed.

Especially Trevor.

Gideon had been unable to protect his sister from him the first time. And now she still suffered from his cruelty. It sickened Gideon that he'd failed her, despite the fact that he hadn't known until it was too late. As her older brother, the man in the family, he should've been there. Should've asked questions. Should've...

Damn it. He ruthlessly scrubbed his hands down his face.

Never again. Trevor Neal wouldn't get away unscathed this time.

He would pay. Pay for them all.

Five

Shay approached the dining room entrance, pausing just outside, preparing herself for the first meal of the day. It was breakfast; it shouldn't be an event worthy of deep-breathing techniques. But depending on her brother's mood, it could go either way—calm and pleasant or tap dancing on her last damn nerve. Sighing, she straightened her shoulders and entered.

"Good morning," she said to Trevor, pulling out her chair to his left. As soon as she lowered herself into it, Jana, their maid, appeared at her elbow and set a plate with steaming hot food in front of her. "Thank you, Jana." She smiled at the other woman.

Trevor glanced up from the tablet next to his plate. "You're running late this morning," he said in lieu of a greeting.

"A little bit of a restless night," she explained.

Several restless nights, actually. But she kept that bit of information to herself, since there was no way she could tell her brother what—or rather *who*—had been interrupting her sleep lately.

"Are you okay?" His eyes, hazel like her own, narrowed on her face. "Feeling well?"

There were moments like this, when concern shone in his gaze, that made it hard to remember the increasingly cold and callous man her brother could be. Right now, he was the caring big brother from her childhood who'd affectionately teased her, who'd spent hours watching TV with her when she'd been sick with the flu and bored. That man had started to make rarer appearances over the last few years—since their father had fallen sick and died.

"I'm fine," she replied, cutting into her vegetable omelet. "What am I running late for?"

"The office. You have a meeting with the representative from the ASPCA. You can't afford to be late for that, not with the fund-raising gala for Grace Sanctuary just a few nights away. I'm counting on you to make this a success for not just RemingtonNeal but for Mom's memory," he reminded her.

No pressure. She swallowed the retort. Barely.

While she firmly believed Trevor had created her position and department specifically for her—vice president of Social Development—she did her best for it. Yes, it was an important job—anything bettering their city and the people living there was worthy—but it wasn't her passion. And it damn sure wasn't what she'd attended college and earned a BBA and MBA to do. She'd wanted to join her brother in running RemingtonNeal, but like their controlling, domineering father, he'd shot down that idea.

Usually, Trevor took no interest in her work unless a photo op happened to be attached to it. But Grace Sanctuary belonged to their mother—it had been her pet project before she died, when Shay was eleven and Trevor sixteen. Their father had continued its legacy until he passed, and now they did. The foundation funded various shelters throughout the city, as well as paid veterinarian, adoption and fostering fees for families taking in the animals. The fund-raising gala was important, as the donations from the attendees encompassed a large portion of the budget.

Still, Shay had headed the committee for the gala the past three years, and the last thing she needed was Trevor breathing down her neck or trying to micromanage.

"Everything is going smoothly, and the benefit will be a success like it always has been," she said.

"I know it will. After all, it's in your hands," Trevor praised softly. "I'm sorry if I'm being overbearing, Shay. And if I haven't said it before, thank you. Believe me, I would be a lot more of a pain in the ass if you weren't in charge. I trust you to make this gala the best yet."

Warmth spread through her chest, and she swallowed past the lump of emotion lodged in her throat. Here was the big brother she knew and loved. The one whose approval she valued because it meant so much to her.

"Thank you," she murmured. Then, clearing her throat, she asked, "How's Madison?"

His fiancée had been joining them for breakfast more often lately. Actually, spending more time at the house, period. As if she were already preparing to be mistress of the home.

"She's fine." He picked up his napkin and dabbed at his mouth. "Just so you're aware, I gave her a key. She's dropping by later with an interior designer. There're some things she wants to change in the living and dining rooms, as I do most of my entertaining in those two places. And since she'll soon be living here..." He shrugged. "I didn't think you'd mind, so I told her to go forward with it."

Irritation twinged inside Shay's chest. As usual, Trevor didn't consult her about anything, even when it had to do with her home. Yes, Madison would soon be moving in as his wife, but it'd been Shay's home for twenty-five years. Yet it hadn't occurred to him to ask her opinion, which didn't count for much with her older brother. Again, like their father.

The irony of it always struck her. Trevor and their father had had a...complicated relationship. He'd loved and revered Daniel Shay, constantly seeking his stingy approval, while at the same time, resenting his my-way-and-there's-no-such-thing-as-a-highway attitude when it came to running his company and his family. Especially when it came to raising his only son, who would one day inherit his financial kingdom. Yet, over the years, Trevor had become the reflection of their father. And the battle inside her—the warring factions of anger at his overbearing arrogance and protective-ness for the brother she loved—continued to wage.

But, as she was discovering, it was pointless to argue with Trevor regarding anything having to do with Madison Reus. Winning the hand of a senator's daughter had been a coup for him, and he spoiled her like a princess. And like royalty, Madison accepted it as her due.

That sounded catty even in her own head. *God.* Shay winced, sipping the coffee Jana had set before her.

Doesn't make it any less true, her inner bitch whispered.

"Of course not," she said evenly.

"Good." He nodded. "What're your plans for lunch? We could meet so you can give me an update on the benefit."

She shook her head. "I can't. I'm meeting Bridgette."

Trevor's mouth thinned into a flat, grim line.

Yes, she already got that he didn't like her friend-ship with the other woman. Bridgette's mother had worked for the Neal family when they were younger. Lonely, Shay had immediately bonded with the preco-cious, funny little girl who'd wanted a friend regard-less of the difference in their families' tax brackets. Continuing that friendship had been one of Shay's very few rebellions against her father's and brother's edicts about being a Neal. She loved Bridgette like a sister, and Trevor's disapproval wouldn't make her give up her friend.

"Which reminds me," Shay continued, not giving him a chance to offer yet another opinion on her relationship with Bridgette. "I won't be able to make dinner tonight, either. I made other plans."

His gaze narrowed on her. "Dinner is with the senator, his wife and several of his friends."

"I'm aware, and I apologize for backing out at the last moment, but something came up that I can't reschedule."

She returned his stare, not offering an explanation about the "something" even though his eyes demanded one. The words actually shoved at the back of her throat, but she refused to soothe him, to cave just to keep the peace. Especially since he'd been the one to make the plans for this dinner without even checking to see if she was available. Sometimes her brother misinterpreted her silence for meekness. And sometimes she let his high-handedness go. But not when it mattered. And tonight mattered. To her.

"Shay," he murmured, leaning back in his chair, his mouth hardening even more. "I know I don't need to remind you how important the next few months are to me, to our family and, therefore, to Remington-Neal. This wedding isn't just gearing up to be the social event of next year, but it's also only months before Senator Reus's campaign kicks off. We can't afford to have anything go wrong. We're Neals, with a name and reputation above reproach. Don't do anything to taint either."

Anger at his thinly veiled admonishment surged within her, and she fought down the barrage of words blistering her throat. The same throat that constricted as the noose of the Neal name tightened, suffocating her. She'd always been the dutiful daughter, the proper socialite and, except for in her head, had done it all without complaint. But lately, the constraints were chafing, leaving her raw and irritated. In emotional pain.

Well, you haven't been that *proper.*

The same snarky voice that had taunted her about Madison mocked her again, this time following it up with a parade of vivid, explicit images of the night she'd spent with Gideon Knight. Her belly clenched, a dark swirl of desire eddying far south of her navel. Flashes of those lust-drenched hours burst in her head like fireworks across a dark July night. Gideon kneeling before her, lips glistening with the evidence of the desire he'd coaxed out of her with that same talented mouth. Gideon leaning over her, midnight hair tumbling around them, his big body moving over hers...in hers.

Gideon sleeping as she quietly dressed in the murky morning light, the sharp angles and planes of his face not softened by slumber.

Heat rushed up her chest and throat and poured into her face. She ducked her head over her plate, concealing the flush that surely stained her cheekbones.

"Shay?"

She jerked her head up, freeing herself from thoughts of Gideon. Inhaling, she refocused on their conversation. "No, I don't need to be reminded. And missing one dinner isn't going to mar the Neal name or threaten the senator's campaign," she replied. Ignoring the narrowing of his eyes, she pushed her chair back and stood. "I need to get to the office. I'll see you later."

Leaning over, she brushed a kiss across his cheek, then left the room before he could attempt to dig into her reasons for not complying with his plans. As soon as she stepped over the threshold, she heaved a sigh. The tension that seemed to be more of a common occurrence when she was with Trevor eased from her shoulders.

Shoulders that were aching from carrying the heavy burden of her brother's expectations.

Six

Shay smiled up at her server as she accepted the black folder containing the check for the meal she'd just finished. Well, a little more than a meal. Her smile widened at the warm glow of satisfaction radiating inside her chest. A business meeting with the two women who had just left the restaurant, and one that had gone extremely well.

This had been her reason for ducking out on dinner with Trevor, Madison and her family. As much as Shay's job at RemingtonNeal bored the hell out of her, she was grateful for it. Without the six-figure salary, she wouldn't be able to finance her own secret company—an investment firm that funded innovative, promising start-ups—start-ups founded by women.

Shay made it possible for women to achieve their

dreams, and with a percentage of the profits, she was able to continue growing her own business. Leida Investments—named after her mother—was hers alone, without any connection to her family. Even the incorporation documents weren't in her name. The anonymity—and the NDA she had all her clients sign—allowed her the freedom to use the degrees she'd earned without anyone trying to pigeonhole her. Yes, enduring the time she put in at her brother's company was well worth it when she could be her own boss.

If Trevor discovered her secret, he would do more than disapprove of it; he would sabotage it. As archaic as it sounded, he possessed firm ideas about her role in the family and the business. He might have created a lip service position for her at RemingtonNeal, but he intended for her to be a replica of their mother—wife, mother, philanthropist, socialite and the perfect hostess. The philanthropist part wasn't bad, but the rest of it? She mentally shuddered.

Tonight was a reminder of why she went to such measures to maintain her subterfuge. The excitement and joy that had lit Jennifer Ridland's and Marcia Brennan's faces as Shay slid an investment contract across the table had reinforced for her why her company must continue to thrive without any interference from her brother. The two women could revolutionize the travel industry, and she wanted to be the one who helped them do it.

Oh yes, this was well worth missing out on Trevor's dinner.

"Good evening, Ms. Neal. Do you mind if I join you?"

That voice. Shock blasted through her, and under it wound a current of something darker, sultrier. Her voice and breath crowded into her throat like an angry mob, strangling her for a long, panicked moment.

Even when Gideon Knight slid into the chair across from her, she remained speechless, frozen. It was as if her thoughts of him earlier that morning had conjured him. The bottomless onyx eyes no longer glittered with lust, but they held the same piercing intensity. It had her wavering between ducking her head and allowing him to pilfer her darkest secrets. The angular but beautiful face with its sharp angles and unsmiling, sinfully full lips... The tall, powerful body that seemed to dwarf the chair and table...

A shiver shuddered through her body, and she prayed he didn't notice. *What are you doing here?* almost tumbled from her lips before she hauled the words back. But recognition didn't shine in his eyes. Then, why would it? He'd spent a hot, sex-drenched night during a blackout with Camille, a member of the waitstaff. Across from him sat Shay Neal, composed heiress with long, dark brown hair instead of a wig, no glasses, hazel eyes instead of brown contacts and an eggplant-colored, long-sleeved cocktail dress instead of a uniform.

She bore no resemblance to the woman he'd known. Touched. Brought such immense pleasure.

"I'm afraid I'm just finishing up dinner, Mr..." She trailed off. God, she felt like such a hypocrite, a liar. Intentional deception wasn't her. But she couldn't confess how they knew one another, either. One, she'd lied to him about her identity. Two, if he discovered that she and Camille were the same person, he could use that to embarrass her family. If Trevor found out… She mentally shook her head. No, not an option.

"Gideon Knight," he said, setting a brown folder on the table. "And I promise not to take up too much of your time. But I believe you will want to hear what I have to say."

Though every instinct for self-preservation inside her screamed to run and run *now*, she remained seated. His almost emotionless tone didn't conceal the faint warning in his words.

And then there was the part of her—the part she struggled not to acknowledge—that trembled with desire from just being near Gideon. If she could just erase that night from her head…

"I'm sorry, Mr. Knight, but I don't know you." Not a lie. Biblical knowledge didn't equate *knowing* someone. "Therefore, I don't believe there is anything we need to speak about. So if you'll excuse me…"

She set her napkin on the table and started to rise from her chair. Yes, she was being rude, but desperation trumped manners. She needed to get away from him before she did something foolish. Such as beg him for a repeat of a night that never should've happened.

"I know your secret, Ms. Neal."

Shay froze. Except for her heart. It pounded against her sternum like an anvil against steel. Hard. Deafening.

Slowly, she lowered herself to her seat, forcing her expression into one of calm disinterest. Hiding the fear that coursed through her like a rushing current.

He knew about the night of the blackout? What had she done to betray her identity? Oh God. *What did he intend to do with the information?*

"I'm afraid I have no idea what you're talking about," she replied.

His aloof, shuttered demeanor didn't alter as he cocked his head and studied her. "Is your brother aware of where you are tonight? Does he know about the meeting you concluded just minutes ago?"

Wait. What? "I'm sorry?" she asked.

"Does he know about Leida Investments?" he clarified, leaning back in his chair. "I must admit, I can't imagine Trevor Neal supporting his sister running a company that is outside of RemingtonNeal. More specifically, out from under his control."

Equal parts relief and unease swirled in her belly. Relief because he still hadn't equated her with Camille. But unease because how did he know about her business? Better question, why did he care?

"Forgive me for not seeing how it's any of your concern," she answered, ice in her voice.

"Forgiveness. Oh, we're so far past that," he murmured, and as she frowned at the cryptic words, he slid the brown folder across the table toward her.

That sense of unease morphed into dread as she stared at the banded file. She lifted her hand, but at the last moment, she froze, her fingers hovering above it as if it were a scorpion, ready to strike and poison her with its venom.

Yet she grasped it, then opened it.

Minutes later, her heart thudded against her chest

wall like a hammer against stone. The pounding clang in her head deafened her. God, she wished it would blind her to what she was reading.

Report after report detailing shady business deals involving her brother, and even some with his future father-in-law, Senator Reus. Bribery for product placement, undercutting bidding contracts, predatory practices, procuring illegal campaign contributions on behalf of the senator. And these were just some of the accusations leveled against Trevor and RemingtonNeal.

"Why are you showing me these…these lies?" She dropped the stack back on the table as if it singed her fingertips. If it didn't betray weakness, she would've shoved her chair back from the table just to place more space between that file and her.

"Lies?" He arched a black eyebrow, the corner of his mouth lifting in the faintest of sneers. "Facts, Ms. Neal. Your determination to believe they're false doesn't make it so."

"And your determination to believe they're true doesn't make it so," she snapped, throwing his words back at him. "I don't know you, and I damn sure don't know the people who gathered this defamatory conjecture." She flicked a corner of the folder. "Let's face it, Mr. Knight. If any of this was provable in court, you wouldn't be sitting here across from me at a restaurant table. You would be meeting with the DA or SEC."

"That's where you're wrong," he said, cruel satisfaction glinting in his eyes. "It's amazing how the court of public opinion will try and convict someone much swifter than a court of law."

Her stomach rolled, bile churning before racing for the back of her throat. She hated to admit it, but he was right. Good God, if *any* of this information leaked, it would destroy Trevor's reputation, his engagement, and irreparably harm the family company. It wouldn't matter if the claims couldn't be proved; the speculation alone would be detrimental and the damage irreversible. Since their father died, Trevor's one goal—no, his obsession—had been to enlarge RemingtonNeal, to make it even more successful and powerful than what their father had done. None of that would be possible if even an iota of the data in this dossier was true.

Not that she believed it. She *couldn't*. Yes, Trevor could be merciless and cut-throat. She'd increasingly seen more and more evidence of this, personally and professionally, in the last few years. And it worried her. The glimpses of the brother she'd revered and adored as a child and teen were becoming further and further apart.

But it was those glimpses that gave her hope. That reminded her that underneath the often cold demeanor existed a good man. A man incapable of the things noted in that defaming file.

And bottom line… She loved him.

Love and loyalty demanded she believe in him.

"What do you want?" she asked, forcing a calm into her voice that was a farce. Questions, thoughts and *fear* whipped through her in a chaotic gale.

The man who'd fed her and provided her protection and light in a blackout didn't sit across from her. No, this wasn't the man who'd introduced her to such pleasure she still felt the echo of it weeks later. This man… He was a stranger. A cold, calculating, beautiful stranger.

"You."

The blunt announcement doused her in a frigid blast, stunning her.

"Excuse me?" she rasped.

He couldn't mean…?

No. No way.

He didn't want her. He had to mean something else.

But God, her body was having one hell of a time getting the message. *You*. Heat prickled at the base of her spine, and desire wound through her veins like a molten stream. A barrage of memories assaulted her—the sound of his ragged breath in her ear as he thrust into her body, all that dark, thick hair tumbling around his lust-tautened face, his whispered "moonbeam" as he stroked her damn skin… Her breath evaporated in her lungs, and she struggled to keep any hint of arousal from her face.

"I want you." He leaned forward, his midnight gaze pinning her to her chair. "More specifically, I want you to be in love with me."

The images in her head splintered like glass, dousing the passion-kindled flames inside her. She gaped at him. Couldn't help it. After all, it wasn't every day that she sat across from a lunatic.

"Are you crazy?" she demanded, clutching the edge of the table as if it were the only thing keeping her from leaping out of her chair. "I don't even *like* you. And we've never met," she continued, ignoring the memory of skin pressed to damp skin that flashed across her mind's eye. "How could you believe you love me?"

He flicked a hand, the gesture impatient, dismissive. "Of course I don't love you. And I don't need your affection or professions of an emotion that is nothing but an excuse for fools and liars to behave badly."

Shay shook her head, confused. "But you just said—"

"Pretend," he interrupted. "You're going to pretend to be deeply enamored with me, and our whirlwind relationship will be as fake as that sentiment."

"You *are* crazy," she breathed. "That's ridiculous. Why would you even propose something like that?"

"Why?" he repeated, that damn eyebrow arching again. "Your brother."

She barked out a harsh crack of laughter. "My brother? Do you really think Trevor cares if I'm in a relationship with you?" Hell, he might be happy. Yes, he and Gideon were business rivals, and Trevor had been trying to acquire the other man's company for years, but her brother would probably consider it a coup for his sister to date such a successful and wealthy man.

But for the first time since sitting down across from her, Gideon smiled. The curling of his sensual lips was slow, deliberate…and menacing. "Oh yes. Your brother will care. And he'll understand."

"Another enigmatic message, Mr. Knight?" She waved a hand, frustrated. "I'm too old for games. Whatever your play is here, make it plain."

"I'll make this very plain, Shay," he said, using her given name even though she hadn't granted him permission to do so. His voice, as dark and sinful as his eyes, caressed her name like a long, luxurious stroke. It was damn near indecent.

"You can pretend to be my significant other, and convince your brother that you are mine. Or…" a steely edge that was both lethally sharp and smooth entered his voice "…I can let the truth about Leida Investments drop into your brother's lap. Imagine his fury when he realizes the secrets his sister has been keeping. And then, while that little bomb detonates, I will release the information in that file to not just the SEC but to every news outlet and journalist I have access to. And believe me, the list is long. As would be the jail sentences your brother and his precious senator would face for everything they've been up to. What effect do you think the meltdown of your family name and company will have? How many people will want to accept funds from a woman associated with a man whose name will be synonymous with financial scandal and fraud? Even the desperate will think twice about that. So both of you would be ruined, if everything in that dossier leaks. That leaves us at an impasse, Shay."

He paused, and the import of his words—no, his *threat*—sank into her like the realization of a floundering person being swallowed by quicksand.

Slow but no escape.

"And the choice is yours."

Seven

Gideon inhaled as he entered his mother's Lincoln Park home, and the sense of calm that always settled on him when he was with his family wrapped around him like a warm embrace.

Though his mother and sister had lived in the six-bedroom, seven-bathroom home for only four years, it was home because they were there. It was as much his sanctuary as his own downtown Chicago condominium. As the sound of his mother and Pat Benatar singing about love being a battlefield on her ever-present radio reached him, he shook his head, amending his thought. No, it was *more* of a haven for him.

Because family was *everything*.

Striding past the formal living and dining rooms with their soaring twelve-foot ceilings, and the sweeping, curving staircase, he headed toward the rear of the house. His mother might have initially balked at him purchasing this home for her and Olivia in one of Chicago's wealthiest neighborhoods, but there'd never been any doubt about how much she adored the airy, state-of-the-art kitchen. With its wall of windows, restaurant-style ranges and cooktops, top-of-the-line appliances, large marble island and butcher block and dual workhorse sinks, Ai had instantly fallen in love. And it was in this room that he usually found her.

Like now.

Ai stood at the stove, still clothed in her professor outfit—elegant gray pantsuit with crimson blouse and hair in a loose bun at the nape of her neck—and barefoot. Her slim body swayed back and forth to the eighties' rock anthem, and Gideon stifled a snort as she perfectly executed an arm-and-hip dance move he recognized from the classic MTV video.

He gave her a slow clap.

She whirled around with a gasp, brandishing a tea strainer like a club. "*Gideon*," she scolded, splaying the fingers of her free hand over her chest. "Are you trying to give me a heart attack?" She replaced the strainer in the waiting cup of steaming water and shot him a look over her shoulder. "I warn you, if I go, all of my money has been left to your grandmother's Maltese puppy."

Chuckling, he crossed the room and pulled his mother into a hug. Her familiar scent of gardenias greeted him like a childhood friend. Only with his family could he be Gideon Jian Knight, the oldest son of Ai Knight, former cafeteria worker who busted her ass to provide for her children and earn her PhD in educational studies at the same time. With them, he could lower the guards he'd erected between him and the rest of the world, especially those who greedily grasped for money, connections, time or sex from Gideon Knight, CEO of KayCee Corp.

He jealously guarded his moments with his family. Zealously protected *them*.

"That's fine," he assured her, with a quick kiss to her forehead. "I have the very best legal department, and they would be capable of breaking that will." He smiled as she swatted at him. But then he noted the two cups on the gleaming countertop, and his amusement faded. "How is she?" he murmured.

The light in his mother's eyes dimmed. "Better," she answered. She sighed, turning back to preparing the hot tea. "She's still sleeping more than I like and hasn't left the house since coming home from the hospital a week and a half ago. But…better." She checked the strainer in the second cup. "I was just about to take this up and sit with her for a while."

"I can do that, Mom. You obviously just arrived home." She didn't have to continue to work as a social sciences and history professor at the University of Chicago. He was more than willing to provide for her, as she'd done for him and Olivia. But Ai Knight wouldn't hear of it, and Gideon was proud to have one of the most loved professors at U of C as his mother. "Go upstairs, relax and I'll take care of Livvie."

"Thank you." She turned, smiling softly and extending her hands toward him. He enfolded hers in his, squeezing them. "But no, I want to spend some time with her before I grade papers. Although she always loves to hear you play. Maybe you could bring your guitar by sometime this week."

"I'll do that," he agreed.

His mother had been responsible for him first picking up the instrument. She'd found a battered acoustic Fender at a garage sale, and from the second he'd held it, he'd been enamored. Though extra money had been almost nonexistent during his childhood, she'd still found a way to pay for lessons. No one outside the family had ever heard him play, because it was for him. His peace. His way to lose himself and get away from the stresses of running a multimillion-dollar tech company.

Ai cupped his cheek, giving it an affectionate pat before lowering her arm. "Now, not that I don't enjoy you dropping by, but is everything okay?"

"Yes. There's something I do need to speak with you about, though." He propped a hip against the island and crossed his arms over his chest.

She studied him, then nodded, copying his pose. "Okay. What's going on?"

"I had a…business meeting last night," he said. "With Shay Neal. Trevor Neal's sister."

Surprise widened his mother's eyes. "I didn't even know he had a sister," she whispered, then shook her head. "Why, Gideon? What could you possibly have to discuss with her?"

"Our common interest," he said. "Her brother."

"Gideon," she murmured, tilting her head to the side. "What did you do?"

Meeting his mother's gaze, he relayed his conversation with Shay, including his revelation of all he'd dug up on Trevor, the ultimatum he'd delivered and her refusal to give him an answer.

"What are you thinking, son?" she asked, worry crowding her gaze. "She's innocent in all this."

Innocent. His fingers curled around his biceps, tightening even as blood pumped hot and fast through his body. *Innocent* was one word he wouldn't have associated with Shay Neal.

He'd done his homework on her before ambushing her at the restaurant. Twenty-five years old. Graduated with honors from Loyola University's Quinlan School of Business with a bachelor's in finance and entrepreneurship and a master of business administration. A member of Women in Business and International Business Society. Currently worked as vice president of the Social Development department at Remington-Neal. And from what he could tell, the position was nothing but a fancy term for event coordinator, and definitely underutilized the education she'd received. All this information could be found on her social network platforms or the company's website.

Only a deeper dive below the surface uncovered her ownership of Leida Investments. The degrees and obvious intelligence had made her interesting. But this—the company she owned in secrecy—fascinated him. This society princess who organized brunches and galas was a mystery wrapped in an enigma. And anything he couldn't dissect and analyze he mistrusted. Tack onto that her last name, and he wouldn't dare to blink around her, vigilant of the knife that might slide into his back in that flick of time.

Still…nothing, not his caution, his preparation or even the pictures included in his private investigator's file, could've prepared him for the impact of Shay Neal face-to-face.

His grandmother owned an antique locket that she'd brought with her from China. Inside was a black-and-white picture of her older sister, who'd died in childbirth. In the image, his great-aunt had been composed, stoic. But in her lovely features—in her eyes—there glimmered emotion, vitality. *Life*. It emanated through the aloof expression like dawn breaking through the last, clinging shadows of night.

And staring at Shay Neal had been like gazing upon that faded photo. Yes, she was gorgeous. No one could deny she was beautiful—the refined bone structure with high, proud cheekbones, the patrician nose with its flared nostrils, or the full curves of a mouth that belonged on a pin-up model and not a demure socialite. And he couldn't deny that just for a moment, his wayward, rebellious mind had wondered if her gleaming golden brown skin was as butter-soft as it appeared.

But it'd been none of those features that had drawn him. Fueled an insane impulse to drag his chair closer and discover what scent rose from the corner where neck and shoulder met. Had his fingers itching to pluck the strings of his guitar and find the melody that would encapsulate her.

No, it was the intelligence, the spark, the *fire* in those arresting hazel eyes.

It made him mistrust her even more.

And then there was the niggling sense of familiarity that had hit him the moment he'd sat down at her table. As if they'd met before… But like he'd done last night, he dismissed the feeling. If he'd ever met Shay Neal, no way in hell he wouldn't remember.

"She's a Neal, Mom," he said, shoving thoughts of her—of the unsettling effect she had on him—away. "She doesn't have clean hands."

"That's probably the same logic Trevor employed when he went after your sister," she pointed out, and the words struck him in the chest, burrowing into his heart.

"I'm nothing like him," he ground out, lowering his arms and curling his fingers around the edge of the marble top. "He stalked Livvie, lied to her, used her, then tossed her aside like yesterday's trash. I've been completely up-front with Shay, laying my intentions out and offering her a choice. Trevor stole Livvie's choice from her." He broke off, tipping his head back and deliberately cooling his rising temper. "You might not agree with my methods, and I'm sorry for that. But I didn't do anything when he damn near broke my sister, because you both asked me not to. I can't let it go this time. I'm not going to allow Trevor Neal to continue mistreating women. By the time I'm finished with him, he will have nothing left, and no woman will fall victim to him again."

It was the guilt that drove him.

Because it was his fault Trevor had sought out Olivia in the first place. If not for their mutual hatred and ongoing feud, she would've been safe.

"Gideon." His mother shifted forward, once more cupping his cheek. "You're right. I don't agree with your methods. I believe they will more than likely backfire, and not only will an innocent woman be hurt, but you will, too, son. If you have a conscience—which I know you do—there's no way you can't be affected by this path. And I wish you would end it now before this goes too far." She sighed, her gaze searching his. "But I also know you. And from the moment you refused to be born on your due date, I figured out you're stubborn. I'm not going to change your mind, I get that. So just…please. Be careful."

"Don't worry about me. I have everything under control," he assured her, hugging her close.

She didn't reply, instead squeezed him tighter.

He hated disappointing her, but nothing, *nothing* could dissuade him from his plans. Not her disapproval. Not Shay's reluctance and refusal to give him a decision.

He had one purpose. To bring down Trevor Neal.

And hell couldn't stop him from accomplishing it.

Eight

"Trevor, the gala is a wonderful success. You should be proud. I'm certain your parents would be," Senator Julian Reus praised, pumping his future son-in-law's hand.

I don't know how you can say that, since you never met either of them.

Shay mentally winced over the snarky comment echoing in her head. God, she really wanted to like the influential man who would soon be part of her family. But he was such a…politician. Charming. Affable.

And phony.

Good thing she never voted for him.

"Thank you, sir." Trevor smiled, then slid an arm around Shay's shoulders. "I wish I could take the credit, but it belongs to Shay. She's the reason we've already surpassed the donations from last year."

Pride glowed like an ember in her chest, and for the first time that evening, a genuine smile curled her lips.

"Thank you, Trev," she said, wrapping an arm around his waist and briefly squeezing.

"Next year, it'll be even more of a success, with Madison by your side. I'm sure she will be more than happy to step in and help organize this special event." Senator Reus announced his daughter's involvement in Grace Sanctuary as a foregone conclusion.

"Of course I will, Daddy," Madison agreed, tilting her head back expectantly, and Trevor obliged her with a soft, quick kiss on the lips. "Shay and I will make a wonderful team."

Madison turned that wide smile to Shay, and even though all the warmth that had filled her faded away, Shay returned it with one of her own.

Trevor's fiancée had been nothing but cordial to Shay, but again, there was something not quite genuine about her. Madison reminded Shay of the ice sculpture in the lobby outside the ballroom. Beautiful but cold. To stand too close would send a shiver through the body.

"Let's get through tonight first before thinking about next year," Shay said, not committing to anything. Trevor stiffened beside her, but she ignored the telltale sign of his irritation. Her mind jumped to that dark brown file Gideon Knight had slid across the table. She thought about how her brother donated significant funds to the senator's campaign. And she couldn't help but wonder if some of that money came from their mother's organization.

Stop it.

The sharp order ricocheted off her skull. Damn Gideon Knight. She hated that he'd infiltrated her head, and she couldn't evict him. Not his damn dossier or the man himself. It'd been four days since that meeting—no, ambush. Four days since she was supposed to give him her decision about his preposterous ultimatum.

Four nights of heated fantasies that left her twisting and aching in her bed.

What kind of sister did it make her that she woke up shaking and hungry for the man who blackmailed her? Who threatened her brother's livelihood and freedom?

A sad excuse for one.

Smothering a sigh, she excused herself from their small group on the pretense of checking with the catering staff, and headed across the room. She'd taken only a dozen steps before tingles jangled up her bare arms and culminated at the nape of her neck.

She sucked in a breath and immediately scanned the crowded ballroom for the source of the unsettling, *exciting* feeling.

There. No...*there.*

Gideon Knight.

The unexpected sight of him glued her feet to the floor.

Unexpected? Really?

Okay, maybe not. As soon as that prickle had sizzled over her skin, a part of her had instinctively known who'd caused it. Only one man had ever had that kind of effect on her.

She stared at him, trapped in an instant of déjà vu. Seeing him in his black tuxedo, she was swept back to the first night they'd met. Once more he seemed like the imposing but regal warlord surveying his subjects, his armor traded for perfectly tailored formal wear, his hair emphasizing the stark but gorgeous lines of his face. The distance of the ballroom separated them, but she somehow sensed those black eyes on her, just like then.

Just like then, she fought the dual urges of fight or flight.

And by fight she meant the warring of their mouths and bodies for dominance.

Damn.

She balled her fist, forcing her feet to maintain a steady, unhurried pace forward. Even as her heart pounded a relentless rhythm against her sternum.

"How did you get in here?" she gritted out.

Conscious of any gazes that might be leveled on them, she kept her polite, social mask in place, when in truth she wanted to glare daggers at him.

His aloof expression didn't change…except for the arch of that damnable dark eyebrow. "I expect like everyone else. The front entrance. And paying the seven-thousand-dollar-a-plate fee."

"That's not possible," she snapped. "I looked over and approved the final guest list myself. Neither you nor your company's name was on it."

"Then you missed it. Maybe other matters distracted you," he added. A beat of charged silence vibrated between them. No need to name the "other matters." They both were well aware of what he referred to.

"Is that why you're here?" she demanded, and in spite of her resolve, her voice dropped to a heated whisper. "To pressure me for an answer?"

"It's been four days, Shay," he replied, and in that moment, she resented his carefully modulated composure.

The rash and admittedly foolish urge—no, *need*—to shatter his control swelled within her. She wanted the man from the blackout, the one who stared at her with flames of desire burning in his onyx eyes as he drove them both to impossible pleasure.

"I've given your four days longer than I'd usually grant anyone else."

"Well, I'm flattered."

"You should be."

She clenched her teeth so hard an ache rose along her jaw. "The answer is n—"

"Is this man bothering you, Shay?" Trevor appeared at her elbow, and both the venom in his question and his sudden, hard grasp elicited a gasp from her.

Gideon's gaze dropped to her arm, and anger narrowed his eyes.

"Get your hand off of her," he ordered. The volume of his voice didn't rise, but only a simpleton could miss the warning. "You're hurting her."

Scowling, Trevor glanced down at his fingers pinching her arm, then jerked his hand away. He lifted his regard to her face, and she glimpsed disgust, but also regret. She dipped her chin in a silent acknowledgment of his equally silent apology.

Turning back to Gideon, he snarled, "What are you doing here? You weren't invited. Leave. Now."

"I'm afraid that's not going to happen," Gideon said, with no hint of remorse. If anything, satisfaction rang loud and clear in those words. "I paid to attend just like everyone else here, and made a hefty donation on top of that. I'm staying."

"You can have your money back. We don't need it," Trevor spat, nearly trembling with rage as he edged closer to Gideon. "We both know why you're here. You lost. Get over it. It's not like it's the first time, and it damn sure won't be the last."

Fear spiked inside Shay's chest. *Good God.* She'd never seen her brother this angry. His reaction to Gideon's presence had to be more than a business rivalry. This was…personal.

"Trevor," she quietly pleaded, gently but firmly grasping his arm. "Please."

Gideon shifted his attention from her brother to her. And the same fury that twisted her brother's face lit his eyes like a glittering night sky. But as he studied her, some of the anger dimmed.

He retreated a step, his gaze still pinned on her.

Shock pummeled the breath from her lungs. Had he backed away…for her?

No. That was impossible. He didn't give a damn about her or her feelings.

Still…

"Have a nice evening. Both of you," he said, though

his regard never wavered from her. "It was wonderful seeing you again, Shay," he murmured, then turned and headed farther into the room, not toward the exit as Trevor had demanded.

"What was he talking about, 'seeing you again'?" Trevor hissed as soon as Gideon was out of earshot. "When did you meet him?"

With Herculean effort, she tore her gaze from Gideon and met her brother's glare. Hurt and hints of betrayal lurked there. And guilt pricked her. For what, though? She'd done nothing wrong.

"A few nights ago when I had dinner with friends. He was at the same restaurant." She delivered the half-truth with aplomb. *God, when did I become such an accomplished liar?* "He just introduced himself, that was all. What in the world was that all about, Trevor?"

"Nothing," he snapped. Then, sighing, he dragged a hand over his closely cropped hair. "I'm sorry. I didn't mean to bark at you. Just…stay away from him, Shay. I don't want you to have anything to do with him. Do you understand?"

"I'm not a child, Trevor," she murmured, meeting his fierce stare. "And this isn't the proper place for this discussion, either. We have guests."

With that reminder, she turned and strode away from him and the disturbing scene that had just unfolded.

Oh yes, there was bad blood between him and Gideon. Now more than ever, she felt like a pawn in whatever twisted game the two of them were engaged in. And she hated it.

As the evening progressed, she couldn't uproot the bitterness. Maintaining her not-a-care-in-the-world socialite persona became a weightier burden, and by the time dinner was being cleared away, she was bone-deep exhausted. Peeking at the slim, gold watch on her wrist, she thanked God she had only about an hour more to do her hostess duty before she could escape.

"I noticed you talking to Gideon Knight earlier," Madison said, her tone low enough that Trevor, who was engrossed in conversation with Senator Reus, didn't overhear.

Surprised that she knew of him, Shay nodded. "Yes."

"Do you know him well?" she asked, and unease niggled at Shay. The air of nonchalance in Madison's seemingly innocent question seemed forced.

"Not really," Shay replied cautiously. "Though Trevor seems to."

"Oh, you don't know, do you?" Madison studied her, a gleam in her dark brown eyes. "Trevor didn't tell you?" she prodded before Shay could answer. "Gideon and I were…close before I met your brother."

"Close," Shay repeated, though the twisting in her stomach interpreted the coy choice of phrasing.

"Engaged, actually," Madison confessed, and this time, there was no mistaking the cat-that-ate-the-whole-damn-flock-of-canaries smile that curved her mouth. "We were engaged for a year before we ended our relationship. He wasn't happy about it." She chuckled, apparently amused at her understatement.

We both know why you're here. You lost. Get over

it. It's not like it's the first time, and it damn sure won't be the last.

Trevor's accusation echoed in her head, and it now made sickening sense. As did Gideon's reason about why he'd proposed his ridiculous plan, that night at the restaurant.

Your brother, he'd said. All of this—hatred, blackmail, rivalry—was over a woman.

Her belly lurched, and she fisted her fingers, willing the coq au vin she'd just eaten not to make a reappearance.

"If I may have your attention, please?" Senator Reus stood, his booming politician's voice carrying through the ballroom and silencing the after-dinner chatter.

"Thank you. Now I know this evening is about Grace Sanctuary, and I speak on behalf of both the Reus and Neal families when I thank you for your generosity in both spirit and donations." Applause rose, and Julian Reus basked in it, his smile benevolent. No, the evening wasn't about him, but somehow, he'd managed to make it all about him.

"I'd just like to take this moment to recognize this wonderful charity, as well as Trevor Neal, who has spearheaded it since the passing of his dear parents. I'm so proud that I will be able to call him son in the very near future, as he and my beautiful daughter, Madison, embark on a journey together as man and wife. Trevor..." he accepted a glass of champagne from a waiter who suddenly appeared at his elbow, and lifted it high "...congratulations to you and my daughter. You are the son I wasn't blessed with, but am so fortunate to now have."

Around them, people hoisted their own wineglasses and echoed "To Trevor," as her brother stood and clasped the senator's hand, his huge grin so blinding, Shay had to glance away. The sight of him soaking up the senator's validation like water on parched earth caused pain to shudder through her.

Their father would've never praised him so publicly—or privately. Lincoln Neal had been a hard man, huge on demands and criticism, and stingy with compliments. She, more than anyone, understood how Trevor had craved his approval. And it'd been their father's refusal to give it that had changed Trevor. Their father had been dead for five years, and Trevor still drove himself to be the best…to be better than their father. This high regard from such an important man had to be like Christmas to Trevor. A thousand of them packed into one short toast.

Oh God. She dipped her head so no one could glimpse the sting of tears in her eyes.

She was going to cave to Gideon's ultimatum.

Family. Loyalty.

Those were the tenets that had been drilled into them from childhood. Definitely by their father, and even in one of the last conversations she'd had with her mother before she died. She'd stressed that Shay and Trevor always take care of one another.

Family loyalty wouldn't allow her to let Trevor lose everything. The family name. His company. His fiancée. His future father-in-law. There was no one left to protect him, except her. And until she could verify the truth of the information Gideon held—and she still doubted the veracity of it, especially given what she'd learned from Madison—she couldn't permit her brother to be ruined. Not when the kind but wounded boy she remembered still existed inside him.

He was her brother.

And to keep that happiness shining on her brother's face, she would make a deal with the devil.

And Gideon Knight was close enough.

It wasn't difficult to locate him in the crowded room. The entire evening she'd been aware of his presence, and when she glanced over her shoulder to the table several feet away, their gazes immediately locked. As if he'd only been waiting for her to look his way.

She gave him a small nod, and he returned it.

Exhaling, she turned her attention to the glass of red wine she'd barely touched throughout dinner. Now it, and about four more, seemed like a fabulous idea.

She would need all the courage she could get.

Nine

"When I agreed to meet you, I assumed we would go to another restaurant, not your home."

Gideon stepped down into the recessed living room of his downtown Chicago penthouse and slipped his hands into the pockets of his tuxedo pants. Shay hovered at the top of the two steps leading into the room.

He surveyed his home, attempting to view it through her eyes. The dual-level, four-bedroom, three-bath condominium was the epitome of luxury with its airy, open-floor plan, floor-to-ceiling windows, game and media rooms, indoor and outdoor kitchens and private rooftop lounge that boasted its own fireplace. But it'd been the stunning views of the Chicago River and Chicago skyline from every room that had sold him. It was like being a part of the elements while protected from them.

He'd left most of the simple, elegant decor to his interior designer, but scattered among the gray, white and black color scheme were pieces of him, if Shay cared to look close enough. Next to the god-awful piece of metallic abstract art on the fireplace mantel that he'd never gotten around to tossing stood a framed photo of him with his family, including his grandparents, at last year's Mid-Autumn Festival in Chinatown.

On top of the white baby grand piano where his sister sometimes plucked out "Mary Had a Little Lamb" sat the guitar pick he'd forgotten to put away the night before.

Peeking from between the couch pillows was the ear of a pair of Bluetooth headphones that he used to listen to music with while working from home.

Yes, if she paid attention, she might glimpse those hints into him. And part of him tensed with the need to go through the room and remove those clues from her sight. But the other half... That half wanted her to spy them, to ask questions. Which was bullshit, since their arrangement didn't require that kind of intimacy.

He shouldn't hunger for that—especially not from her. Not just sister to his enemy, but another beautiful woman who didn't want the real him. The last time he'd allowed a woman to enter into the space reserved for family, she'd betrayed that trust. Had left him so disillusioned, he'd vowed to never be that foolhardy, that reckless, again.

Only family could be trusted. Only family deserved his loyalty...his love.

Definitely not Trevor Neal's sister.

"This kind of conversation deserves more privacy than a crowded restaurant," he said, finally addressing her complaint. "Would you like a drink? Wine? Champagne? Water?"

"Champagne?" she scoffed, stepping down into the living room. "I guess this would be a victory celebration for you. But no. I'll take a Scotch. This situation calls for something strong that tastes worse than the deal I'm about to swallow."

Her acerbic retort had an inappropriate spurt of amusement curling in his chest. He squelched it, turning to fix her a finger of Scotch and a bourbon for him. Moments later, he handed the tumbler to her and silently watched as she sipped the potent liquor. Not even a flinch. His admiration grew.

When she lifted those beautiful hazel eyes to him, that niggling sense of familiarity tugged at him again. He cocked his head to the side, studying her. What was it…?

"Can we get this started, please?" she asked, setting the glass on the small table flanking the sofa. She rubbed her bare arms, and the sign of nerves pricked a conscience he'd believed to be impervious. "I'm sure you've already guessed that I'm going to agree to your ridiculous plan. Or let's just call it what it is. Extortion."

"You have a choice, Shay," he reminded her, sipping his bourbon.

"Yes," she agreed, bitterness coating the word. "Sacrifice myself or my brother to the beast. That's a hell of a choice."

He shrugged. "But one, nonetheless."

"You're not really this cold and unfeeling. I know you're not," she whispered, her green-and-amber gaze roaming his face as if trying to peer beneath the mask he chose to let her see.

Unbidden, the night of the blackout wavered in his mind. No. Those dark, hungry hours had proved he wasn't cold or unfeeling. For a rare instant, he'd lost the control he was much lauded for. But those circumstances had been extreme, and she wasn't a hardworking, passionate and fiery server named Camille. That woman had disappeared without a trace, filling in for another member of the waitstaff, and not leaving behind a hint of her identity. She'd seen the man he rarely let anyone see.

One Shay would never witness.

"If you need to make up an idea of who I am in order to fulfill the pretense of falling in love with me, then go ahead. Whatever will allow you to deliver an award-winning performance for your brother and everyone else watching."

"Everyone else being Madison Reus."

The accusation punched him in the chest, and he braced himself against the impact. By sheer will he forced himself not to react. But inside…inside he snarled at the mention of *her*. The woman who'd taught him that love could be bought by the highest bidder. Who'd knowingly betrayed him with the one man he hated. Who'd shown him that placing his heart and trust in a person outside of family was a costly mistake—to his bank account and to his soul.

He would never repeat that particular mistake.

"You must have loved her very much to go to such lengths for your revenge," Shay continued when he remained silent. "That's what this is all about, right? How dare my brother date the woman you were once engaged to? You're punishing both of them by flaunting me in their faces?"

He caught the threads of hurt beneath that calm tone. And in spite of his resolve to maintain his distance, both emotionally and physically, he shifted forward. She didn't retreat, but instead tilted her head back to meet his gaze. Courageous. He hadn't been expecting that from her.

Just like he hadn't been expecting this inconvenient attraction. Even now, her scent—the fresh, wild lushness of rain right before a storm and roses in bloom—called to him like a siren's lure, urging him closer, until his hard, solid planes pressed against her soft, sensual curves.

Though all common sense railed at him not to touch, he ignored it and reached for the thick strands of hair that fell in a sleek glide behind her shoulders. Pinching a lock between his fingers, he lifted it, indulged himself and brushed it over his lips.

Never breaking his stare, he murmured, "You don't know what you're talking about."

He heard the slight catch of her breath. Noticed the erratic beat of her pulse at the base of her neck. From nerves? Desire? The hardening of his body telegraphed which one it voted for.

Step back. Remember the plan. Stick to the plan.

But he stayed. Playing with sin-wrapped-in-bronzed-skin fire.

"No?" she breathed, the corner of her mouth lifting in a sardonic smile. "Is this the part where I just blindly trust what you say because my lying eyes and lil' ol' brain can't possibly grasp the intricacies involved here?" She scoffed, jerking her head back, and he released her. "Please. I'm patted on the head and patronized every day, so forgive me if I call bullshit."

She turned away from him, and he ground his teeth together, his fingers curling into his palms to battle the urge to grab her and bring her back against him. She didn't understand. This wasn't about Madison; it was about another woman—his sister. And that bastard who'd abused her heart and shattered her mental state.

An eye for an eye. A sister for a sister.

But he couldn't admit any of that to her. Not when she would no doubt run back and tell Trevor everything.

"You're forgetting I know the secret about your job. And I don't mean that joke of a title at Remington-Neal. I would be a fool to underestimate you, Shay."

She pivoted and something flashed in her hazel eyes, but before he could decipher it, she briefly closed them and pinched the bridge of her nose.

"Can we just get this over with?" she asked, weariness coating her voice. "Tell me what you need from me so you won't burn my brother's world to the ground."

"Like I told you at the restaurant. You and I will pretend to be a couple. A real couple, Shay. Which means convincing everyone that we're hopelessly in love." He couldn't prevent the bitter smile from curving his mouth. "I read that you took several drama classes in college. Time to dust off those old skills and bring them out of retirement. I'll require you to attend several events and dinners with me, and the same for you. The first time you try to twist out of this arrangement, it's off, and your brother's dirty dealings become public."

This time he clearly interpreted the emotion turning her gaze more green than brown. Anger. "Don't worry about me. I'll hold up my end of the bargain. But I won't carry this lie on indefinitely. You have a time limit of six months. That's all I'll agree to."

Six months would be more than enough time to carry out all he had planned. "Fine."

"And at the conclusion, you promise to destroy the report and all copies of it."

He nodded again, although he had no intention of doing that. Only a fool would reveal his hand. Did he feel a twinge of guilt for deceiving her? Yes, it didn't sit well. But he'd meant what he'd told his mother. His number one goal was to prevent Trevor from ever hurting another woman as he'd hurt Olivia. This arrangement with Shay was only one part of his plan.

"Okay, then." Shay inhaled a breath and tilted her chin up at a haughty angle, every inch the socialite. "One more thing. I'm not a whore. We might have to pretend affection for each other, but I won't have sex with you."

Irritation flashed inside him, and he took a step toward her before he drew to an abrupt halt. "I can promise you that when I take a woman to my bed, she wants to be there. I don't give a damn about love, because there's something much more honest—fucking. There are no lies when a woman is coming for me, and I don't want one in my bed who doesn't want to be there. If she can't give me the truth of her pleasure, then I don't want her under me. And any man who's satisfied with just getting a woman between the sheets, without giving a damn about her desire to be there, isn't a man."

Silence plummeted into the room, and that sense of déjà vu hit him again. He'd said something similar to Camille weeks ago when she'd accused him of using his position of power to screw her. He shook his head. He had to stop thinking about her. He couldn't afford to show any weakness or distraction around Shay.

"But you need to understand one thing, Shay, and come to terms with it." He moved forward again, lowering his head so their mouths were inches apart. So close he glimpsed the golden striations in her eyes and inhaled the heady scent of Scotch on her breath. "I'm not the other men you might have had dancing to your tune. For the next six months, you're mine. And while you might not be in my bed," he murmured, brushing the back of his finger over a sculpted cheekbone, "you'll act like you are. Which means you'll pretend to desire my touch, my hands on you. You'll behave as if you crave what I, and only I, can give you. Pleasure. Passion. A hunger so deep you don't know how you ever existed without me to take care of it for you. So, moonbeam, even if you loathe me, those beautiful eyes better convince everyone that I'm yours. And *you're mine.*"

She wrenched away from him, stumbling backward, her panting audible testimony to the arousal that stained her cheeks and glinted in her eyes.

Fuck.

Need gripped his stomach, grinding and squeezing like a vise. He'd overplayed his hand. His aim had been to teach her a lesson, and he'd ended up the student with his knuckles rapped.

"Don't call me that," she ordered hoarsely. He frowned, at first not grasping what she meant. Then it hit him. Moonbeam.

Where had that come from? Why had he called her *that* name?

"Pet names, like we're something we're clearly not, aren't part of this, either." She tugged her shoulders back, and that delicate but stubborn chin went up again. "And for the record. I belong to *me*. Not my brother. Not RemingtonNeal. And definitely *not you*."

Shay spun around. Snatching up her coat, which he'd laid over the back of the foyer chair when they'd entered the penthouse, she strode out of his home.

He stood there, staring at the closed door, and a small smile played on his lips.

Whether she realized it or not, she'd just issued a challenge.

Accepted.

And he more than looked forward to winning.

Ten

Shay grimaced at the vibration of her cell phone in her back pocket as she served up an order of green papaya salad and tom yum to another hungry customer standing outside Bridgette's food truck. Her best friend's delicious Thai cuisine made hers one of the more popular trucks stationed at Hyde Park during the lunch hour.

Bridgette was a wonderful chef, and when she'd proposed starting a food truck business, Shay had insisted on investing. The love of food and cooking were just a couple things the two of them bonded over. And because they were such good friends, when Bridgette had called this morning, frantic because she'd been down a person, Shay had been more than willing to jump in and help. It hadn't been the first time she'd volunteered, and if Bridgette needed her, it wouldn't be the last. Just another reason Trevor resented her "lowbrow" relationship with Bridgette.

Good thing that she'd never told him about cooking and serving on her food truck.

Another insistent buzz of her cell, and she sighed. She knew who was calling her.

Gideon.

He'd left a message about joining him for lunch about a half hour after Bridgette's panicked call. She'd shot a text off to him, letting him know meeting wouldn't be possible. But had he accepted that? Hell no. Well, that fell under the category of His Problem.

Yes, she'd agreed to attend events with him, but she'd also meant it when she told him he didn't own her. She was more than willing to accompany him to dinners, lunches, parties, whatever. But she also needed notice, and not just a couple hours. She had a life and refused to hand it over to him.

She was already an indentured servant to the Neal name and reputation. He wouldn't become another master.

You're mine.

Those two words had played over and over in her head like a rabid hamster in a wheel. It'd been two days since she'd left his penthouse, and she hadn't been able to erase the declaration from her mind.

Or deny the spark of desire that had erupted into a conflagration inside her. Her thighs had clenched at the dark, sensual note so dominant in his voice. And in that moment, she swore she could feel the heavy, thrilling possession of his body taking hers, filling hers.

Claiming hers.

God, it wasn't fair. Not the words he uttered to her. Not the out-of-control reaction of her body to his.

She didn't have to pretend to know his touch. No, she had intimate knowledge of it.

Which was why she'd reacted so strongly—and unwisely—to the "moonbeam" he'd so carelessly tossed at her. That endearment had been special to her, meant for her alone. But it hadn't been. God only knew how many women he'd said it to.

She wasn't special.

And damn, that had hurt. More than it should've.

Another buzz, and she gritted her teeth. Probably a threatening message this time. The tenacity that had made him so successful as a businessman was working the hell out of her nerves.

Six months. She just had to hold on for six months. Then she would be free. From both this "agreement" with Gideon and from under the yoke of the Neal name.

Gideon didn't know the significance of her time limit. In that time, she would turn twenty-six and be in control of the trust funds from her mother and maternal grandmother. With that came financial independence. She wouldn't need her paychecks from RemingtonNeal to help finance Leida Investments. With the money from her trust funds, she would have more than enough capital, and while she wouldn't totally be able to escape the assumptions because of her last name, she would no longer be under the restrictions and expectations of her brother and her family reputation.

From birth, she'd been under a man's thumb: her father's, her brother's and now Gideon's.

In just six months, she would be liberated from them all.

"Here you go, babe." Bridgette handed her an order of pad thai, disrupting her thoughts of emancipation. "That's number 66."

"Thanks." Shay accepted it, bagged it and carried it to the window. "Here you go." She passed the food to the customer with a smile and turned to the next person in line. "Hi, how can I—"

Oh hell.

Gideon.

Her eyes widened as she stared at his cold, harsh expression. "What are you doing here?" she asked, and in spite of the "you don't own me" speech she'd just delivered to herself, apprehension quivered through her at the anger glittering in his gaze.

"Wasting my time hunting you down, apparently," he ground out. "You're already reneging on our arrangement, and it hasn't even been two days. I warned you about thinking I would dance—"

"Hey, man, order and move on. Some of us have to get back to work," someone yelled from in back of Gideon. And when several more grumbles of agreement followed, Gideon whipped his head around. Immediately, the mumbling ceased.

Good Lord. That was some superpower.

He returned his attention to her and in spite of his glare, she hiked her chin up. "I'm helping a friend out. She needed me today."

His gaze narrowed further, and he growled, "Open the door."

Before she could reply, he stalked off and disappeared. But seconds later, a hard rap at the side door echoed in the truck. From the grill, Bridgette tossed her a "what the hell?" look, and, bemused, Shay shrugged and unlocked it.

The door jerked open, and Gideon strode through it. His big body and intense presence seemed to shrink the interior to that of a toy truck.

Bridgette stared at him, openmouthed and struck silent. Which wasn't an easy feat. With sharp movements, he jerked off his coat and suit jacket and hung them on a wall hook. Then he rolled his sleeves up to his elbows and pinned both her and Bridgette with that dark glare.

"Well?" he snapped. "Where do you need me?"

Need him? What was happening?

Bridgette recovered first. "Can you cook?" At his abrupt nod, she handed him a knife. "You get an order of cashew chicken going, and I'll get the green curry."

Without a word, he crossed to the sink, washed his hands, then accepted the utensil and started chopping fresh vegetables and chicken like a pro. Bridgette again shot her a look, but Shay shrugged, still stunned and confused.

"You have customers waiting," Gideon reminded her, without turning around.

Now the man had eyes on the back of his head as well as cooking skills?

Again...w*hat the hell?*

Shaking her head, she returned to the window and the ever-growing line outside. For the next couple hours, the three of them worked like a well-oiled machine. Shay still couldn't quite grasp that Gideon Knight was there in the cramped quarters of a food truck, cooking Thai entrées like a professional.

She tried to imagine Trevor jumping in and helping out and couldn't. The image refused to solidify, because her brother would never have done it. Not many men of her acquaintance would've bothered getting their hands dirty. But then again, two hours ago she wouldn't have been able to picture Gideon getting his hands dirty, either. And especially not for her.

As Bridgette closed the serving window and hung the Closed sign, questions crowded into Shay's head. But before she could ask them, he turned, tugging down his sleeves and rebuttoning the cuffs.

"I'll be by to pick you up at seven tonight for a dinner party. This time, be there and ready," Gideon ordered, thrusting his arms into his jacket, then his coat, his tone warning her not to argue. And for once, she heeded it. "And don't keep me waiting."

With a brisk nod at Bridgette, he stalked out the door, leaving a weighty silence behind.

Bridgette was the first to break it.

"What in the hell just happened?" she yelled, voicing the same question that had been plaguing Shay since Gideon's sudden appearance.

And her answer was the same.

Damned if she knew.

* * *

Hours later, Shay stood in the foyer and stared at the front door as the ring of the doorbell echoed through her house.

Seven o'clock. Right on the dot.

Her pulse raced, and the roar of it filled her head, deafening her. Nerves. They waged war inside her, turning her belly into a churned-up battlefield. Any sane woman would be anxious about entering a charade and perpetrating a fraud on everyone she knew and cared about.

But she would be lying to herself if she attributed the lion's share of the nerves to their arrangement. No, that honor belonged to the man himself.

Who was Gideon Knight?

The attentive, protective and devastatingly sensual stranger from the night of the blackout? The aloof billionaire and brilliant CEO of a global tech company? The ruthless, revenge-driven ex-fiancé? The man who barged into a food truck, rolled up his sleeves and selflessly helped serve the Chicago masses?

Which one was real? And why did they all fascinate her?

Exhaling a breath, she rubbed her damp palms down her thighs. No fascination. Or curiosity. Both were hazardous and would only lead to a slippery, dangerous slope. One where she could convince herself that the tender, generous man was the true one, and the one who held her brother's future over her head was the aberration.

What had been one of her mother's favorite sayings? "When someone shows you who they are, believe them." Well, Gideon had shown her he would go to any lengths, no matter how merciless, to achieve what he wanted. Even if it meant using and hurting other people in the process. She needed to believe this truth.

And accept it.

The doorbell rang again, and it unglued her feet, propelling her forward. She unlocked and opened the door, revealing her date for the evening. No, correction—the man she was madly in love with for the next six months.

Gideon stared down at her, his black eyes slowly traversing the curls and waves she'd opted for tonight, down the black cocktail dress with its sheer side cutouts and sleeves, to the stilettos that added four inches to her height. When his eyes met hers again, she barely caught herself before taking a step back from the heat there. It practically seared her skin.

Hazardous. Dangerous. She silently chanted the warnings to herself like a mantra.

He would set fire to her life and leave her covered in ashes.

"Seven o'clock," she rasped, before clearing her throat of the arousal thickening it. "Just as you requested."

"You're beautiful."

Struck speechless, she could only stare at him. His expression hadn't changed from the cool, distant mask, but those eyes, and now his voice… If his gaze made her tremble, the low, sensual throb in that dark velvet voice had her squeezing her thighs against the ache deep inside her.

"Where's your coat?" he asked, glancing past her into the house.

"I have it."

Get it together, she silently ordered herself as she briefly returned inside to grab her coat off the stand.

"Here. Let me." He stepped inside the foyer and took the cape from her, holding it up while she slipped into it.

Fastening it, she turned back to him, and her voice did another vanishing act when he offered her a crooked elbow. Her breathing shallow, she hesitated, then slid her arm through his and let him guide her out of the house and to his waiting Town Car. A driver stood at the rear door, but Gideon waved him away and opened the door for her himself.

God, she was too old for Cinderella-like fairy tales. If she'd ever had stars in her eyes, they'd been dimmed a long time ago. But here, sitting with Gideon Knight in the back of a car that was more elegant and luxurious than any limousine she'd ridden in, with the heat from his body and his earthy sandalwood scent invading her senses, she could almost understand why Cinderella had lost a beautiful shoe over a man.

"I didn't have a chance to tell you earlier, but… thank you. For stepping in and helping Bridgette this afternoon." She glanced at his sharply hewn profile. "How do you know how to cook? I wouldn't have expected it of…a man like you."

He turned to her, and even in the shadowed interior, his dark eyes gleamed. Dim light from the streetlamps passed over his face, highlighting then hiding his too-handsome features. She fought the urge to stroke her fingertips over those planes and angles, over the full curves of his mouth. Free those thick, silken strands and tangle her fingers in them…

"A man like me?" he repeated, the sardonic note relaying that he understood exactly what she meant. "I hate to tarnish your image of me, Shay, but my beginnings aren't as rarefied as yours and your brother's. My grandparents immigrated from China with nothing more than they could carry, and both of my parents worked barely above minimum-wage jobs when I was a kid. When my father died, Mom often worked two jobs to provide for us. And as soon as I was old enough, I took any kind of employment I could to help her. One of those happened to be as a short-order cook. If you ever need your yard landscaped or your gutters cleaned, I can do those, too."

Shame sidled through her in a slick, oily glide. She'd unknowingly spoken from a lofty place of privilege, but her ignorance didn't excuse it. True, she didn't subscribe to the idle lives some of those in high society did—she believed in working hard and making a difference in the world—but she couldn't deny that she didn't know what it was to go without. To go to bed exhausted from menial labor or worried about how the next bill would be paid.

Gideon's mother, and even Gideon, obviously did.

"I'm sorry," she murmured. "I spoke out of turn." She paused, debated whether to say anything else, but ended up whispering, "Your mother must be proud of you."

He studied her for several silent, heavy moments. "She is. But then again, she would've been proud of me if I'd decided to remain a short-order cook in a fast-food restaurant."

Shay digested that, turned it over and analyzed it again. Could she say the same for her parents? *No.* Her father would've easily disowned her. And as much as Shay adored her mother, Leida Neal wouldn't have been proud of or happy for her daughter if she had been anything less than what her name demanded— respectable, wealthy, connected and married to a man who fit those same qualifications.

The certainty in that knowledge saddened her. Did Gideon realize how fortunate he was?

"She sounds lovely," Shay said, ready to drop the unsettling subject. But then, because her mouth apparently had no allegiance to her, she blurted out, "I'm sorry about your father."

Another heartbeat of weighty silence.

"It was a long time ago."

"My mother died fourteen years ago. And I still miss her every day," she admitted softly.

Slowly, he nodded. "I remember," he finally said, surprising her. "Your brother and I went to high school together, and later attended the same college. But I recall when your mother died. The principal came for him in the middle of class and took him out."

"I didn't know you and Trevor went to school together." Shock whistled through her. "He never mentioned knowing you." Not that he mentioned Gideon at all unless it regarded acquiring his tech company.

Or more recently, not unless a blue streak of unflattering adjectives followed his name.

His sensual mouth curved into a hard, faintly cruel smile. "Your brother and I have a long history. He was decent until that day. I was a scholarship student at an elite, private prep school. That already made me a target for most students there. But your brother wasn't one of them. Until after your mother died. Then he became one of the worst. That he and I were often head-to-head competitors in academics and athletics didn't help matters. Neither did the fact that I didn't take his or any of the other assholes' shit."

"He changed after Mother passed," Shay murmured, the dagger of pain stabbing her chest all too familiar when she thought about the boy who'd become a hardened man. "She was the...buffer between him and my father. My dad..." Shay shook her head, turning to stare at the passing scenery outside the car window, but seeing Lincoln Neal's disapproving, stern frown that was often directed at his children. But more so at his first-born child. "He was demanding, exacting and nearly impossible to please. And Trevor desperately wanted to please him. Which became impossible after our father died. Yet, even now..." Again she trailed off, feeling as if she betrayed her brother by revealing even that much.

"That doesn't excuse his behavior," Gideon replied, ice coating his voice.

"No," she agreed, more to herself than him. "But no one is created in a bubble. And no one is all bad or all good. Sometimes it helps to understand why people behave the way they do. And it helps us give them compassion and mercy."

Strong, firm fingers gripped her chin and turned her to face him. Gideon's touch reverberated through her, echoing in the taut tips of her breasts, low in her belly, and in the pulsing flesh between her thighs. He'd clutched her like this the night of the blackout, holding her in place, so he could watch her as she came. Now, like then, she couldn't tear her gaze away from his. Like then, her lips parted, but now, she swallowed down the whimper that clawed at the back of her throat.

"Your brother doesn't deserve compassion or mercy, Shay. So don't try to convince me differently with sad stories of his childhood." He swept the pad of his thumb over her bottom lip, and this time she lost the battle and released that small sound of need. His eyes narrowed on her mouth, then after several moments, lifted to meet hers. "Why does it feel like I've—" He frowned, but didn't remove his hand.

"Why does it feel like you've what?" she breathed, dread filtering into the desire. He'd heard her plead for him, for his touch, many times during the night they'd spent together. Had the sound she'd released just now triggered his memory?

God, in hindsight, she should've been up front with him about her identity from the beginning. If she came clean now, he would only see her as a liar.

Maybe because you're lying by omission?

Shame crept in, mingling with the dread. She hated deception of any kind, and this didn't sit well with her. At all. But self-preservation trumped her conscience at this point. Her reasons for initially remaining quiet still stood. She didn't trust Gideon. Didn't know what he would do with the information that Shay Neal had masqueraded as waitstaff at one of the biggest social events of the year and then slept with him under false pretenses. Would he use it as another source of ammo in this war he waged with her brother, leaving her reputation and her company as casualties?

Possibly.

No, she couldn't afford to find out.

"Nothing." He dropped his hand from her face, his customary impassive expression falling firmly back in place. Turning from her, he picked up a small, rectangular box from the seat beside him. "Here. I have something for you."

She glanced down at the gift, then back up at him. After several moments, she returned her attention to the box and, with slightly trembling fingers, removed the lid. And gasped.

Delicate ruby-and-gold bangles nestled on black velvet. Tiny diamonds rimmed the bracelets, making the jewelry glitter in the dark.

They were beautiful. Just…beautiful.

"There're eight of them," he said, picking up the bangles when she didn't make a move toward them. "In Chinese culture, eight is a lucky number. Red is also lucky."

Gently grasping her hand, he slid the jewelry onto her wrist.

"Thank you," she whispered. In the past, she'd received earrings, necklaces and rings from men who hoped to win her over—or rather win over the Neal heiress. But none of them had been bought with thought or meaning. None of them had been for *her*, Shay. Whether he'd intended it or not, Gideon had given her a piece of himself, of his heritage. And for that alone, she'd accept. "They're gorgeous."

"You're welcome," he murmured, his fingers brushing over the tender skin on the inside of her wrist before withdrawing. For a moment, she caught a flicker of emotion in his eyes before he shut her out once again.

She felt the echo deep inside her.

And for some inexplicable reason—a reason she refused to explore—it hurt.

A charade, she reminded herself. They were both playing their parts, and gifts to his fake girlfriend were part of those roles.

As long as she kept that truth forefront in her mind, she wouldn't get caught up in the beautiful enigma that was Gideon Knight.

Eleven

"I feel like a zoo animal in a cage," Shay muttered, lifting a glass of white wine to her lips. "They could at least be subtler about the staring."

Gideon arched an eyebrow, scanning the large formal living room. Several pairs of eyes met, then slid away from his, caught ogling the newest couple in their midst. Satisfaction whispered through him. He'd accepted this particular dinner party invitation because of who would be in attendance. Not just business associates, but members of the social circle Shay was intricately a part of. Talk of their appearance together would rush through Chicago's society elite like a brush fire.

"They're wondering why you're with the beast," he said.

"Probably."

He snorted at her quick agreement, earning a dazzling smile from her. He had to hand it to her—Shay was a brilliant actress. As soon as they'd crossed the threshold into Janet and Donald's mansion, she'd immediately charmed his client and her husband. And though he knew the truth behind their arrangement, even he could almost believe Shay was smitten with him. Small, but intimate touches to his arm and chest. Gentle teasing. Special smiles. Yes, she deserved an award for her performance.

And as their hosts approached them, and she slid her arm through his, her soft breast pressing into side, he ordered his dick to stand down for about the fifty-fifth time...in two hours.

If he was a better man, he would insert some distance between them, not enjoy the sensual lure of her scent. Or savor each time he settled a palm at the small of her back—a back covered only by the same sheer material that "covered" her shoulders and arms. She was sex and class in this dress that skimmed every delicious curve.

Damn if the heat from her didn't seep into his palm and ignite every greedy need to stroke her skin, sift his fingers through the thick, dark strands of her hair... claim her saint-and-sinner body for his own.

The only woman to have stirred this unprecedented reaction in him had been Camille. It unsettled him. The mysterious waitress was no longer in his life. But Shay... Everything about her tested his control, his reason, his plans.

How he kept touching her when every rule of logic demanded he keep all displays of affection public to cement the facade of a happy, in-love couple. How she challenged him with those flashes of temper when no one except his best friend and business partner dared. How she surprised him with things like working in a food truck. How he couldn't jettison the sense that there was something familiar about her...

And then there was his jewelry on her wrist. The gold and rubies gleamed against her skin like sunlight and fire. And that fierce surge of possessiveness that had blindsided him in the car swelled within him again. He braced himself against it.

This wasn't the first time he'd bought a woman jewelry. Hell, the amount he'd bought Madison could have filled a store and still left enough diamonds to pay for a small city. He'd gone into the store this time intending to purchase a necklace or earrings, something that screamed wealth. But none of the pieces had felt...right. So he'd left, and instead had driven to a smaller jeweler. One where he'd bought his grandmother's birthday gift. And the bangles had been there, waiting. He hadn't intended to purchase something so personal to him, so...intimate, for what should've been just a flashy statement of ownership, with the sole purpose of making others take note. But he had. And unlike almost everything in his life, he didn't analyze it, instead going on impulse.

Because in that moment, as he'd handed his credit card over the counter, his need to see Shay wearing the pieces he'd personally chosen far outweighed caution.

And that need hadn't abated.

As he slid his hand up her spine and cupped the nape of her neck, the need deepened, sharpened.

"I should be annoyed with both of you," Janet Creighton said, her smile erasing the reproach from her words. Leaning forward, she dropped her voice to a conspiratorial whisper. "But the two of you outing yourselves as a couple tonight has made my little dinner party the social event of the season."

Shay smiled, glancing up at Gideon, and the warmth reflected in the gold-and-green depths of her eyes had his breath stumbling in his throat. "I told Gideon he should at least give you some warning of who his plus one would be, but…" She tipped her head to the side and murmured, "The rumors are true about that stubborn nature of his."

"I find myself giving in to you way too often, though. My reputation might not survive it," he replied, squeezing her neck and bringing her closer, brushing his lips over the side of her head.

Her fingernails bit into his arm, and he barely managed to fight back a groan. The tiny prick of pain echoed lower in his body, and he locked his jaw against asking her to do it again. But harder.

"You shouldn't let me know I'm a weakness," she teased, but only he caught the undercurrent of faint sarcasm. "I might be tempted to take advantage."

"I might be tempted to let you," he rejoined softly.

Silence thrummed between them, taut and tension-filled. Their gazes clashed, tangled, locked. The pretense seemed all too real. As did the desire that flared inside him, the excitement that flashed through him, as bright and hot as a bolt of lightning. What would she do if he lowered his head and took her soft mouth? Would she jerk away from him? Or would she use their act as an excuse to surrender, to let him taste her?

"Well, damn." Janet's awed, but amused whisper infiltrated the haze of arousal that had clouded him and his judgment. *Damn it,* he silently swore, returning his attention to his client. This was a facade, an act. One he'd set in motion. He couldn't afford to forget that. "Honey, I need you to take notes."

Beside Janet, her husband snorted lightly. "We've been married thirty-two years. My hand is cramped."

Shay's laughter drew more gazes in their direction, and Gideon smiled, both at the other couple and the pure delight in Shay's amusement.

"Dinner is almost ready," Janet said, shaking her head and throwing Donald a mock-irritated glance. "Let's go, you."

"That went well," Shay murmured, as soon as they were out of earshot. She slowly released his arm. "You can let go of me now."

Instead of obeying, he turned into her body, his hold on her drawing her closer until her breasts brushed his chest. He caught her sharp gasp, felt the puff against the base of his throat. Tiny flickers danced under his skin at that spot.

She stiffened, and he softly tsked, lowering his voice so it carried only as far as her ears. "You're supposed to enjoy my touch, Shay. Want more of it. But definitely not shy away from it." When she lifted her hands and settled them at his waist under his jacket, her fingernails digging into his skin through his shirt, he didn't hold back his low rumble of hunger. "I think you're intending to punish me, moonbeam," he growled above her mouth, pinching her chin with his free hand and tilting her head back. "But I don't mind a bit of pain with my pleasure. Would you sink those claws in deeper if I asked nicely?"

He expected her to wrench away from him; his muscles tightened in anticipation of controlling the reaction he purposefully coaxed from her.

But she sank her nails harder into his flesh, and the stings were a precursor of how she would scratch and grip him if they were stretched out on his bed. He tried to swallow his groan, but some sound escaped against his will. And the molten gold in her eyes almost eclipsed the brown and green.

She'd played him. Turned the tables so completely he ground his teeth together, imprisoning the words that would reveal she'd knocked him on his ass. Those words being *more, harder, please...*

"Gideon," she whispered.

"Well, don't you two look cozy," a new, all-too-familiar and despised voice drawled from behind them.

Gideon released Shay, shifting to her side and slipping an arm around her waist. He faced Madison and Julian Reus, careful to compose his features so they betrayed none of the disgust and hatred that burned in his chest for her, or the disdain he harbored for her father.

Underneath those emotions, satisfaction hummed

through his veins. *Good.* He'd been waiting for their arrival. He'd expected Trevor to be with them, but since he wasn't glued to Madison's side, the other man must not be in attendance. That was a disappointment, but Gideon's cheating ex and her equally deceptive father were good enough.

He switched his attention to Madison. It stunned him that he'd once missed the avaricious, calculating gleam in her brown eyes. Given her long dark hair, sensuous features and curvaceous body, he couldn't deny her beauty, but it was hard, like a lacquer that distracted from the coldness beneath.

Love had truly been blind. No. It'd made him dumb and deaf, too.

"I must admit, when we heard the rumors of you being here with Gideon, Shay, we didn't believe it at first," Julian said, his tone as amicable as any good politician's. But his eyes blazed, yelling the things one would never want heard on an open lapel mic. "Your brother didn't mention you were attending tonight. Or that you were…" he paused deliberately "…seeing someone new. I'm sure he'll be interested to discover this turn of events."

If the senator had expected Shay to quail under his not-so-subtle condemnation, he'd sadly underestimated her. "Trevor is a wonderful brother, but he's just that— my brother. And I don't require his approval for who I choose to spend time with. Just as he didn't ask for mine with Madison." Shay smiled, and it could've cut glass. "Although I would've gladly offered it."

Julian blinked, his mouth hardening at the corners.

"Your brother and I have much in common. We both admire honesty—and loyalty."

"You don't really want to go there, do you, Julian?" Gideon interjected, arching an eyebrow. He forced his voice to remain even, bored, but injected a thread of steel through it. He'd be damned if he'd let the man intimidate Shay or belittle her with his condescending bullshit. Especially not in front of him. "I'd be willing to discuss both with you. At length."

"Let's go, Daddy." Madison chuckled, the sound strained, her lovely features tight. Like her father's, her gaze ordered Gideon to do unnatural things with his own anatomy. "There are more people we need to speak with."

Shay waited until her soon-to-be sister-in-law and her father were out of earshot, then sighed. "God. This evening just became infinitely longer."

"I beg to disagree." He settled a hand on the small of her back again, guiding her forward. "The fun has just begun."

Shay breathed deeply as she washed her hands in the Creightons' bathroom. This moment alone, without the narrow-eyed glares from both Madison and the senator, or the microscopic attention of the other guests, was a mercy.

She hated being the subject of all that speculation. They'd reminded her of vultures, waiting to see who'd get their pick of carrion. Gideon seemed unfazed. But all those sidelong, greedy glances and not-so-quiet whispers… They'd crawled over her like ants attacking a picnic. By the time dinner concluded, she'd nearly raced to the bathroom. To be free. If only for a few moments.

"Can't stay in here forever," she said to her reflection.

That was the first sign of losing it, right? Talking to oneself. She smiled, shaking her head as she headed toward the restroom door. Her mother used to do the same, mumble to herself as she puttered around the kitchen when Dad wasn't there to catch her. God, Shay missed her. Missed her hugs, her quiet assurances, her confidence in Shay.

Well, one thing Leida Neal would've reprimanded her about was hiding like a coward in the bathroom during a dinner party. Snorting lightly, Shay exited the powder room…and nearly collided with Madison.

Damn.

"Hi, Madison." She greeted her brother's fiancée with a smile. "I'm sorry if you had to wait. The bathroom's all yours."

She shifted to the side, prepared to walk around the other woman, but the futile hope of avoiding a confrontation died a quick death when Madison stepped to the side as well, blocking Shay's escape. Madison smiled in turn, but it didn't reach her chilly brown eyes.

"No hurry, Shay. I was hoping to catch you alone for a few moments," she purred. "We have so much to catch up on, seeing as we apparently have more in common than I thought."

"I'm assuming you're referring to Gideon," Shay said, resigning herself to this conversation. It wasn't

one she could've circumvented, but she hadn't anticipated having it outside of the guest restroom.

"You're a cool one, aren't you, Shay?" Madison
asked, slowly shaking her head. "The other night you
never mentioned you knew him. And when I told you
about our past, you pretended to be dumb. It seems I
underestimated you. I won't repeat the mistake."

Anger flickered to life, crackling like dry wood set
ablaze. "I didn't pretend to be dumb, as you put it. Discussing my private life while you were at the table with
my brother, your fiancé, didn't strike me as appropriate. And like I told your father, I don't need approval
for my relationships," she said, working to keep the
bite of rising irritation from her tone. After all, this
was her future sister-in-law. Even if more and more
she was beginning to question the wisdom of Trevor's
choice. "Now, if I'd known you were attending this
dinner party, I would've informed you so you weren't
taken by surprise. But I wasn't aware."

Several silent moments passed, and a fury-filled
tension thickened between them.

"Your brother always brags about how smart you
are." Madison tsked softly. "Shay earned this degree.
Shay graduated with honors from this program. So
intelligent. And yet, when it comes to men, you're so
naive." Her expression softened with a sympathy that
was as false as her lashes. "What are the odds that *my
ex* would turn around and fall for *my new fiancé's sister*? A little too coincidental, don't you think?" She
chuckled, the sound taunting. "It's almost pathetic in
its transparency. He's using you, Shay. Gideon still

wants me, and you're caught up in his little plan to make me jealous."

Pain, serrated and ugly, slashed at her, the truth of Madison's words the razor-sharp knife. Why did it hurt? She'd gone into this charade knowing the reason behind it. Gideon hadn't tried to deny it. But reason had no place when humiliation and pain pumped out of her with every heartbeat.

Forcing her lips to move and her arm to lift, she waved away Madison's barb-tipped claims as if they were petty annoyances. "I don't see how any of this is your business, Madison. What is between Gideon and me is just that. *Between us*. Now if you'll excuse me…"

She moved forward again. If Madison chose to get in the way, this time she'd find her ass meeting the floor. Thankfully, Madison didn't try to block her, and Shay headed toward the dining room with a smothered sigh of relief.

"Ask him who broke it off with whom. He hasn't let go of me. If I wanted him back, Shay, he would be mine."

Madison's parting shot struck true. By sheer force of will, Shay kept walking.

But it was with a limp.

Twelve

"You ambushed me. Again."

Gideon turned from his silent—okay, brooding—study of the scenery passing by the car window to look at Shay. She'd been quiet since they'd left the Creightons' mansion ten minutes earlier. No, she'd been distant since returning to the dining room after dinner.

And Madison had followed a couple minutes behind her, wearing a sly grin. Personal experience had taught him his ex could be a malicious bitch. Had she said something to Shay? Had Madison hurt her? A wave of protectiveness had surged inside him, and he'd just managed to check the impulse to drag Shay onto his lap and demand answers. To ease the tension that had strung her shoulders tight. To assure her that if Madison had sharpened that dagger she called a tongue against Shay, he would fix it.

Instead, he'd remained sitting beside her at the table, continuing the charade until they could politely leave.

Disgust ate at him like a caustic acid. Disgust with himself. He'd led her into the lion's den and hadn't shielded her.

Every war has casualties.

He mentally repeated the reminder like a mantra. He'd been aware when he'd included Shay as part of his plans that she might be wounded, but the end justified the means. He intentionally conjured an image of his sister lying on that hospital bed, black hair limp, skin pale as she stared listlessly out the window. Oh yes. The end justified the means. *Olivia*—her suffering, her brokenness, her loss—justified it.

"Am I supposed to know what that cryptic comment means, Shay?" he asked. "Because I can assure you, I don't."

She didn't flinch from his flat, indifferent tone or the dismissal in his question. "You knew Madison and the senator would be there tonight."

Gideon stared at her, not even debating whether to give her the truth or not. "Of course I did. Janet and Donald are business associates of Julian's."

"You didn't think to warn me?" She shook her head. "What if Trevor had been there?"

"And?" he asked, anger igniting inside him. "I hoped he would be. But it doesn't matter. Maybe him hearing about his sister dating his enemy from his future father-in-law or his fiancée might work out better than I intended."

"Do you care that your schemes and plans are hurting people?" she whispered.

The disappointment in her voice, as if he'd somehow let her down, raked over his skin. Burrowed beneath it.

He hated it.

Dipping his head, he leaned closer until only inches separated them. So close her breath ghosted over his lips. "Your brother?" He paused. "No."

"All this for her," she breathed, her gold-and-green eyes roaming his face. Summer on the verge of autumn. That's what they reminded him of. Shaking his head as if he could physically rid himself of the sentimental thought, he leaned away from her, turning back to the window. "Madison was right."

He stiffened, his suspicions confirmed.

Slowly, he straightened and shifted on the seat, meeting her gaze again.

"What did she say to you?" he growled.

"Nothing I didn't already know," she replied, her full bottom lip trembling before she seemed to catch the betraying sign. Her teeth sank into the sensual curve.

"What did she say to you, Shay?" he repeated, grounding out the question between clenched teeth.

"That you were using me to get back at her and Trevor. That she could have you back if she wanted. She…" Shay paused, and something flickered in her eyes. "She told me to ask you who broke up with whom. From that, I'm assuming she left you."

He didn't answer. Couldn't.

What did it matter if Shay knew the dirty details? Of how he'd walked in on her brother in Madison's bed. How the woman he'd believed he would spend the rest of his life with had told him she'd upgraded with Trevor.

None of it mattered now. Yet he couldn't shove the words past his throat.

Shay shook her head, chuckling softly. Except the sound contained no humor. "So is that your master plan? Was the file on my brother your way of ensuring I cooperated while you plotted to steal back your ex? That would show Trevor who the better man was, right? Teach him—"

"You don't know what you're talking about."

"That's another thing Madison accused me of being. Dumb. But I'm not. You're fighting over her like she's some ball you lost on the playground. And in the end, I'll look like the idiot she called me. But that doesn't matter to you, does it? Not as long as you win."

Her accusation struck too close to the doubts that had pricked at his conscience only moments before. That only stirred his anger.

He didn't give a damn if she knew the truth.

"Win?" He arched an eyebrow, not bothering to prevent his sneer. "Win what, exactly? A relationship based on lies and greed? A woman who would jump to the next dick as long as he was willing to pay hand-

somely for the privilege? Tell me, Shay, doesn't that
sound like a terrible grand prize?"

She gaped at him, no doubt stunned by the ferocity
of his reply. "What do you mean?" she asked, her gaze
roaming his face, as if searching for the truth. As if
she actually wanted the truth. "Do you mean she—"

"Cheated on me? Oh yes." He nodded, and the smile
on his mouth felt savage. "We'd been together a year
and a half, engaged to be married. Gorgeous, fun,
witty, exciting—I didn't care who her father was or
about her family name. All I wanted was her. And all
she wanted was what I could give her. At least, until
she found someone else who could give her more. Care
to guess who that someone was?"

Her lips formed her brother's name, but no sound
came out.

"Yes, Trevor. I came home early from a business
trip and stopped by her place. I had the key, so I went
in and found them together. In the bed I'd just made
love to her in two days earlier. It hadn't been the first
time they'd been together. The next day, when giving
me back my ring, Madison informed me that it'd been
going on for some time—six months. According to her,
I might be rich, but Trevor had prestige, connections
and a family name. She'd upgraded."

Shay's chin jerked up as if he'd delivered a verbal
punch to her jaw. Sorrow flashed in her eyes, and for
a second, he resented her for it. He didn't want her
pity; he wanted her to understand the kind of bastard
she called brother.

"Your brother did it on purpose, Shay," he pressed.

Just as he'd used Gideon's sister to get to him. "He went after Madison because she was my fiancée, and faithless bitch that she is, she had no problem sleeping with a man she knew I hated. She not only betrayed me with her body, but with her loyalty, her heart. So I don't need to prove to Trevor who the better man is. Because, Shay, your brother isn't a real one."

"Gideon," she whispered.

"No." He slashed a hand down between them, done with the topic. Done with laying out his stupidity before her. "And to address the second part of that statement, you're not dumb. Far from it. But you are blind." He narrowed his eyes on her. "Why are you so quick to believe the manipulative claims of a jealous woman?"

She blinked. "What do you mean?" She frowned. "Madison's not—"

"Jealous," he interrupted again. "Why is that so hard to accept?" He didn't wait for her to answer, but continued. "And this doesn't have anything to do with me. You're everything she wants to be. Respected. Admired not just for your beauty but for who you are—successful, brilliant, esteemed. She, like me, like Julian, watched as you charmed everyone around you tonight, and as they damn near competed to have a moment of your time. And that has nothing to do with your last name. That's all you. I'm the toy in this scenario, moonbeam," he murmured. The thought of being her plaything roughened his voice, tightened his gut. "And she wants me only because you—a woman she could never be—has me."

If he hadn't been watching her so closely, he

might've missed her flinch before she controlled it. "Why are you calling me that?" she rasped.

"The other women there tonight… They were like the sun—bright, obvious. Trying so hard to be noticed. But you, Shay, you don't have to try to grab someone's attention. Like the moon, you're distant, cool and beautiful. Men can't help but notice you. Be drawn to you, ready to beg for some of your light rather than be lost and alone in the dark."

Only the harsh grating of their breaths filled the back of the car. Part of him demanded he rescind those too-revealing words. But the other part—the greedy, desperate part—refused to, instead waiting to see what she would do with them.

"What game are you playing now, Gideon?" she whispered, her eyes wide…vulnerable. "I don't know how to play this one."

"Then set the rules," he said, just as softly. Unable not to touch her any longer, he cupped her deceptively delicate jaw, stroked the pad of his thumb over the elegant jut of her cheekbone. "Set the rules, and I'll follow them."

It was a dangerous allowance. In this "relationship" the balance of power couldn't shift; he couldn't hand her a weapon to use against him. Not when revenge for his sister's pain, his family's torment hung in the balance. But that knowledge didn't stop him from shifting closer to her, from tipping her head back and brushing a caress over her parted lips. From staring down into those beautiful eyes and letting her see the desire that hurtled through his veins.

"Just one. Make…" She paused, briefly closed her eyes, but then her lashes lifted. "Make me forget."

"Forget what, moonbeam?"

The answer was already yes. He'd surrender anything to her if she'd permit him to continue touching her.

But that same hunger to brand her vied with the need to conquer what haunted her. He'd never considered himself some knight facing dragons, not for anyone, but for Shay, he'd forgo the armor and charge into the fire.

One hand rose to his wrist, the slender fingers wrapping around and hanging on to him. The other slipped inside his jacket and settled on his chest before sliding up to his neck, her thumb resting on his pulse.

"Forget that you're trying to destroy my brother, my world," she whispered. "Forget that you're going to break me. And I'm going to let you."

A vise gripped his chest and tightened until the barest of breaths passed through his lungs. If he was a good man, he would release her, promise not to touch her again. Walk away from this whole plan that already ensnared her like barbed wire. She was right; he would probably end up hurting her, and if he had a conscience, he would warn her to protect herself from him.

But he'd never claimed to be good.

Still, he could do what she asked. He could make her forget.

"Kiss me," he ordered in a low rumble. "Take what you want—what you need from me. And, moonbeam?"

He lowered his head, pushing his thumb past the seam of her lips and into her mouth. Moist heat bathed the tip. "Don't be gentle," he growled.

She studied him, and as he watched her in turn, desire eclipsed the vulnerability that lingered in her gaze. He felt her teeth first, and the tiny sting arrowed straight to his lower body.

"Don't be gentle," he repeated, harder.

Her eyes still on him, she moved the hand on his neck so her fingers encircled the front. She squeezed just as her lips closed around his thumb, and she bit him.

"Fuck," he groaned, the sting arcing through him like a sizzling bolt of electricity. "Baby." Her gaze darted to the side, toward the front of the car and his driver. "The divide is soundproof," he assured her, pulling his thumb free and rubbing the dampness over her bottom lip. Before repaying her with a nip of his own.

Another moan clawed free of him. Damn, he'd been aching—literally *aching*—to get his mouth on her. To taste her. Reaching for the console in front of the seat, he lifted the hood and hit a button, and another panel, this one smoke-tinted, slid across, concealing them.

"Are you good?" he asked. His dick throbbed, and he gritted his teeth.

He could wait until they reached their destination, but fuck if he *or* his dick wanted to. He needed to be inside her. From the moment he'd sat down across from her in that restaurant, he'd craved this. No, damn that. Longer. From the second he'd opened his private investigator's file and laid eyes on her picture. Even as he'd spun his plans of revenge, he'd envisioned those hazel eyes gleaming with the arousal he'd stirred. Pictured her sweet body bowing and twisting for him. Wondered if she would take him slow and easy, or hard and wild. God, he'd almost driven himself insane wondering that.

She nodded, but he shook his head. "Tell me, moonbeam. You good?"

"Yes," she breathed, giving his neck one last squeeze. She removed her hand, replacing it with her mouth, trailing a path up his throat, over his chin until she hovered over his lips. "I've set the rules," she reminded him, kneeling on the seat so she rose over him. "Now follow them like you promised."

She crushed her mouth to his.

The kiss wasn't patient, wasn't tentative. Her tongue thrust forward, parried with his, tangling and dueling. She took him as if she knew exactly what he liked, what he needed. It was…familiar. Something—a thought, a warning, maybe—tickled the back of his skull, but as she sucked on his tongue, drawing on him as if he were everything she needed to survive, that inkling winked out. Nothing mattered but the intoxicating, addictive taste of her. And in that instant, the question that had plagued him since he first gazed on her picture was answered: Shay would be hard and wild in bed. Or in the back of a Town Car.

"I want to…" She didn't finish her request, but reached behind him, removing the band holding back his hair.

The strands loosened, and her heavy sigh differed from the ones she'd been emitting during their kiss. This one? It matched the delight that softened her beautiful features as she drew his hair forward and up to her face. Tangling her fingers in the strands, she tugged on them, and the prickle across his scalp tripped down his spine, crackled at the base. He clutched her hips, digging his fingertips into the soft flesh.

"Beautiful," she whispered.

Only one other woman had ever called him that, and with that same note of awe coating the compliment. It'd shaken him then, and it did now. Once more that niggling sense of…something…teased him. But he shoved it away. Now, with his hands on Shay, with her storm-whipped rain and fresh roses scent embracing him, there wasn't room for thoughts of another woman. Especially one that was a ghost. Shay was sensual, golden-bronze flesh-and-bone. She was hot, pounding blood coursing through him. She was his insanity, his hunger brought to vivid life.

She was *here*.

For him.

With a growl, he skated his palms up the sides of her torso, and the zipper of her dress abraded his skin. Desperate to discover if his imagination matched reality, he impatiently tugged it down and wasted no time in pushing the material over her shoulders and down her arms. She obliged him, freeing his hair and joining him in getting rid of the clothing.

"No." The word escaped him before he could trap it.

"No?" she repeated, and he caught the hint of insecurity that crept into her voice. She started to lift her arms toward her torso, but he latched on to her wrists, lowering her arms back down before she could cross them.

"My imagination doesn't match reality. Doesn't even fucking compete." He cupped a breast and hissed at the delicious weight of her flesh filling his palm. Warm, soft, perfect. Reverently, he whisked his thumb over the nipple, watching in fascination as it beaded. No, she wasn't the first woman he'd touched like this, but none had been *her*. He tore his gaze from his hand on her to meet her eyes. "Nothing or no one could fucking compete."

Her lips parted, but no words emerged. Good. He was saying enough for both of them, and he needed to stop that before he took them somewhere they had no place being. Bending his head, he sucked a tip deep, flicking his tongue against her flesh before drawing hard. Shay shuddered, her hands cradling his head, holding him to her with a strength that telegraphed her passion. That and the nails pricking his scalp.

Switching breasts, he treated the other to the same devotion. She writhed against him, as if seeking to get closer. Cooperating, he fisted the hem of her dress and shoved it up her thighs. With a whimper, she straddled him, dropping down and pressing them sex to sex.

He growled around her flesh, suckling harder. And she rewarded his attention with a dirty grind of her hips that had him throwing his head back against the seat, eyes squeezed closed. Her panties and his pants and underwear separated them, but none of those inconsequential details mattered. Not when her hot, wet heat rode him. Not when each drag of her flesh over his cock shredded his control.

"Give me your mouth again," he ordered, in a voice so guttural he barely understood himself.

But she must've translated it, because she gave him what he asked for, her hips still working over him. She didn't stop, and the thrust of her tongue and pull of her lips mimicked each stroke below. Even as she yanked his jacket open and attacked his shirt, damn near ripping buttons loose to get her hands on his bare chest, she didn't lose him.

They groaned into each other when she touched him. Those slender, clever hands swept down his chest, lingering over his tattoos, tracing the ink with almost worshipful strokes.

"How is it possible that you just get more beautiful?" she whispered. He parted his lips to tell her she was the stunning one, not him, but she ripped away his ability to talk by brushing her fingertips over his nipples, rubbing them. His hips bucked into her. Live wires connected from her touch to the tip of his dick. He swelled, throbbing, *hurting*.

"I need to be inside you," he rasped against her mouth. He abandoned her breasts and burrowed his fingers in her hair, gripping it, holding her still so he could stare into those slumberous eyes. "Are you going to let me?"

"Yes," she breathed, trailing a route of fire over his clenched abs to the band of his pants.

"Are you going to take me like this?" he pressed,

thrusting upward so she fully understood what he meant. "Take me like you own me?"

"Yes."

Almost too rough, he released her, reaching into his inner jacket pocket for his wallet. Quickly withdrawing a condom, he tossed the billfold to the floor. Within moments, he had his pants opened, his erection freed. Her swift intake of breath preceded the hot, tight clasp of her fist around him by seconds. His back bowed under the whip of pleasure, and his free hand wrapped around hers, so they pumped his flesh together. For several torturous and blissful moments, they stroked him, pushing closer to an ending that wouldn't include him balls-deep inside her.

"Enough," he muttered, and, removing their hands, tore open the small foil package and slid the protection over him. Above him, she fumbled under her dress, trying to push black lace panties down her hips. "Fuck that," he growled.

Shoving her dress higher until it encircled her waist like a band, he fisted the front of her underwear and jerked it to the side. For a couple seconds, he savored the vision of her bare, glistening sex and the erotic beauty of her silken thigh-high stockings against silkier skin. But then the lure of that feminine flesh proved too enticing, too much.

He slid his finger through the dark cleft, moaning at the wetness coating his skin. The sound dragged from her echoed his, and her head tipped back, shuddering when he circled her, applying minute pressure. Just enough to have her shaking like a leaf, but not enough to catapult her over the edge. That honor belonged to his dick.

Hands grasping his shoulders, she eased down his length, and though the drugging pleasure had his eyes nearly closing to savor the tight, smooth fit of her sex, he kept his attention on her. Because nothing—not the rippling clasp of her body, the quiver of her thighs, the sight of her taking him—could compare with the slight widening and darkening of those beautiful eyes. Those eyes conveyed how much she craved him, needed him.

Those eyes gave him all of her.

And greedy bastard that he was, he wanted it all.

Except for the very fine tremble of his tautly controlled muscles, he held completely still. Allowing her to claim him at her own pace. Even if each interminable second she took to inch down threatened to send him careening into insanity or orgasm—whichever came first. Finally, she sat on his thighs, and he was fully embedded inside her. And still he wouldn't free her from his gaze. Not when, in this moment, surrounded by her sweet flesh, everything clicked into place. He finally knew this gaze.

Knew *her*.

"Fuck me, moonbeam," he whispered. "And don't look away from me."

Sliding her hands over his shoulders and into his hair, she grabbed fistfuls of the strands and glided up his length. Air kissed his tip before she sank onto him again, swallowing him in the firmest, but softest heat. Again. And again. She released him, took him. Eased off him, claimed him.

She rode him, rising and falling over him, driving them both toward the rapidly crumbling edge of release. Her cries mixed with the litany of his own and still she continued to look at him. Letting him see what he did to her. Gifting him with that. Electric pulses zipped up and down his spine, crackling in the balls of his feet. He couldn't hold back much longer. He wasn't going to last.

He loosened a hand from her hair and tucked it between their undulating bodies and slicked it over the top of her sex. Once, twice. A third and a pinch.

She flew apart with a scream, stiffening, her sex gripping him, milking him. Daring him to dive into the abyss with her. Grabbing her hips, he slammed into her, plunging so deep he almost doubted he would ever find his way out of her.

She fucking leveled him.

Her arms closed around his shoulders, cradling him as he bowed his head, groaning out his release into her neck. He inhaled her thick, heady scent as his body calmed and his breathing evened. His senses gradually winked back online after pleasure short-circuited them.

Silence filled the interior of the car. Carefully, he withdrew from her, disposing of the condom and righting their clothes. Shay didn't look at him, paying undue attention to pulling down her dress and settling it around her thighs.

"Are you okay?" he asked, his voice seeming overly loud even to his own ears.

"Yes," she said, still not glancing in his direction.

Camille.

The name shivered on his tongue. He almost said it aloud just to see if she would respond. If her reaction would give her away. But he swallowed the name of the woman who'd haunted his thoughts since the night of the blackout.

The woman who was one and the same as Shay Neal.

It explained the nagging sense of familiarity. The feeling that they'd met before. Sinking into her body had sealed the knowledge for him. How had Shay thought she could continue to fool him once he was deep inside her? How could she believe he would ever forget the too-tight and utterly perfect fit of her?

She'd lied to him. All this time, she'd recognized him—how could she not?—but she'd kept the secret of her identity from him.

Why?

Several reasons entered his mind—embarrassment, protecting her reputation—but one kept blaring in his head, gaining validity.

Had meeting him at the Du Sable City Gala been a setup? Not the blackout, of course, but had she gone to the gala with a plan to meet him? To get close to him? Yes, he'd approached her, but what would've happened if he hadn't? Would she have found a way to get close to him? Found a way to get him to talk to her, to reveal information?

Had Trevor sent her to the gala with that purpose?

Minutes ago, Gideon would've said no. But with the haze of pleasure quickly evaporating and leaving him with a clearer mind, he couldn't know for sure. First and foremost, Shay was a Neal and her loyalty belonged to her brother. Hadn't she been willing to surrender to blackmail and sleep with the enemy— literally, now—to save Trevor? Gideon couldn't see her going so far as to fuck him in that dark break room for her brother. As she'd defiantly told him before, she didn't whore herself out for anyone. But…doing a little subterfuge on Trevor's behalf? Maybe that wasn't out of the question…

He studied her proud profile, waiting to see if she would tell him the truth now, after she'd allowed him back inside her body. Maybe she'd explain her reasons for deceiving him.

But she didn't.

Her silence was a punch-in-the-gut reminder of who she was—who they were to each other. She said she wanted to forget. But they never could. Especially when forgetting for even a moment meant letting his guard down and the enemy in.

And that's who she was.

The enemy.

Thirteen

Shay shrugged into her suit jacket, studying herself in her room's cheval mirror. The slim fit of the gray, pin-striped jacket and pencil skirt were flattering, emphasizing the curves of her waist and hips. The cream blouse with the throat-to-waist ruffle lent it a feminine flair. She'd gathered her hair into a loose bun and fastened a pair of her mother's favorite diamond studs to her ears. The whole look was professional, fashionable...

And armor.

Yes, she needed it today. Hopefully, no one looking at her would guess that the previous night she'd had hot, wild sex in the back seat of a car.

God. She closed her eyes, pinching the bridge of her nose. What had she been thinking? But that was just it. She hadn't been.

Groaning, she turned from the mirror. It would've been so easy to stay in bed today and burrow under the covers. Just pretend last night hadn't happened. After all, that was her forte lately. Pretend to be in a relationship. Pretend to be in love with Gideon Knight. Pretend she hadn't just thrown all common sense and family loyalty out the window and screwed the man who was blackmailing her.

Regret weighed down her chest, so she couldn't inhale without feeling its bulk. Not regret about the sex. It had been as cataclysmic as the first time, and though it'd been foolish to give in to him, she didn't have remorse over experiencing passion.

No, it was what happened after that earned her regret. For a time, she'd forgotten that Gideon hated everything and everyone associated with the Neal name. That he planned on taking down her brother if she didn't capitulate to blackmail. That they stood on opposite sides of a Hatfield-and-McCoy-esque feud.

But as soon as the pleasure ebbed from her body, he'd returned to his aloof, distant self. She'd practically felt the wall slamming up between them. He'd been gentle when he'd shifted her off his lap and adjusted her dress, but unlike the hands that had cupped her breasts, tangled in her hair and stroked between her legs, his touch had been cold, almost clinical.

Other than asking if she was okay and wishing her good-night when he'd dropped her off at home, he hadn't spoken. And she'd never felt so vulnerable, so… alone. Not even after the night of the blackout.

And to think she'd been so close to telling him she was Camille. That would've gone over well. Not.

Well, lesson learned. Last night was a mistake she wouldn't repeat. She refused to let herself be vulnerable to him again. Get through the next six months. That was her goal. Protect Trevor from Gideon, come into her trust fund, then leave RemingtonNeal to concentrate on her own business.

The days of being under the thumb of the men in her life would come to an end.

To achieve the dream of independence, she could endure six more months of Gideon Knight.

With a sigh, she glanced at the clock on her bedside table. Well, no time for breakfast, and she could grab coffee at the office. If traffic cooperated, she would just make her nine o'clock meeting with the event planners for RemingtonNeal's huge annual holiday party.

Grabbing her coat and purse, she descended the steps, her mind already locked on the multiplying items on her to-do list today.

"Shay."

She halted at the front door, shooting Trevor a hurried smile as she set her purse on the foyer table to slip into her coat.

"Morning, Trevor. I'm sorry I don't have time for breakfast. I have a—"

"You'll need to make the time. I need to talk with you immediately. And it's too important to put off. I'll meet you in the study." He didn't wait for her agreement, but pivoted on his heel and strode toward the rear of the house.

Bemused, she stared after him. Removing her arm from her coat sleeve, she tossed the garment over her purse and followed her brother.

"Shut the door, please," he said, when she entered the room he considered his domain. As their father had done before him.

Trevor hadn't changed much in the room. Except for the dark chocolate office chair that sat behind the massive oak-and-glass desk, everything else was the same. The tall bookshelves that lined two of the walls, the heavy floor-to-ceiling drapes, the two armchairs flanking the big fireplace. She'd hated being called into this room when her father had been alive; it'd meant she'd somehow screwed up. And she didn't like it any better now with her brother.

"What's going on, Trevor?" she asked, crossing her arms over her chest. Another thing she hated. Feeling defensive.

"Why did I have to find out about you and Gideon Knight from Madison and her father?" he snapped, stalking around his desk. "Do you know how humiliating that was for me, receiving that phone call?"

Of course. How could she have forgotten about Madison and the senator?

Gideon, that's how. Gideon and sex in the back seat of his car.

"I'm sorry, Trevor," she said, truly remorseful. She'd fully intended to tell him about her and Gideon's "relationship" when she arrived home last night, but it'd slipped her mind. "I wanted you to hear about us from me first."

"Us?" he sneered, his hands closing on the back of the chair several feet from her. "There shouldn't even be an *us*. I told you to stay away from him," he reminded her with a narrowed glare. "Do you remember? It was when you told me you barely knew him and there was nothing going on between you two."

"Like I told Madison last night, the fund-raiser wasn't the place to discuss my personal life. Especially when you didn't try to hide your hostility toward him. I've been seeing Gideon for a while now, but because of who we are, we decided not to make our relationship public until we knew we were serious about it." Great. Now she was lying about her lie. "But like I also told the senator, I don't need to run my relationships by you for permission. I did intend to give you the *courtesy* of telling you about Gideon last night. So again, I apologize if you were embarrassed discovering it from someone else."

"Where's your loyalty, Shay?" he hissed. "Your duty to family first?"

Pain struck her like a fiery dart to the breast. It spread through her until she vibrated with it. Reason whispered that he didn't know all she sacrificed—was still sacrificing—for him. But it didn't halt the hurt from his condemnation, his disgust.

"My loyalty is always to this family," she whispered. "Who I'm seeing socially should have nothing to do with you or my love for you."

"It does if you're screwing a man I hate. Have always hated," he snarled.

"Why?" she asked, lowering her arms and risking

a step forward, closer to him. "Tell me why. Gideon told me you went to school together."

That hadn't been all he'd said, but even as shameful and horrible as her brother bullying him was, surely there had to be more to the story. Especially on Trevor's end. Yes, he was a snob, but she'd never seen him actively hate someone just because they came from humble beginnings.

"Yes, we went to school together, and he didn't know his place back then, either."

"Didn't know his place," she repeated slowly, not believing that he'd uttered those ugly, bigoted words. Yes, they were fortunate enough to be in that elevated percentage of wealthy Americans. But they were still black. They still endured racists who gave them the "you're not our kind, dear" looks when they dared enter some establishments. How dare *he*...

"Why? Because he's Chinese-American?" she rasped.

"No." He slashed a hand through the air. "I don't give a damn about that." The vise squeezing her chest eased a little, and relief coursed through her. "After Mom died, all I had left was Dad."

Oh God. "Trevor," she said, moving forward, holding a hand out toward him.

"No," he repeated, coupling it with another hand slash. "I know you were there, but she was something different to me than to you. She was the shield, the... insulation between him and me. When she died, she left me exposed to him. To his expectations, his impossibly high standards, his disapproval. I didn't get time to grieve for her because I had Dad riding my ass, wanting to make a real Neal man out of me without my mother's babying. His words," he added, his tone as caustic as acid.

"I know," Shay murmured. "I saw how hard he was on you. But, Trevor?" She lifted her hands, palms up. "What did that have to do with Gideon? Dad didn't know Gideon."

"But he did," Trevor snarled. "Who do you think funded the scholarship that enabled Gideon to attend the prep school? One of RemingtonNeal's charities. And Dad never let me forget it. Sports, academics, even the damn debate team—Gideon and I were always head-to-head in everything, and when he beat me, Dad was always right there to remind me that a poor scholarship kid was better than me. That maybe he should hire him to run the family company because he was smarter, stronger, quicker, more clever. He constantly compared us, and it didn't end with high school, but continued in college and beyond, even following Gideon's career after he graduated. The one thing I'm grateful for is that he's not alive today to see you with him. He probably would claim him as his son, give him RemingtonNeal."

Shock pummeled her. She'd had no clue. But now his animosity toward Gideon made sense, because she knew her father. Knew how denigrating and belittling and cruel he could be. Especially toward Trevor. Lincoln Neal probably didn't even like Gideon, but using him as an emotional weapon against his son sounded like something he would do.

And Trevor… God, if her brother didn't let go of his bitterness, he would live trying to prove to their dead father that he was better than a man he might have counted as a friend once upon a time.

"Do you understand why you can't be with him, Shay? That man has been the source of my pain and unhappiness for over a decade. I won't allow him in my home or to eat at my table, much less date my sister." He shook his head. "End it."

I can't.

The words bounced off her skull, pounded in her chest. To call off her relationship with Gideon would be to destroy her brother. But even in an alternate universe where she and Gideon had met under normal circumstances without blackmail and revenge, she still wouldn't have broken up with him based on what her brother had shared. Trevor's antagonism for Gideon wasn't his fault—it was their father's. But with Lincoln Neal gone, Trevor had transferred all his resentment and pain to the one who was still alive.

"No, I won't end it with Gideon," she said. Sighing, she moved across the small distance separating them and covered his hand. "Trevor, I—"

He jerked away from her, taking several steps back and glaring at her. A muscle ticked along his clenched jaw. "You won't break this *thing* off with him?"

"No, Trevor, I won't." *I'm doing this for you*, she silently screamed. But the words remained trapped in her throat.

"I didn't want to do this, but you've left me with no other choice. Leida Investments, Shay."

For the second time in the space of minutes, shock robbed her of speech. Icy fingers of astonishment and dread trailed down her spine.

Trevor cocked his head to the side. "You believed I didn't know about your little company all this time? Nothing gets by me. And as long as you were discreet, I didn't see the harm in letting you dabble in business. It didn't interfere with your responsibilities to this family. But now, your actions are jeopardizing us. If you don't end it with Gideon, I'll ruin every business that has received money from you. And with my name and reputation, you know I could do it with just a whisper. Now, while you take some time to make your decision about who you're giving your loyalty to, I'm going to insist you step back from your job at RemingtonNeal. I've already asked Madison to take over some of your duties for the next few weeks. Consider it a leave of absence while you choose between a man you barely know and your family."

With that parting shot, he exited the room, not pausing to spare her a glance. Not even bothering to glimpse the devastation he'd left behind.

Not only had he dismissed her easily, replacing her with his fiancée, but he'd threatened her company, as well as the hard work and livelihoods of those she'd invested in.

He would cavalierly ruin others' lives to bring her to heel.

Forcing her feet to move, she left the study and retraced her steps to her room. There, she removed her suit and went to her closet for her suitcases. Forty minutes later, she once more descended the stairs, not knowing when she would return.

She couldn't stay here any longer.

Not when she wasn't sure who she was selling her soul to protect.

Fourteen

Gideon pulled up in front of the small brick house in the Humboldt Park neighborhood. With its white trim, meticulously manicured front lawn and currently empty flower boxes, the home was cute and obviously well taken care of.

But Shay still had no business being here.

Not when she had a home.

So why had she sent him a text informing him he'd need to pick her up here tonight, as she would be living in this place for the foreseeable future?

What the hell was going on?

The questions had burned in his head, then twisted his gut into knots. The need for answers had propelled him out of his mother's house, where he'd been visiting her and Olivia. He hadn't bothered replying to

Shay's text but had entered the address in his GPS and driven directly there.

He shut off his car and walked up the tidy sidewalk to the postage-stamp-size porch. Maybe she'd heard him arrive, because before he could knock on the storm door, Shay appeared in the entrance, wrapped in a cashmere shawl and evening gown. She joined him on the porch, scanning his attire, her gaze running over his peacoat, down his black jeans to his boots, then back up.

"You're going to the ballet dressed like that?" she asked, frowning.

"No," he answered shortly. "Come on."

He'd offered her his hand before considering the gesture. They weren't in public, so the display of affection wasn't necessary. But when she wrapped her fingers around his, he only tightened his hold. And didn't think about why he did it.

Moments later, with her safe in the passenger's seat, the full skirt of her gown tucked around her legs, he started the car and drove away.

"What's going on, Shay?" he asked. "Whose house is that?"

"My best friend, Bridgette. You met her that day in the food truck," she replied, keeping her gaze straight ahead.

Impatient, Gideon pressed, "And? Why are you staying with her—how did you put it—for the foreseeable future?"

She sighed, and he steeled himself against the punch

of that tired sound. "Because I left home. And I don't know when, or if, I'll return."

Surprise winged through him, and quick on its heels was fury. Cold, bright fury. "Did you leave or did Trevor kick you out?"

Another sigh, and when he glanced over at her she shook her head. "I left. We…had a disagreement, and I thought it best if I gave us both space."

"You're trying to make me drag it out of you, aren't you?" he growled.

"I'm not trying to make you do anything," she said, every inch of the society princess in that reply. "What's more, I don't *want* you to."

His fingers curled around the steering wheel, his hold so tight the leather creaked. Part of him longed to jerk the car over three lanes to the side of the road and demand she confess everything to him, because he knew there was more to the story. And from those sighs and the tension in her slender frame, he sensed the "disagreement" with Trevor hadn't been pretty. It'd hurt her. And for that Gideon wished he could strangle the man.

But the other part… That part longed to pull over, too, but for a different reason. It wanted to park, release her seat belt and tug her onto his lap so he could hold her. Comfort her. Murmur into her ear that everything would be all right, that *she* would be all right.

Which was ridiculous. If there was a woman who didn't need comforting—didn't need *him*—it was Shay Neal.

Quiet settled in the car like a third passenger as he

drove to his home. It wasn't until he pulled into the underground parking garage that she stirred.

"I can wait here or in the lobby while you change if you're not going to be long. The ballet starts in about thirty minutes," she said, straightening in the passenger's seat.

"Don't be ridiculous," he snapped, her obvious reluctance to be alone with him irritating him. Did she expect him to jump her? "I promise to keep my hands and dick to myself. Now can you please get out of the damn car?"

He didn't wait for her answer, but shoved the door open. But he still caught her grumbled, "Speaking of dicks…"

In spite of the anger and frustration churning in his chest, he couldn't suppress the quirk of his mouth. This woman gave as good as she got.

Minutes later, they entered his penthouse, and as he took her wrap to hang up, lust joined the cluster of emotions he was feeling. While the champagne-colored skirt of her dress flowed around her legs, the top clung to her shoulders, arms and torso—except for the deep V that dipped between her breasts and even lower in back. He briefly closed his eyes, turning away from the alluring sight of her. Immediately, images of the night in his Town Car skated over the back of his lids like a movie trailer. Him, cupping those breasts, drawing them into his mouth…

Cursing under his breath, he jerked open the closet door and, with more force than necessary, hung up her shawl and his coat.

How could she flaunt sex and sophistication at the same time?

"Would you like a glass of wine? Scotch?" he asked, stalking into the living room and toward the bar.

"Do we have time for that? If you don't hurry and dress, we're going to be late," she reminded him, following him, but halting on the top of the steps that led into the living room.

He removed the top of a crystal decanter and poured himself a finger of bourbon. Only after he'd downed a sip did he turn and face her. Staring at her golden skin and the inner curves of her breasts, he took another. He needed the fortification.

"We're not going to the ballet," he informed her.

She frowned. "What? Why not?" She stepped down into the room. "And why didn't you tell me you changed your mind at Bridgette's house?"

"Why?" he repeated, lifting the tumbler to his lips and staring at her over the rim as he sipped. "Because even though you won't admit it, you're hurting. Something more than a 'disagreement' had to have occurred to make you leave the only family you have left, as well as the only home you've known. I'm a self-confessed asshole, Shay, but even I wouldn't make you attend a social event and fake a happiness you're far from feeling. Especially when your brother might be in attendance." He swirled the amber liquor in his glass and arched an eyebrow. "And as for why I didn't tell you when I picked you up, that's simple. You wouldn't have come with me if I had. The last thing you need right now is to be alone. And since I know your friend supplements her food truck income with a part-time job, you would've been very much alone tonight. So that leaves me."

Her frown deepened. "It's a little creepy how you know so much about me and everyone I'm close to."

He shrugged, taking another taste of the bourbon. "Before going into battle, it's wise to be prepared and know everything you can about your enemy."

"Enemy," she breathed, then scoffed. "You just proved my point. We're not friends—far from it. So why do you care how I spend my night? I'm not your responsibility," she said softly.

"No," he agreed just as softly. "We're not friends. But can we call a truce and resume hostilities tomorrow?" He risked drawing nearer to her. "You're right, you're not my responsibility. But I am responsible. The argument was about me, wasn't it?" When she didn't reply, he gently pressed, "Shay?"

"Yes," she reluctantly admitted.

"Let me guess," he said, his anger rekindling. "Trevor wanted you to break it off with me and you refused."

"Correct again." She notched her chin up at a defiant angle, but he caught the slight tremble of her bottom lip. "But if I'd given in to his demand, then it would've meant destroying everything he cares about, destroying him. Still, it's not like I could share that with him. Instead, he threatened to dismantle my company, starting with ruining all the businesses I've invested in. Oh, and he fired me—or placed me on a temporary leave of absence. So those are my choices. End our relationship and destroy everything my brother loves. Or continue upholding our bargain and lose the company I love."

Fury blasted through him, and for a moment a red haze dropped over his vision. Trevor had threatened his own sister? Gideon grasped the tumbler so tightly the beveled edges dug into his flesh. He pictured that thick, brown file in his office safe, and had no regrets about his intentions to expose Trevor. A man like him deserved the hell Gideon planned to rain down on him.

"I won't let him do that," Gideon promised. Soon enough her brother would be too busy trying to pick up the flaming pieces of his life to worry about harming her company.

"It's not your concern." She waved a hand, dismissing his vow and the topic. "And you mentioned a truce? I accept." Moving forward, she extended her arm. "Should we shake on it?"

Gideon glanced down at her open palm before lifting his gaze to meet her eyes. Though his mind ordered him not to touch her, he wrapped his hand around hers. For several long moments, they stared at each other. An electric shock ran through him at lightning speed and jolted his body to attention. It would be an impossibility to be skin-to-skin with her and not respond. But he didn't pull her closer, didn't try to seduce with his words.

Space and sanctuary, that's what he'd promised her.

"Are you hungry?" he asked, lowering his arm to his side. "I can order in anything you'd like."

"I…" She hesitated, shrugged a shoulder and

started again. "I can cook if you have something in the kitchen."

Since meeting Shay, he'd been surprised so many times, he should really stop being taken aback by her. But once more, she'd done the unexpected.

"You can cook?" Dubious, he scanned her beautiful hair, gown and shoes. "In that?"

She snorted. "You're not starting off this truce thing well. And yes, I can cook." If he hadn't been watching her so closely, he might've missed the flash of insecurity that was there and gone in an instant. "Show me to the kitchen? That is, if you don't mind me…?"

"No, this I have to see for myself," he assured her, and strode past her toward the room he rarely used. His housekeeper often prepared dinners for him that she left warming in the stove. So the pantry and refrigerator should both be stocked. "I'll even supply you with clothes so you don't get anything on your dress. See how accommodating I am?"

"Until tomorrow," she added from behind him.

"Until tomorrow," he agreed.

"I wouldn't have believed it if I hadn't tasted it for myself," Gideon exclaimed with wonder, staring down at his empty plate.

Shay shook her head, smothering a smile, although her cheeks hurt with the effort. Forking the last of the chicken carbonara to her mouth, she tried not to blush under his admiring scrutiny. She was twenty-five and an heiress—needless to say, she was used to compliments. But coming from this man… She returned her gaze to her plate, not wanting to analyze why it was different.

"Can I say something without breaking the tenuous bonds of our truce?" he asked, cocking his head to the side.

She wanted to duck her head and avoid his piercing contemplation. It cut deep. Exposing her. Even with the distance of the breakfast bar separating them, she had the sudden urge to lean back, insert more space between them.

But she remained seated and met his gaze. "Sure."

"I would've never pegged you for someone who enjoyed getting their hands dirty in a kitchen. I know you helped your friend out that day in the food truck, but I thought that was a fluke. What you did in there—" he dipped his head in the direction of the kitchen "—was skill. And spoke of someone who really enjoyed it. You're a walking contradiction."

"So your all-knowing file didn't include that information?" she mocked. Picking up her wineglass, she sipped the moscato, silently debating how much to tell him. Then, before she could make up her mind, her mouth was moving. "My mother loved to cook. We had a personal chef, but when Dad wasn't home, she'd commandeer the kitchen and cook for all of us. She would let me help, and some of my happiest memories are of the two of us preparing a pot of gumbo or baking a quiche. I learned to cook from her, but I also inherited my love of it from her."

God, where had all that come from? Embarrassment rose in her, swift and hot.

"Anyway, now your dossier is complete," she added flippantly. "I'll clean up."

She rose from her chair and, grabbing both their plates, circled the bar and headed toward the sink. As she set the dishes in it, a long-fingered hand settled over hers, stilling her movements.

"She would've been proud of you," Gideon murmured in her ear. Heat from his body pressed into her side, her shoulder. "Now, go relax. You did all the work, the least I can do is clean up."

Her first instinct with Gideon was always to defy his orders. She wasn't a puppy. But this time, she accepted his offer and slid from between him and the counter.

Coward.

Maybe.

Okay, definitely. But his unexpected displays of tenderness and the potent, dark sexuality that he emitted like pheromones combined to undermine every guard she'd erected since that night he'd so coldly rejected her after giving her devastating pleasure.

She went in search of the restroom, and after locating it and washing her hands, she continued her tour of his place. At least the downstairs. A formal dining room. A bedroom done in soft blues and cream. Maybe this was where his sister, Olivia, slept when she came over; he'd said the T-shirt and leggings he'd given Shay were hers. Until that moment, she hadn't even known he had a sister. But he didn't offer more information, and for the sake of their temporary cease-fire, she didn't ask.

Another bathroom. A study. A den.

She paused at the open door of that last room. With its two couches, love seat, numerous end tables, large coffee table, massive television screen mounted above the fireplace, this space appeared more lived-in than the rest of the penthouse.

She glanced behind her, but the hallway remained empty. *Just a peek*, she promised herself, then she'd leave. Moving into the room, she stroked a hand over the leather couch that bore a distinct imprint in the middle cushion.

Must be where Gideon sat the most. She could easily imagine the man she'd spent this evening with—in his black, long-sleeved, V-neck sweater, black jeans and bare feet—relaxing in this room. Feet up on the table, remote in hand, scanning through the no-doubt-numerous channels before deciding on…what? Funny. She knew how he had sex, but had no clue about his favorite TV shows or movies.

For some reason, that struck her as sad.

It also lit a hunger to discover more about him. Some things they'd shared in the blackout, but not nearly enough to satisfy her curiosity. What was his favorite color? His favorite band? Snack? Boo—

Oh God.

Breath trapped in her throat, she crossed the room toward the instrument that had captured her attention. No, *instruments*. Plural. A glossy black stand with padded interior cradled six guitars. She knew nothing of guitars, but she could tell the three acoustic and three thinner, sleeker electric guitars had to be expensive. And obviously well cared for.

A flutter tickled her stomach, launching into a full-out quake. She reached a slightly trembling hand toward the guitars.

"Do you play?"

She whipped around, guilt snaking through her. "I—I'm sorry," she stammered, backing away from the instruments. Damn, she was a sneak. And not even a good one. "I didn't mean to snoop, I…" She paused and inhaled a deep breath. "I was taking a self-guided tour of your house and saw the guitars. They're beautiful," she whispered. "I don't play, but obviously, you do…?"

He nodded, crossed the room on silent bare feet and halted next to the stand.

"For years," he said, brushing an affectionate stroke over the gleaming wood of an acoustic guitar. Her thighs tightened, the touch reminding her of how he'd caressed her skin. A lover's familiar caress. "We didn't have a lot of money when I was growing up. But when I showed an interest and aptitude for guitar, my mother somehow managed to scrape enough together for lessons. I didn't find out until I was a teenager, but my father played the guitar, too. I don't remember it, but I like to think I inherited my love of music from him, as you did cooking from your mother."

"Will you—" She broke off. God, she was pushing her luck. From his explanation, she sensed he didn't share this part of himself with many people. It didn't line up with the image of ruthless business tycoon. But in this moment, she wanted to see his clever, talented fingers fly over those strings. To witness him coax beautiful music from that instrument. To watch him lower that damnable shield and let her in. "Will you play for me?"

He stared at her, and her heart thudded against her rib cage. Finally, *finally*, he dipped his chin and reached for the acoustic guitar on the far end. He almost reverently lifted it off the stand and carried it to the love seat. She trailed behind him, not saying anything. Afraid if she uttered a word, he might change his mind. Once he perched on one end of the small love seat, she sank to the other.

Propping the instrument on his thighs, he plucked a few strings, turned the knobs at the top. Once he seemed satisfied, he cupped the neck, fingers at the ready there. And the other hand hovered over the big, rounded body.

Then he started to play.

And...*Jesus*.

She'd expected something classical, reserved. But no. Passion flowed from beneath his fingers. Passion, and anger, and joy and grief. So many emotions soared from the music, which sounded almost Spanish, but bluesy and a little bit of rock. It was fierce, soul-jarring and...and beautiful. So. Beautiful.

Pain swelled in her lungs, and she expelled a huge breath, just realizing she'd been holding it.

When his fingers stilled, and the music faded away, she remained speechless, breathless. Like she'd been transported to Oz and offered this rare peek behind the wizard's curtain. Only she didn't find a fraud, but a rare, wonderful truth about this man. One that few people were gifted with seeing.

He lifted his head, and those fathomless black eyes studied her. A faint frown creased his brow, and he reached for her, swiping his thumb under her eye.

"You're crying," he murmured.

"Am I?" she asked, shocked, wiping her fingers over her cheeks. Well, hell. She was. "I didn't notice."

"Was I that bad?" he teased, with a soft smile she'd never witnessed on him.

"You were—" *are* "—amazing," she whispered. "Thank you for sharing that with me."

The smile disappeared, but his midnight gaze glittered as if dozens of stars lay behind the black.

"I shouldn't want you." She blurted out the confession. "I shouldn't. But… Even knowing who we are… Even knowing this can only end one way, I still want to grab on to those moments when we're just Gideon and Shay, not someone's enemy or sister. When we're being honest with each other the only way we truly can."

Sex. Need. Passion—they're honest. The body can't lie. Lust is the great equalizer regardless of social status, race or tax bracket.

It was a risk saying those words to him, since he'd uttered them to Camille, not her. And from the gleam in his hooded gaze and the tightening of his sensual mouth, maybe he remembered giving them to another woman.

Honesty. Though her pulse slammed her ears, she had to drag her big-girl panties on and tell him the truth. She couldn't justify keeping it from him anymore, especially when he'd offered her the gift of playing for her.

"There's something you should know," she murmured. "I've been keeping something from you. The night of the blackout, Bridgette had come down with a bad cold and asked me to take her place at a job so she wouldn't lose it. Gideon, that was at the Du—"

"Shay, I already figured it out. You're Camille."

Her lips parted with a gasp. She blinked, staring at him. How had he…?

"Did you really believe I could be inside your body and not remember?" he murmured. "Not remember every detail of how tight and sweet you are? No, moonbeam." He shook his head. "I'd never forget that."

"Wait." It suddenly made sense now. His rejection afterward. "Is that why you were so cold to me? Because I hadn't told you?"

He studied her for a long, quiet moment. "It wasn't so much that you lied, but wondering *why* you were at the gala and why you kept the truth from me."

"Bridgette would've lost her job if she'd called in on such short notice, and with her business just getting off the ground, she can't afford that. And I had to use a disguise and a fake name. I've attended the gala in the past, and my brother also…" She trailed off, a dark inkling beginning to stir in her head. "My brother," she whispered. "Did you think I'd been there because of him? That I sought you out for him?"

After a slight hesitation, he nodded. "The thought occurred to me."

"Someone must have hurt you terribly for you

to be so mistrusting and suspicious," she continued softly. And she had an idea about the identity of that "someone."

"Trevor had no clue I was there. There were only two people in that break room, Gideon—you and me. What happened between us was the scariest and most exhilarating, *freeing* thing I've ever done. That's what you make me feel. Terrified out of my mind because no one has ever affected me so viscerally I don't recognize myself. While at the same time, I'm excited because I like it…crave it."

As soon as the confession escaped her, she recognized that he could use it to his advantage. But she mentally shook her head. Gideon wasn't like her brother. He might utilize blackmail to gain her compliance, but never once had he tried to use her passion against her. He might be ruthless, but he possessed his own code of honor.

Sex. Desire. It was their Switzerland.

And she'd seek asylum there for a while before they found themselves on opposite sides of a war again. Because that was inevitable.

But for now…

She shifted closer to him, covered the hand that still rested on the body of the guitar. Lightly, she explored those fingers, amazed at how they could draw such magic out of the instrument and her. She wanted him to cradle, strum and play her.

She trailed a caress up his arm, over his shoulder and neck, until she reached his jaw. Cupping it, she mimicked the many times he'd held her in the same grip. She swept her thumb over his full bottom lip.

His gaze never leaving hers, Gideon carefully set the guitar on the table, then clasped her hand in his. He turned his head, placing a kiss in the center of her palm, then tracing a path to her wrist. His lips pressed there over her pulse, and her lashes fluttered down. But at the damp flick of his tongue, she gasped, eyes flying open. Liquid heat pooled between her legs, and she didn't even try to contain her whimper.

He rose, gently tugging her to her feet. Without releasing her hand, he led her out of the room, down the hallway and up the curving staircase. They entered a cavernous bedroom lit only by a single lamp on a nightstand. Not just any bedroom—his. The big king-size bed covered in a black spread and white pillows, two chairs flanking a large, freestanding fireplace, a couple glossy bedside tables, a rug—the almost austere decor was relieved by the breathtaking view of the Chicago River and city skyline through the three floor-to-ceiling windows, and the one wall that bore a black-and-white mural of a bare, leafless tree on a lonely plain. It was gorgeous. It was him.

Turning to her, he captured all her attention by cradling her face between his palms, tilting her head back and claiming her mouth. Slow, tender; raw and erotic. His tongue relayed all that he wanted to do to her—would do to her. And as she cocked her head to the side, granting him deeper access, she consented to it all.

"I've had you on a couch and in the back seat of my

car. I want to take you on a bed," he muttered against her lips. "*My* bed."

As soon as her whispered "Please," passed her lips, he stripped her, haphazardly tossing her borrowed clothes to the floor. His clothes followed and, hiking her in his arms, he carried her to the bed. Her back hit the covers and his big, hot body pressed her into the mattress. He kissed her harder, wilder, more insistently, as if that leash on his control had unraveled. She dug her fingers into his hair, yanking off the band that corralled it and freeing the strands so they tumbled around both their faces. With a hot, low rumble, he kissed her again, then every inch of her received attention from his mouth, his fingers. By the time he tugged open the drawer on a bedside table and pulled a condom free, she shook with need, twisting and aching for him to fulfill his promise and take her.

Linking their fingers, he drew her arms up, their joined hands bracketing her head.

"Open for me, moonbeam," he murmured, desire burning hot in his dark eyes. The head of his erection nudged her entrance, and she willingly, eagerly widened her thighs and locked them around his slim hips. "Thank you, baby."

He groaned as he sank inside her, not stopping until her sex fully sheathed him. She arched under him, grinding her head into the pillow. God, he stretched her, filled her. Branded her. When he started to move in long, hard thrusts that rocked her body and her soul, she felt claimed. And when her channel clenched around him, and she hurtled into an orgasm that threatened to break her apart, she shut her eyes and became a willing sacrifice to it.

Soon, the aftershocks rippling through her eased, and the fog of ecstasy started to fade. She tensed, waiting for him to roll away from her, to reject her. But when he drew her into his arms, his still-labored breathing bathing her neck, she slowly relaxed.

Right before she drifted away, his low, hoarse voice penetrated her heavy blanket of drowsiness.

"Don't let me break you, Shay. Protect yourself from me."

She didn't reply, but carried that warning with her into sleep.

Fifteen

Shay nabbed the slice of bread out of the toaster and spread avocado on it. She ate it leaning against the counter, alternating between sips of fresh coffee. Gideon had already left for the office, and with a glance at her wrist, she realized she didn't have long before she had to leave, too. Since she no longer had a position at RemingtonNeal, she'd scheduled a meeting with a potential client.

Staying the night hadn't been in the plan. But when he'd curled around her after he'd made her body sing its own special melody, she hadn't wanted to go anywhere. And then he'd woken her with a cup of steaming coffee, keys to one of his cars and a sweet but wicked kiss that left her toes curling into the mattress.

But those lovely gestures couldn't completely erase

the kernel of apprehension that lingered at the edge of her consciousness.

Don't let me break you, Shay. Protect yourself from me.

His murmured warning stayed with her, and dread wormed its way through the warmth. He didn't caution her to be careful because he might hurt her, but because he would. And she would be foolish to ignore that truth. Real life was blackmail, revenge, vendettas and pain. Only in fairy tales did frogs turn to princes. Or wolves to heroes.

Cold seeped into her veins. Suddenly losing her appetite, she dumped the remains of her breakfast. She needed to get going and return to the real world outside this penthouse.

She was heading toward the closet to collect her wrap and dress when the front door opened. Startled, Shay stared as a woman who looked to be about her age entered. With wavy black hair that tumbled over her shoulders, smooth, unlined skin and a tall, slender frame wrapped in a camel cashmere coat, she was obviously too young to be the housekeeper Gideon mentioned last night. Jealousy, unbidden and bright, flared in Shay's chest. Whoever she was, she must be close to Gideon to have a key to his penthouse.

But then the other woman lifted her head, and the truth slammed into Shay. With those heavily lashed, beautiful onyx eyes, she had to be related to Gideon. And considering her age, she was most likely his sister.

"Oh, hi," Olivia said, arching a dark eyebrow in a manner so similar to Gideon's, it confirmed her identity. "I'm sorry. I didn't know Gideon had company. I can come back."

"No, you're fine," Shay objected, finding her voice as his sister half turned to grasp the doorknob. "Gideon's not home, and I was just leaving, too. You must be Olivia." Shay moved forward, her hand extended. Gideon's sister stepped away from the door with a smile, her arm lifting. "My name's Shay. Shay Neal."

Olivia froze, except for the arm falling woodenly back to her side. "Neal?" she repeated in a tremulous whisper. "Are you related to Trevor Neal?"

Unease crawled through her. "Yes. Do you know him?"

Olivia paled, her eyes widening. Visibly trembling fingers lifted to her lips and pressed against them. "I didn't—no, he wouldn't—"

Her fractured sentences made little sense to Shay, but the woman's obvious distress amplified the dread until it was full-out fear. "Olivia, are you okay?" she asked, risking moving closer.

Olivia jerked her head from side to side, tears glistening in her eyes. "Why are you here?"

"Gideon and I are..." She paused, unsure of how much to expose. "...seeing each other. Would you like to sit down? Can I get you anything?"

Again, Olivia shook her head, the tears streaming down her cheeks now. Unable to stand the woman's pain, Shay reached for her, wrapping her in a hug. She half expected Olivia to shove her away, but instead, the woman clung to her, sobbing now.

God. Shay tightened her embrace, her own eyes

stinging. What kind of agony must Olivia be in to cause this kind of reaction? It burrowed inside Shay, and she wanted to soothe it, to take it from her. Gently, she guided the crying woman to the living room and lowered them both to the couch. She continued to hold Olivia, gently rocking her as her mother used to do when Shay ran to her in need of comfort.

She didn't glance at her watch to see how long they sat there. If Olivia needed her to remain the whole day, she would. Anything so those awful, tearing sobs would stop. Gradually, Olivia calmed, and only when she went silent and the trembles eased did Shay slip her arms away. Her shoulders twinged, but she ignored the slight ache. She left for the bathroom. Minutes later, after a quick stop in the kitchen, she returned with a box of tissues, a warm, damp cloth and a bottle of water.

"Thank you," Olivia whispered, her voice hoarse from her tears. "I—I'm sorry. I didn't mean to—"

"Please don't apologize. It's okay," Shay assured her. The woman's clear air of fragility stirred a sense of protectiveness in Shay. "I'm a stranger to you, and you don't have to talk if you don't want to, but I'm here. And whatever you say will stay between us."

For several moments, Olivia clutched the bottle between her hands. Though she'd wiped her face with the cloth, her eyes remained stark, her cheeks and lips pale. Shay waited, ready to listen if Olivia chose to confide in her, ready to just sit with her if she decided not to.

"I know your brother," Olivia finally said, haltingly

at first. "I met him a year ago, and we…we fell in love. Or at least I did. I don't know if he ever did love me. But he told me so. And I believed him. I would've done anything for him—and I did. He asked me to keep our relationship a secret because he and Gideon were business rivals, and he didn't want any of that interfering with us. I'd heard Gideon mention Trevor before and knew he had no love for him, so I agreed. Also, I figured once he saw how much we loved each other, he would come around. Especially since I became pregnant."

Shay gasped, unable to contain her shock and dismay. At the sound, Olivia lifted her gaze from the water bottle. The grief and unadulterated pain there shook Shay, and she wanted to gather the other woman in her arms again. But she didn't, sensing Olivia needed to get this out, like lacerating a festering wound so it could heal faster.

"I thought he would be happy about the news. I was overjoyed. All I dreamed about was marrying him and starting a family. We would be doing it a little out of order, but I didn't care. But—but…" She paused, and a sob escaped her.

Shay grabbed her hand, offering her support, and Olivia went on. "When I told him about the pregnancy, he told me he didn't want me or the baby. To get rid of it because I was no longer useful to him. Then he walked away, like I was garbage he'd tossed out the window. He used me to get back at my brother. At the time, I worked at Gideon's company as his executive assistant. I was so naive, so snowed by Trevor, that when he asked me questions about Gideon's agenda, who he was meeting with, I gave him the information. He worded it to make it sound like he was only asking about my day, what I had on my plate, but he was pumping me for inside information. He never loved me, never had any intention of creating a family with me." She shook her head, her throat working, as if swallowing back another sob. "I refused to end the pregnancy, but it didn't matter. I miscarried and lost the baby."

Shay remained sitting next to Olivia, but inside she reeled, enraged screams slamming against her skull. Part of her longed to deny the story, to label Olivia a liar, but she couldn't. Not only could she not violate this woman all over again by not believing her, but deep inside her soul where only honesty existed, she knew Olivia wasn't lying. Her utter agony bore witness to it, and Shay believed her.

Grief assaulted Shay, welling up in her, and she silently wept. For Olivia. For her pain. For Shay's own pain. For Trevor's coldness, controlling behavior and dismissal of her hopes, dreams and needs. For her disillusionment about her brother. If Trevor could treat his own sister so callously as well as do something as despicable as take advantage of this woman for personal gain, then what else was he capable of? Maybe those things in Gideon's dossier?

Gideon. Was Olivia the reason behind his plans? The night in the restaurant, when he'd first showed her the incriminating file, he'd scoffed at her claim that Trevor wouldn't care who she was dating.

Oh yes. Your brother will care. And he'll under-stand.

Then, his assertion had been cryptic, but now, understanding dawned on her. No wonder he hated Trevor and had no qualms about blackmailing her. This was more than a business deal; Trevor had come after Gideon's family. If she'd harbored any fledgling hope after waking up in his bed this morning that maybe they could have something more than a truce, this knowledge obliterated it. She would always be a living reminder of the harm and damage her brother had inflicted on his sister, his family.

There was no forgiveness for that. Not for her brother.

And not for her, being guilty by association.

Sixteen

"I still don't think this is a wise decision."

Shay stared out the rear window of Gideon's Town Car at the Gold Coast historic mansion lit up with a cheerful glow. A steady stream of people climbed the front stone steps of the place she'd called home for nearly twenty-six years, entering for Trevor and Madison's engagement party.

"You and Trevor might not be seeing eye to eye right now, but I'm sure he wouldn't want to celebrate his engagement without his sister," Gideon said from beside her.

She glanced at him, irritation and something deeper, sadder pressing against her breastbone like a large boulder. "You won't pass up an opportunity to turn the screw, will you?"

With his aloof mask firmly in place, he met her gaze, onyx eyes steady and unblinking. "No."

She faced the window again, that heaviness gaining weight. It'd been a week since she'd walked out of her childhood home. A week since her and Gideon's truce, which had stretched longer than the next morning. A week since she'd held Olivia as the woman broke down in her arms and revealed Trevor's betrayal.

Yes, now Shay understood the motives behind Gideon's blackmail. And a part of her couldn't blame him. But another part—the part that remembered the man who'd played guitar for her, the man who'd cuddled her close in his bed after tearing her apart with pleasure—longed for him to put all of this aside.

For her.

To want her more than revenge.

She shut her eyes, making sure to keep her head turned away so he couldn't glimpse the yearning that she was certain leaked into her expression. In spite of knowing it was the epitome of foolishness, she'd started to fall for Gideon.

No, that was a lie. The fall had started some time ago, at what moment, she couldn't pinpoint. Maybe when he'd revealed his own pain to her in the back seat of the car. Maybe when he'd raced to Bridgette's house and decided to place her comfort above putting on another episode of the Gideon and Shay Show at the ballet. Maybe when he'd sat on that couch with his guitar and revealed a part of himself that he didn't with most people.

Not that narrowing down the exact instant mattered.

The truth was she loved Gideon Knight.

His fierceness. His heart, which he tried to hide. His passion. His love for his family.

Yes, he was a hard man, a merciless man, but never a cruel one. And when she looked at him, gazed into those midnight-and-stars eyes, she dreamed. She stupidly dreamed that he could love her as he'd once adored Madison before she'd scarred him with her disloyalty and infidelity.

Maybe she did believe in fairy tales, after all.

The door to the car opened, and with a sigh, she climbed out, murmuring a thank-you to the valet who stood next to it. Seconds later, Gideon's body heat warmed her back, and his palm settled at the base of her spine. A spine she straightened.

No time for self-pity now.

She had the performance of a lifetime to give.

Because she was walking into the lion's den knowing her arrival on Gideon's arm would announce her decision to her brother—she'd chosen his enemy over family loyalty. That's how Trevor would see it.

And she wasn't naive; there would be consequences to her decision. No job at RemingtonNeal. She would most likely have to find a place to live because she couldn't stay with Bridgette forever. And, most importantly, Leida Investments and the businesses she'd invested in would be affected. Especially if Trevor followed through on his threat of tampering with the start-ups she'd funded. She had savings, and she could use most of it to provide capital. But the possibility of having to scale back or rebuild her company was very real without her salary.

The cost of loving Gideon was high.

And, God help her, she was willing to pay it.

Gideon walked silently beside her, but the tension rolled off him, and it ratcheted higher when they entered her home and handed their coats to a waiting servant.

She seamlessly fell back into the role of Chicago socialite and, pasting on a smile, mingled with the other guests. Many of whom didn't seem surprised to see her with Gideon, so the gossip about them as a couple must've made the rounds. Still, they were aware of the enmity between Gideon and Trevor as business rivals, and watched her and Gideon with an avid, greedy curiosity.

Especially when a path seemed to open, and they stood only feet away from Trevor, Madison and Senator Reus. Shay looked up, and her gaze connected with her brother's. Though he smiled for the benefit of those around them, fury blazed from his hazel eyes, so like hers. His glare shifted from her to Gideon, and a frightening rage hardened his expression before he controlled it.

"Stand tall, moonbeam," Gideon murmured in her ear. His big palm slid up her back and under her hair, curling around the nape of her neck. "He can't hurt you."

But you can. The words rang in her head, her chest. Tipping her head back, she said, "That's debatable. Cutting me off emotionally and financially and targeting my company definitely falls under the 'hurting me' category."

"Correction, then," he growled. "I won't let him hurt you."

That ship had sailed and was a faint glimmer on the horizon.

She straightened her shoulders and added a little more wattage to her smile. "We should go greet the happy couple."

"You mean, get it over with?" he retorted, dark eyebrow arched. She'd once detested the gesture, but now counted each one.

"That's what I said."

His low chuckle tripped over her bare arms. Inhaling a deep breath, she allowed him to guide her over to the trio who stoically watched their approach.

"Trevor, Madison, congratulations." She leaned forward and stiffly kissed Madison's cheek. Although she did return the feigned embrace, most likely for those closely observing them, Madison's rigid posture didn't relax. Straightening, Shay nodded to her brother's future father-in-law. "Senator."

"Shay," he murmured coldly.

"Your sister wanted to see you, wish you well," Gideon said to Trevor, his tone frigid, but she detected the undercurrent of anger. Of hatred. "She has a forgiving heart considering you put her out of her own house."

Oh God.

"She left by her own choice," Trevor snapped, the fury in his eyes leaking into his face. His lips twisted into an ugly snarl. "But come now, Gideon. We both know how trying *sisters* can be."

Nausea churned in her belly and raced for the back of her throat.

Dark waves of rage poured off Gideon, and he moved forward. Terrified, she latched on to his arm, fearful of what he might do to her brother. And she feared *for* Gideon, for the consequences he might suffer for his actions. She harbored no doubt that Trevor would enjoy pressing charges and using it against him.

"Gideon, no," she pleaded softly. "It's what he wants."

Trevor sneered. "Shay, I need to speak to you. Alone," he stressed.

"Fine," she agreed, more to separate Gideon from Trevor than to be amenable. "Gideon," she whispered. When he tore his still-frightening stare from her brother, she squeezed his arm. "I'll be right back."

"You don't have to do this," he reminded her, just as softly, but the fury still vibrated in his voice.

"Yes, I do," she returned. Rising onto her toes, she placed a kiss on his jaw. "They're not worth it." She waited for his abrupt nod before she turned back to her brother. "In the study, I assume."

Not waiting for his confirmation, she strode toward the rear of the house. Anger bristled under her skin, poking her like thousands of tiny needles. When she entered her brother's domain, she could barely look at him.

"How dare you bring that asshole into my house?"

Trevor ground out through clenched teeth as soon as he closed the study door behind them.

"Your house?" She crossed her arms. "You were right when you told Gideon that I chose to leave. Chose. Because this is *our* home, Trevor. I can bring whoever I want here, and you have no say. I don't need to ask your permission."

"I would've never thought you were a traitor," he snarled. "Mom and Dad wouldn't recognize you right now."

She absorbed the power of that blow and fought not to stagger from it. But the pain ebbed and flowed inside her.

Stand tall. He can't hurt you.

Inhaling a deep breath, she pushed past it.

"You're such a hypocrite," she said, surprised at her even tone. "So righteous and high-and-mighty. And to think I defended you. Believed in you. Trusted you. But you didn't deserve any of it."

"What the hell are you talking about, Shay?" he demanded. "I've done nothing but honor this family, the Neal name, *you*. You, baby sister, betrayed me."

"By thinking for myself, wanting something for myself? For daring to defy you? I'm not a sheep, Trevor. I have a mind. I have feelings. I have a heart, but there's only one Neal who can claim to possess the last two. Because somewhere along the way, you lost them to jealousy, pettiness and hate. No, *big brother*," she said, throwing his taunt back at him. "I've done nothing but stand by this family. I've protected it when you would've destroyed it with your greed and ambition."

"You need to stop right there," he warned in a dark growl, taking a step forward.

But he didn't intimidate her. Didn't control her. Not anymore. She didn't wait for him to advance, but marched forward and met him halfway.

"No, you stop. And listen. I know what you and your precious senator are up to," she said. "Insider information. Fixing contracts. Kickbacks. Illegal campaign contributions. And that's just the tip of it." When he rocked back in shock, his eyes flaring wide, she nodded. "Yes, Trevor, I know about it all. Because Gideon has a file on you, inches thick. I've seen it, read it. I'm aware of all your dirty dealings, which if made public could topple RemingtonNeal, ruin the Neal name and send you and Julian to jail."

"How long have you…?" His voice trailed off, but she understood his question.

"Weeks. Since before the Grace Sanctuary fundraiser. I made a deal with the devil to save you. I agreed to pretend to be in a fake relationship with him so he wouldn't expose you. That's why I couldn't break things off with him. Because if I did, you would've been destroyed. But that's not all," she whispered, eliminating the small space between her and the man who wore her brother's face, but was a stranger. "He did all this because of Olivia. You remember her, don't you?" At his stony expression, she nodded again. "Of course you do. The woman you seduced, used to get back at her brother, impregnated, then tossed aside. All for your petty hatred and resentment. Now, who wouldn't Dad and Mom recognize?"

"You don't understand," he spat, but the anger in his eyes had been overshadowed by worry. By fear. Because he understood that his greatest enemy had the dirt on him, no doubt. "You could never understand…"

"Not understand what? How hard it is to live up to our name? To live under the yoke of it for so long that sometimes you feel like your back's going to break from the burden? Yes, Trevor, I do. The difference between you and me is that I'm choosing not to let it poison me until I make unconscionable decisions that hurt other people. I decided to help people rather than harm them. But just to get your way, you would steal that from me, too."

For too long, she'd allowed him and the duty of being a Neal to dictate her life, her behavior, her decisions. No longer. She might have been quiet, but she'd learned from the best.

Not him. Gideon.

"I love you, Trevor. For the brother and man you were, I'm giving you a choice now. Come after Leida Investments or any of the businesses I've invested in, or my trust fund, and Gideon won't have to leak any of that information to the press and SEC. I will. He gave me a copy of the file, and right now, it's tucked away safe. But if you dare touch anything that's mine—and when I say mine, that includes Gideon Knight and everything he loves—I'll take you down. And I won't lose sleep over it."

Trevor stared at her, shocked. But she didn't wait for his response. He couldn't say anything that would fix what he'd broken. She would just have to accept that some men changed for the worse instead of the better, and as much as it tore her heart apart, Trevor was one of them.

"I have to admit, Gideon, I never expected you to go to *these* lengths." Madison tsked, appearing at his side, her familiar scent teasing his nostrils.

At one time, he'd found the floral fragrance alluring. Now it was just cloying. She trailed fingertips down his arm and over the back of his hand. Tilting her head to the side, she offered him what she probably considered a coy smile. She didn't pull it off. Not when he knew the real woman behind the mask.

He shifted his arm, knocking her hand away. Foolish as hell of him to think he could slip unseen into the closed-off room that reminded him of his den. He'd needed space and time to walk off the killing rage that had consumed him when Trevor had alluded to Olivia.

If not for Shay, he would've put that bastard through the wall, his hands around his throat, and damn the consequences. But his name in that soft voice and the fear darkening her lovely eyes had stopped him. He'd put that hated emotion in her gaze, and he detested himself for it. Still, even with rage roiling inside him like a volcano set to blow, he would've accompanied her to that meeting with her brother. He hadn't wanted to leave her alone. That protective streak toward her had only widened and deepened in the time they'd spent together. Yet he also understood she needed to have it out with Trevor, to stand up to him on her own.

And she couldn't do that with his life in imminent danger from Gideon.

But right after he marched into an empty room to cool off with a glass of bourbon from the bar, Madison had appeared.

Goddamn, he didn't have the patience to deal with her machinations right now.

"What lengths, Madison?" He lifted the tumbler to his lips, downing the last of the dark alcohol before setting the glass on the mantel. "I don't have time for your games."

"Time for me," she corrected, assuming a hurt expression. "That's what went wrong with us, you know? You spent so much time at the office or out of town at meetings, I felt neglected. I missed you and couldn't stand the loneliness."

He snorted. "Is this your way of trying to explain why I walked in on you sitting on Trevor's dick? Forget it, sweetheart. This guilt trip not only isn't going to work, but it's months too late. I don't give a fuck now."

"We both know that's not true, Gideon," she crooned, clutching his arm. He stiffened, hating her hands on him. It felt…wrong. There'd been a time when he'd enjoyed her teasing caresses, her heated strokes. But now? Now his skin prickled and crawled as if his very body rebelled against her. These days, he welcomed the touch of only one woman. Shay.

Again he shifted away, dislodging her touch.

"If you'd answered any of my phone calls this week, you'd know—"

"I didn't answer them because we have nothing to talk about," he said.

"So you're going to tell me that your love for me just died? Went away just like that?" She snapped her fingers, eyes flashing. "I don't believe it."

"Believe it," he growled. "You killed it. And you don't get a do-over. Get it through your head, sweetheart. I. Don't. Want. You."

Tired of this, he went to move around her, but she sidestepped, blocking him. Unless he wanted to grab her, pick her up and shift her out of the way, he couldn't pass. And at the moment, the thought of putting his hands on her caused his stomach to curdle.

"Then what was this whole…act with Shay about? You don't expect me, or anyone for that matter, to actually accept that you're madly in love with her? The sister of the man who stole the woman you love? You don't have to continue this silly pretense anymore, Gideon." She shoved into his personal space, so her perfume clogged his nose, crawled down his throat. He grabbed her shoulders to prevent her from coming any nearer. She flattened her palms on his chest. "I love you. I made a mistake leaving you for him. It's been you all along. And I know you still love me if you'll go to these lengths."

Screw this. He tightened his grip on her, prepared to move her. "Madison…" he growled.

"Yes, Gideon." She moaned, and shooting up on her toes, wrapped her arms around his neck and crushed her mouth to his.

Shock froze him. But just for a second. Bile scorched

a path to the back of his throat. Muttering a curse, he jerked his head back, circled her wrists and yanked her off him.

"Dammit," he snapped. But any more words died on his tongue.

Shay stood in the doorway to the den, her shuttered gaze on them.

"Oh, Shay," Madison cooed, panting lightly. "We didn't see you there." Perverse satisfaction threaded her tone.

"Shay," he breathed, already leaving the unfaithful bitch he'd almost married behind, forgotten, and moving toward the woman with the wounded eyes.

"I'm ready if you are," she said, her voice flat, hideously polite.

She turned on her heel and left, leaving a void in his gut.

Seventeen

Shay stared out the window of the Town Car, watching the landmarks that defined Chicago passing by in the distance. What she wouldn't give to be in one of those monuments right now. Just anywhere as long as it wasn't here, sitting in the back of this car, tension thick, her pain crushing her chest like an anvil.

Tonight had been a special hell. Between the confrontation and probable loss of her relationship with Trevor and walking in on Madison and Gideon kissing, she just wanted to hole up somewhere and wait out this pain. But how could she hide from it, when she embodied it, breathed it?

Next to her, Gideon was silent, brooding. She'd never seen him brood. Distant, yes. Taunting, yes. Passionate, God yes. But never this dark heaviness that seemed to reach out to her, wrap around her.

Hold on, she reminded herself. Just hold on until she could get out of the car and into her temporary home, where she could break down. But not now. Not in front of Gideon.

"Shay."

His deep, silken voice stroked over her skin even under her coat, and she flinched away from it.

"I didn't kiss her, Shay," he rasped.

She squeezed her eyes shut. As if she could block out the sight of Madison, her arms thrown around him, her mouth pressed to the one that she adored, needed. But that image would no doubt be branded onto her brain for all eternity. As well as the slashing pain on her heart.

Yet... "I know, Gideon."

A pause, and then an audible exhale. "You believe me," he stated.

She nodded. "Yes."

"Then, baby, look at me. Please." It was the "please" that had her turning her head and meeting that midnight gaze. "Then what's wrong? Why haven't you spoken to me, looked at me since leaving the party? Tell me what I've done and let me explain it."

"You haven't done anything," she said, scanning his features. Committing them to memory. "But I can't go through with this charade. Our agreement is over."

His head snapped back, his eyes narrowing on her face. "Why? Did your brother convince you to leave me?"

"Leave you?" She chuckled, and it grated her throat

raw. "You once accused me of being blind, Gideon. It seems to be contagious. You can't see that I would do anything to stay with you. But not as a pretend girl-friend or a lover-for-now. I want the real thing. I *deserve* the real thing."

"Shay," he said, and her heart squeezed so hard, she placed her hand over her chest. "What are you saying?"

"I'm saying I love you. Desperately. Completely. Finally. There's no going back for me. There's no one else. And that's a problem, because you don't love me. You don't want me other than as a bed partner and a means to an end."

"That's not fair," he rumbled, the skin tautening over his cheekbones, anger diamond-bright in his eyes. "You mean more to me than a fuck. I've never treated you like that. I never would."

"No," she agreed. "You've been one of the few men in my life who saw past the socialite, the family name and money. You saw the business owner, the capable woman. When no one else respected me, you did… even as you used me to get back at my brother. And that's the problem. Because above all, the first thing you will always see is Trevor Neal's sister." She hesi-tated, but in the end, she had nothing to lose in laying it all out there. "I know about what he did to Olivia," she said.

Gideon transformed into living stone. Except for his eyes, which blazed with anger and another darker, more heartbreaking emotion.

"How did you find out? Surely *Trevor*," he spat her brother's name, "didn't confess his sins to you."

"No." She shook her head, hurting for him, for Olivia. Shame for Trevor's despicable actions coating her in grime even though she wasn't responsible for him. "I didn't tell you, but Olivia came by the morning after I moved out of my house. She broke down when she realized who I was, and she ended up revealing everything to me. She's the reason behind the file, the blackmail, the revenge, not Madison. Your hatred goes much deeper than him cheating with her."

"Yes," he confirmed, still cold, still impenetrable. "You saw for yourself what he did to Olivia. She's been emotionally fragile ever since he left her, and she lost the baby. The morning after the blackout, she'd found out about his engagement to Madison. And it sent her to the hospital. She's recovering, but she hasn't been the girl I remember since before your brother came along."

"And you'll never be able to get past that. Not that I blame you. He crossed an unforgivable line, and there's nothing that could justify it. But even realizing this, I can't waste one more day hoping you will let it go. Not one more day living a lie. It's time for me to live for me, to determine and shape my own future, and I can't do that with a man who insists on remaining in the past. A man for whom revenge is more important than love...than me."

"I didn't ask for your love," he snapped, and the tone, razor sharp, flayed her already wounded and bleeding heart. "I told you not to let me break you, Shay. I warned you."

"And I didn't ask for your permission to love you,"

she countered softly. "Don't feel guilty, Gideon. I'm used to not being enough for the men in my life. But the difference—what you've taught me—is I no longer give a damn. I'm enough for *me*."

At that moment, the car stopped in front of Bridgette's house. Shay didn't wait for the driver to come around and open her door. She unlocked it and did the honors herself. It was like a metaphor for her new life. She was tired of waiting on others. She was in control of her own fate; she could open her own doors.

And she would.

Starting now.

"Shay." Gideon's strong fingers grasped her wrist. "Please."

"Goodbye, Gideon," she whispered.

Then, pulling free, she stepped out of the car.

And didn't look back.

Eighteen

Gideon entered the numbers into the spreadsheet, then several seconds later swore under his breath and deleted them. *Dammit*. He'd been doing a repeat of this same thing for hours now.

Hours, hell. His fingers fisted on top of the keyboard. Days.

His concentration had been shot for five nights and six days. Since the five nights and six days ago when Shay got out of his car. When she'd announced she loved him, then walked away without looking back. As an image of her leaving him, spine ramrod straight, glide elegant and proud, wavered in his head, he squeezed his eyes shut. Bowing his head, he didn't will the mental picture away. No, he conjured it up over and over, punishing himself with the memory of the pain and soul-deep sadness that had darkened her eyes, of the words that had driven daggers into his chest.

Of the resolve and strength radiating from her that let him know if he didn't say something, *do* something to prevent her from exiting the car, he would never see her again. Never inhale her rain-and-roses scent. Never hear her husky voice. Never have her body pressed to his, fitting like a missing puzzle piece.

But he'd done nothing.

That grab at her wrist had been weak, and they'd both known it.

"Damn you, Shay," he whispered harshly. "Damn you."

Like he'd told her that night, he hadn't asked for her love. Didn't want it. He'd earned a PhD in how faithless love was. People threw that word around to abuse, betray and abandon others. Madison had claimed to love him. Trevor had vowed the same to his sister.

Love deceived, used and…died. It left pain and disillusionment and loss behind. It changed people for the worse, not the better. Intuition had warned him that if he allowed Shay in, if he risked opening to her, when she left—because experience had taught him the leaving was inevitable—the wreckage would be much worse than the damage Madison had inflicted. Shay would level him.

He refused to be played for the fool by *love* again. Ever.

With that "ever" ricocheting off his skull, he turned back to his computer screen and the report he'd been trying to finish for the past two hours.

His desk phone buzzed. "Mr. Knight, there's a Mr. Trevor Neal here to see you. He doesn't have an appointment—"

"Send him in," Gideon snapped.

What the hell was Trevor doing here? Scratch that. He didn't give a damn.

For the first two days after dropping Shay off, Gideon had tried to drown her out with alcohol. When that had failed, work had been his next attempt to erase her from his mind. Apparently, that wasn't succeeding, either. While meeting with Trevor was most likely a terrible idea, he was also spoiling for a fight. A grim smile stretched across his mouth. For the first time in days—six days and five nights, to be exact— he looked forward to something.

Seconds later, his office door opened, and the man he'd resented for thirteen years and actively hated since he'd harmed Olivia stalked inside. Harsh lines etched his forehead and bracketed his mouth, and his eyes, so like his sister's, blazed with anger. His hands curled into fists at his sides. Seemed like Gideon wasn't the only one looking for a fight.

His smile widened.

"Good afternoon, Trevor. I'd say it was nice to see you again, but we both know that would be bullshit. So we'll skip the pleasantries and get to what are you doing here." Gideon leaned back in his desk chair and templed his fingers beneath his chin.

"You son of a bitch," Trevor snarled.

"Well, that didn't take long," Gideon drawled with a sigh, his voice heavy with mock disappointment.

Rising, he flattened his palms on the top of his desk. "What the fuck do you want?"

"Where's my sister?" Trevor demanded. "I checked with Bridgette. She's no longer staying there. So where is she?"

"I don't know," Gideon replied calmly. Though inside, alarm clanged in his head, his chest. As far as he'd known, she'd still been with her best friend. *Was she okay? Was she safe?* The questions barraged him, but he forced his focus back to the man across from him. "Why do you care? You let her leave the only home she ever knew because she wouldn't bend to your demands. Are you suddenly having an attack of conscience?"

Doubtful, since the man didn't have one.

"Not that it's any of your business, but I need to speak to her. Last time we spoke, she made some… irrational accusations and threats. We need to clear this up. As a *family*," he sneered.

Gideon arched an eyebrow. "Threats?" Pride and admiration warmed him. "There's an interesting turn of events."

"You would find it funny." Trevor scowled. "She wasn't like this before. I'm thinking it's the company she's been keeping."

"Thank you." Gideon dipped his head in acknowledgment. "And just for the record, your sister has always been strong. You were just too busy playing lord of the manor to recognize it. If you had, maybe you would've used her brilliance for the advantage of your *family* company instead of sticking her in some bullshit position. Then she might not have had to go form her own business, but could've helped yours grow."

"You know nothing about Shay," Trevor growled, shifting forward as if ready to leap over the desk. "Don't pretend that your *relationship*," he spat the word, "was real. She told me the truth about your blackmailing her into pretending you two were a couple. She also informed me about the file of lies you have on me."

Shock reverberated through him. When she'd claimed she wouldn't go one more day living a lie, had she been referring to confessing to her brother about their arrangement?

Flipping these new revelations over and over in his mind, Gideon returned his attention to Trevor. "You might have tried that argument with Shay, but don't bother with me. Everything listed in that file is the least of your crimes. We both know who you are, Trevor. We both know what you're capable of," he growled. "You used my sister, then tossed her aside like she was something beneath your shoe. No, I take that back. You would've at least paused and scraped something off the bottom of your precious loafers. You didn't even give her that courtesy. And for what? A grudge against me from high school? You broke her, and for you it was business as usual."

"Like you broke my sister?" Trevor accused. "Eye for an eye? Don't stand there and preach to me like you're so self-righteous, when you turned around and did the same thing to Shay. You used her to get back at me. That doesn't make you the hero in this story."

"You're right."

Trevor's mouth snapped closed, his eyes flaring in surprise at Gideon's quick agreement, before narrowing. He was probably wondering what Gideon's game was now. But there wasn't any game. There wasn't any trickery to slide another point home as if this was a contest to be won.

He'd used Shay. Oh yes, he'd justified it as righting a wrong against Olivia, as protecting future women from being hurt by Trevor. But the truth couldn't be denied any longer. His actions hadn't been noble—they'd been selfish, vengeful…and reprehensible. Maybe unforgivable.

Not because of Trevor. He still had zero fucks to give about Trevor. But because he'd dragged an innocent into it. As blameless as Olivia had been in Trevor's schemes, Shay had been just as blameless. His mother's warning haunted him, ringing in his head like a premonition that had come to pass. He *had* ended up hurting others. And the most important person he'd hurt was Shay. No, he wasn't Trevor—could never deliberately deceive and devastate someone, then walk away from a child he'd created—but he'd also blackmailed, hurt, then turned his back on the woman he loved.

God. He loved her.

The force of the revelation struck him with the blow of a mallet to the chest. He sank to his chair, staring blindly ahead.

He loved Shay.

Somehow, despite every wall, every barrier and

shield he'd thrown up, she'd wedged herself into his heart, his soul. No wonder he'd felt so empty these past days. The one who'd given him life again was gone. Because, yes, she'd resuscitated him, jolting his heart so it beat again. She'd given him more than work to be excited about—she'd given him her quiet humor, her defiance, her wit, her loyalty, her body...her love.

And what had he done? Thrown it back at her like it meant nothing.

Don't feel guilty, Gideon. I'm used to not being enough for the men in my life.

Pain, razor sharp and searing hot, razed his chest. He gasped at the agony of it. Nothing—absolutely nothing—could be further from the truth. She was more than enough. She was *everything.* But he'd been willing to throw away a future with her for revenge.

"Gideon," Trevor snapped, hauling Gideon out of the hell he'd plummeted into.

He jerked his head up, blinking. God, he'd forgotten all about this man standing in his office. And now he didn't have time for him or the vendetta that had brought both of them low. Urgency spiraling through him, Gideon shot to his feet and strode across the room. Removing a large picture from the wall, he revealed the safe behind it and quickly punched in the code to open it. He withdrew the thick, brown file inside, then slammed the safe door shut, not bothering to replace the painting.

"Here." He marched over to Trevor and shoved the dossier containing all his damning information into the other man's chest. "Take it. There aren't any more copies other than the one I gave your sister."

"What?" Trevor gasped. He clutched the folder, glancing at it before his gaze whipped back to Gideon. "What's your angle now? You can't seriously just hand this over to me without wanting something in return."

Gideon stepped back, shaking his head. "No angle. No ulterior motive. But you're right. I do want something in return. Or rather, someone. I want Shay. More than that file or revenge against you. But that's for me to fix, not you."

How he'd go about doing that, he had no clue. Hell, by all rights, she shouldn't forgive him. But he needed her. He loved her.

And he'd fight to have her. Harder than he'd ever fought to pay back Trevor.

Because winning Shay was more important than any battle he'd ever faced.

Nineteen

"Order up, babe."

Shay turned around and rushed across the minimal space inside the food truck to grab the two cartons of larb served over thin noodles. Snatching up napkins and plastic utensils, she placed everything in a bag and handed it to the waiting customers through the window. Smiling and thanking them, she turned to the next person and took his order for green papaya salad.

Bridgette had called that morning, asking if she would help her out on the truck again. Though Shay suspected her friend had arranged this sudden lack of help to keep her busy and her mind off a certain person, she'd jumped at the chance to get out of her newly leased, empty Edgewater apartment. More specifically, she'd been eager to get out of her head.

In the almost two weeks since she'd walked away from Gideon, she'd found an apartment—despite Bridgette's argument that she could stay with her as long as she wanted—located a small office space for Leida Investments, officially resigned from RemingtonNeal, opened a safe deposit box for the damning file on her brother and done more research on start-up companies that she could invest in.

Yes, her family and love life had exploded, but she refused to stop living. A gaping hole existed where her heart had once been, but that didn't mean she would roll over and give in. She'd meant every word she'd uttered to Gideon.

This was her time. Her life. And no one but she was in control of it.

She might have lost the man she loved because he wanted revenge and hate rather than her, but for the first time in longer than she could remember, she loved herself. She *valued* herself. And she was demanding it from everyone in her life.

As Bridgette had put it, Shay was a boss.

Dammit, yeah, she was.

She'd learned something in the last couple weeks. She would've loved having Gideon in her life. But he *wasn't* her life.

And she was okay with that.

"Have another order for the larb, but by itself, without the noodles," she called out to Bridgette over her shoulder before returning her attention to the window and the next customer. "Hi, how can I…" She trailed off, the sudden lurch of her heart to her throat preventing the rest of the words from escaping.

No.

No.

She stared into midnight eyes with stars and the scream inside her head increased in volume. It wasn't fair. What the hell was he doing here? Telling him she loved him and having him reject her had been agonizing, humiliating. How did he not know that? Was he a sadist getting pleasure from her pain?

Well, *screw that.*

She schooled her features into the cool, polite mask she'd mastered since she'd been old enough to sit at the adult table. He wouldn't get anything else from her. She didn't have it in her to give.

"What are you doing here, Gideon?" she asked, proud when not so much as a tremor shook her voice.

Behind her, Bridgette appeared next to her elbow like a bodyguard. "What the hell is this?" she demanded, spatula still in hand.

"I got this," Shay murmured to her friend. "We're busy, as you can tell," she said to Gideon. "And you and I don't have anything left to say to each other."

Again, she sounded calm even to her own ears. Sounded as if her fingertips didn't tingle with the need to touch him.

But inside…

Inside she quaked. Love, hurt, yearning, desire—they all coalesced and swirled in her chest, leaving almost no room for air. She dragged in what little she could and waited.

"You don't have to say anything, moonbeam. All I ask is for you to listen."

"Don't call me that," she snapped, and silently cursed herself for betraying that much emotion. She shouldn't care if he murmured that endearment. It shouldn't affect her.

"Two minutes, Shay." His dark gaze searched hers. "Please."

Please.

Like before, it gave her pause.

"Two minutes. That's it," she agreed.

"Thank you," he said, then hesitating, he dragged his hands over his head. Taken aback by the uncharacteristically nervous gesture, Shay narrowed her eyes on him. Noting for the first time the faint smudges under his eyes, the two-minutes-past-five-o'clock shadow that darkened his jaw. Where was the clean-cut, reserved man she'd known?

He gave a rough, abrupt chuckle. "Now that I'm here, I don't know where to begin." Sighing, he dropped his arm. "First, I should apologize. And I am sorry, Shay. I used you. There's no getting around that fact. I rationalized and defended my actions by claiming I wanted justice for Olivia. That your brother had gotten away with hurting people long enough, and if no one else would make him pay, then I would. But what I didn't want to admit is that I blamed myself.

"I hated myself as much as, if not more than, him. It was my job to protect my sister, and I failed. If I'd been a better brother, she would've felt free to tell me about the relationship with Trevor instead of keeping it a secret. And most of all, if not for me, she wouldn't have even been on his radar. Me. It all came back to me, and I couldn't bear the guilt, the shame and, God, yes, the anger. It was that anger that led me to do what I had judged him for—ruthlessly using you to get to him. I convinced myself I was more honorable than him, but in my rage, I'd *become* him. And worst of all, I hurt you. That, I will never forgive myself for."

Soul-deep shock robbed her of speech. Even the long line of people behind him had stopped grumbling and were quiet. A few even had their phones out. She mentally winced. Gideon wouldn't be happy to know he was probably live-streaming on social media.

"Gideon, you don't have to—" she began, only to be cut off.

"Yes, I do. I'm desperate, Shay. I don't have any pride left. Not when it comes to you. And I don't want it. Don't need it. Not when it kept me from telling you how important you are. God, baby, you're *vital*. Nothing is the same without you in my world. Before you, work, family, money, success—those were priorities. Hell, they were everything. But since you walked away from me, I still have all of those, and aside from my mother and sister, they don't fulfill me anymore.

"I can't concentrate at work because I'm wondering where you are, what you're doing…if you're thinking about me. I could escape into all the things wealth buys, I could travel to the most exotic places on this earth, but I'd see nothing, appreciate nothing, because you wouldn't be there with me. Success?" He held up his hands, palms out. "Until you, I measured success by how many clients I had, the profits, how many doors opened for me. But now? Success is how many times I can make you smile. How many times I can hear you say I love you. How many nights I can fall asleep beside you. How many ways I can prove to you that you're loved. So far, I've been damn unsuccessful."

"Wow," Bridgette whispered beside her. Shay shot her friend a look, and she shrugged, smiling sheepishly. "I mean, bastard."

Shaking her head, Shay returned her gaze to the man who'd captured her attention and that of an increasingly growing lunch crowd in Hyde Park. She blinked back the tears stinging her eyes, and her heart pounded thickly against her rib cage. Hope tried to rear its foolish head, but she slapped it back down. She'd been stupid enough to spin impossible dreams around this man once, even though he'd never made promises to her. And that was just it. She could no longer afford to pin nebulous hopes on a man who refused to put her first. No matter how lovely his speech.

"Thank you for the apology, Gideon. I really do appreciate it. But I can't risk taking a chance on you. How long before you realize you're sleeping with the enemy—literally—and resent me for it? I can't live waiting for that day to happen."

"You don't get it, moonbeam," he said, moving closer to the service window. And in spite of her resolve, she leaned forward, a part of her—the part that woke up aching for him every night, the part that refused to stop believing in fairy tales—desperate to hear what she didn't get. "I love you. I don't know when it happened. When I sat down across from you in that restaurant and you essentially told me to go to hell? When you refused to answer my phone call and cater to me because you were helping a friend? When I played my guitar for you? Maybe..." He hesitated, swallowed hard. Then whispered, "Maybe the first time I saw you as Camille."

"Saw you as Camille? What kind of kink are y'all into?" Bridgette muttered from behind her.

Shay ignored her, latched on to every word falling from Gideon's lips. Ensnared by those onyx eyes that she couldn't tear herself away from.

"I don't deserve you. But there's no man on this earth who does. But that won't stop me from fighting for you. From fighting for *us*. From begging you to not throw me away, even though I almost did. Moonbeam, you complete me in a way revenge never could. Without you as my conscience, my lover, my friend, I'm empty. I want to be full. I want to be found. Please, don't leave me out there again. I love you, Shay Neal. Desperately. Completely. Finally. There's no going back for me. There's no one else."

He gifted her with the words she'd given him. Only this time, he was the one standing on the ledge, hoping she would grasp his hand and pull him back to safety, to love. He'd pushed her over that night. And now, she could do the same. Pay him back. Turn away to a future that he wouldn't be in, but would still be good. Or she could reach across, risk her heart again and jump off the edge, trusting him to catch her. And hold her forever.

There was no choice.

Running, she barreled out of the truck, but before she could round it, she crashed into Gideon. He hadn't waited, but met her halfway. That's what they would always do—meet each other. Never fail to be there for one another.

Dimly, she heard a roar of applause and cheers, but as his arms closed around her, and she wrapped hers around his neck, everything else ceased to exist. He captured her mouth in a kiss that stole her breath and sent heat roaring through her. But most of all, it shattered every remnant of fear and doubt, promising her with the thrust of his tongue, the molding of his lips, that he would love her, cherish her, worship her. And she returned the vow.

"I love you," she whispered, peppering his mouth, jaw and chin with kisses. "I love you so much."

"I thought I'd never hear you say that again," he rasped, pressing his forehead to hers.

"I promise you I'll never stop telling you." She took his mouth this time, leaving them shaking against each other. "I love you."

"Forever?"

"Forever."

Epilogue

One Year Later

"Mrs. Knight, your husband's here to see you."

Shay smiled, pressing the speaker button on her desk phone. God, she never tired of being called that. "Please send him in, Jackie." Seconds later, her executive assistant opened the door, grinning as Gideon strode past her. Leida Investments was still small, but now Shay could afford a staff. Even if that staff was just Jackie. Still, the business was steadily growing, and Shay couldn't be happier.

Well, she took that back, her smile warming as Gideon crossed the room and took her into his arms. With the news she'd just received not minutes ago, she could indeed be happier. And she was.

Her lips parted under his, and as always, his kiss kindled the desire that only he could stir within her. She tilted her head back farther, opened her mouth wider, and he dived deeper. By the time he lifted his head, their rough breaths echoed in the office.

"I'm supposed to be taking you to lunch," he reminded her with a sensual smile that was reflected in his eyes. "But with you kissing me like that, hell, moonbeam, you might *be* lunch."

She chuckled. "You're bad. And I refuse to keep your mother and sister waiting. I had to twist Bridgette's arm to let me have Olivia for an afternoon, so nope, not missing lunch."

Gideon's eyes brightened at hearing his sister's name. And no wonder. Olivia had come a long way in a year. After hearing the whole story about what Trevor had done to her, Bridgette had decided to take her under her wing. And Olivia hadn't had much of a choice. Bridgette had bulldozed her way into Olivia's world, and assumed the role of big sister, as Shay had. Soon, she had Olivia in the food truck, working beside her, and to Olivia's surprise, she'd enjoyed it and was wonderful with people and the business side of it. Bridgette had taken her on as a partner, and now the two of them were planning to buy another truck.

And Trevor… A sliver of sadness wormed its way into Shay's happiness. It happened whenever she thought of him. She hadn't shared the file she had on him; he was her brother, and no matter what he'd done, she couldn't destroy him. But things like that had a way of exposing themselves. He and the senator were in trouble with the law and SEC now. Soon,

Trevor would lose not only his wife, the family business and reputation, but also his freedom. He'd caused a lot of pain and loss to people both emotionally and financially, and now he faced the consequences of his actions. She loved him, but she also hadn't seen him since the night of his engagement party.

"Are you sure about lunch?" Gideon asked, cupping her chin and tipping her head back for another press of his lips to hers. "I'm sure Mom and Olivia would understand."

"Yes." Shay laughed, then cradled his cheeks between her palms. "I'm hungry." She paused. "And especially since I'm eating for two now."

Shock blanked his features. Slowly, understanding dawned, and his black eyes glittered.

"What?" he rasped. "Are you telling me that we're… that you're…"

"Pregnant," she finished with a wide grin, slipping her arms around his neck again. "We're going to have a baby."

"Moonbeam," he whispered, awed. With a reverence that brought tears to her eyes, he stepped back, and her arms fell to her sides. He knelt in front of her, his big hands spreading over her still-flat abdomen. "Jesus, Moonbeam. How can you continue making me the happiest, richest, most loved man in the world?" He dipped his head, brushed his mouth over her belly. Rising to his feet, he pulled her into a tight, hard embrace and buried his face in her neck. "I love you, Shay. I love you so much."

"I love you, too. Forever."

* * * * *

A BRIDE AT
HIS BIDDING

MICHELLE SMART

CHAPTER ONE

ANDREAS SAMARAS POKED his head into the adjoining office to his own. Having spent the day on a multinational conference call, he needed to check in with his PA.

'How is everything going?'

Debbie sighed. 'The world is going to hell in a handcart.'

'Quite.' His PA's theatrical tendencies were infamous throughout Samaras Fund Management. Andreas would find it wearing if she weren't the best business PA he'd ever had. 'Apart from that, is there anything I need to know? With regards to the business,' he hastened to add in case she started harping on about polar bears and Arctic ice melt again.

'Nothing important.'

'Good. How did the interviews go? Have you come up with a shortlist for me?' Rochelle, his domestic PA, had quit. The smitten fool was getting married and had decided that a job requiring a great deal of travel was not a good fit for domestic bliss. He'd offered to double her wages and increase her holidays but still she had said no. He'd dragged his heels for weeks about finding a replacement for her in the hope she would change her mind. She hadn't and finally he had accepted defeat.

Debbie held up a stack of papers. 'I've whittled the candidates down to five.'

Andreas stepped into the office. Debbie had been tasked with doing the preliminary interviews. She knew exactly what kind of person he was looking for to take on the role that basically entailed organising his domestic life. It was a live-in role that would see the successful candidate travel wherever he went, ensuring his domestic life ran as smoothly as his business. The person needed to be honest, loyal, unobtrusive and flexible, have impeccable references, a clean driving licence and no criminal record.

He took the papers from her hand and flipped through them. All had a square photograph of the candidate attached to the corner of their applications. It was a requirement he insisted on. Three candidates would make it to the shortlist and he liked to be familiar with their appearance before he met them for the final interview, which he would undertake personally.

By Debbie's computer was a stack of the applicants she'd already rejected. The top one caught his eye. There was something familiar about the direct gaze staring back…

'Why have you rejected this one?' he asked, picking up the form and studying it. Dark hazel eyes stared right back at him. Dark hazel eyes he knew instinctively that he'd seen before.

Debbie peered at it with a frown. 'Oh, her. Caroline Dunwoody. She interviewed well but there was something about her I didn't trust. I don't know what it was. A feeling, nothing more, but it made me check her references in more detail. One of them checks out okay but I'm suspicious of the other one. She says she worked as Head of Housekeeping at Hargate Manor for two years and has a letter in her file to that effect. I spoke to the gentleman who wrote the reference, the Manor's butler, and he verified everything.'

'Then what's the problem?'

'Hargate Manor doesn't exist.'

His eyebrows rose. 'Doesn't exist?'

'There is no Hargate Manor within fifty miles of this one's supposed location.'

If Debbie said it didn't exist then it didn't exist. She was the most thorough person Andreas knew.

He looked more closely at Caroline Dunwoody's photograph, racking his brain trying to remember where he could have met her. He usually had an excellent recall for faces but on this occasion he couldn't put a finger on it. She had dark chestnut hair that fell in a neat line to her shoulders and pretty if angular features, a short straight nose, a top lip slightly fuller than the bottom and a cute heart-shaped chin. Yes, a pretty face but not one familiar to him.

But he had seen those eyes before.

Just as he opened his mouth to order Debbie to do some more digging into this woman, it suddenly came to him.

Digging. Journalists did lots of digging.

Caroline. The extended version of Carrie.

Carrie Rivers. The journalist sister of his niece's old best friend.

The journalist for the *Daily Times* who had made a name for herself by exposing the illegal and often seedy practices of rich businessmen.

He doubted he would still remember their tenuous association were it not that her most recent undercover investigation into James Thomas, an old business acquaintance of his, had revealed James's business to be a cover for drugs, arms and people trafficking. A month ago, Carrie's meticulous work had seen James sentenced to fifteen years in prison. Andreas had read about the sentencing and silently cheered. He hoped he rotted in his cell.

With the feeling of a ball bearing pressing down on his guts, Andreas did an Internet search on his phone for her. There were no photographs of Carrie online. He supposed this wasn't surprising given the nature of her work.

But it was her. He was certain of it.

He'd only met Carrie once, three years ago. It had been such a fleeting moment that it was no surprise he'd struggled to remember. Three years ago, she had been blonde with rounded cheeks.

Her eyes were the only thing about her that hadn't changed. Their gazes had met as he'd left the headmistress's office of his niece's boarding school. Carrie and her sister Violet had been sat in the corridor waiting for their turn to be admitted. Violet had hung her head in shame when she'd seen him. Carrie should have hung her head too.

Neither had known it would be the last time they would be admitted into the headmistress's office. Violet was to be expelled with immediate effect.

Three years on and Carrie was applying for a domestic job with him under a different name and supplying fake references in the process. This did not bode well and his brain groped for reasons as to why she might now be targeting him. Andreas ran a clean business. He paid all his taxes, both personal and corporation, in all the relevant jurisdictions. He followed and exceeded local employment law. His romantic affairs over the years had been consensual and discreet, guilt and responsibility for his family overriding the urge to bed as many beautiful women as possible, something he intended to rectify now all the burdens had been lifted from his shoulders.

One thing Andreas had learned over his thirty-seven

years was that when problems cropped up, the only thing to do was keep a clear head and deal with them immediately, stopping the problems escalating into catastrophe.

A plan quickly formed in his mind. He inhaled deeply then smiled. 'Debbie, I want you to call Miss Dunwoody and invite her back for a second interview.'

Debbie looked at him as if he'd sprouted blossom from his head.

'Back it up with a letter. This is what I want you to say...'

Carrie sat in the spacious reception room of Samaras Fund Management's London headquarters and tried to get air into lungs that seemed to have forgotten how to breathe. Her heart was beating erratically, the thuds loud in her ears, and she had to keep wiping her clammy palms on her thighs.

She'd woken from fractured sleep with her stomach churning so hard she'd had to force her coffee down. Food had been unthinkable.

She had never known nerves like it, although calling this sensation nerves was like calling a river a small trickle of water. Soon she would be taken through to Andreas Samaras's office and she had to contain these mixed and virulent emotions that threatened to crush her.

She hadn't suffered any nerves while going undercover and investigating James Thomas. She'd been ice-cool and focussed as she'd systematically gathered the evidence needed to prove his heinous crimes and expose him, using the same mind-set she used on her regular investigations, her focus never swaying. The day James had been sentenced had been the brightest spot of the last three night-marish years.

Andreas might not have fed her sister the drugs that had

destroyed her young fragile body but his contribution to Violet's descent into hell had been every bit as lethal as James's and far more personal, and now it was his turn for justice. Carrie could not allow her nerves or conscience to blow it for her…but this time it was different.

It had been common knowledge that James Thomas was a shady figure deserving of proper investigation. Getting permission and backing to go undercover in his workforce had been easy—the whole of the *Daily Times* had wanted that scumbag brought down.

Andreas Samaras, Greek billionaire investor and owner of Samaras Fund Management, was a different kettle of fish. There was nothing in his past or on the rumour mill to suggest he was anything other than clean. Only Carrie knew differently, and when she'd seen the advertisement for a Domestic PA mere days after James had been sentenced, she had known Andreas's time had come. She knew infiltrating his personal life carried a much greater risk than investigating him as an employee in his business life but it was a risk she was willing to take.

Three years ago she had written two names on a piece of paper. She had since struck James's name off. Now it was time to strike Andreas's off too.

To get her newspaper's backing to go undercover though, she'd had to tell a little white lie… A few surprised eyebrows had been raised but the go-ahead had been given. No one had disbelieved her.

As the clock ticked down to the moment she would be taken to see Andreas, the ramifications of her lie rang loudly in her head. If the truth that Carrie was undertaking a personal vendetta was revealed her career would be over. The *Daily Times* was no shady tabloid. It was a highbrow publication that had made it through the trials and tribulations all the British press had been through over the past decade with its reputation largely intact. It was a good employer too.

If they could print only a fraction of what was suspected about some of the world's most powerful people the public would need vodka spiked into the water system to help them get over the shock. The rich and powerful threw money into silencing the press and making problems disappear. They forced their staff to sign cast-iron non-disclosure agreements and were ruthless about enforcing them. Super-injunctions were *de rigueur*.

If Carrie got the job with Andreas she would be thrown directly into his personal world. She would be closer to her target than on any of her prior investigations. Who knew what she would find? When she'd first gone undercover with James in his accounts department she'd known he was a drug-abuser with a predilection for teenage girls but had had no idea of his involvement with people trafficking or arms. Andreas was that criminal's friend. Who knew what *he* was involved with?

She'd known the odds of getting the job with Andreas were slim, even with her rigged CV and falsified references. On paper, they'd made her the perfect candidate for the role but it had been a rushed job, hurried to meet the application deadline. She couldn't help worrying that there was a giant hole or two in it.

She hadn't thought the preliminary interview with his PA had gone well and had left the building certain she'd messed up. When she'd received the call inviting her to a second interview, she was so shocked a mere breeze would have knocked her over.

And now, as that ticking clock echoed louder in her ears, all she could see when she closed her eyes was the burning hatred Andreas had thrown her way the one time their eyes had met.

* * *

'Miss Dunwoody?'

Carrie blinked and looked up to find the superior young receptionist staring at her quizzically.

She'd gone under the name of Rivers for so long it had become a part of herself. Hearing her real name sounded foreign. She'd been known by the surname of Rivers since her mother had remarried when she'd been four and had thought it wise to continue using it when she embarked on her career in investigative journalism. There were a lot of sickos out there. In this instance, that decision had been fortuitous. She'd never legally changed her name. People in her world knew her as Carrie Rivers. Her birth certificate, driving licence and passport had her as Caroline Dunwoody. The advert for the job had explicitly stated it involved lots of travelling.

Falsifying references was one thing. Trying to fake a passport was a whole different ballpark.

'Mr Samaras is ready to see you now.'

He'd kept her waiting for an hour.

Swallowing back a sudden violent burst of nausea, Carrie tightly clutched the strap of her handbag and followed the receptionist down a wide corridor lined with modern artwork.

It had taken her ages to find the perfect outfit for this interview. She'd wanted to look professional but not as if she were applying for a job within Samaras Fund Management itself. She'd settled on a cream high-necked cashmere top with a dozen small buttons running the length, a pair of smart grey trousers and simple black heels that gave her a little extra height for confidence but which she could comfortably walk in. Now she felt as if she'd dressed in a smothering straightjacket, the heels a hindrance to her unsteady feet.

A door opened and Carrie was admitted into an office twice the size of the one she shared with the rest of the crime team and a hundred times plusher.

There, behind an enormous oak desk, working on one of three computers, sat Andreas Samaras.

Her heart slammed against her chest then thudded painfully and for one frightening moment Carrie thought she really was going to vomit.

He didn't look up from what he was doing.

'One minute please,' he said in the deep, quick, sharply staccato voice she remembered from their one telephone conversation instigated by Andreas five years ago.

Carrie's sister and Andreas's niece had been weekly boarders and roommates at school together. Their friendship had deepened and soon they had wanted to spend weekends and holidays together too. Andreas had phoned Carrie to agree on some ground rules. They had found much to agree on. It helped that they had both been in the same position, both of them the sole carers of their vulnerable teenage charges. After that one conversation, they would text message each other to confirm if Natalia was due at Carrie's for the weekend or if Violet was due at Andreas's. It had become a rhythm in Carrie's life, right until Andreas had engineered Violet's expulsion.

Finally, he looked up from his computer, pushed his chair back and got to his feet. The sheer size and power of the man was as starkly apparent as it had been when he had swept past her three years ago.

'It is a pleasure to meet you, Miss Dunwoody.'

She stared at the huge hand extending towards her and forced herself to lean forward and take it. Large, warm tapered fingers covered hers as he shook her hand briskly before letting go.

'Take a seat,' he commanded amicably, sitting back down and picking up a thin pile of papers from his desk.

The skin on her hand buzzed where he'd clasped it and she fought the urge to rub it against her thigh as she took the seat he'd directed her to, and expelled the tiniest sigh of relief.

There had been only a teeny ounce of doubt he wouldn't recognise her. Physically she'd changed a lot since that one fleeting glance three years ago outside the headmistress's office, when his light brown eyes had lasered her with such ferocity she had recoiled. Stress alone had made her lose three stone since then, which had altered her facial features as well as her body shape. She'd long stopped her quest for the perfect shade of blonde hair and reverted to her natural brown colour.

If Andreas had the slightest idea of who she really was, she would not be there. She wouldn't have got past the initial application.

It hadn't seemed feasible that he would recognise her or her name but she had learned through five years of her job to take nothing for granted.

Light brown thoughtful eyes studied her rather than the paperwork in his hand, which she guessed was a copy of her job application, and she fought hard against the flush of colour crawling over her skin. When she finally forced herself to meet his gaze, the raw masculinity staring back at her intensified the flush, enflaming her bones, taking her so unawares that for a moment her mind emptied of everything but the rapid tattoo of her heart reverberating in her ears.

Carrie swallowed, desperate for moisture in her parched throat, desperate to suck air into lungs that had closed in on themselves. Whatever kind of a man Andreas was, there was no denying that he was divine to look at. He had thick dark brown hair sun-kissed on the tips, barely tamed to flop onto a gently lined forehead, cheekbones you could ski down, a chiselled square jaw already dark with stubble and a sharp nose with a slight bend on the bridge. Deeply tanned and weather-beaten, he looked every one of his thirty-seven years.

He was the most overtly virile and handsome man she'd ever laid eyes on.

Then he gave her a crooked grin.

It was like being smiled at by the big bad wolf the moment before he ate Grandma.

'Congratulations on making it to the final shortlist,' he said in his impeccable English. Carrie knew, as she knew so much about this man, that he'd learned English at school in his Greek homeland and then perfected it at his American university. He spoke the language with true fluency, firing the words out so quickly his accent sounded like a musical cadence to her ears. 'I will be honest and tell you that you are my preferred candidate.'

She was taken aback. 'I am?'

His eyes sparkled. 'Before I go into more detail about my requirements, there are things I wish to know about you.'

She attempted to hide her fear with a smile that didn't want to form on her frozen cheeks.

Had he spotted the holes in her résumé?

After a moment of silence that seemed to echo between them she got her paper-dry throat to work. 'What do you want to know?'

'References and application forms only give a narrow perspective on a person. If I give you the job then we will spend a lot of time together. You will be my right hand in my domestic life. You will be privy to my most intimate secrets. So, Miss Dunwoody…may I call you Caroline?'

She nodded faintly. The only person who had ever called her Caroline had been her mother but she hadn't made her name sing as Andreas did. Even as it occurred to her, that struck Carrie as an odd thought to have.

'Caroline. If I give you the job I need to trust you and trust that we'll be able to work well together.' His relaxed frame, the musical staccato of his voice and the amusement enlivening his handsome features all worked together to reassure her that her ruse had worked but the scent of danger still lingered.

Her instincts were telling her to take her bag and coat and leave this office right now.

'Are you married or do you have a partner?' he continued. 'I ask because if you do, you should know you will be spending a lot of time apart from them. Your personal life must be conducted in your own time and you won't have much of that.'

'I have no significant other.' She never had and never would. Men could not be trusted. She'd learned that before she'd reached double digits.

'Children?'

She shook her head, immediately thinking of Violet, who she loved as much as if she'd given birth to her.

'Any other dependants? Dogs, cats, goldfish?'

'No.'

'Good. I make no apologies. I am a demanding employer and this job is a twenty-four-seven one. What did Debbie tell you about it in the preliminary interview?'

'That it entails the day-to-day running of your homes.'

His head tilted and his face grew thoughtful. 'That is how the job is advertised but you should know it is more about the day-to-day running of *me*. My domestic PA does oversee the running of my homes but they're not expected to do any of the manual chores themselves—I employ other domestic staff for that. I work long and demanding hours. When I am at home I like to live in comfort and I want all my needs and comforts met by someone who is capable of turning their hand to anything, without argument. I need someone on hand to tend to all my personal needs—pour my drinks, prepare my clothing for me, make sure a towel is on hand if I do any physical activity, that kind of thing.'

It wasn't a domestic PA the man wanted, Carrie thought in mute outrage as she listened to his seductive voice, it was a slave.

'In return, I offer a *very* generous salary.' He mentioned a figure that made her blink, it being four times what she earned at the newspaper.

She imagined that any genuine applicant would bite his hand off for it. It was an extortionate amount of money for what was essentially nothing more than being Andreas's dogsbody.

Now he put a forearm on his desk and leaned forward to stare at her with an intensity that made her stomach do a strange flip.

The more she looked into his eyes, the more startling she found them, the light brown having a translucent quality that still contained real depth.

If he gave her the job she would have to tread carefully for as long as she lived under his roof. This man was dangerous.

'Now, Caroline,' he said, the tempo of his speech finally slowing down a notch, 'I do have one more requirement from the person I give this role to.'

'Which is?'

'I require someone who has a cheerful disposition.'

She might as well leave, then. How could she be cheerful around the man who'd caused such damage?

'What I mean by that is that I get enough stress in my

work life. When I come home I like to be welcomed with a smile and not be bothered by petty gripes. *Can* you smile?'

He framed the question with such faux earnestness that Carrie found her facial muscles softening and the smile she'd been trying to produce since she'd stepped into his office breaking out of its own accord.

His eyes gleamed in response. 'Much better.' Then he sat back and folded his arms across his chest. The cuffs of his sleeves moved with the motion revealing a tantalising glimpse of fine dark hair.

He nodded slowly. 'Yes. I think you're going to suit me very well. The job is yours if you want it.'

She blinked her gaze away from his arms as his words sank in. 'It is?'

She hadn't expected it to be this easy...

Her heart started to thunder beneath her ribs.

This was *too* easy.

Andreas was one of the richest men in the world. He was highly intelligent—unverified reports placed his IQ in the world's top one per cent and he had the street smarts to match it. In short, he was no fool, and this job that he was giving her after less than fifteen minutes in his company would take her straight into the heart of his life.

'*Do* you want it?' he challenged, breaking the silence that had fallen.

'Yes.' She nodded for emphasis, trying to muster her enthusiasm, and forced another smile to her face. 'Yes, I do, definitely. Thank you.'

'Good.' His teeth flashed wolfishly. 'Did you bring your passport?'

'Yes.' The letter discussing the second interview had been specific about it. She assumed it was needed for him to photocopy as proof of her identity.

Andreas rose to his feet. 'Then let us go. We have a flight slot to fill.'

Carrie stared at him blankly. 'Go?'

'The letter you were sent clearly explained that the successful candidate for the job would start immediately.'

'It did…' But she hadn't thought immediately meant this immediately. 'Are we going abroad *now*?'

That gleam she was beginning to seriously distrust flashed in his eyes again. 'Yes. Right now. Do you have a problem with that?'

'No problem.' She hurried to stand. The job was hers and she wouldn't give him reason to change his mind. She would practise smiling as soon as she found a mirror. 'It's just that I have no change of clothes with me.'

'You will be provided with everything you need when we get there. Give Debbie your dress size as we leave.'

'Where are we going?'

'To one of my homes where it isn't raining.' And with that he opened his office door and ushered her through it.

CHAPTER TWO

ANDREAS SAT AT his desk on his private jet with his laptop open before him. Barely ten feet away, Carrie was at the dining table reading through the thick folder that contained the working details of all his properties. He had no doubt she would find it excruciatingly tedious to read through.

All his properties were listed except one—the one they were flying to.

'Which one should I concentrate on?' she'd asked when he'd given it to her, subtly letting him know he hadn't given her their final destination.

'All of them.' He'd smiled. 'I'll give you a test when we arrive.'

'Which will be when?'

He'd looked at his watch. 'In approximately eleven hours.'

Her eyes had flickered but she'd made no further comment. He'd seen her thoughts racing and had enjoyed watching her bite the questions back.

He'd enjoyed himself enormously throughout their meeting too, far more than he'd expected. The knowledge that he'd rumbled her before she'd even set foot in his office had bubbled away inside him, satisfying enough to smother the anger that had fought for an outlet.

Anger clouded logical thinking and he needed to keep his mind clear if he was to continue outwitting this viper.

He'd determined that getting her out of England and as far from her home and true employment as he could and as quickly as he could was the best way to proceed. Disorientate her. Put her at the disadvantage without her even realising it and then, when he had her in his private home, unable to escape or communicate with the outside world, he would demand answers. He wanted to know everything—why she was investigating him, what she expected to find and who had put her up to it. He'd made his own discreet enquiries amongst his media contacts but had come up blank. No one was aware of even a hint of a brewing scandal about him.

Instinct told him that Carrie's reasons for being here were at least partly personal. The coincidence was too great to be explained any other way.

He would discover her reasons in due course but rather than question her immediately, he decided he'd have some fun with her first. Let her suffer a little. It was the least she deserved.

Did Carrie really think him such a useless human being that he required someone to live by his side pouring his drinks and mopping his brow? Andreas liked his creature comforts but he was no man-child and he'd seen the flicker of surprise in her eyes when he'd outlined the duties expected of her, duties he'd made up on the spur of the moment just to see what her reaction would be.

For the next few days he would embrace the man-child role and make her wait on him hand and foot. She would hate every minute of it.

Excellent.

He would enjoy every minute of it.

He watched her put aside the notepad she'd been scribbling on as she'd read through the folder and remove her phone from her handbag. She angled her body away from him and switched it on. A few moments later her shoulders rose and she tugged at her hair.

Andreas grinned, enjoying her silent frustration to find it not working. He dealt with highly sensitive information. To get onto his jet's network required a password. He wondered how long it would be before she cracked and asked for it.

It took her three hours, an impressive length of time he thought, before she lifted her head, cleared her throat, and said, 'Would it be possible for me to have the Wi-Fi password?'

'I didn't think you had anybody to check in with,' he commented idly, enjoying the flush of colour that crawled up her slender neck.

'I don't,' she said with only the smallest of hesitation. 'I just wanted to check my emails.'

'Expecting anything important?'

She shook her head, her whole neck now aflame. 'Don't worry about it. I'll check them later.'

Carrie Rivers, Caroline Dunwoody, whatever her real name was, had a beautiful neck. He'd seen by her photograph that she was pretty but in the flesh she was so much more, her features softer, her skin dewy and golden. She was beautiful.

He thought back to the slightly plump woman he'd caught that momentary glimpse of three years back. Her eyes had been striking enough for him to remember but at the time he'd been too angry to think properly let alone remember any other detail about her. He'd been angrier than he'd ever been. The previous evening, he'd come home early from a rare evening out to find his niece and her best friend off their heads on drink and drugs. What had followed later that night had been almost as bad.

Taking guardianship of an orphaned teenage girl had

never been easy but that weekend had been the hardest of his life, harder even than the night he'd received the call telling him his sister and brother-in-law had been found dead or the day he'd learned his parents faced financial ruin.

Where was the manual that gave step-by-step guidance on how to handle the discovery that your niece, your responsibility, was creeping towards drug addiction, or how to handle waking to find your niece's sixteen-year-old best friend naked in your bedroom intent on seducing you? Where had Violet learned that kind of behaviour? From her older sister? Was the seemingly prim and proper woman sitting just feet away from him as wanton and reckless as her sister had been?

Despite his best attempts, he'd been unable to discover anything significant about Carrie. Her page on the *Daily Times* website listed her awards and achievements but nothing of a personal nature. He only knew her age because of their old personal links. Twenty-six. An incredibly young age to have achieved so much in her career. That took real commitment and dedication, something he would have admired had those traits not now been aimed at him. But unlike the men—and they had *all* been men—she'd brought down before him, Andreas had nothing to hide. His business was clean. So why had she set her sights on him? Why was the award-winning investigative journalist Carrie Rivers after him? *Was* this personal?

Whatever the reasons, he would learn them and nip whatever trouble was brewing in the bud. The old maxim of keep your friends close but your enemies closer stood the test of time.

Until he learned the truth, he would keep Carrie *very* close to him and then...

And then, unless he could think of a better plan than the

one formulating in his head, Carrie would be kept close by his side for the foreseeable future.

It was dark when they landed. The early spring storms London had been dealing with were but a distant memory as Carrie disembarked Andreas's jet and found herself engulfed in a heat the like of which she had only ever read about. She removed her jacket and looked up to find a cloudless black sky glittering with stars.

'Where are we?' She'd diligently read the folder Andreas had given her, pored over the location of all his homes and, as time had extended on their flight, convinced herself they were going to Tokyo.

'The Seychelles.' Andreas stood beside her. 'Welcome to Mahe, the largest island of the Seychelles Granitic Archipelago.'

Her mind turned frantically. How could she have missed a home in the Seychelles? She'd read his property folder from cover to cover three times, and there had been nothing about a home there in any of her prior investigations into him.

'It's the most private of my properties,' he said in a low voice close to her ear. The tangy freshness of his expensive cologne swirled around her.

Carrie casually sidestepped away from him and swallowed the sudden rush of moisture filling her mouth. 'What time is it?'

'One in the morning. We have a short flight on my helicopter before we reach my home.'

They were whisked through security and within twenty minutes of landing were climbing into a sparkling helicopter.

'Have you been in a helicopter before?' Andreas asked as he strapped himself in beside her.

There were six seats to choose from and he had to sit right next to her?

Carrie shook her head and determinedly did not look at the thigh resting so close to her own she could feel its warmth on her skin.

'It's an enjoyable experience and the quickest way to my island.'

'*Your* island?'

He pulled a thoughtful face. 'It's more of a peninsular off another island but the peninsular belongs in its entirety to me.'

Carrie silently swore as, under the heavy noise of the rotors twirling, the helicopter lifted off the ground.

She hadn't had an inkling about any of this. What else had she missed in her research on him?

Whose name had this property and accompanying land been bought in? Was it a secret shell company? She would get digging into it as soon as she had some privacy and a decent Internet signal. She needed to check in with her editor and let him know where she was too. But after she'd had a shower and, hopefully, some sleep. She'd been in the same clothes for almost a whole day, not having dreamt when she dressed that morning that she would end the day in the famed wedding and honeymoon spot of the Seychelles.

By contrast, Andreas had showered an hour before landing and changed from his suit into a fresh, crisp white shirt and light grey tailored trousers.

She dragged her attention away from the powerful body brushing so close against her own and the tangy scent playing under her nose by envisaging the shower she would have when they reached his home. She wouldn't have the temperature scalding as she usually did. To rid herself of the stickiness clinging to her pores she would lather herself under refreshingly cool water.

Her thoughts dissolved as a particularly sharp movement from the pilot caused Andreas's thigh and arm to compact against hers. An immediate shock of awareness crashed through her, so acute and so sudden and so totally unexpected that she froze.

It felt as if she'd been tasered.

For long moments she couldn't breathe.

A large hand covered hers and squeezed.

'It's nothing to worry about,' he murmured. 'Just a little turbulence.'

Carrie swallowed and forced a nod, trying desperately to get a coherent thought into her scrambled brain, her lungs finally opening back up again when he let go of her hand.

She was just tired, she assured herself, digging her nails into her palms.

Better he think she'd been frightened by the sudden turbulence they'd flown into than know of the turbulence that had exploded inside her at the feel of him pressed so tightly against her.

She looked out of the window and made an effort to relax her frame.

Come on, Carrie. You've always wanted to fly in a helicopter. At least try *and enjoy it.*

Violet had always wanted to fly in a helicopter too. She remembered how excited her sister would get during sunny days when their mother was still alive and they would go out for walks and spot helicopters zooming overhead. Her chubby little arms would wave frantically and she was always convinced the pilots waved back.

What was Violet doing at that moment? Her sister had been in California for three months now, her recovery from addiction and all her other issues a slow, fragile process.

Carrie had called her a couple of days ago, their weekly conversation as stilted and awkward as they had been since Violet had woken from her coma and it was spelled out how close to death she had come. Whenever she spoke to her sister now it was like talking to a stranger. The little girl whose first word had been 'Cawwie,' and who had followed Carrie like a shadow from the moment she could crawl was gone. In truth, she'd been gone for a long time and it tore at Carrie's heart to remember the sweetness that had once been there.

Blinking away hot tears at all that had been lost, Carrie continued to gaze out of the window. The moon was bright, allowing her to see the small landmass they were approaching in the middle of the Indian Ocean. Soon they flew directly over a beach gleaming white under the moonlight, the form of a large house emerging from the shadows as the pilot brought the helicopter down.

Andreas got out first then held out his hand to assist her, his eyes holding hers with a look that made her stomach knot in on itself.

Knowing she didn't have any choice, she took the hand. His fingers tightened as they wrapped around hers, solid and warm, keeping her steady as her feet reached for the ground.

'Thank you,' she muttered, glad the darkness cloaked her flaming cheeks from his probing gaze.

'My pleasure.' His fingertips swept gently over hers as he released his hold and then he climbed back inside to speak to his pilot.

Alone for a moment, Carrie inhaled deeply and found her senses filled with the heady scent of unseen flowers. The breeze of the ocean had cleared the humidity away, a fresh warmth brushing over her skin. It was all she could do not to close her eyes and savour the feeling.

Savouring the feeling would have to wait as suddenly lights came on and Andreas's house—villa—mansion—which the pilot had landed in the back garden of, was revealed.

It was breathtaking.

Only two storeys high, what it lacked in height it made up for in width, looking like a white stonewashed Buddhist temple surrounded by a deep red wraparound veranda. Matching deep red roof tiles gave what could easily have been an imposing building a welcoming air.

Andreas had rejoined her. She could feel his eyes on her and knew he was looking for a reaction.

What kind of reaction would a true employee give?

She opted for a truthful one.

'It's lovely.'

'Isn't it?' he agreed. 'Wait until you see it in the daylight. I fell in love with it from a photograph. I was looking for a holiday home and here I've found the perfect place. I can get away from the world but there's people and nightlife only a short flight or boat ride away.'

'This is your holiday home?'

'Of course,' he said with mild surprise. 'Who would want to conduct business on a paradise like this?'

'How long will we be here?'

'Why? Is there somewhere you have to be?'

'No, it's just…' She felt herself getting flustered.

'Relax. I'm teasing you. I know you have no commitment you have to rush back for or you would have disclosed it on your application form. We'll stay here for a while. I haven't had a proper holiday in some time and need to recharge my batteries.'

She hadn't had a holiday in some time either. At least a decade, two or three years before her mother had died.

But this wasn't a holiday for her. She was here to work.

Her job was to ensure the smooth running of this beautiful mansion and take care of the whims of its owner while secretly undertaking her own work of discovering its owner's darkest secrets. What kind of secrets she would find in Andreas's holiday home was anyone's guess. Chances were she would have to wait until they moved on to one of his other homes where he actually conducted business before she discovered anything useful.

Expecting a member of his staff to greet them—all his homes had at least three permanent live-in employees—Carrie was a little disconcerted to step inside and find the house shrouded in silence. Yes, it was the middle of the night, but surely the staff wouldn't retire for the night before their boss's arrival?

'I'll give you a quick tour before I show you to our bedrooms,' Andreas said, leading the way. He headed through an arched doorway without a door and said, 'Here's the living area.'

Her misgivings were put to one side as she slowly took in the beauty of Andreas's house, a home that managed to be both luxurious and yet welcoming. High ceilings and white walls were given colour by an intricate tiled mosaic that covered the floor wherever they stepped, including the large, airy dining room dominated by a large, highly polished mahogany table.

The kitchen was the size of an entire floor of her home.

'This is Brendan's domain,' he informed her.

'Brendan's your chef?'

'Yes. If you're hungry I can call him and he'll make something for you.'

'I'm fine, thank you.' Regular meals, which she'd had to force down into her cramped stomach, had been provided throughout the flight by Andreas's cabin crew.

He shrugged. 'If you need anything before morning I'm

sure you won't have any trouble finding it. I assume the kitchen functions as a normal kitchen.'

'You assume?'

He pulled a face. 'I employ staff so I don't have to do these chores for myself.'

'When was the last time you used a kitchen?' she asked before she could stop herself. Somehow, she doubted Andreas welcomed his domestic employees questioning him.

Her doubt proved wrong.

'In my university days in America—I studied at MIT—I discovered I was a terrible cook so I got a job working as a waiter in an Italian restaurant where they were always happy to feed me. I've not cooked for myself since.'

'An *Italian* restaurant?'

'There were no decent Greek restaurants where I lived then. There was a tapas bar but they didn't do breakfast so I opted for the Italian one.'

His long legs powered on gracefully up the cantilevered stairs to the first floor. Carrie hurried behind him, smothering a yawn. All the travelling on top of minimal sleep had exhausted her.

'My room.' Andreas pushed open a door to reveal a bedroom equal in size to the kitchen, containing everything a spoiled billionaire could need. Carrie hung back, reluctant to enter until he beckoned her inside with the crook of his finger and the hint of a gleam in his piercing light brown eyes. 'Don't be shy, Caroline. You need to become familiar with my room.'

Familiar with it? All she could see was the enormous carved bed heaped with pillows, and her imagination immediately stripped Andreas bare and pictured him sliding with that masculine grace she'd never seen on another man between the navy satin sheets.

She clenched her teeth together, trying to blink the

image away and pretend the rush of blood she could feel pumping around her was not connected to it.

She'd never imagined a man naked before and it disturbed her that she should have such unwelcome thoughts about this particular man.

There was such a sensuous potency about him. It was there in his every move, his every breath, his every word, and all it did was add to her growing sense of danger.

Sheesh, she really, *really* needed some sleep.

'What other staff work here?' she asked. Once she knew where everyone was she would stop feeling as if she'd been trapped in a gilded cage that only Andreas had the key to.

Everything had happened so quickly and smoothly that day that there hadn't been time for her misgivings to do more than squeak at her but now, here, standing in Andreas's bedroom in his secret home in the middle of the night, those misgivings were shouting loudly.

'I inherited most of the staff from the previous owners. The grounds are managed by Enrique and his eldest son. Enrique's wife Sheryl and a couple of her friends take care of all the cleaning. Between them they know everything there is to know about the house and the peninsular and the Seychelles itself.'

'Where are the staff quarters?'

'There aren't any. Brendan and his assistant live in a cottage on the grounds but the others all live on the main island.'

Another chime of alarm rang in her ears. 'So who actually lives in the house?'

Surely she had misunderstood something. Surely she wouldn't be the only person living under this roof with him while they were there?

'We do. You and me.'

'*Just* you and me?'

'Yes.' His eyes seemed to do more than merely sparkle. They *smouldered*. His nostrils flared as he added, 'While we're on this beautiful spot of paradise, the night time belongs to you and me alone.'

CHAPTER THREE

ANDREAS ENJOYED CARRIE'S attempt to hide her horror at this clearly unwelcome revelation.

'I bought this place as a getaway from the world so it's run in a more relaxed way than my other homes,' he said. 'As long as I have someone close at hand to take care of my needs, I don't need much else and that, *matia mou*, is why you are here. Consider it an easy breaking-in for you. The house runs itself so you can dedicate your time here to me and we can get to know each other properly in the process.'

The colour drained from her face, her hazel eyes widening.

Understandable, he thought lazily. Carrie wouldn't want him delving into her life with probing questions that would put her on the spot. She wouldn't want to trip herself up with easily forgotten lies.

He admired that, through the tumult of emotions flickering through her eyes, her composure didn't waver. If he were ignorant of her true identity he doubted he would have noticed anything amiss. If he didn't know the truth he would assume she was a naturally quiet, self-contained woman.

He looked forward to seeing how far he could push her before she cracked and the real Carrie emerged.

'Now for your room. You will find it adequately appointed.' But not as adequately as Rochelle's had been. She was being put in a much different room from the one his former Domestic PA had enjoyed. Rochelle's room had been located at the other end of the house so she could have her privacy.

He didn't intend for Carrie, this cuckoo in his nest, this spy, to have any privacy during her interlude in his life. Her duties would be of the kind he would never dream of imposing on a proper employee.

Andreas turned the handle of a door in the middle of the left-hand wall of his room. It opened into a much smaller, adjoining room.

He spread a hand out. 'See? You have everything you need. A bed, a dressing table, wardrobe and your own bathroom.' But no television or other form of entertainment. Andreas intended to be Carrie's only source of entertainment while she was here.

The colour that stained her cheeks this time was definitely of the angry variety but she kept it in check to ask with only the slightest tremor, 'My room adjoins yours?'

'How would you take care of my needs if you were on the other side of the house? The previous owners used this room as a nursery. I admit it's rather small—it was designed for a small child before they went into a proper room of their own—but I can assure you it's perfectly adequate.' Adequate for a baby or toddler. Barely adequate for a fully grown woman, even one as slender as Carrie. He'd intended to turn it into another dressing room and was glad he hadn't got around to organising it.

'Where's the lock?'

'There isn't one so it will be nice and easy for you to come and go between our rooms.' He winked. 'But do not worry. I am a gentleman and only enter a lady's bedroom when invited.'

And should she be tempted to enter his room without invitation, which she undoubtedly would seeing as her whole purpose for being here was to snoop, then the microscopic cameras he'd had installed in his bedroom and throughout the house would monitor her every movement.

He'd intended to bug her room too with voice-activated cameras but had talked himself out of it. There was a line a person should never cross and bugging a lady's bedroom, even a journalistic spy like this one, was firmly on the wrong side of it. Now that he'd spent the day in such close confines to her, he was doubly glad he hadn't crossed that line.

Carrie had an allure about her that played to his senses like a finely tuned violin.

She also had eyes that looked bruised from exhaustion.

'I can see you're tired. Is there anything you wanted to ask before we retire for the night?'

She shook her head, those soft, plump lips drawing in together. The situation had clearly overwhelmed her. He could sympathise. When she had walked into his offices in the heart of London's financial district that morning she could not have guessed she'd finish the day cut off from everything she was familiar with in the paradise that was the Seychelles. No doubt she was feeling vulnerable.

Good.

He *could* sympathise but he would not. Carrie was a vulture. A beautiful vulture for sure, but a vulture nonetheless.

She deserved nothing less than what was coming for her.

'In that case, I bid you goodnight. The clothes I promised you were flown in while we were travelling. Sheryl has put them away for you. You will find them imminently suitable. And remember...'

A pretty brow rose cautiously. 'Remember?'

He winked. 'I like to be welcomed with a smile.'

As he closed the interconnecting door he smiled himself to imagine her reaction to the clothing selected for her.

His fun with Carrie was only just beginning.

Carrie threw the entire contents of her new wardrobe onto the narrow excuse of a bed and rifled through them with increasing anxiety.

She'd expected to be given outfits akin to what chambermaids in hotels wore, not clothing like this.

Her wardrobe and dresser had been filled with soft, floaty summer dresses, vest tops, shorts that put the meaning into the word 'short', bikinis and sarongs. There was underwear too, all of the black, lacy variety.

Every item had a designer label.

Her skin had never felt so heated as when she'd picked up a pair of knickers and wondered if Andreas had chosen them personally.

But how could he have done? She hadn't left his side since she'd stepped into his office. It must have been his PA, Debbie, who she'd been certain hadn't liked her in the initial interview and who she'd had to give her vital statistics to as Andreas had whisked her out of his building.

Carrie tugged at her hair with a mixture of consternation and fear.

Whoever had chosen the items, which included beach paraphernalia along with all the clothing, this was not right, not by any stretch of the imagination. To make matters worse there was no Internet she could connect to and her phone signal seemed to be non-existent. The text message she'd written to her editor forty minutes ago was still trying to send.

Who knew she was here? Andreas and his PA Debbie, his flight crew and his Seychellois domestic staff. No one from her own life knew she was in the Seychelles, only people employed by Andreas.

Rubbing her eyes, she told herself she was probably worrying over nothing. It had been an incredibly long day and she was sleep deprived. Sleep deprivation did funny things to the brain.

The letter inviting her to the second interview *had* stated the successful applicant would be expected to start the job immediately. It was her own fault that she hadn't taken the letter literally enough.

She was exactly where she wanted to be, with greater access to the man than in her wildest dreams.

But he also had access to her, and she eyed the adjoining unlocked door with nerves fluttering in her chest.

There was no way she would trust his word that he wouldn't enter her room uninvited.

The way he looked at her… Did he look at all his employees with that same intensity? Did he leave the rest of his employees feeling that he was stripping them bare with a glance?

Or was it just her guilty conscience playing at her and making her see things that weren't there?

Movement from the adjoining room made her catch her breath.

Andreas was still awake. They were connected to each other's rooms and she couldn't even lock herself away from him.

She forced herself to breathe.

She needed to take a shower but had been holding it off until she could be reasonably sure he'd gone to sleep. An hour after he'd left her in this tiny bedroom, there was nothing to suggest he was ready to turn in.

What was he going to do? she chided herself. Walk in on her while she showered?

Sexual foibles were the easiest secrets to uncover. Andreas Samaras might be many things but a sex pest was not something that had been flagged up about him, not even on the secret grapevine from which she and other journalists like her got so many of their stories. He rarely dated and when he did it was discreetly. If there was anything along those lines she had to worry about she would already know about them.

She was being over-cautious when she didn't need to be.

Carefully putting the expensive clothing back into its rightful place, she realised what her real problem with it was. These were the sort of clothes a man bestowed on his lover for a holiday, not his employee.

Carrie awoke in the unfamiliar tiny room minutes before the digital alarm clock on her bedside table went off. It had been set for her by some faceless person that she would no doubt meet shortly, a person with whom she would have to pretend to be someone she was not.

Lying on an investigation had never bothered her before. The few she had done before, though, had been office-based. Offices were places where *everyone* wore a mask. She'd fitted in without any problems and without any guilt, knowing she was working for a good cause.

This was different. This was Andreas's home. She had told herself over and over that this was an opportunity that had been gift-wrapped for her but she still felt as if she'd breached an invisible line.

He deserves it, she told herself grimly, focussing her mind on Violet's scarred, emaciated body and its root cause. *He deserves everything he gets.*

She checked her phone and sighed to see the message to her editor still pending. Her room must be in a black spot.

After a quick shower under the disappointing trickle of water in her private bathroom, only mitigated by the expensive, wonderfully scented toiletries provided for her, it was time to select an outfit to wear.

After rifling through her new clothing for the dozenth time she chose a dark blue dress covered in tiny white dots. It was made of the sheerest material, had the thinnest of spaghetti straps and fell to mid-thigh but at least it covered her cleavage. And, she had to admit, it *was* pretty.

Scrabbling through her handbag, she found a hairband wedged in the bottom and tied her hair into a loose bun at the nape of her neck. She had no make-up with her. Usually that didn't matter as she rarely wore it but today she felt she could do with some camouflage.

Dressed and feeling much more alert, she pulled the floor-length curtains open and gasped.

The sight that greeted her could have come from a postcard.

If she'd peeked through the curtains during the night she would have seen her room had its own private balcony. She stepped out onto it now, heart thumping, the sun kissing her skin good morning.

She closed her eyes to savour the feeling then opened them again, hand on her throat, staring in stunned awe at the deep blue sky unmarred by so much as a solitary cloud and at the stunning azure ocean that lapped gently onto the finest white sand imaginable, the cove's shore lined with palm trees. A short distance ahead sat an isolated green landmass that looked, from her dazed estimation, close enough that she might tread through water to it. An artist couldn't have painted a more perfect scene.

'Good morning, Caroline.'

The deep, cheerful voice startled her and she gripped the balustrade before turning her head.

So mind-blown had she been by the view before her, she hadn't noticed her balcony was far too wide to be hers alone.

Hair damp and wearing nothing but a pair of low-slung black shorts, Andreas strolled to stand beside her and grinned. 'What did I tell you about the view in daylight—takes the breath away, doesn't it?'

Her grip on the balustrade tightening, she stared back out at the view and nodded. 'It's stunning.'

But it was the view standing feet away from her that had truly stolen her breath and, though she tried her hardest to keep her attention on what lay in front of her, her senses were leaping to what stood beside her.

His body was even better than her imagination had allowed her to believe. Broad shouldered, muscular without being overdone and deeply tanned, this was a body kept fit by plenty of swimming and enjoyment of the outside life, not by lifting weights or working on a treadmill. This wasn't a body that had been sculptured out of vanity.

'Sleep well?' he murmured, resting his arms on the balustrade.

She inhaled and gave a sharp nod, intensely aware of his penetrative gaze on her.

So much for sleep curing her inexplicable awareness of him.

'Fine, thank you.'

'Good. Ready to start work?'

She nodded again.

'Then let's introduce you to the others and get some breakfast. I don't know about you but I'm starving.'

'Okay.' She turned to go back into her room.

'Caroline?'

She met his sparkling gaze. 'Yes?'

'Have you forgotten my most basic requirement?'

She furrowed her brow as she tried to clear her mind of his semi-nakedness enough to think, pretended her insides hadn't just clenched and heated to see the fine dark hair that lightly covered his chest snaked down and over his hard abdomen to where his shorts rested low...

He shook his head in amusement. 'Where is my smile?'

'Still waking up,' she replied without thinking.

His grin was wide enough to eclipse the rising sun. 'Ah, you *do* have a sense of humour. I did wonder. Now let's get some breakfast.'

And with that, he strolled back into his room.

Carrie was on the brink of laughter for reasons she couldn't begin to understand, although she suspected it would have a hysterical quality to it if it came out, when clarity suddenly came to her.

She was *here*.

She'd got the job.

Everything was in place to allow her to do what she'd spent the last three years dreaming of doing. The last thing she wanted was to blow the opportunity by not performing as required and getting sacked before she'd properly started.

Whatever strange reactions Andreas provoked inside her, she had to ignore them and do her job.

He'd made his requirements crystal clear. She was to be good humoured and cater to all his whims. Well, she would do just that. She would do everything he required of her *and* she would make darned sure to keep a smile on her face while she did it. She would inveigle her way into his confidence and uncover the secrets Andreas Samaras kept hidden from the world.

And then she would expose them.

And then, finally, she would find some peace of mind. Violet would have been avenged and both the men who'd destroyed her life would, in a much different way, be destroyed too.

With that happy thought in her head, she hurried to join him.

Breakfast had been laid out on the sunny veranda, an array of breads, pastries, fruits, condiments and yogurt.

'I take my coffee black without sugar,' Andreas said as he took his seat.

He'd introduced Carrie to his staff but had kept it quick. He'd taken Enrique and Sheryl into his confidence and they'd been outraged to discover an investigative journalist was trying to infiltrate his life. They were honest, upstanding people who he knew would struggle to hide their true feelings towards her for any length of time.

He liked to think he was an honest man too, but dealing with the shysters and scumbags that littered the financial world he inhabited like the dregs of a pot of coffee had taught him how to play the game that the people he employed on this island could never understand.

Carrie, still standing, poured his coffee for him. She even poured it with a smile.

'I will have honeydew melon and yogurt,' he told her.

She took a bowl and, with another smile, spooned chunks of melon into it. 'Tell me when to stop.'

Her disposition since he'd startled her on the balcony had changed considerably, and very much for the better. He would bet her new, cheerful disposition was external only.

He waited until the bowl was full before raising a hand. He noticed her own hand was incredibly slim, the nails long and nicely shaped. If Carrie were to look at the hands of any of his domestic staff she would see none of them had nails as well maintained as hers. She would see her nails were a dead giveaway that her life had not been spent undertaking domestic work.

'Four spoonfuls of yogurt,' he commanded amiably.

Again, she obeyed. 'Can I get you anything else to go with it?'

Tempted though he was to ask her to spoon it into his mouth, just to see if the smile fixed on her face cracked, he resisted. 'That will do for the moment. I will let you know when I want anything else.'

She nodded and folded her hands together over her belly.

Andreas put a spoonful into his mouth and took the opportunity to cast his eyes over her again in an appreciative open manner he would never dream of doing with an ordinary employee.

She was a little smaller than the average woman, the modest dress she'd selected showcasing the lithe legs of a model and breasts he would never have guessed could be so full on so slight a person. The morning sunlight beamed on her face highlighting the soft dewiness of her skin, reflecting off her complexion in glimmering waves.

Carrie didn't need make-up. She was stunning exactly as she was..

It was fortuitous that she wasn't a proper employee of his, he thought, as a thick heaviness pooled in his loins. Boss-employee relationships were disasters waiting to happen and he steered well clear of them, just as he avoided anything that could harm his business and personal reputation. In today's climate, where sexual harassment charges were a mere compliment about a pretty outfit away, he was too conscious of his position and power to risk his reputation.

Carrie would be a challenge to his self-imposed ideals. If he had to work with her in a close environment for real he knew he would find it a challenge to keep their relationship on a professional footing, a notion he found faintly disturbing.

Here and under these unique circumstances, his personal ethics could be safely pushed aside. She wasn't his employee. She was a snake. A beautiful, beguiling, incredibly sexy snake who wanted to destroy him.

'Are you not going to sit down?' he asked once he'd swallowed his mouthful.

Her hazel eyes flickered, her brow furrowed slightly, but the smile stayed in place.

'Are you not intending to eat?'

Now the furrow in her brow deepened.

'I dislike eating alone, *matia mou*. While we're here it is my wish that you dine with me, so, please, sit. Pour yourself a drink and eat something.'

As she complied with his request, he couldn't resist adding, 'Also, if you dine with me, it makes it easier for you to wait on me.'

'Whatever makes your life easier,' she said demurely and with only a hint of teeth being ground together. 'I am here to serve you.'

'That you are,' he agreed. 'And you look beautiful doing it. Are you happy with the clothes selected for you?'

Her spoon, which had been adding a little yogurt into the bowl she'd taken for herself, hovered in her hand. 'Yes. Thank you. Although... I thought I would be given more... practical clothing.'

Poor Carrie. How disconcerting it must have been for her to open her wardrobe and find there was no uniform to hide behind, no means to slip unobtrusively into the shadows of his life.

'Practical clothing has no place in such a beautiful setting.'

'Well, it's very generous of you. I'm amazed you were able to get it all here before we arrived,' she said lightly.

'It's a bespoke Internet service my niece uses. She holidayed here during her Christmas break but flew over on a commercial flight and lost her luggage. Twelve hours later she had a whole new designer wardrobe delivered.' He gave a rueful laugh. 'I did wonder if Natalia lost her suitcase deliberately just so I could buy her new clothing.'

Carrie's face pinched in on itself as he spoke his niece's name but only briefly. If he hadn't been watching her so closely he would have missed it.

It was good to know she was squirming inside.

'Anyway, with all this talk of clothes, I should tell you that you will need to change after we've eaten,' he said.

'Why?'

'The current on my beach is too strong to swim in at this time of year but there's a cove on Tortue Island that's perfect. We will take my boat out there and swim and get to know each other better. Doesn't that sound good?'

Her throat moved before she nodded and smiled. 'I can't think of anything I'd like more.'

CHAPTER FOUR

IF THE WIND CHANGED, Carrie was quite sure her face would freeze with this pathetic smile stuck on it for ever. Her cheeks ached with the effort of it and all she wanted was for the slave-driving Greek egomaniac to let her go to bed and get away from him for some respite.

She'd thought the day before had been long… It had *nothing* on the day she'd just endured, which, despite being late evening, showed no sign of ending soon.

Tortue Island had been the tiny green island paradise she'd spotted from her balcony, a mere five-minute hop on Andreas's speedboat. He'd taken her to a secluded cove surrounded by enormous palm trees and drenched in sunlight. That was where paradise had ended.

Violet as a toddler had been easier to take care of than this overgrown infant. Practically the only thing she hadn't had to do for Andreas was towel him dry after his frequent swims. She'd kept him supplied with constant refreshments, opened his bottles of water, peeled his fruit, fanned him when he'd decided he was too hot, even read news articles off his tablet for him, which had been financial articles and as exciting to read as it was to watch paint dry.

And she'd had to do it all with a cheerful demeanour!

The only thing that had kept her cheerful was imagining his smug face when he discovered her true identity. He'd mentioned that they would be flying back to London before heading on to Frankfurt and she couldn't *wait* to get going. Both of those homes had proper offices set up for him to work from—he was so lazy she was surprised he bothered having offices outside his homes—and she just knew it wouldn't take her long to discover his illegal secrets.

She couldn't get over how spoilt and lazy he was. If someone had told her the rugged Andreas Samaras liked to have his grapes peeled for him as if he were a Roman emperor, she would never have believed it, and she had applied for a job with him with the lowest expectations of the man. It just didn't fit with what she thought she knew of him. But, no, he clearly adored being waited on, a wolfish smile near enough constantly playing on his lips.

Once he'd grown bored of Tortue Island, they'd returned to his peninsular where Carrie had waited on him some more while he'd sunbathed by his swimming pool.

She had never imagined a man like Andreas could do so much sunbathing!

Her duties at the pool had consisted mostly of sitting by his side with a handheld fan aimed at his face in between runs to his fully stocked poolside bar for ever more refreshments for him. Then it had been time to prepare his clothing for dinner and take a super-quick shower herself before they went to sit out on his veranda for their evening meal. Other than her shower, she hadn't had a minute to herself, had only been able to check for a phone signal as she'd chucked a clean dress on after her super-quick shower. No magical signal had been found; her text message still sat pending.

The meal cooked for them by Brendan had been possibly the best food she'd ever tasted, fat succulent tiger

prawn salad—Andreas had got her to shell his prawns
for him—followed by a creamy coconut curry, but she'd
been unable to appreciate it as Andreas had had her running back and forth to the kitchen like a yo-yo.

She hadn't done so much exercise in years.

'Caroline?'

She suddenly realised that while she'd been silently
fuming about his lazy, slave-driving ways, he'd been
speaking to her.

She fixed the wide smile back on her face.

*What do you want this time? Another bowl of water set
at the optimum temperature to dip your fingers into? Another napkin to dry them with or to wipe your mouth to go
with the five I've already had to get for you?*

'Sorry, I missed what you said.'

He drained his white wine and set the glass on the table.
'I'm ready to go in…'

About time.

'…so I need you to run me a bath and turn my bed
down.'

'Turn your bed down?' she answered blankly, not having the faintest idea what he was talking about.

His forehead creased and he tilted his head. 'You've
never turned a bed down before?'

Sensing danger, she hid her apprehension with a smile.
'It's not something that's been asked of me before. Maybe
I know it by another name?'

'I thought it was a universal term.' A suggestive gleam
sparkled in his eyes. 'It just means preparing my bed so
it's ready for me—turning the sheets over so I can slide
into them.'

'Oh, *that*,' she said with feigned brightness. Yes, this
was exactly the sort of thing this spoilt man would demand. She would bet that in colder climates he would de-

mand his domestic PA personally warm his bed for him. 'Of course. Yes. Anything else?'

'I'll let you know if anything comes to mind while you're running my bath.'

I just bet you will.

She got to her feet. 'I'll run it for you now. What temperature do you like it?' Scalding or ice-cold? she prevented herself from asking.

He waited a beat before answering, a smile tugging on his lips. 'Why don't you run it to the temperature *you* like?'

Andreas watched Carrie walk into the house to run him a bath with amusement fizzing in his veins.

He couldn't remember the last time he'd enjoyed himself as much as he had that day.

She waited on him as if she'd been born to serve his whims. Her determination to act the role he'd set for her and act it well had been exquisite to watch.

The little tells that had betrayed her real feelings had been equally exquisite. When this was all over he'd have to arrange for her to be given an acting award because he was quite certain he would never have seen those betraying signs if he hadn't been looking for them.

When this was all over...

That was a thought to knock the smile from his face.

He would have to put Carrie out of her misery sooner rather than later, however enjoyable it was to play the role of spoilt playboy, a role that, despite his riches, he'd never had the time or inclination to play before. With Carrie being the one to act the role of slave, the spoilt playboy role had been one to relish. What a shame he would have to put a stop to it so soon.

Debbie had messaged him earlier with news that made it clear he needed to return to London and start on damage limitation. Whatever Carrie's reasons for being here, she'd prodded a hornets' nest.

He poured himself another glass of wine. Other than shave, it was the first thing he'd done for himself all day. He took a sip, leaned back and closed his eyes.

His graduation from university had coincided with his parents' world falling apart. Since then, his life had been one long conveyor belt of obligations. Family, work, responsibility, with Andreas the one holding everyone and everything together. Then, as he'd seen light at the end of the long dark tunnel, his sister and brother-in-law had died and he'd suddenly found himself guardian to his teenage niece. Natalia had been raised in London and was already a weekly boarder at her school in the English capital when her parents died. Andreas hadn't wanted to uproot her life any further so had uprooted himself instead, moving his life and business from Manhattan to London. Natalia had become his priority.

He had never begrudged anything he'd done for his family. It was what families did—they loved and took care of each other. But it was only when Natalia had left for university and he'd felt the burden of responsibility lifting from his shoulders that he'd realised what a weight it had been on him. That weight had been there most of his adult life.

Now Natalia was approaching the end of her first year at university, that flicker of light beckoning his freedom he'd seen before her parents had died was flickering again, brighter than it ever had before. Technically Natalia was now an adult. She still needed him but not in the way she had before. Nowadays she only needed his money and his London home to 'crash' in, as she put it, when she went out partying with friends in the city. She was young, working hard and enjoying her life, exactly as she should be.

He'd promised himself that once she'd completed her first year he would start living his life for himself. He no longer had to worry about being a good influence or role model. He could enjoy the wealth he had created and experience what life had to offer but which responsibility had denied him for so long.

He never wanted to have any form of responsibility in his personal life ever again.

His business, though, was a different matter entirely and it was this he vowed to protect from Carrie Rivers's poisonous pen.

He drank some more of his wine and reflected that it was fortuitous that Carrie had set her sights on him when he had the freedom to do whatever was needed to stop her. Whisking her to the Seychelles would have been unthinkable a year ago when he'd still planned every minute of his life around Natalia's schedule.

Setting his empty glass on the table, he got to his feet, rolled his neck and stretched.

He would hit Carrie with the truth in the morning. Until then, he intended to extract his last few hours of fun from her.

Carrie marched into Andreas's bathroom, switched the light on and stopped short.

Soft lighting revealed a space that wasn't a bathroom but a marble palace. The walk-in shower alone was bigger than her bathroom.

But it was the deep, sunken bath she approached, as opulent as anything Roman emperors had bathed in. Half a dozen people could fit in it with room to spare.

It took her a few moments to work out where the plug was. Then she turned the taps on. A surge of water gushed out, not just from the taps but from tiny round holes the entire circumference, all pouring quicker than she had ever known water to pour before.

She found bath foam in a cabinet and added a liberal dollop, which immediately filled the room with a delicious warm spicy scent, then adjusted the water temperature some more, resisting the urge to set it on cold. When the bath was run and filled with thick foam, she dried her hands and went back into his bedroom.

Her bravado almost deserted her as she approached his bed.

She'd been in his room a number of times that day but this was the first time she'd had to go near his bed.

She took a deep breath before carefully untucking the sheet. She pulled it back to form a triangle, then smoothed it, trying not to think that only the night before these sheets had covered his naked body.

Because he did sleep naked. She knew that on an instinctive level she couldn't begin to understand and the mere thought made her lower abdomen clench tightly.

You've had too much sun, she told herself grimly, lifting his pillow to plump and immediately releasing Andreas's scent trapped in the Egyptian cotton. She hurriedly put the pillow back down as the scent entered her bloodstream and, for a moment, her pulses soared with such strength she felt dizzy.

She blinked hard to regain her focus and stared at the pillow as if it could bite her.

'Is my bath ready?'

She jumped.

Andreas stood at the threshold of his bedroom, a wry smile playing on his lips.

How long had he been there, watching her...?

'Yes. There's fresh towels on the rail. Everything's ready for you.' How she managed to get the words out with her heart thrashing so wildly and leaping in her throat she didn't know.

'Good.' He stepped into the room, eyes on her as he removed a cufflink from the sleeve of his shirt.

Suddenly terrified that he was going to strip in front of her, she forced her legs to move towards the door to her own room, sidestepping around his huge figure, which somehow seemed even taller and broader than it did in daylight hours.

'I could do with some water,' he said as her hand touched the door handle. 'Can you bring a glass up for me please?'

A please? That was a first.

Carrie nodded tightly and hurried out of his room, down the stairs and to the kitchen, resolutely telling herself over and over that she'd had far too much sun that day and that was why her veins were fizzing so. The young kitchen assistant was just finishing for the night, a reminder that very soon the house would be empty of everyone but her and Andreas...

All she could hope was that this was her last duty of the evening.

Her heart still hammered frantically as she walked back up the stairs with his glass of water.

His bedroom door was ajar. She knocked lightly on it. When there was no response she stepped tentatively inside. His room was empty, the bathroom door wide open.

'I have your water,' she called. 'Shall I leave it on the table for you?'

His reply was muffled by the thick walls. 'I'll have it in here.'

Hoping she'd misheard him, she confirmed, 'What, in the bathroom?'

'Seeing as that's where I am, yes.'

Taking a deep, fortifying breath, Carrie trod slowly to the open door, praying he hadn't removed all his clothes yet.

It was a futile hope.

Andreas was in the huge bath, leaning back, the top of his chest right in her eyeline, facing the door. Facing her.

Knowing her face had gone the colour of sun-ripened tomatoes, she looked everywhere but him, searching for a decent spot to put the glass on.

'Bring it to me,' he commanded casually.

She couldn't get her feet to work.

Water sloshed as he sat up and extended an arm. 'Don't be shy, *matia mou*. I only bite if invited to.'

Flames engulfing her, resisting the urge to throw the water right in his face, she finally put one foot in front of the other, her eyes darting everywhere but at him.

She *couldn't* look at him, not directly. As long as she looked at the beautiful cream tiling around his head she would be fine.

When she reached his side she extended her own arm to put the glass in his waiting hand, careful not to allow their fingers to brush, then quickly stepped back.

'I'll leave you to enjoy your bath,' she said.

'You're not going to stay and keep me company?'

Without her meaning them to, her eyes found his and her heart leapt then twisted.

A breathless, suspended moment passed between them, the only movement the growing ache in her most feminine place and the colour she could feel creeping up her neck.

And no wonder she couldn't breathe. The look in his eyes… The gleam…

This beautiful, ruggedly handsome man was staring at her as if she were a delicacy he wanted to feast on.

Heat rose in her that she was quite sure had nothing to do with the steamy vapours coming from the bath.

Suddenly her imagination ran riot, a feast of its own, racing into places she had never been before of naked limbs and soft sighs…

She'd spent the whole day with this man's semi-naked body within touching distance and had successfully kept him fully clothed in her mind, just as if she'd been a subject in *The Emperor's New Clothes*. Blocking out his near-nakedness had been as hard as keeping that stupid smile on her face but she had done it. Now the veil she'd put over her eyes had been ripped away and she saw *him*, darkly tanned, a homage to rugged masculinity, and the base feminine part of herself responded to it.

And then she saw something else in his eyes, something darker even than the desire that swirled and pulsed, and it was this something, this dark danger, that pulled her out of the hypnotic spell he'd cast over her and snapped her back to herself.

She forced herself to breathe and dragged her lips into a smile.

'You're a big boy,' she said in as light a tone as she could muster. 'I'm sure you can cope with your own company for a while.'

There was a moment of utter stillness before his firm lips curved into an all too knowing smile. 'I didn't think you'd looked.'

Looked…?

Suddenly his meaning became clear and her eyes, with a will of their own, gazed down at the water, at the long, muscular legs laid out, covered in foam but not covered enough that she couldn't see the dark hair between his thighs or his…

Shocked rigid, she quickly blinked and turned away.

But she couldn't blink enough to rid herself of what she'd seen.

She'd never seen a fully naked man before, not in the flesh, and, even with the bath water and foam distorting the image, she didn't need to be experienced in matters of the flesh to know that he was in proportion *everywhere*.

'I'll be in my room if you need me,' she mumbled, hurrying to escape from this seductive atmosphere and all the danger lacing it.

She closed the bathroom door with the sound of his low laughter ringing in her ears.

Alone in her bedroom she sat on her bed and clutched her still-flaming cheeks, breathing heavily.

She despised Andreas, had hated him from that moment outside the headmistress's office when he had stared at her as if she were something dirty he had trodden in.

He had destroyed her sister! How could she feel such attraction to him? How was it possible that her first real flush of desire should be for her enemy?

And how was it possible that he could be so aware of it? She'd seen it in those seductive eyes...

She flopped onto her pillow face-first and gave a muffled scream.

How could she be thinking these thoughts?

Too much sun.

Of *course*. That was the answer.

She'd had more sun in one day than she'd had for at least three years. It had addled her brain in much the same way sleep deprivation had addled it yesterday.

Feeling calmer, she stretched herself out on the narrow bed, closed her eyes and concentrated on inhaling and exhaling in long, regular breaths, the way she had long ago trained herself to fall asleep when her terrified fears for her sister had threatened to stop her ever falling into oblivion.

* * *

A loud rapping woke Carrie from the light slumber she had fallen into.

The digital bedside clock showed it had just turned midnight. She'd been in her room for less than an hour.

The rapping vibrated through the door again. 'Caroline?'

'I'm awake.' She staggered off the bed and took the one step needed to reach the door, straightening her dress, which she'd fallen asleep in.

She braced herself before opening the door only to find her senses hit immediately with the tangy scent of Andreas's cologne and the faint spice of his bath foam.

He was standing in a pair of faded jeans, his torso bare, a smile playing on his lips.

'Were you sleeping?' he asked with one eyebrow raised.

'Dozing.' *I forgot that working for you meant only sleeping when you gave the order.*

'Good. I'm in the mood for a nightcap.'

Of course you are.

'You want me to get it for you?'

He pulled a face that said very clearly that that was what he employed her for.

'Give me a second to put something on my feet,' she added hastily.

'Bring me a tumbler of Scotch—any single malt will do—three fingers, two cubes of ice, and one for yourself. I'll be on the veranda.' Then he winked, turned and headed off.

Taking a deep breath while internally cursing him to the heavens, Carrie slipped her toes into the gold designer flip-flops she'd been given and trudged down the stairs to his den, where he kept his indoor bar.

How could any normal self-respecting employee put up

with this? she wondered. No salary, however large, could compensate for being at Andreas's permanent beck and call.

She fixed his Scotch exactly as demanded and poured herself some lemonade. As tempting as the vast array of liquors and spirits was, she didn't want any alcohol in her bloodstream when dealing with this tricky man. She'd refused wine with her dinner for the same reason.

She carried the glasses outside, where a fresh breeze whispered over her skin, and found him back at the outside table reading something on his phone.

She still didn't have a signal.

His teeth glimmered white in the moonlight as she put the drinks on the table. 'Before you sit down, go to my dressing room and get me a pair of swim-shorts. I might want a swim later.'

Later? It was already the middle of the night. Did the man not plan on getting *any* sleep?

Was *she* not allowed to get any sleep?

Then she caught something in his eyes, an amusement that immediately aroused her suspicions…

Was he…?

Could he be…?

Was Andreas playing a *game*?

He stared right back at her, the amusement no longer just in his eyes but quirking on his lips, as if he were biting back laughter. But something darker lurked in those light brown eyes too, something that sent fresh alarm bells ringing inside her.

She backed away slowly, suddenly wary of taking her eyes off him.

Her job had taught her the importance of listening to her instincts and her instincts were telling her loud and clear that something was off and that some unseen danger awaited her.

Climbing back up the stairs, she realised that she'd had this instinctual feeling of something being amiss since her interview with him but Andreas had kept her so busy running around after him that she'd had no time to listen.

She paused at the threshold of his bedroom and gazed around with narrowed eyes. She'd resisted looking too deeply before as there had always been someone around and she hadn't wanted to seem as if she were doing anything other than what Andreas was supposedly paying her for. The newest members of staff in any organisation always attracted curious glances, whether the work was in a business or domestic environment. It was human nature to watch strangers more closely than people you were familiar with. She'd thought it wise to hold off before she started any snooping.

Slowly she took all the expensive furnishings in, unsure what, if anything, she was looking for.

It was just a bedroom. A masculine, richly opulent bedroom for sure, but still, just a bedroom…

What the heck was *that*?

Right at the end of the curtain pole that covered his French doors, a tiny round object winked at her.

Carrie had been an undercover journalist long enough to know exactly what she was looking at but it still took a few moments before it really sank in.

The tiny round object was a camera. And it was filming her.

CHAPTER FIVE

ANDREAS SIPPED HIS Scotch as he watched Carrie on his phone.

He'd seen the suspicion in her eyes in the moments before she'd gone back inside to cater to his latest whim. Instinct had made him switch his phone over to the live feed coming from his bedroom.

Judging by the stillness in her frame as she stared around his bedroom, he suspected her own instincts had kicked in too.

After a couple of minutes of nothing, her expression suddenly changed, sharpening, her head tilting, brow furrowing as she walked trance-like towards the French door.

And then she was looking right at him...

Her pretty lips formed a perfect O as he watched realisation hit her.

Suddenly she was on the move, her face set, lips now pressed tightly together. She dragged a chair to the curtains and climbed onto it and yanked the camera out. The picture disappeared and he had to wait a few seconds for one of the others to kick in in its place. By then she'd found another, hidden in plain sight on the television. Her face now twisted with rage, she mouthed a curse at him before yanking that one out too.

She made her way systematically around the room until

she'd removed all four hidden cameras and there were no more feeds left.

Andreas sipped more Scotch and prepared himself for the storm that was surely going to follow, breathing deeply to abate the weighty beats of his heart.

This was it, a few hours sooner than anticipated. Time for the truth to be revealed.

He didn't have to wait long.

The patio doors slammed open and Carrie appeared, marching straight towards him. When she reached the table, she snatched the glass from his hands and dropped the four tiny cameras into the Scotch.

He looked her up and down as she faced him, hands clenched in fists at her sides, chest heaving, her furious face pinched, looking ready to punch his lights out.

'Why don't you sit down?' he suggested coolly.

In many respects, it was better for the truth to come out now, when it was just the two of them and no witnesses.

Her lips parted and her jaw moved, clearly struggling to get any words out. When they finally came they were barely audible. 'You know, don't you?'

'That you're the undercover journalist Carrie Rivers?' He hooked an ankle on his thigh. 'Yes, *matia mou*, I know exactly who you are. I've always known.'

'So…this has all been a game?'

He allowed himself a smile. 'And what a game it has been. You have played it exquisitely. You make an excellent skivvy.'

She moved so quickly she was a blur, grabbing her glass and throwing the lemonade in his face.

Carrie, her heart a heavy burr, her stomach a mass of knots, fought for breath, feeling not the slightest bit of satisfaction to see the cold liquid soaking his face and hair.

He hadn't even flinched.

Of all the things she hated about him, at that moment the greatest thing to loathe was that he was sitting there, as cool as a cucumber with lemonade dripping off him while she couldn't even control her own breathing.

But then his eyes clashed with hers and she realised he wasn't as cool as he appeared. His jaw was taut and his eyes as dark as she'd ever seen them, filled to the brim with the danger she had always sensed but had stupidly chosen to ignore.

He'd known who she was all along. Right from the beginning.

Her brain burned just to recall it all. She'd *known* there was something wrong with the way he'd got her waiting on him hand and foot, had been too focussed on the prize at the end to allow herself to think about it. She'd also, she had to admit with painful humiliation, been too busy fighting her reactions to him to pay attention to all the dangers and warnings.

She'd ignored everything her instincts had been telling her.

It had all been a game and she had fallen for it.

She had infiltrated his life to bring him down but he had turned the tables on her and played her like a toy.

Slowly and deliberately, he wiped his sodden face with his hands and shook the liquid away, his piercing eyes never leaving her face.

'I believe it is time for you to tell me why you are really here, *Carrie Rivers*.'

His tone cut through her along with the words he used.

'But before you start, tell me your real name. Are you Carrie or Caroline? Or would you prefer I address you as Lying Snake?'

'I'm not the snake here.' Why did her voice have to

tremble so much? 'How many cameras have you had spying on me?'

'Enough to have monitored your every move if the need had arisen.'

'You spied on me while I slept? While I...?' She shuddered, unable to voice her thoughts.

He must have read them though for he frowned. 'There were no cameras in your bedroom or any of the bathrooms. Unlike you, I have boundaries.'

'Boundaries?' she shouted. 'You had me bring you a drink while you were in the bath!'

'And didn't you enjoy looking at me?' he mocked. 'Now answer my question. Your real name.'

Cheeks burning, she glared at him, willing him to feel the hate vibrating out of her and to be scorched by it. Then she straightened her spine and spoke steadily. 'My legal name is Caroline Fiona Dunwoody, exactly as it says on my passport. I have been known as Caroline Rivers since my mother remarried when I was four but my name was never legally changed. I have always been called Carrie.'

'So, Caroline Dunwoody Rivers, why are you investigating me?'

She put her hands on her hips and glared at him. 'I'm not answering that.'

'You are,' he contradicted amiably. 'I promise that by the time the sun comes up you will have told me everything I wish to know.' He leaned forward. 'You are an award-winning journalist. You specialise in exposing the illegal practices of rich businessmen. You went to a lot of effort to infiltrate my life. You supplied false references. Debbie spoke to the people you stated were your referees. I assume these were your colleagues and that this sting has been carefully orchestrated by you and your newspaper. Investigations are not started on a whim. I want to know what started this whole ball rolling. I want to know *everything*.'

She listened to his words, delivered in such a reasonable tone but with steel lacing the staccato, with mounting fury at herself.

Why had she not listened to her instincts when she'd walked into his office and every nerve in her body had told her to turn on her heels and run?

And how was she supposed to answer any of his questions without dragging herself deeper into the hole she'd stupidly and unwittingly allowed herself to fall into?

When she remained tight-lipped, he sighed. 'Caroline...'

'Carrie.'

His broad shoulders raised nonchalantly. 'I don't care. What I *do* care about is the truth and we're not going anywhere until you give me answers. You've lied and lied and now you owe me the truth.'

She put her hands on the table and glared at him. 'I don't owe you a damned thing and you lied too. You didn't have to go along with the pretence. You could have confronted me in the interview.'

'And have you run straight back to your newsroom and out of my reach?'

'But why have me skivvy after you? What was the point in that?'

'You really need to ask?' Amusement flared in the darkness of his eyes. 'You wanted to destroy me. The least I could do was let you suffer a little humiliation in return. I haven't enjoyed myself so much in years.' The amusement dropped. 'Someone is out to destroy me. It is either a business rival or a disgruntled ex-employee, or you are on a personal vendetta...because you and I have history, don't we, Carrie Rivers, sister of Violet?'

It was the way Carrie's face contorted at the mention of her sister's name that was the clincher for Andreas.

His intuition had been right all along. For Carrie, this was personal.

He got to his feet. 'Stay here. I'm going to get us a drink.'

'I don't want anything.'

'*I* do. And when I get back you will sit down and you will tell me everything because I promise you this—you won't be leaving the Seychelles until you do.'

He left her standing there, white-faced in her fury, and strode inside to his bar. He looked through the rows of bottles and plumped for a bottle of whisky, a brand with the spicy bite he needed right then.

Grabbing two crystal tumblers, he headed back to the veranda, part of him expecting Carrie to still be stubbornly standing where he'd left her but she'd sat down, legs crossed and arms folded across her chest, giving him what he could only describe as a death stare.

He took his seat opposite her, unscrewed the lid and poured them both a hefty measure. He pushed one of the tumblers to her. 'You're welcome to throw this in my face or smash the glass but it won't change anything.'

She picked it up with a scowl and sniffed it. 'It smells disgusting.'

'Don't drink it, then.'

She took a sip and pulled a face. 'It tastes worse than it smells.' That didn't stop her taking another sip.

He settled back and stared at her. She met his gaze, the hazel of her eyes reflecting fire at him. The effect gave her beauty a majesty.

Whatever had motivated Carrie to set out to destroy him, she thought she had right on her side. She was set for a humiliating disappointment.

'Okay, let us establish some facts to begin with. The paper you work for has a reputation for excellent journalism and I include you in that. When it splashes on a big story the rest of the media follows. It is rarely sued for libel and when it is it rarely loses—namely, it backs up its stories. It is a serious, weighty newspaper. It doesn't print spurious gossip. It stands to reason that there was evidence for your editor or whoever is in charge of signing investigations off to think it worth their time and expense sending you to investigate me. What was that evidence?'

She dropped her gaze from his and took another sip of the whisky she professed to hate.

'The evidence?' he repeated, his patience waning.

'There were rumours.'

He drummed his fingers on the table. 'Rumours? About what?'

Her chin lifted. 'That you were embezzling your clients' funds.'

'What a pile of rubbish. Where did these rumours come from? Because I can assure you they are lies. Markets go up and down but I invest my clients' money with the same care I would if it were my own. I defy you to find a single investor who would say otherwise.'

Something flickered on her face, a shamed, guilty expression she tried to cover by taking a bigger sip of her whisky.

But it was too late. He'd seen it. Seen her guilt.

'The rumours came from you, didn't they? What did you do? Go to your editor and say you had a credible tip-off about me that was worth investigating?'

She lifted her head to look at him, her lips drawn tightly together. The truth was right there in her eyes.

He breathed deeply, trying to contain the anger swirling like a maelstrom in him. 'Come on, Carrie. It is just you and me. There is no one to hear what we say. We have both been playing games and now it is time for them to stop. Be honest and admit the truth. You went to your editor with a pack of lies about me, didn't you?'

Carrie's chest had compacted so tightly that she couldn't draw breath.

They'd both been playing games?

This had *never* been a game for her. This had been her sister's life, which Andreas had destroyed.

Everything she had done, the risks she had taken, the lies she had told, had all been for Violet and now she had to face that it had all been for nothing.

He'd rumbled her before she'd even set foot in his office and any secrets he had would remain secret.

She would never be able to expose him. Violet would never see justice.

Pulling air into her cramped lungs, she looked him square in the eyes. 'Yes.'

'Yes?'

'Yes. It was a pack of lies. I told my editor that I'd had a tip-off from a credible source that you were embezzling funds and, yes, he believed me.'

'He authorised your investigation into me on nothing more than your word?'

She leaned forward, willing him to feel every atom of her hate for him. 'I have spent three years dreaming about bringing you down and when the time came, there was no way I was going to let it slip through my fingers. Believe me, I was *very* convincing.'

'You have been plotting this for three years?' He shook his head slowly. 'I assume this has something to do with your screwed-up sister?'

His words cut through her like an arsenic-laced blade. 'Do not speak of Violet like that.'

Now he was the one to lean forward, close enough for her to see the stubble breaking out on his jaw. 'I have no idea what kind of a woman she's grown into but do not delude yourself as to what she was like three years ago. She was a mess.'

Carrie's rage consumed her so totally that it took what felt an age before she could speak. When she finally managed to get the words out, they tumbled from her, three years of pent-up heartbreak and anger spilling out in a torrent.

'Yes, Violet was a screwed-up mess. And do you know why? It was because *you* let your drug-peddling friend seduce her under your own roof. Between you and your bastard friend, you ruined her life, so yes, the reason I'm here *is* for Violet. I knew all I had to do was find a way into your life and I would find the evidence I needed to expose you as the monster you are and kill the squeaky-clean image you've fooled the world into believing.'

'What the *hell* are you talking about?'

Andreas had listened to the venom pouring from Carrie's tongue with growing incredulity and outrage. He'd suspected her motives were personal, that she had a grudge linked back to her sister's expulsion, but had assumed she had seized the opportunity to investigate and potentially expose him when the opportunity had come.

While he could take some relief that there was no business rival trying to blacken his name or anything nefarious going on within his company he was unaware of, it felt like ice in his veins to know he'd spent the past three years unaware he had such a dangerous enemy patiently biding her time and working against him.

'As if you don't know!' Putting her hands on the table, she rose to her feet like a phoenix emerging from the ashes, her face more animated and alive with colour than he could have believed. 'James Thomas. Violet met him when she was staying in your home, under your care. He groomed her—what teenager wouldn't be thrilled to have a rich, handsome man showering her with expensive gifts and attention? He bedded her for the first time on her sixteenth birthday, the clever, underhand bastard. He was *thirty-six*! They had a six-month affair and in that time he introduced her to drugs and all manner of perversions, and then he dumped her.

'When she refused to go quietly, he threatened to destroy her—five days later and drugs were found in her school bedside table and she was expelled, her life destroyed exactly as he'd promised. *You* instigated the search of her bedroom, *you*, his friend, and don't you dare deny it—the headmistress told me that you had informed her Violet and Natalia had been taking drugs and urged her to search their room. What an amazing coincidence that drugs were only found in Violet's possessions and only Violet was expelled. Your niece got off scot-free.'

Andreas took a deep breath, veering from rage to horror and back again, furious at the accusations being levelled at him but also revolted that Carrie—that anyone—could think him capable of covering up such depravity.

'Let me make one thing very clear,' he said levelly. 'James Thomas is no friend of mine and never has been. I knew nothing of this.'

'You would say that,' she scorned.

He downed his whisky before looking her in the eye. 'Be very careful, *matia mou*. I can see you are emotional right now but you have made many slanderous accusations against me and I *will* defend myself. James Thomas came to my home once, years ago, with a number of other potential investors for a business dinner. That is the only time I met him because I disliked him on sight and refused to take his business. I don't remember Violet being there that weekend but accept she could have been. I knew nothing of any affair between them.'

'If you weren't in cahoots with him—and I congratulate you on keeping your association with him out of the public eye—then why did you get Violet expelled?'

'Because I came home early from an evening out and discovered Violet and Natalia off their heads on drugs and alcohol. It was the weekend before her expulsion. Do you remember? Because I sure as hell do. That is a weekend I will never forget.'

The rage had turned to bewilderment. 'You caught them taking drugs?'

'Yes.'

'And you didn't think to tell me?'

'I would have called you in the morning but events took a turn that changed everything. After letting them know how disgusted I was with their behaviour, I sent them to bed to sleep it off and sober up. An hour later Violet came into my bedroom naked.'

'Liar.'

'I do not lie. In her intoxicated state she thought I was going to call the headmistress to warn her of what I had found. She thought seducing me would soften my anger and stop me reporting them. Violet had left cannabis and cocaine in her bedside table at school and knew it would be found if their room was searched and that she would be expelled. She was already on a final warning for disruptive behaviour as you know perfectly well.'

Carrie looked as if she were going to be sick.

She would look worse if he relayed how Violet had tried to climb into his bed and the filthy language she had used. He dreaded to think what kind of films she'd watched to imagine he would find such language a turn-on.

'I will spare you the details but Violet became hysterical when I rejected her. The noise woke Natalia. She tried to calm her and got a smack in the face from Violet for her trouble. If Violet hadn't been only sixteen I would have kicked her out onto the street. As it was, I waited until morning and sent her home in a cab.

'You are correct that I influenced Violet's expulsion. I make no apologies for it. Natalia confessed in the morning that Violet had been running wild and using drugs for months. Natalia was being drawn into a world she didn't know how to escape. That is what prompted me to call the school—I was protecting my niece. I am not in cahoots with James Thomas. I despise the man.'

As he'd been relating the sordid details, Carrie's face had turned ashen. She paced a few steps then spun around. 'Why didn't you tell me? If Violet tried to seduce you... If *any* of this is true...' Her eyes found his, censure merging with the bewilderment.

'I left it to the school to fill you in on what your sister had been up to.'

'The school...?' Fresh fury wiped the ashen complexion from her face. 'The headmistress didn't give us even two minutes of her time. All she told us was that drugs had been found in Violet's personal effects and that she was expelled. She kicked her out just like that.' She snapped her fingers for emphasis. 'You should have called me as soon as you found them. I was her guardian. I should have been told.'

Andreas hardened himself to the guilty feeling pooling in his stomach and rose to his feet, walking over to look her in the eye. 'After the stunt Violet pulled I wanted nothing more to do with either of you. If I am being honest I assumed she had learned her tricks from you...'

Almost too late he saw the hand come flying towards him and only just managed to snatch hold of the wrist before the fingers connected with his face.

CHAPTER SIX

HOLDING HER STRUGGLING wrist up in the air, Andreas stared into the furious hazel eyes. 'Let me finish. At the time I made the assumption she had learned to seduce a man through watching you, her older sister. That was my mistake and I apologise for it—I was angrier than I have ever been and incredibly worried for my niece, who told me the next morning that Violet had been in and out of different boys' beds for months. What would you have done in my position? What would you have done if it had been Natalia running wild and dragging Violet down with her?'

She'd stopped her struggle against his hold. For a moment the anger disappeared to be replaced with sadness. 'If it had been the other way round I would have told you. Violet needed help not condemnation. If I had been told then…' She sighed, seeming to deflate with the motion. 'It probably wouldn't have made any difference. The damage had already been done. Violet *had* been sleeping around— the naïve fool thought it would make James jealous. She was desperate for him to take her back, totally unable to accept they were over, and she had no one to talk to about it. He'd made her keep it a secret and I think that screwed with her head as much as anything but she'd been completely under his spell. I only discovered the truth after the expulsion.'

And now, as she recalled the horror and despair she'd felt when Violet had made her confession, she felt the same guilt that she'd been so unaware that her darling baby sister had had an affair with a rich man old enough to be her father and who had fed her all the drugs she could consume.

Slowly it penetrated that Andreas's hold on her wrist had loosened and slid down to cover her hand. She shook it off and stepped back. She didn't want his sympathy.

Even with all the anger and hate that had flown between them there had still lived in Carrie a basic toxic awareness of him that her brain had no control over. Her hand zinged from his hold, causing a thrashing in her chest that echoed loudly in her ears.

She forced out a long breath and fought to think clearly.

She mustn't let his touch affect her thoughts.

But he didn't even need to touch her to make her react.

Moments ago she'd been inches from hitting him. She'd never hit anyone before, never even come close, and the violence she felt towards him terrified her as much as anything else.

When she next spoke, she did everything she could to keep her tone more moderate. 'Why did Violet say you set her up if it wasn't true? She was adamant about it. I took her home after that awful meeting with that condescending witch of a headmistress and she swore you had planted the drugs. That's when it all came out about James.'

'Revenge?' he suggested with a deep sigh. 'For rejecting her? For informing the school? For telling her she wasn't welcome in my home any more? For telling her to keep away from Natalia?'

'I suppose that makes sense,' she admitted heavily. 'She hates you as much as she hates him.'

Andreas inhaled. As much as he felt for the screwed-up Violet and the atrocious, immoral way she had been used by that monster, he couldn't rid himself of the anger that Carrie had thought of him in the same light, had been willing to think him corrupt and immoral too, had used her position as a journalist to get vengeance for something in which he was innocent.

'You know, it would have saved a lot of grief if you had confronted me with Violet's allegations when she made them.'

'Truth or lie, you would have denied it,' she answered flatly. 'I wouldn't have trusted your answer.'

'Natalia would have confirmed it if you had asked.'

'Natalia hero-worshipped you. She would have said anything you told her to.'

'Are you saying you still don't believe me?' he asked with incredulity.

'I don't know what I believe.' Suddenly, she laughed, the sound startling, cutting through the heavy sadness that had brewed between them. But it contained no humour. 'You've led me on an un-merry dance for two days. I would have to be mad to trust you, of all people, and quite frankly I don't trust anyone, especially not rich, powerful men who are used to bending people to their will and stamping on anyone who gets in their way and think the laws of the land are for lesser mortals to obey. And you're one of the richest and most powerful of the lot.'

She turned her back on him and stepped over to the lawn, walking to the stone wall that separated his immaculate garden from the rocks and sand that led to his beach, and put her hands on it, tilting her face to look up at the stars. The moonlight cast her silhouette in an ethereal glow. Seeing her like that sent a strange ache through him.

He wanted to touch that effervescent skin. He wanted to grab those shoulders and shake the truth into her.

Her reached her in four long strides.

'You know damn well I speak the truth,' he said, standing behind her and placing a hand on her shoulder. 'I saw it in your eyes. Your sister lied to you about me. You know it and I know it.'

She went rigid under his touch. When she spoke, there was a breathless quality to her words. 'I'm a journalist. I deal with proof.'

'You lied to infiltrate my life,' he reminded her. 'Where was your proof then?'

'I infiltrated you in the hope of finding it but it doesn't matter any more, does it? You're safe. You rumbled me. Any dirt or skeletons in your closet will stay hidden. You'll get on with your life and I'll return to London and try to forget this whole mess ever happened. At least I can take comfort that I managed to get James put down for his crimes. Now take your hand off me.'

Although Carrie stood with her back to him, she was painfully aware of his stare burning into her just as his touch was doing.

He removed his hand as she asked but before she could exhale he leaned into her, his warm breath breezing through her hair as he spoke into her ear.

She squeezed her eyes shut and held her breath.

'Ah, *matia mou*, you think this is the end of it and I'm going to let you leave? Just like that?'

Closing her eyes was no barrier, she realised with silent desperation. The heat emanating from him seeped into her, the warmth of his breath playing through the strands of her hair and tickling her earlobes, sending tiny shivers dancing over her skin and into her bloodstream.

How could she *still* react like this to him? Whether or not he spoke the truth about his acquaintance with James and his role in Violet's expulsion—and if she believed that then she would have to believe Violet had lied to her—he'd played her like his own personal puppet.

She clenched her hands into fists and turned to look him in the eye. 'You said I couldn't leave here until I'd told you the truth. Well, you've had the truth and now I can go.'

He gave a sound that was like the antithesis of a laugh and stepped back but not far enough for her to dare move. He was still too close. She could still breathe in his scent and feel his warmth.

His eyes bore into hers, mesmerising her with the depth of their strength.

'I said you couldn't leave until I'd had the truth, that is correct,' he mused thoughtfully, his voice as hypnotising as his stare. 'But I never said you would be leaving without me. I foiled your attempt to infiltrate my life and my business but now I have the staff of your paper, some of the most respected journalists in the world, thinking about me and wondering what kind of man I really am. There are already whispers in the media circulating about me. You have set something in motion, *matia mou*. Suspicions have been roused.'

Carrie's heart was beating so hard she had to fight to speak through its heavy echo in her throat. 'I will tell them I made a mistake.'

'Enough of the lies,' he whispered. 'You still think I am corrupt. Even if I believed you would say you had made a mistake and was able to say it convincingly, it wouldn't be enough. The doubts will linger. Every time a journalist sees my name the kernels of doubt will start again. My business will come under much closer scrutiny.'

'If you have nothing to hide then you have nothing to worry about.'

'If only it were that simple.' He grimaced and finally stepped away from her and walked back to the table.

Carrie rubbed her arms, the sudden removal of his warmth producing chills on her skin.

'All it takes is a few enquiring words in the wrong ears and the seeds of doubt are sown,' he said, picking up the whisky bottle. 'My clients invest their money with me because they trust me. They trust my ethics. It is a reputation I have cultivated with great care—it is the reason I refused James's business; I didn't trust him or his ethics. Once that trust is cast into doubt the repercussions can be disastrous, something I know from my parents' bitter experience. I am not prepared to take any risks with my business's health or with my reputation.'

He poured himself another drink, shaking his head with such faux regret that Carrie's internal danger signals fired back into red alert.

Raising his glass, he said, 'There is only one thing that will kill your colleagues' suspicions and the suspicions of anyone else who knows you've been investigating me. You will have to marry me.'

She stared at him, her brain freezing, her vocal cords stunned into silence.

He had to be playing more games...

'It is the only thing that will work,' he said with a decisive nod. 'You are a respected journalist. You have a reputation for fearlessness. You fight the underdog's corner. You fight for justice. If you marry me any lingering doubt about Samaras Fund Management will be killed stone dead.'

The idea of marrying her had first occurred to Andreas on the flight over, a plan he had sincerely hoped he would never have to enact. Embezzlement, though, was too serious an accusation to let slide. He had to nullify the rumours before they gained traction.

'It's the most stupid thing I've ever heard,' she whispered, her voice barely discernible in the breeze.

He took a drink and welcomed the spicy burn. 'Either you marry me or I send a copy of your confession to the proprietor of your newspaper, to my lawyer and to the police. I don't know how many laws you've broken but you've certainly broken all the ethics you're supposed to aspire to. Marry me or you're finished. Your career will be over, you might even go to prison.'

'What confession?' Her voice had strengthened. 'I haven't signed anything.'

With slow deliberation, he pulled his phone out of his top pocket where he'd put it since she discovered the hidden cameras.

'No,' she breathed.

'Yes.' He smiled grimly. 'I recorded every word.' To prove his point, he pressed play. Interference crackled loudly through the stillness of the night, then:

'You know, don't you?'

'That you're the undercover journalist Carrie Rivers?'

'You hateful bastard!' She stormed so quickly over to him she appeared to fly, until she was before him, her entire body trembling and her shaking hand held out to him. 'Give me that phone.'

'I think not.' He stopped the recording and tucked it back in his pocket. 'If you're thinking of stealing it from me, it's backed up automatically. But you're welcome to try.' He stood still and raised his hands in the air as if in supplication.

The look on her beautiful face could freeze lava. 'I can't believe you would be so underhand and deceitful.'

He lowered his hands and shrugged, unmoved. 'You're the journalist. Deceit is second nature to you as you have already proved. You were attempting to destroy me. I reserve the right to protect myself with whatever means I deem necessary. Under the circumstances, I would say I'm being generous. I am giving you the chance to save your career, your freedom and your privacy. And let us not forget your newspaper's fine reputation. Oh, and your sister.'

'Violet?' Her eyes widened alarmingly. 'You leave her out of this.'

'How can I when this is all about her? She is on the transcript. Everything we discussed is recorded. I don't imagine that everyone who hears it will be discreet—how long do you think before the tabloids get hold of it? Loose lips, *matia mou*...

'All you have to do is marry me for...let us say six months. Yes, that is a decent amount of time. Give me six months of marriage and then I will destroy the recording and all back-ups.'

'You can't expect me to give up six months of my life for you!'

He gazed at her pityingly. 'You should have thought of that before you began your vendetta against me. I am a good man. I am loyal to my family and my friends. I do not cheat in life or in love. But I am not a man to cross and you, *matia mou*, have crossed me and now you must accept the consequences.'

Her shoulders rose and then sagged as if in defeat, and she took the steps back to her seat and slumped onto it.

'Drink?' he asked, sliding into the seat next to hers and stretching his legs out.

She shook her head blankly before looking at him. 'You can't want to marry me.'

'I have no wish to marry at all, least of all to a poisonous viper like you.'

'Then *don't*.'

'I will do whatever is necessary to protect my business and my reputation.' He rolled his shoulders and looked at her. 'I've been waiting more than fifteen years for the freedom to do whatever the hell I want; I can wait another six months for it. And, you know, I think a marriage to you could be fun.'

'It will be hell. I'll make sure of it.'

He laughed. 'I'm sure you will, *matia mou*, but you *are* going to marry me. My cousin is marrying a week on Saturday. You will come as my guest and we will announce our engagement then.'

'What?'

Ignoring her outrage, he continued. 'We will marry by the end of the month. The sooner we do it, the sooner we can separate and get back to our real lives.'

'No one will believe it.' Hysteria crept into her voice. 'I don't want to marry, especially not a rich man, and everyone I work with knows that.'

'You have made your feelings about rich men very clear,' he said drily. 'One could accuse you of having a prejudice against us.'

'I *do*.'

'Then you will have to act to the very best of your ability to convince people that you've fallen in love and changed your mind, won't you?' He reached out a hand and fingered her hair.

She slapped it away. 'There is no way I can pretend to have fallen in love with you; I hate everything about you.'

'That is good because I hate everything about you too. Won't that make everything much more fun?'

'Fun?' she practically shrieked. 'You're mad!'

'Not mad,' he corrected. 'Practical. I could look at your beautiful face and allow myself to be furious with you for your vendetta against me and the potential it has to destroy everything I've spent a lifetime working for, or I can flip it around and enjoy the fact that the woman who would have done me such harm is locked to my side. You can behave exactly as you want behind closed doors but you can and will make the world believe you have fallen madly and passionately in love with me, because if anyone doubts it the deal is off and I expose your underhand, illegal dealings to the world and your sister's name will be dragged into it. Do it my way and we both keep our reputations and Violet gets to stay under whatever rock she is currently hiding under.'

She breathed deeply through her nose, the baleful glare she was casting him developing an air of resignation. 'How do I know I can trust you to destroy the recording?'

'It is a gamble you're going to have to take but I *am* a man of my word and if you stick to your part of the arrangement I will stick to mine.' He cupped her cheek and brushed his fingers over the satin skin and felt the tiniest hitch of her breath before her hand rose to slap his away again. He caught it and pulled it to his chest.

'Don't pretend you don't welcome my touch, *matia mou*,' he murmured. 'We've finally been honest about everything else so why pretend? There is an attraction between us, a desire. You know it and I know it. We are going to live together for many months so why deny it?'

Her eyes held his for the longest time, a dozen emotions flickering through them, her lips pulled in tightly. Then they parted, the hazel eyes flashed and she tilted her head. 'You are suffering from what I like to call Rich Man's Delusion.'

He brought her hand to his lips and razed a kiss over her fingertips. 'Oh, yes? And what is that?'

'It's a syndrome only found in the ridiculously wealthy

man.' Her voice had dropped, become breathy. Seductive. It whispered through his skin and seeped into his loins. 'It makes him think he's irresistible. I quite understand why a man like you would suffer from it—your wealth acts as a magnet to many women, I appreciate that, but sufferers, in their arrogance, then think *every* woman is attracted to him. It's beyond your concept that a woman can look at you and not want to drop her knickers.'

Rising from her seat, she gently removed her hand from his hold and palmed his cheek so she stood over him, the tip of her nose almost touching his.

Her pretty fingers caressed his cheek and, *Theos*, his skin revelled in the sensation, little sparks firing through the rest of him, heating him like a gently firing furnace.

She moved her hand to thread through his hair. 'I don't desire you,' she whispered, her lips so close to his that if he made a sudden movement they would fuse together, her sweet breath warm on him. 'I don't want you. If I did, I wouldn't be able to do this...'

The plump lips he'd stared at for hours imagining their feel and taste brushed against his in the whisper of a kiss.

For a moment Andreas did nothing but close his eyes and savour what might possibly be the most erotic moment of his life.

Her lips pressed a little more to his, still not fused, tentative but breathing him in, sweet yet sensuous, his loins, already charged, responding as his blood thickened and all his senses sprang to life.

Right at the moment he sensed her nerve failing her, he hooked an arm around her waist and jerked her to him. As he pulled her onto his lap she gave a tiny gasp and he took ruthless advantage of it, sweeping his tongue into her mouth and holding her tightly, primal lust surging through him. Her lips were softer than a pillow and moulded to his perfectly as he deepened the kiss, savouring her taste and the shape of her body pressed so compactly to his, the furnace heating his blood fired to a roar.

Her hands clasped at his skull, her fingers massaging into him, her mouth moving with his own as if they had fused into one entity.

She fitted perfectly into him, he thought dimly, sweeping a hand over her back and then round to stroke her stomach, which pulled in with a spasm at his touch, a moan so faint it could have been the breeze vibrating from her. He slid his hand up and rubbed his thumb on the underside of her breast, felt its softness through the fabric of her dress, but before he could touch any more she jolted and dragged her mouth from his.

Her fingers still clasping his skull, her breathing erratic, kiss-bruised lips parted, she gazed at him with confused heavy-lidded eyes before whipping her hands away and scrambling off his lap.

Looking anywhere but at him, she ran her hands through her hair and straightened her dress.

Andreas swallowed and took in air, the aching weight in his groin making it hard to think let alone speak. Only the heaviness of their breaths and the beats of his thundering heart cut through the stillness of the night.

When she looked at him again some semblance of composure had returned that would have fooled him if her voice didn't sound so breathy when she said, 'See? If I desired you I wouldn't be able to walk away from that.'

Then she turned and walked away from him to the French doors, her head high, her back magnificently straight. Only the tiny missteps she took showed she was as affected by what they had just shared as he.

'Next time, *matia mou*,' he called after her, his own voice hoarse, 'you will not be able to walk away.'

She didn't look back. 'There won't be a next time.'

'Do you want to put money on that?'

She didn't answer.

A moment later she had disappeared into his house.

CHAPTER SEVEN

CARRIE LAY FULLY dressed and wide awake under the covers of the narrow bed, kicking herself for not finding another room to sleep in, one far away from Andreas. If she weren't so afraid of bumping into him on the landing she would move to another room now. She didn't need to stay in this one any more. He was hardly going to fire her.

She laughed into her pillow, a maniacal sound that she immediately smothered.

If she'd heard that noise from anyone else she would assume they were mad.

Was she mad? Had all the glorious sun that had shone on her these past two days infected her mind and driven her out of it?

It was as good an explanation as anything, she supposed, to justify her behaviour.

Twenty minutes after crawling under the bedsheets and she still couldn't get her head around what had possessed her to play with fire like that.

She'd wanted to prove a point to him and wipe that smug grin off his face but it had gone too far. *She* had gone too far.

His touch...it had scorched her. She could still feel the imprint of his lips on hers and had to stop herself from rubbing her fingers over them. And she could still feel the contours of his body pressed against her. Her blood still felt fizzy, an ache in her loins she'd never known before.

Her brain burned just to remember it. It burned to remember the effort it had taken to walk away. They had been the hardest steps she'd ever taken, fighting her own yearning body.

Her first kiss.

She gritted her teeth and wished she were in a place where she could scream her frustration. She shouldn't be reliving their kiss, she should be trying to think of ways to get out of marrying him.

Marriage! To him!

And he was deadly serious about it too.

Violet was his trump card. If it were only Carrie's future at stake she would tell him to stuff it and take her chances. She'd been prepared to lose her job and her freedom before she'd embarked on investigating him, but that recording had changed everything. Andreas was too well known and her professional name too renown for that recording not to be dynamite to the tabloid press. Andreas would probably deliver a copy of it to them himself or upload it onto social media if she refused to go ahead with his plan, and then the whole world would hear him talk of how her sister had tried to seduce him and her affair with James and all those other awful things.

She screwed her eyes tight shut, fighting the fresh panic clawing at her chest.

That recording must never find its way into the public domain. Violet's recovery was too fragile and nebulous to cope with that. She didn't want her sister to have an excuse to dive back into the horrid, seedy world that had almost killed her.

A sliver of hazy light filtered the gap in the heavy curtains. Night was fading, the sun was rising and Andreas still hadn't come to bed.

Rubbing her hand over her forehead, she rolled over so her back was to the door.

What was the point in moving rooms? she thought as hot tears prickled her eyes. She would be sharing a roof with him for the next six months.

She was trapped.

Andreas stepped onto the veranda and breathed in the hot salty air, trying to clear the last of his lethargy away.

Going to bed after the sun had risen had not been conducive for a decent sleep but he'd thought it safer to wait until he could comfortably walk before putting himself an unlocked door's distance from Carrie.

He'd dreamed of her, hot lusty dreams as disturbing as they had been erotic, waking to the taste of her kisses on his tongue. He hardly ever remembered his dreams but these were still vivid, playing like a reel in his mind.

The real kisses they'd shared were still vivid in his mind too. He smiled to remember the little stumble she'd made when she'd walked away from him, her nonchalant charade not fooling either of them.

She wanted him. It had been there in the heat of her kisses and the heat from her flesh.

She really thought she could resist the attraction for the six months they would be married?

He'd known her for mere days but knew, as he knew his own name, that Carrie would resist until her stubborn little feet got sore.

It was more than mere stubbornness. When she set herself on a path it needed a bulldozer to steer her off it. Look at her work, the powerful men she had exposed, the focus and dedication it had taken to infiltrate their organisations and find the evidence needed to expose them.

And then there was her unflinching support for her sister and her stubborn refusal to accept the truth about what had happened those years ago when she knew—and he was certain that deep down she did know—that he spoke the truth.

She'd believed him to be the friend of a monster, a thought that darkened his mood. Carrie had believed him capable of setting up a teenage girl with drugs. She believed him to be the same as the men she'd described who didn't think twice about stamping on lesser mortals if they got in their way.

There were many men in his circles who did behave like that, men who believed their wealth and position in society gave them free rein to do exactly as they pleased and generally they were right. Society turned a blind eye unless irrefutable evidence of the kind that tenacious journalists like Carrie produced meant action had to be taken.

She believed he was just like them. She believed he'd become seduced by the trappings of his wealth and lost his soul.

He inhaled even more deeply and closed his eyes, letting the burst of anger flow into his lungs and then expelling it out of his body.

His father had held onto his anger at the business rivals who had used such cruel tactics to destroy his business and it had put him in hospital with a failing heart. Deal with the root cause of the anger, punish those that needed it and move on—that was Andreas's way.

Carrie had held onto her hatred towards him for three years. She'd bided her time, taken out James first and then had decided the time was right to strike at him.

He took much satisfaction in knowing he'd cut her off

at the head and foiled her plans. Marrying her ensured his business and reputation would be safe. And what were six months? As he'd told Carrie, he'd already waited fifteen years for his freedom so a few extra weeks were nothing.

At least those months would be eventful, something he'd not had the luxury of allowing his life to be since he'd left his Greek Island of Gaios for the adventure that was America. He'd planned out his whole life: work hard and play hard at university then work hard and play hard as he built a financial business for himself and then, and only after he'd enjoyed everything life had to offer, find someone to settle down with.

Of those three goals only the first had been achieved and he looked back on his university days with nostalgia.

No sooner had he graduated than he'd discovered the dire mess his parents were in.

Movement behind him made him turn. A member of his staff had brought him a tray of food, a light mezze to sustain him, the time being closer to lunch than breakfast and the sun already burning hot.

'Have you seen Carrie?' he asked. He'd knocked on her door before leaving his bedroom and, when there had been no answer, had taken a quick look and found her room empty, her bed neatly made.

A shake of the head. 'Do you want me to look for her?'

'Don't worry about it. Let me know when she turns up.'

She couldn't have gone far, he assured himself. He kept just one car here, in an outhouse and for emergency purposes only, and there was only one road off the peninsular. It would be impossible to take his car or his speedboat without someone seeing or hearing.

Pouring his coffee first, he was helping himself to melon and yogurt when he caught a glimpse of a figure walking along the beach in his direction.

The tightness he hadn't noticed in his chest loosened.

He watched her while he ate as, step by step, she came into clearer focus, the memory of their kiss playing in his mind all over again.

'Good morning, *matia mou*,' he said when she reached the table. 'Have you eaten?'

She shook her head, her eyes hidden behind the designer shades he'd bought her. They were the only things he could see that she was wearing that he'd provided her with. Today, in temperatures already in the high-twenties and guaranteed to rise much higher, Carrie wore the outfit he'd interviewed her in, her cashmere jumper and grey trousers, which she'd rolled up to lay mid-calf. Her feet were bare.

'Coffee?' he asked, reaching for the pot.

There was a tiny hesitation before she nodded and sat down in the seat furthest from him. 'I didn't think you knew how to pour coffee.'

'Now that my minion has been upgraded to fiancée I thought I should reacquaint myself with the simple tasks I have always done for myself. And for the record, I have never expected a proper employee to perform the slavish chores I got you to do. I'm no man-child.'

He poured the coffee, added a splash of milk and one spoonful of sugar, and pushed the cup over to her.

'Thank you.' A tiny smile played on her lips. 'I didn't realise you'd paid attention to how I take my coffee.'

'I pay attention to everything, *matia mou*, especially with you.'

She tilted her head to look up at the sky then gathered her hair together and tied it into a knot without using any kind of device to hold it in place.

'Feeling hot, are you?' he asked drily. 'Maybe you should consider changing into clothing more suited to the weather.'

She took her cup and cradled it in both hands. 'Now I'm no longer your minion I can wear what I like, and what I like to wear are clothes that don't expose all my flesh.'

'Afraid you will drive me wild with desire?'

'You're putting words in my mouth,' she said stiffly.

'I have managed to keep my hands to myself since we arrived here and you have had plenty of flesh on display.' As he spoke he helped himself to a fresh bread roll and cut into it. A delicious yeasty aroma was released, a smell almost as good as Carrie's scent, and he inhaled it greedily. 'After all, you were the one to kiss *me*, *matia mou*. Do you need to cloak yourself to resist me?'

The knuckles holding her cup had turned white. 'I kissed you to prove a point. It meant nothing to me.'

'And you proved it very well. If I'd had any doubt that you desire me, your kiss dispelled it.'

'The fact I walked away proves I felt nothing.'

Digging his knife into a pot, he slathered jam over his roll. 'It proves that you have mastered the art of walking. For the avoidance of doubt, I am prepared to be used by you whenever you want to prove that you don't desire me. Any time at all. Day or night.' Then he bit into his roll.

Carrie fought hands that wanted to shake and put the cup to her mouth to drink her coffee, closing her mind to the vivid images playing in her mind of being in his arms and the hunger of his mouth on hers.

After three hours of sleep she'd woken from dreams already fading into haziness but which her body ached to recapture. Then everything that had passed between them had come back to her in one huge rush, all the words, their kiss…

She'd jumped out of bed, dug her own clothes, which had been laundered by Andreas's staff, out of the wardrobe and put them on as a form of armour. Then she had escaped to walk on the beach, desperate to exercise the ache deep inside out of her system and clear her mind. It had all been pointless. She could cover herself from head to toe in sackcloth and she would still feel naked before him. She could walk a thousand miles and her stomach would still flip over when she looked into those piercing light brown eyes.

And he seemed to know it.

Putting the cup back on the table, she strove to compose herself, a difficult task when she felt as if she were sitting in a sauna, the heat from the sun and her body's reaction to merely sitting and talking to Andreas combining together to be almost unendurable. But endure she would. He had the upper hand over her life now but she wouldn't allow him to have the upper hand over her emotions and feelings too. 'I don't need to prove anything to you.'

He swallowed his food. 'You have six months to convince yourself of that. For now, you should eat something. We will be leaving soon.'

'Where are we going?'

'Back to London.'

Thank God for that.

It would get better when they were back there, she assured herself, when cold drizzle and concrete greeted her rather than brilliant blue skies and palm trees.

London was her home. Her territory. It was where she belonged.

She hid her relief to ask, 'What happened to your holiday?'

'We have wheels to set in motion, *matia mou*…a wedding to prepare.'

'You said we wouldn't announce our engagement until your cousin's wedding.'

'We still need to arrange our own and you need to return to work and inform your colleagues that the tip-off you had been given about me is completely unfounded and that you are so convinced of my innocence that you have fallen madly in love with me.'

She scoffed.

He laughed loudly. 'I'm sure faking mad, passionate love will not be a problem for such an accomplished actress as yourself.' Getting to his feet, he stretched his back. 'I'm going to have a swim in the pool before we leave. Can I tempt you to strip off those clothes that are making you so uncomfortable to join me?'

'I can't think of anything less tempting.'

He shrugged and whipped off his T-shirt, the movement sending a wave of his cologne into her senses. The sun shone down on his bare torso, his toned and oh-so-masculine physique seeming to shimmer under it.

Tiny pulses set off low inside her as she remembered just how good it had felt to be held so tightly against that body...

Moisture filled her mouth and she fisted her hands against her thighs while striving to keep her features neutral, fighting the fresh hunger uncoiling itself inside her.

For a long moment he stared at her. A smile played on the lips that had kissed her so thoroughly, before he placed his T-shirt on the back of his chair. 'Are you sure you're not tempted?'

'Very sure.' But she wished her voice sounded more convincing and that she was the only one to have heard the husky rasp that had come into it.

His eyes gleaming, he hunched over to whisper into her ear, 'Your mouth says one thing, *matia mou*, but your eyes say another. I know which I believe.'

The sensation of his warm breath against her skin was

all too fleeting for no sooner had he spoken than he was striding away from her.

'You've only just eaten so try not to get a stitch while you're swimming,' she called out, forcing strength into her voice. 'It would be dreadful if you were to drown before we marry.'

He turned but didn't stop walking, surefooted even as he trod backwards. 'But it would mean you having to give me the kiss of life so it would be an excellent way to meet my maker.'

Then he winked and hardly broke stride to turn around again.

Carrie put a hand to her chest, her heart thumping hard against it, watching the long, muscular legs walk away from her.

Once he was out of sight, she took some deep breaths and closed her eyes.

It would all feel different when she was back on home soil.

It had to.

CHAPTER EIGHT

THE ELEGANT FIGURE stepped out of the revolving doors with an older woman a pace behind her, the two women chatting between themselves.

The older woman was the first to spot him standing against a black Bentley watching them. She nudged Carrie and nodded in his direction.

He raised a hand in greeting.

Carrie's eyes found his. Even with the distance separating them Andreas could see the high colour slashing her cheeks as she mimicked his greeting, then used the same hand to smooth a loose strand of hair that had fallen from the knot it had been tied into off her face, then to smooth her long cream overcoat. Her movements were rapid but her colleague noticed, a smile spreading on her face as she watched Carrie subconsciously groom herself.

After a beat, Carrie said something to her colleague, then walked steadily to him, chin aloft, her right hand clutching the strap of her handbag to her chest.

'This is a pleasant surprise,' she said when she reached him, speaking in a voice loud enough that those of her nearby colleagues, all hurrying to the nearby underground station in their eagerness to get home, would be able to hear. The inflection of surprise she put in it was a masterstroke.

Andreas had been waiting by his car for twenty minutes. He estimated a dozen of the people who had come out of the building that housed the *Daily Times* had done a double take at his presence outside their offices.

He gave a slow smile, feasting his eyes on the face that had consumed his thoughts all day. The wind picked up the strand of hair she'd only just smoothed down and he reached out to tuck it behind her delicate ear.

Her already coloured cheeks went a few shades darker, and her throat moved.

'I have been thinking of you all day,' he murmured for her ears only, delighting at the way her eyes pulsed at his words.

He'd dreamed about her again. She'd been the first thing on his mind when his eyes had opened that morning. By lunchtime he'd taken to checking his watch every few minutes, the time ticking down until their prearranged meeting outside her work offices slowing to a lethargic snail's pace. He assured himself this restlessness, this yearning to see her again was due to his impatience to get the ball rolling in the fake relationship they were about to establish. He desired Carrie but more than anything his desire was to protect his business from the lies she had told her zealous colleagues about him.

In a clearer tone that anyone passing would hear he added, 'I know it must sound crazy but I was hoping you would let me take you out for dinner.'

She swallowed, her eyes pulsing again before she blinked it away. 'That sounds totally crazy but...that would be lovely.'

'Excellent. Can I give you a lift home?'

'If it's not out of your way.'

'I wouldn't care if it was.' He grinned then opened the back door for her and followed her in.

The moment the door closed them in, her demeanour changed. Carrie perched herself rigidly beside him, knees tucked tightly together, hands clasped on her lap.

Once they were moving in the heavy London traffic, she said in a clipped voice, 'That must have been difficult for you, having to ask politely rather than just bark orders at me.'

'It was a nightmare. I'm used to people asking how high when I tell them to jump,' he replied drolly. 'How did it go today?'

She rested her head back on the leather seat and closed her eyes. 'We had a meeting about you. I said my tip-off had been wrong and that the person who gave it to me is refusing to answer my calls.'

'And that sounds plausible?'

'I've made it sound like my source is avoiding me. I'll give it a few days and say I met up with him and that he confessed he'd made it up for money.'

'And does *that* sound plausible?' He watched her response closely, looking for signs of an untruth or the bending of facts.

'It's not uncommon. We do pay for tips that are verified and lead to a story being printed, but it doesn't happen much. Most of the people who give us tip-offs do it because it's the right thing to do—we're not a tabloid, we deal with weighty stories that are often in the national interest.'

'Will they want to check with your source?'

'Our sources are sacrosanct. We never reveal them without the source's permission, not even to each other.' Carrie rolled her shoulders, trying to ease the tension in them. Her colleagues had seemingly taken her story at face value— Andreas's instincts had been proven right in that regard— but the cramped feeling of guilt had spread its way inside her and through to her muscles.

It nauseated her to think of all the barefaced lies she had told her colleagues in recent weeks. When she'd embarked on the single-minded task of bringing Andreas down, she'd been so certain of his guilt and so filled with anger at what he'd done to her sister that she had smothered her own screaming conscience. Now she was lying to her supportive colleagues for a second time but what else could she do? If she didn't go ahead with Andreas's plan then her sister's name would be dragged into the world's consciousness and whatever recovery she'd made would be destroyed. Violet would be back on the drugs quicker than a wannabe vegetarian lion passing by a wounded gazelle; unable to resist.

'How did you explain my learning your true identity?' Andreas asked.

She could happily scream. She'd had almost a whole day away from him but he'd been breaking into her thoughts the whole time. She might as well have taken him to work with her. Her morning had been devoted to talking about him in the staff meeting, her afternoon fielding female colleagues' whispered questions about what he was *really* like, if he was as handsome in the flesh as in pictures...

Every time she'd been asked her cheeks had flushed. It had been excruciating. Half the office thought she had a crush on him without her having to say a word.

Andreas would be delighted if she told him, which of course she would not.

Instead, she told him in as cool a voice as she could muster—anything to counteract the skipping warmth being back with him was inducing, 'I said your PA had learned my references didn't check out after all—at least that wasn't a lie—and that by the time this was discovered, I was already convinced of your innocence. Exactly as we agreed.'

She felt him relax beside her, pressing his own head back against the seat and facing her. She kept her eyes facing forward, not looking at him.

He inched his face a little closer to her. 'You didn't like lying to your colleagues, did you?'

How could he read her so damn *well*? He barely knew her.

Her throat caught. 'I hate it,' she muttered. 'Lying on an investigation is never real because I always know I'm getting the facts needed to expose corrupt and illegal practices. This is very different.' She turned her head to meet his gaze. 'You know I'm only going along with this to protect Violet, don't you? If it was just my own future at stake I would let you throw me to the wolves.'

He brushed his thumb over her cheekbone lazily but there was an intensity in his stare. 'She is lucky to inspire such devotion.'

Carrie grabbed his hand, intending to push it off her face but instead wrapped her fingers around it tightly and stared back with matching concentration to his. 'Do we have to do this…this marriage thing?' she asked on impulse. 'My colleagues all believe I made a mistake. I've convinced them there's nothing worth investigating about you.'

His light brown eyes continued to ring into hers for a long time before he answered. There was none of the usual staccato beat to his voice, his tone slow and thoughtful. 'A good reputation takes years to build but can be knocked down in minutes by nothing more than careless words. Do you know what happened to my parents' business?'

She shook her head.

'They owned their own water taxi company. Do you know what that is?'

'Like a regular taxi firm but on water?'

He nodded. His face had inched so close to hers she could feel his warm breath on her skin.

A voice in her head warned her to shift away from him, not allow him to get any closer.

Carefully she released her hold on his hand but his eyes...

This was why she tried to avoid looking into them.

It was as if he were hypnotising her.

'They took tourists and locals island hopping or from one side of the island to another. They also had a handful of larger boats they chartered out for daytrips through the holiday companies. It was a good living for them.' His lips tightened, the mesmerising eyes darkening. 'When I was in my final year at university a rival company set itself up. These rivals were predators. They sabotaged my parents' fleet. One of the charter boats sank; it's a miracle none of the passengers were killed. Then rumours were spread that they knowingly employed paedophiles—can you imagine the impact that had on an island built for families? People stopped using their taxis, the holiday companies cancelled their contracts...in months the business they had spent their whole marriage building was in ruins.'

Chills raced up Carrie's spine. 'That's...horrific. What did your parents do?'

He grimaced and rolled his face away from hers. 'They tried to fight but did not have the resources. They had used all their savings to get me through university. I went on a scholarship but they paid for all my accommodation, flights back home for holidays... I thought they could afford it. If I had known they were putting themselves in such a precarious financial situation I would have worked more hours to support myself...' He cut himself off and shook his head before straightening in his seat.

His gaze fixed on the screen separating them from his

driver, he continued, 'It is done. I cannot change what they did or what I did. I didn't go home at all in that last year. There was too much going on in my life. Studying. Girls. Parties. Too busy to call home and only listening with one ear when we did speak. I didn't have a clue what was happening with them. They didn't want to worry me and made my sister promise not to tell me. I learned the truth when I graduated.'

'Would you have been able to do anything if you had known?'

His jaw clenched before he answered. 'If they had told me when it first started I might have been able to scare their rivals off. I could have at least shared the burden with them. Once I did know, I helped as much as I could. Their financial situation was an incentive for me to work all hours so I could support them through it and pay for lawyers who were able to take the case to court. To prove the allegations wrong and prove that their rivals deliberately sabotaged their business. It took four years to get there but they went to prison for it.'

'Good,' she stated vehemently.

He turned his face to look at her. A faint smile appeared on his lips. 'I should have guessed that what happened to my parents would make you angry. You are a one-woman crusader against injustice.'

'I'm surprised I didn't already know about it.' She swallowed before giving a small, apologetic smile. 'I did a *lot* of research on you.'

His low laugh showed his lack of surprise at her confession. 'The press coverage was minimal and all in Greek. My name wouldn't have been in any of the reports—it all happened before I became well known.'

'How are your parents now?'

'In a good place, thank God, but it took them a long

time to recover. The whole thing did not just affect their finances but everything else too. Their reputations and health were ruined. Friends, neighbours, people who knew them well, all shunned them. By the time it went to court what mattered most to them was having their reputations restored. It was a bitter thing for them to accept, that people believed them capable of knowingly employing child abusers. My mother has since fought two different forms of cancer and my father has had a quadruple heart bypass. Losing Tanya almost finished them off.'

'I'm sorry.' Her heart twisted for this couple she had never met who had been through so much pain and heartache.

And Andreas had lost his sister.

Carrie knew what the pain of loss felt like. Her mother had been dead for seven years now but there were still times when grief caught her; a song playing on the radio, seeing her shampoo on a supermarket shelf, little things that could poleaxe her.

She felt her heart wrench to imagine all the little things that could poleaxe Andreas with grief too.

When he reached for her hand and brought it to his lips she didn't snatch it away.

'It does not take a lot to destroy a reputation and a business,' he said sombrely as he brushed his lips over her fingertips. 'I will not take the risk of assuming the damage can be prevented with some carefully chosen words. Even a *whisper* of embezzlement could cause irreparable harm to my name and then who can say what the repercussions would be? Marrying you, the woman who started the whispers, is the best way to kill it.'

Her hand tingled, her fingers itching to open up and explore his face and touch all the hard, masculine features her eyes could not help but drink in…

'We are here.'

Blood roared so hard in her ears his softly delivered words sounded distant. 'What?'

'Your home. We have arrived. Are you going to invite me in?'

Coming to her senses with a jolt, Carrie snatched her hand from his and jerked back, then fumbled with the door handle, her sudden desperation for air that wasn't filled with his scent making her all fingers and thumbs. Before she could break the handle off, the driver appeared and opened it for her.

She practically threw herself out of the car. The cold drizzle was a welcome relief on her flushed skin.

'Carrie?'

She dragged the fresh air into her lungs before looking back at him. 'Yes?'

His eyes were alive with amusement, as if he knew exactly what had got her so flustered.

He probably did know. He seemed to be able to read her like a book.

'Tomorrow, we book our wedding.'

She shrugged, pretending a nonchalance she absolutely did not feel.

'And you need to book leave from your work.'

'I can hardly marry you if I'm in the office.'

He grinned. 'I meant for my cousin's wedding. It's being held in Agon, an island near Crete. We'll fly over at the weekend.'

'But the wedding's not for a fortnight.'

'We can spend the week before it there. I'm already bored of the English rain.'

'I can't just take a week off at this short notice.' She'd thought they would spend the weeks leading up to their marriage in London, in her home territory, where she was safe…

She hadn't been safe in the back of his car.

The cold English drizzle had proved no barrier to her ever-growing awareness of him.

'Tell them I've agreed to an exclusive interview with you.' His lively eyes carried steel in them, clearly saying, *You will do exactly as you are told or our deal is off.*

He had her exactly where he wanted her and he knew it.

'Fine. But you'll have to actually give me an exclusive interview in exchange.'

Now his eyes gleamed with more than mere amusement. 'There are many exclusive things I can give you, *matia mou*. An interview is just one of them.'

The gleam deepened, his suggestive words hanging in the air between them for what felt like a whole epoch before she got her vocal cords to work, her cheeks flaming like a bonfire. 'I'll book the time off.'

A knowing smile played on his lips. 'I will pick you up in two hours.'

'What for?'

'I am taking you out to dinner, *matia mou*.' The smile turned into the wickedest of grins. 'Unless you wish to invite me into your home and cook for me?'

'Hell will freeze over before I lift a finger for you again.'

He gave an ironic shake of his head at her defensiveness. 'It is funny how your mouth tells me one thing but your eyes and body the other.'

It was with great delight that she slammed the car door in his face.

When her front door was closed and locked for good measure she stood with her back against it, trying to breathe properly.

Being on home soil hadn't changed a thing.

* * *

The knock on the front door Carrie had been anticipating
for the past ten minutes still made her jump and set her
already skittish heart thrumming maniacally.

She took one last look in the mirror and smoothed her
hair, then breathed deeply as she walked down the stairs.
Her shoes were ready by the front door and she slid her
feet into them and removed her coat from the hook before
she opened it.

After a mere five days in London it was time to get her
passport out again.

Andreas stood at the threshold, dressed in a sharp navy
suit with an open-necked white shirt, that wicked, wolfish
grin on his face. 'Good morning, *matia mou*. You look as
beautiful as ever.'

She rolled her eyes. 'Cut the cheesy lines, there's no
one to hear you.'

Over the past five days they'd been on four 'dates', all
in restaurants where the paparazzi liked to camp out. As
he was a man who had always kept his private life discreet, the paparazzi responded to Andreas's presence as
if he were Father Christmas bearing early gifts.

The lengths she had gone to in the past to keep her face
hidden from public view, like all journalists who worked
undercover, had been for nothing. That the Greek billionaire Andreas Samaras was dating the respected journalist
Carrie Rivers had generated more excitement than even
she had expected.

Her name would be linked to his for ever.

'It cannot be a line when it is the truth.' The pulse in
his eyes shot straight through her flesh and into her bloodstream. 'You *are* beautiful.'

Heat rose inside her, a now familiar throbbing ache.

When they dined out together he would stare at her with

that same look, his eyes holding hers as he probed her with questions about her job and her interests, drawing her into conversation as any other dating couple behaved.

She'd been surprised at how...*easy* it had all been. She'd expected there to be awkwardness between them but Andreas had carried all the conversations with an easy-going wit, always keeping talk in safe territory, displaying a droll humour that often made her laugh without her having to fake it for the paparazzi lenses.

There had been moments when she had forgotten why they were there, forgotten that she hated him. Forgotten *why* she hated him; struggled to reconcile him with the man she'd spent three years dreaming of destroying.

And underlying everything lay the strange chemical cocktail that snaked between them. Always she refused to drink wine with their meals; his intoxicating presence enough for her to fight against without adding alcohol to the mix. She had to keep her defences up as much as she could, not blithely allow herself to lower them.

'Are you packed?' he asked.

She blinked sharply to clear her head—it seemed she was always having to clear it when with him—and nodded. 'My case is in the kitchen. Give me a...'

'I'll get it for you,' he interrupted with a wink, then swept past her and into the house. 'I have some papers for you to read through before we leave.'

Carrie couldn't help the laugh that burst out of her.

Until that moment, she had continued to refuse him admittance into her home. This was her territory, her sanctuary away from him, the one place she felt safe from all the turbulence that her life had become and the wild emotions he continually evoked in her.

She sighed and rolled her eyes. She had only been delaying the inevitable and, frankly, she was surprised she'd been able to keep him out of her home for this long. Andreas had proved himself to be a steamroller when it came to getting what he wanted done. Even at the registry office the other day when they'd gone to book their wedding, the date he'd wanted had been fully booked and yet somehow the registrar had been able to accommodate him for that particular date and for the exact time he wanted.

Carrie followed him down the long hallway behind the trail of his tangy cologne.

Breathing in his scent drove away her momentary amusement and replaced it with the tell-tale flutters of panic and with it a certainty that she would never be able to walk down this hallway again without thinking of him...

How could she know that?

Stop being so melodramatic, she chided herself grimly.

'This is nice,' he commented as he stepped into the airy high-ceilinged kitchen. 'It's much bigger than it looks from the outside.'

'Yes, it's a regular Tardis.'

'It's a good location too. It must have cost a lot of money to buy.'

'I guess so. It costs a fortune to maintain and heat.' The front looked out over Hyde Park but as a child the monetary value of such a prime location had meant nothing to her. She remembered sunny days there, going for picnics, curling up on her mother's lap under a tree as she read her stories, remembered teaching Violet how to do cartwheels and walk on her hands. Remembered dropping her ice cream and trying so hard to be grown up and not cry about it and Violet, chubby legged and her hair in pigtails, toddling over to her.

'You eat mine too, Cawwie...'

She blinked the bittersweet memories away before they could lance her heart any more.

She'd spoken to Violet only the day before, another stilted conversation but this time it had been stilted on both sides, the question Carrie most wanted to ask she'd found herself incapable of saying: *Did you lie about Andreas setting you up?*

She hadn't asked because she was afraid of the answer. She was afraid that even if Violet's answer was negative, she might not believe it.

'I've lived here since I was four,' she explained, speaking over the fresh roil of nausea that was induced whenever she allowed those doubts to gain too much space in her head. 'My stepdad bought it when he married my mum. She got it when they divorced.' And Carrie and Violet had inherited it when she'd later died. 'What were the papers you wanted me to look at?'

He pulled a thick envelope out of his inside pocket and held it out. 'It's a draft of our pre-nuptial agreement.'

'What pre—?' She caught herself and shook her head. 'Of course. You're protecting yourself.'

'Anyone in my position would protect himself but you will see I have made more than adequate provisions for you.'

'Unless that document says we both walk away with nothing from each other I don't want to read it. I don't want your money.'

Andreas stared at her beautiful set face.

Had there ever been a more stubborn person in the history of the earth?

He thought of the thousands of pounds' worth of designer goods she'd left behind in the Seychelles, giving them to one of Sheryl's young daughters who was the same dress size. He only knew this because an anxious Sheryl had called him to make sure it was okay for her daughter to have them.

That Carrie had done this shouldn't have surprised him when he considered she'd spent their last day there sweltering in her own clothes rather than changing into any of the items he'd bought for her. It had still stung though, just as her refusal to take the envelope from his hand and read it also stung. She would much rather overheat than wear something paid for by him. She would rather struggle to pay her heating bill than accept a cash sum from him that would keep her comfortable for life.

If she were starving she would still refuse his money.

And he'd thought they'd been making progress.

She still believed him to be corrupt.

'Carrie,' he said, making sure to keep his tone moderate although he wanted to snarl his words at her, 'I'm only giving you what a court would award you on our divorce.'

'I don't want it. I earn my own money.'

He shook his head, incredulity and anger merging like a toxin inside him. 'You are unbelievable.'

'Why? Because I won't play the money roulette game? I'm only marrying you to protect my sister. I don't want your money. The only thing you could give me that I would want is a time machine that can fast forward the next six months.'

He held the envelope up. 'You are sure about this? You are certain you want to give up a small fortune?'

'Yes,' she answered without any hesitation.

'I'll get a new one done, then, that spells out you receive *nothing*.' He ripped the envelope in half and let the pieces fall to the floor. Then he stepped over them to the large old-fashioned suitcase by the kitchen table. 'And now that that is settled, we can go. Maybe some sunshine will make you more agreeable although I doubt anything could.'

CHAPTER NINE

CARRIE OPENED THE French doors of the living room of the lavish Mykonian-style villa she had been given for her stay on Agon and looked out over its beautiful garden. Fruit trees had come into blossom, filling the air with the most wonderful spring scent. She breathed it in deeply, letting it calm her ragged nerves.

The island itself was dazzling, mountainous and overlooked by blue skies, but that was where the similarity with the Seychelles ended. Andreas's peninsular had been remote, his and the chef's cottage the only homes for miles and miles. Agon was filled with pristine white homes, its beaches golden where the Seychelles sand was white. There was a different feel to it too, different smells and a much different vibe. This was a rich island and a growing financial powerhouse. Carrie's villa would befit royalty and if she were in a different frame of mind she would be delighting to find herself staying in such a beautiful place for the next week.

She didn't know if the villa was hers alone or if Andreas was sharing it with her. She hadn't seen him since his driver had dropped her off and brought their cases in while Andreas waited in the car. His only words as she'd got out of the vehicle had been, 'I'll be back by seven to take you out for dinner.'

Since they had left her London home that morning he had hardly exchanged three sentences with her. His cases were still by the front door. If he were planning to stay here they would have been taken to whichever of the six bedrooms had been appointed as his.

A housekeeper and a general handyman had been in the villa to greet her and show her to her room, the handyman carrying her case up the marble stairs for her.

Her bedroom had taken her breath away; it was the complete opposite of the box room she'd been given in the Seychelles. She'd then been given a tour of the rest of the place and given the phone number for the staff house, where a small army of workers lived, all available twenty-four-seven for whatever she needed.

She'd been alone now for three hours and time was dragging insufferably. She'd had a bath in her en-suite bathroom, feeling decadent in the freestanding roll-top bath, and then had changed into a pretty summer top in a light peach colour with spaghetti straps and a full matching skirt that fell to mid-calf. The top half of it especially was very similar to the summer dresses Andreas had bought for her but…this didn't feel as good. The clothing he'd bought for her had caressed her skin in a way she hadn't realised until she'd put her own, much cheaper clothing back on.

She'd paced from room to room ever since, checking her watch every few minutes.

She checked it again and bit her lip.

It was almost seven.

Nerves were accumulating in her belly at an ever-increasing rate, far more violent nerves than she'd become used to when waiting for him to pick her up for their dates in London.

She'd angered him and while it was a thought that should make her glad, it made her stomach feel all coiled and acid-filled. In all that had passed between them in the past week she'd forgotten what it felt like to be on the receiving end of his anger, as she had been three years ago when he'd lasered her with his stare outside the headmistress's office.

He'd been angry the night when the truth had been revealed between them but that had felt different. They'd both been angry—furious—with each other. Since then he'd been all charm and geniality and she didn't think it was an act. He was that way with everyone, treated even underpaid and always undervalued waiting staff in restaurants as if their opinions on the dish of the day truly mattered, made a point of learning their names and *remembering* them.

She couldn't help thinking that her refusal to open his envelope had wounded him in some way, which she knew was a ridiculous notion…

Footsteps treading on the marble floor sounded out behind her and she spun round to find him standing there holding an enormous bunch of red roses.

Their eyes met and held, and her heart made the most enormous thud against her ribs, the motion knocking all the air from her lungs.

There was no humour in his eyes, no knowing gleam, not even any anger, just a steadfast openness that made the thuds in her heart morph into a racing thrum.

He'd changed into fresh clothes, tailored dark grey trousers and a black shirt, since he'd dropped her at the villa. But there was something unkempt about him, his hair a little messier than he usually wore it, his jaw thick with stubble when he'd always been freshly shaved on their dates.

He held the flowers out to her. 'Peace offering.'

She paused for only a moment before taking them from him.

'Thank you,' she whispered.

She'd never been given flowers before.

Keeping her eyes on his, she rubbed her nose against the delicate petals. They smelt wonderful.

'You look beautiful,' he said simply.

Her heart now racing so hard she could imagine it bursting out of her ribs, she attempted a smile but found one impossible to form.

'I'll find a vase to put these in.' Forcing her feet to uproot themselves from the floor, she walked past him and headed to the vast kitchen on the other side of the villa.

Andreas kept step beside her. 'Have you settled in all right?'

'Yes, thank you.' She hadn't found it this awkward to talk to him since the interview in his office. Back then, her tongue had been tied with the fear of being discovered. Her fear now was of a completely different hue. 'Have you had a good afternoon?'

'It has been productive.'

'Oh?' They'd reached the vast kitchen.

Carrie put the flowers on a worktop and immediately busied herself opening cupboards and drawers, ostensibly to find a vase but more to keep her attention diverted from him and the terrifying things happening inside her.

'I had a meeting.' He opened a high cupboard and took down a crystal vase. 'Is this what you're looking for?'

She took it from him with a small smile of thanks and almost dropped it when their fingers brushed.

A shock of electricity skipped over her skin and danced into her veins, and she hurriedly turned her back to him as she muttered her thanks.

Just breathe.

First she filled the vase with water and added the sachet of feed to it.

Breathe.

She'd spotted scissors earlier when she'd made herself coffee, and she grabbed them out of the drawer and cut the pretty cellophane wrapping around the roses, then took the first rose—thankfully the thorns had been removed—and cut an inch of the base off and put it in the vase. She grabbed another, certain she remembered her mother doing something else when she was given roses but her brain was overloaded, trying to focus on the task at hand while tuning out the huge figure standing so close to her.

She could feel his eyes on her.

As she reached for another rose, a warm hand pressed into her lower back while another wrapped around her reaching wrist.

She couldn't move. She couldn't breathe. Her blood had thickened to a sludge that pulsed through every crevice in her body.

Andreas felt the pulse in Carrie's wrist beat madly against his thumb, the only movement on her still frame.

Theos, he wanted her so badly it had become a constant ache he carried everywhere with him.

He'd been so damned *angry* with her and her stubborn refusal to take her blinkers off when it came to him.

When he'd dropped her at the villa he'd had half a mind to check himself into a hotel for the night but then he'd left his meeting hours later and a woman in a soft-top convertible had driven past him, roof down. She'd had chestnut hair almost identical in colour to Carrie's. His chest had contracted so tightly in that moment he'd had to fight for breath.

Why should he care what Carrie thought of him? he'd told himself as he'd dragged air into his lungs. She was only going to be in his life for a short period. All that mattered was that she marry him and kill the rumours before they properly started.

But even as he was thinking all that he'd found himself walking into a florist and asking for their largest bunch of roses.

He'd never bought flowers for a woman before.

It had been the look in Carrie's eyes as he'd passed the flowers to her that had driven the last of his anger out. There had been a vulnerability in those eyes he'd never seen in her before.

He leaned forward to breathe in her cloud of hair, the silky strands tickling his nose, and heard a jagged inhalation.

His need for her, the compulsion to touch her, the yearn to taste her… He had never wanted a woman more.

He breathed the fragrant scent of her hair in again then cupped her cheeks in his hands, his body almost touching hers, close enough to feel the tiny quivers vibrating through her.

Stark, frozen hazel eyes stared into his, her trembling lips parted but no sound coming out.

'I'm going to kiss you,' he said huskily. 'I'm going to kiss you until you tell me to stop.' Then, caressing her cheeks with his fingers, he pressed his lips to hers…

At first she remained stock still, not even breathing, her body like soft concrete. Slipping his hands round to spear her hair and cradle her head in much the same way she had cradled his what now felt like a lifetime ago, he moulded his mouth a little more firmly to hers, gently coaxing her into a response he knew she was fighting with everything she had.

Stubbornly, she continued to resist, her body still rigid, her soft plump lips refusing to move with his. But she didn't push him away or tell him to stop.

Emboldened, he gently moved his mouth over hers and ran a hand down the length of her back.

He felt her give the tiniest of shivers.

Then she took the tiniest of breaths.

And she still didn't push him away or tell him to stop.

He pressed himself a little closer, trapping her against the worktop.

She gasped into his mouth then quickly closed her own again but made no effort to break away from his kiss.

And still she didn't push him away or tell him to stop.

His mouth still covering hers, Andreas brushed his hands lightly down her sides and clasped her hips, then in one movement broke the kiss to lift her onto the worktop. Her hands sprang to life and grabbed his arms as if to steady herself.

Her eyes fluttered open.

For a moment that passed like an age, they stared into each other's eyes, Carrie's hooded gaze pulsing dazed desire at him. The hands holding his biceps like a vice loosened but she didn't let go.

Suddenly desperate to feel the softness of her lips against his again, he crushed his mouth to hers and gently pushed her thighs apart through the fabric of her skirt and stepped into the space he'd just created so the unmistakable feel of his arousal pressed against her pelvis, obvious even with all the layers of thin clothing separating them.

Her breaths were now coming in sharp ragged motions, her sweet yet coffee-laced scent whispering over his mouth and seeping into his pores, but still she made no effort to kiss him back.

And nor did she push him away or tell him to stop.

And nor did she push him away or tell him to stop when he found the hem of her top and slipped his hand under it.

The texture of her skin was silkier and softer than he remembered, as if some benevolent creator had wrapped her in satin.

Needing to kiss more than just her mouth, he dragged his lips over her cheeks and jaw then made a trail down her neck, the scent of her flesh firing into senses already fit to burst.

He was fit to burst. Never—*never*—had he felt sensation and heat like this and it was everywhere in him, from his heart that battered against his ribs to his loins that weren't aching, they were burning.

And never had he felt he would give all his worldly goods to receive just one kiss.

Carrie was letting him kiss her. She was letting him touch her. But she was giving nothing back. She was clinging onto that last ounce of stubborn denial for dear life.

But still she didn't push him away or tell him to stop.

He brushed his lips over her mouth again and nuzzled his nose against hers. His hands swept over her back then moved to her belly, which quivered under his touch as it had when she had kissed him on his veranda. She jolted again when his fingers brushed the underside of her breast, her own fingers tightening reflexively on his arm, but this time she made no attempt to escape.

For a moment he thought fevered wishful thinking had imagined her rubbing her pelvis tighter to his until he heard her swallow between the shallow breaths and her fingers tighten on him again.

Cradling her head in his hand, he tilted her back a little to stare deep into her eyes.

She stared back mutely, everything those stubborn, beautiful lips wanted to say, everything she was feeling reflecting back at him.

Wordlessly he brought his other hand up to her throat then slowly dragged it down, over the breasts he longed to touch without a barrier, feeling the heavy beats of her heart through it, skipping over her quivering belly, down her thighs until he could reach no further and he gathered the material of her skirt into his fist. Then, working slowly, he brought it up to her knee before letting the skirt go so it covered his hand, which now rested on her bare thigh.

Her left hand still gripped his biceps, her right hand…

Her right hand was now splayed on his abdomen, the heat from her touch penetrating through his shirt.

Andreas gritted his teeth. He wanted nothing more than to escape the straightjacket his clothes had become but instinct told him to wait just a little longer…and Carrie pressed her pelvis into his again, her body making spasmodic movements, her lips parting as if readying herself for his kiss again…

He obliged, covering her mouth with his. He felt the lightest of movement beneath it before she clamped her lips back together and turned her head to rub her soft cheek against his. Her fingers on his abdomen had slipped around to splay across his back in short grabbing motions.

He traced his fingers further up her thigh until he found the heat he was seeking and brushed his thumb against the damp, burning cotton.

She jerked against him, the hand holding his lapel moving up and gripping his neck. When he slid his hand under the cotton and found the damp, downy hair that covered her most intimate secret, she jerked again and pressed her cheek even tighter against his.

He slid his fingers lower and discovered her in full bloom, the feminine complement to the painful constriction in his underwear.

Closing his eyes to everything but this moment, he breathed her in as he continued to touch her, finding a rhythm with his fingers that had her grinding against him, her breaths so shallow and rapid he couldn't distinguish where one breath started and another began until she flung herself tightly against him and buried her face in his neck, crying out. Shudders rocked through her frame as she clung to him, her breaths rapid and hot in his neck.

Andreas, his cheek pressed into her hair, now had both arms wrapped around her, stroking her back.

And she held him tightly too.

'Don't say it.' Her words were spoken into his neck but then she shifted and loosened her hold on him, disentangling herself to cup *his* face with *her* hands. Dark, ringing hazel eyes beseeched him. 'Please, don't say it.'

He gave a short, sharp shake of his head. Blood roared in his ears, his chest the tightest he had ever known it.

Even if she hadn't asked, he couldn't look at her and smugly say, *See, I knew you wanted me.*

That had been the most erotic, mind-blowing and... *touching* moment of his life, and he would never diminish it.

Her eyes still gazing into his, she swallowed then slowly brought her face closer and covered his lips with her own.

It was the sweetest, most tender kiss of his life.

And then her lips parted, her tongue danced into his mouth, her arms locked around his neck and he was kissing her back with all the passion his soul possessed.

Carrie shut off the part of her brain shouting at her in increasingly terrified shrill tones to stop this madness *now*.

She shut it down completely.

She had never felt so alive, had never known her body capable of such intense, concentrated pleasure.

He had done this to her. Andreas. His touch, his scent... him. It was as if every part of her body had been tuned to a frequency only he had the dial to.

She had fought her desire with everything she had and it hadn't been enough. He'd broken through her resistance completely. And now she wanted the rest of it and she wanted him to have the pleasure he had just bestowed on her too.

He tasted so darkly masculine, she thought headily, as she drank in his kisses and razed her fingers up and down the nape of his neck. Why fight something that felt so right? Just what was she scared *of*?

But she had to shut her mind off again when the shrill voice tried to break back through to tell her exactly what she was scared of.

She was giving her body to Andreas, nothing more. Nothing more…

For the first time in her life she was going to let her body guide her. Consequences only happened when people allowed foolish dreams to overtake their reality.

Dimly she was aware of him gathering her tightly to him and lifting her off the worktop.

Later, she would have no concrete memory of them getting to a bedroom, just floating images of being carried in his arms and them falling onto the nearest bed in a tangle of limbs.

Their eyes locked.

Carrie lifted her top up and over her head, discarding it without thought.

His throat moved before he held out a hand.

With fingers that fumbled with inexperience, she undid his shirt buttons. As soon as she had the first three opened she put her lips to his chest and breathed in his clean musky scent, a pulse rippling through to her core when he groaned. His skin felt so smooth yet so different from her own, hard where she was soft and so very warm. Brushing her lips all over his chest, rubbing her cheek against the fine hair covering much of it, feeling his raging heartbeat thrum through his skin, she worked the rest of the buttons until the shirt was undone and Andreas shrugged it off, then his arms wrapped around her waist to undo her bra. He flung it away and sat back to stare at her naked breasts for the first time.

His eyes dilated, a moan dragged from his throat. He raised a hand that belied the faintest tremor and cupped her.

A bolt of need pulsed through her, so pure and so shockingly strong that she snapped her eyes shut and struggled for air.

Breasts that had always just…been there, a part of her like her arms and legs, suddenly felt heavy and swollen and needy. He massaged them gently then replaced his hand with his mouth.

She gasped and clenched her hands into fists.

All those wonderful feelings he had brought about in her such a short time ago were building up again but this time they felt so much more, the need being evoked no longer concentrated but *everywhere*, every part of her aching for his touch and yearning for his kiss.

As if he could sense her need, Andreas stripped off the rest of her clothes, trailing hot moist kisses all over her flesh, increasing her hunger.

Her skirt was unbuttoned and pulled off, thrown to the floor, the plain cotton knickers quickly following and then she was naked, lying fully exposed to a man's gaze for the first time in her life.

Andreas stared down at her, his eyes a colour she had never seen before, dark and molten. He'd removed his trousers—how, *when*?—and now all that was left to remove was his underwear.

Not taking her eyes from his, Carrie sat up to kneel before him and placed her hands on his heavily breathing chest. She dragged her fingers slowly down, over the hard muscles of his abdomen, to the band of his snug-fitting grey boxers.

Swallowing the moisture that had filled her mouth, she gripped the band between her fingers and tugged them down over his hips.

Released from its tight confines, his erection sprang free.

She swallowed again, unable to hide her shock.

The glimpse she had seen when he'd been in the bath... that had been nothing to seeing it loud and proud in the flesh. She'd already gauged that he was well endowed but had been unprepared, not only for his size but also the unexpected beauty of it.

She looked back into his eyes and drank him in, a languid, floaty feeling seeping through her. *How could it have been anything but beautiful when it belonged to the most beautiful man in the world?*

The molten eyes seemed to drink her right in too. He took her hand and brought it to his lips, then gently lowered it down to his erection, holding her loosely enough that she could snatch her hand away if she wanted.

She did not want to snatch it away, she thought dreamily. She *wanted* to touch it. Tonight, she wanted everything.

Letting him guide her, she took it into her hand and felt it throb beneath her fingers.

He moaned, his throat moving.

With his hand covering hers, showing her without words how he liked to be touched, she followed his lead. Thrills raced through her to hear his tortured groans and see the ragged movements of his chest. She could feel the heat bubbling inside her, every bit as turned on with what she was doing and the effect it was having on him as she had been when he'd been touching her.

She didn't hide her disappointment when he suddenly pulled her hand away.

He speared her hair and brought his face to hers to growl, 'I want to come inside *you*.' And then he kissed her, a kiss so deep and passionate she felt her bones turn to heated liquid.

The kiss was over all too soon as he pulled away from her and climbed off the bed. Stepping out of his boxers, he grabbed his trousers and pulled out his wallet. From it, he removed a small box of condoms.

He flashed her a tortured grin. 'I have been living in hope, *matia mou*.'

He was back by her side on the bed before she could blink.

He dropped the box on the pillow and pinned her down beneath him, kissing her again, her mouth, her cheeks, her neck, his hands roaming her body, muttering words she didn't understand into her ear but which added to the sensations already consuming her. The weight of his erection lay heavy on her thigh and she made to touch it again but he grabbed her wrist to stop her.

'Later,' he whispered hoarsely. 'You can do whatever you want to me later but right now I need to be inside you.'

She kissed him, sweeping her tongue into his mouth, letting him know with her body how badly she needed him inside her too.

It didn't matter that this was something she had never done before. She hadn't done *any* of this before, had spent her adult life denying herself something so beautiful and… *necessary*. Not any more.

Keeping his body so deliciously flush on hers, he groped for the packet and quickly extracted a square foil from it, which he ripped open with his teeth. Then he shifted slightly onto his side and deftly sheathed himself.

His mouth found hers again as he twisted back to lie on top of her, using his thighs to nudge her legs a little further apart so his erection was right there…

He entered her with one driving thrust, plunging her straight into a world where heaven and hell collided.

Hell; the sharp pain she hadn't expected and that made her suck in a shocked breath…and which Andreas either felt or sensed because he stilled.

'Carrie?' He lifted his head a little to look at her, confusion appearing in the molten depths of his eyes.

But already her body was adjusting to the feel of him inside her, the pain already diminished.

She smiled and tilted her chin to press her mouth to his. For long moments they simply touched lips together and breathed each other in. Then she closed her eyes as he began to move, and then…

Then she found herself in heaven.

He made love to her slowly, his thrusts tempered. His hands held hers tightly as he ground his groin against hers, stimulating her as he filled her.

Yes, she had found heaven.

Then he raised himself onto his elbows to lock eyes with her, causing the stimulation to deepen in rhythm with his deepening thrusts. Sensation pulsed like bolts of lightning in her core, a burning need growing and intensifying.

Wrapping her arms tightly around him, she ran her hands down his back exulting in the feel of his muscles and sweat-slicked skin beneath her fingers, then closed her eyes to everything but the sensations taking control, submitting to them, submitting to the pleasure and magic of everything they were creating together until the lightning exploded.

Pleasure shattered through her like a tsunami, bolts tearing down her spine and into her every crevice with an intensity that sent white light flickering behind her eyes and a cry from her mouth that sounded distant with the drumming in her ears.

Electricity danced on her and through her, almost stunning her. She held onto Andreas as if he were an anchor in this world, a dim acceptance that this was all because of him and only him, that there could never be another...

His lips crashed onto hers as he gave a roar that seemed to have been dredged from his very soul and drove into her for one last powerful thrust that made him shudder with the force of his own release.

Shocked eyes fell on hers before he gave one last groan and lowered himself onto her with his full weight, and buried his face in her hair.

Carrie tightened her hold on him, sighing to feel his breath tickling her scalp.

The sensation that had erupted through her with such violence was now a gentle ripple and she closed her eyes, wishing with all her heart that she could bottle this moment for eternity.

CHAPTER TEN

ANDREAS AWOKE ON his side to find Carrie's face pressed against his chest, an arm and thigh slung around him.

He also awoke to find himself fully aroused.

He took a deep breath and rolled onto his back, careful not to disturb her sleep. She rolled with him, her face now buried in his side, her hand drifting to rest on his abdomen.

The room was shrouded in such darkness he knew without having to look that he'd slept for many hours. He smiled ruefully to know he'd done that most male of male things and fallen asleep almost immediately after sex.

Yes, a most male of male things but not something he had ever done before. But then, he had never known sex to be like that before, an experience so intense that climaxing had felt as if his brains might explode from his head. He'd made it to the bathroom to dispose of the condom then fallen back into bed, scooped Carrie into his arms to cuddle against her, and fallen straight into blissful sleep. The evening had still been light outside.

He'd never done that before either: fallen asleep with his arms wrapped so tightly around someone.

He had good reason to believe Carrie had never done any of this before.

The little spot of blood he'd seen on the sheets when

he'd climbed back into bed had only consolidated what his body had told him when he'd first entered her.

Carrie had been a virgin.

He hadn't bedded a virgin since he'd lost his own virginity. Then, they had both been seventeen and full of raging hormones. He'd promised faithfully to marry her if she slept with him, a blatant lie told by horny teenage boys the world over. They'd given each other their virginity and afterwards he'd ridden off on his scooter, cigarette dangling from his mouth, feeling like a king.

He smiled at the memory. He hadn't thought of Athena for years. She'd dumped him for one of his friends a few weeks later, which he was sure had broken his heart for at least five minutes. As far as he knew, Athena and Stavros were still married with an army of children running them ragged.

He was quite sure she was the last virgin he'd been with. The irony of him actually marrying the second virgin he slept with after promising to do that faithfully with the first did not escape him.

He ran a hand gently over Carrie's hair, smoothing it, enjoying the silky feel of it on his skin.

What had made her wait so long?

To have missed out on those heady teenage years where hormones dictated every part of your life? No office romances either? He kept a strict hands-off rule with his staff but he didn't expect them to keep their hands off each other. So long as it didn't interfere with their work he couldn't care less what the consenting adults he employed got up to.

Had Carrie been waiting for someone special?

He brushed his finger along her cheek, his chest tightening to imagine the myriad reasons why she had chosen to remain a virgin and what the implications for them were.

She stirred against him and nuzzled into his chest. Her movements were enough to tighten the other, much baser part of him that had already been wide awake and aroused and when her fingers began to drift lightly down his abdomen...

Minutes later and he was inside her again.

Carrie was awake for a long time before she dared move. She was pretty sure she had the huge bed to herself. The heat that had enveloped her throughout the night had gone.

Eventually she plucked up the courage to slowly roll over and confirm what her instincts were telling her.

Andreas had left the room.

She stared at the indentation on his pillow and was horrified to find tears filling her eyes.

Quickly she averted her gaze to the ceiling and breathed raggedly through her mouth, a hand on her chest, blinking frantically as she fought the tears back.

What had she done?

Oh, dear God, what had she *done*?

She had slept with him. Not once, but three times.

She had become someone new in his arms. She'd felt like a beautiful butterfly that had emerged from its cocoon for the very first time and found its wings.

Andreas had taken her to paradise but now, with the early morning light streaming through the shutters, paradise seemed as distant as the moon. Now she wanted to find her old cocoon and crawl back inside it.

What was the protocol for dealing with this? *Was* there a protocol lovers kept to when seeing each other for the first time after making love?

Lovers?

Heat suffused her everywhere and she covered her face with both hands, fighting back the sobs desperate to break out.

She didn't want to be Andreas's lover. She didn't want to be anything to him, not his fake fiancée, not his fake wife, not anything…

The door opened.

As quick as lightning, she turned back onto her side and squeezed her eyes shut.

If she pretended to be asleep maybe he would leave her alone.

Footsteps padded over the floor tiles. New scents filled the room. Coffee. Fresh bread.

She heard another door slide open and cool air filled the room.

A minute later the bed dipped. A hand brushed against her hair.

She couldn't stop her shoulders moving in reflex at his touch.

Holding her breath as tightly as she held the sheets around her, she rolled onto her back.

Andreas was sitting on the edge of the bed wearing nothing but a pair of jeans.

His eyes were on her, a wariness underlying the intensity of his stare. 'Good morning,' he said quietly.

She managed the semblance of a smile but couldn't get her throat, echoing with the vibrations of her hammering heart, to move enough to speak.

'I've got breakfast for us,' he said after an impossibly long period of silence between them during which they did nothing but stare at each other. 'It's on the balcony.'

She hadn't known this room had a balcony.

She didn't even know what room they were in. It certainly wasn't the one she'd been given.

'Give me a minute to get changed and I'll join you out there,' she whispered.

His eyes narrowed slightly before he nodded and got to his feet.

She watched him step out onto the balcony, sliding the glass door shut behind him. Only when he was out of her eyeline did she slide out of the bed and snatch her discarded clothes from the floor. She found the en-suite and locked the door behind her.

Barely twelve hours ago she had felt not a modicum of shyness in showing her naked body to him. He had kissed and touched every single part of her and she had thrilled at the sensual pleasure of it, a pleasure she had never imagined; seductive and addictive.

She had been drunk with it all. Drunk on Andreas.

Now she wished for nothing but to hide back in her protective cocoon and forget it had happened.

Throwing her clothes on, she splashed her face with water and smoothed her hair as best she could with her fingers, trying not to look too hard at her reflection in the mirror so she couldn't see the bruised look of her lips or the glow on her skin that had never been there before.

Andreas was eating a Greek breakfast pastry when she joined him on the balcony.

'Coffee?' he asked amiably.

'Yes please.' She sat opposite him and looked at the huge spread laid out between them. 'Did you do all this?'

'Of course not. I called the chefs in and got them to make it.' The mockingly outraged face he pulled as he said this, that *How dare you even suggest I soil my hands by preparing my own food?* expression, tickled her and she found herself fighting back a grin.

But then she met his eye and the smile formed of its own accord. Not a full grin, but her lips loosened enough to curve a touch.

His features relaxed to see it. He pushed her cup of

coffee to her then leaned back. 'Eat something. You must be starving.'

That reminded her of their missed dinner. And his roses...

'What's wrong?' Andreas asked, seeing her brow suddenly furrow.

'Those poor roses. I never...' She dropped her gaze from his and snatched a bread roll, opening it with her fingers.

He knew exactly what had caused her face to look as if she'd been dipped in tomato juice and his loins twitched to remember lifting her onto the worktop, the roses abandoned, and all that had followed.

And what had followed had been one of the best nights of his life. Maybe the best. He couldn't think of a better one.

'The housekeeper has revived them,' he assured her, remembering the way Carrie had rubbed her nose against the petals when she'd taken them from him.

She'd rubbed her nose over his stomach in the exact same way...

The twitch in his loins turned into a throb, the memory of her nails digging into his back as she'd orgasmed strong enough that he could feel the indentations on his skin as fresh as if she were making them still.

'That's good,' she said, nodding a little too vigorously. She stretched for the jar of honey with a hand that trembled and said in a voice so low he had to strain to hear her, fresh colour smothering her entire face, 'Does she know I, err, we, slept in the wrong room?'

'It doesn't matter, *matia mou.*'

'She needs to know.' She struggled to remove the lid. 'When we're gone someone else will stay here. The sheets...'

'Carrie.'

She stopped talking and reluctantly met his gaze, eyes shining with what looked suspiciously like unshed tears, her chin wobbling.

She'd been a virgin.

Until twelve hours ago she had reached the age of twenty-six untouched.

He could not shake that thought from his mind.

'Let me open that for you,' he said gently, nodding at the honey jar clasped so tightly in her hand.

She pushed it across the table to him, her shoulders slumping.

He twisted the lid off and pushed it back to her, resisting the urge to force her to take it from his hand.

She had been a virgin.

She had never made love before.

She had never faced a man the morning after before.

The vulnerability he had seen in her when he'd given her the flowers was even more starkly apparent now and it tugged at his heart to see it and with it came a compression in his chest, an overwhelming punch of emotion he couldn't begin to comprehend but which set alarm bells ringing inside him, a warning that he was steering into dangerous territory and it was time to back away.

'There is no wrong or right room here because the villa is mine,' he said in as even a tone as he could manage.

She darted a little glance of gratitude at him before dipping a teaspoon into the honey jar. 'What do you mean?'

'I signed the paperwork for it yesterday. That's where I went after I dropped you here, to meet with the previous owner.'

'You bought it? But why?'

He shrugged. 'I was looking for a villa to rent for the week. I didn't see anything I liked so I looked at villas for sale and this was available.'

'You bought a villa on a whim? Without even looking at it?' She spread the honey on her roll.

'I saw the pictures. I know the island pretty well—I've had an eye on buying something here for a while. I knew it was in a good location with plenty of privacy. Why not?'

'You already have a holiday home.'

'This will not be a holiday home for me, not like my property in the Seychelles. I can work from here. Agon is a prosperous, independent country with a growing economy. It has many residents looking to invest their cash. It is close enough to fly or speedboat to Athens. It has staff familiar with the house and I get to speak my native tongue for a change. It ticks all the boxes and best of all it has year-round sunshine.'

'Why do you run your business from London?' she asked. 'You clearly hate the city.'

'I don't hate it. In the summertime it is beautiful but the rest of the year it is so grey and dreary. I grew up with the sun on my back. But to answer your question, London was never my first choice to run my business from. When I was younger I wanted to live in America. That's why I went to university there. I had many ideas in my head about what America was like and assumed it had year-round sunshine like my home in Gaios.' He grinned, remembering his youthful naivety and lack of geography skills.

Her lips twitched with humour as she took a bite of her honey-slathered roll.

The tension in her frame was loosening.

'The winters in Massachusetts came as quite a shock, I can tell you,' he continued. 'When I graduated from MIT I was offered a job with an investment firm in Manhattan who were offering an obscene amount of money for a graduate. As you know, that's when my parents were on their knees, financially speaking, so I took the job, worked hard and built many contacts so I could strike out on my own, and tried not to freeze to death in the dire winters. When I started Samaras Fund Management, my intention had been to build the American side up then set up European headquarters in Athens. London and the other European capitals would have been subsidiaries. I'd reached the point where I was earning serious money, my parents were in reasonable health and settled in their new home...'

'Did you buy it for them?' she interrupted, eyes alive with curiosity.

'As soon as I could afford it. They didn't want to stay in Gaios any more, which I could not blame them for after the way they had been treated by the people there, so I brought them a house on Paros. We all thought the worst of what life could throw at us was over and then my sister and brother-in-law died.'

Carrie sucked a breath in.

Andreas said it so matter-of-factly that if she hadn't seen the flash of pain in his eyes she could believe his sister's death had meant nothing to him.

'It was carbon monoxide poisoning, wasn't it?' she asked softly.

He nodded, his jaw clenching. 'They were on holiday celebrating their wedding anniversary. The apartment they were staying in had a faulty boiler.'

She remembered reading the inquest report and wanting to cry for Natalia, their orphaned daughter, a girl Carrie had welcomed into her home and loved fiercely. Violet hadn't been the only one hurt when Natalia stopped staying at their home. Carrie had missed her too, missed the sunshine the girl had brought to their home.

In the year before the expulsion it had been rare for Violet to be at home without Natalia. Had that been why Carrie had failed to see how badly off the rails Violet was falling, because Natalia's cheerfulness and sweet nature had masked it?

But hadn't Carrie herself noticed the sunniness in her demeanour wilting those last few months before Violet's expulsion? A strain in both girls' eyes she had put down to teenage hormones.

Natalia had been so comfortable in their home. She would make herself drinks if she was thirsty, help herself to cereal if hungry…

Natalia would never have dropped Violet like a stone if something major hadn't occurred. If she'd wanted to keep seeing Violet she would have done; not even a strict uncle could have kept her from making contact if that had been what she wanted.

But she hadn't wanted to contact Violet because Andreas had been speaking the truth.

Violet had tried to seduce him, had punched Natalia in the face and blamed Andreas for her expulsion in revenge and, Carrie deduced, her mind ticking frantically, ice plunging into her veins, because she hadn't wanted to admit to the one person in the world who loved her that she had bought the drugs herself, and admit what she was becoming. An addict.

Violet had lied to save face and for misplaced revenge against the man who'd rejected her advances. Her vengeance was misplaced because the man she'd truly wanted to get back at, namely the vile specimen who had taken her virginity on her sixteenth birthday, had become unreachable. In Violet's mind at that moment, Andreas had been interchangeable with James; two rich, handsome men of a similar age. The expulsion, her desperate, wanton behaviour in the months leading to her expulsion…

Caught in her reckless heartache, Violet had managed to discredit herself without even trying. No one in their right mind would believe her story about the fabulously rich, media-friendly James Thomas grooming and seducing her. No one other than her big sister.

The ice in her veins had moved like freezing sludge to her brain.

Carrie had never followed a story without some initial proof. Violet had produced plenty of proof against James; blurry photos on her phone taken slyly when he hadn't been looking and screenshot messages—he'd been clever enough to insist on using apps where messages deleted themselves after being read but not clever enough to guess a lovestruck teenager would still find a way to save them.

There had been no proof against Andreas. Not a shred.

Carrie had gone after him on nothing but her damaged sister's word and that word had been a lie.

'Carrie?'

She blinked and looked into the eyes of the man she had tried to ruin.

'Are you okay? You are very pale.'

How could he even bear to *look* at her, never mind with concern?

She could still feel his touch on her skin, his kisses on her lips. He had made love to her as if she were the only woman in the world.

He should hate her.

He probably *did* hate her.

She hated herself.

What she had done…

Her chest had tightened so much it hurt to draw breath.

She needed to speak to Violet, she thought, as fresh panic clawed at her chest. There was still the chance Carrie might be wrong. She couldn't condemn her sister without giving her the chance to defend herself.

'I'm fine,' she managed to say. 'I was just thinking of Natalia.'

And I was thinking that you are not the monster I've been telling myself you are for the past three years.

This conversation they were having...

Andreas had started it to calm her down.

He knew she'd been a virgin. He'd known it the moment he entered her. He could have chosen to embarrass her about it and demand to know why she, a seemingly confident twenty-six-year-old woman, had spent her adult life as a singleton.

Instead he had given her a way to face being with him without making her burn with humiliation.

'Did you move to London for her?' she added.

He gave her another narrow-eyed unconvinced look before nodding. 'My sister used to read all those wizarding books to her. Natalia thought all boarding schools were like that and asked if she could go.' He smiled though his eyes saddened at the memory. 'I could afford it so I offered to pay the fees for any school my sister thought suitable. They chose London. I bought Tanya and Georgios a house close to the school so Natalia could spend weekends with them. When they died I moved to London and kept Natalia at her school. I couldn't put her through any more disruption.'

So he had uprooted his own life instead and moved to a city he didn't particularly like with a climate he hated.

'Is that what you meant when you said you'd spent fifteen years waiting for your freedom and that another six months wouldn't make any difference? Because you'd had to make your parents your priority and then your niece?'

'Natalia is at university, my parents are happy and settled and have all the home help they need... Now I want to spend as many of my days as I can where the sun shines and live my life as I please.' The wolfish grin she'd once so hated but now tugged at her heart curved on his lips, the gleam returning to his eyes. 'And if delaying my freedom for another six months means I get to see your beautiful face every day then it will make the delay a little sweeter.'

She swallowed. 'How can it be sweet when I tried to destroy you?'

'Because living with me is the price you have to pay to put it right. When it is over we will be even.'

'And last night?' The question was out before she could take it back.

He gazed into her eyes a long time before answering. 'Last night was nothing to do with you putting things right. I make no apologies for desiring you and you should make no apologies for desiring me. Attraction is bound by no rational thought. I have wanted you from the minute you stepped into my office and my bedroom door will always be open to you. If you enter is up to you.'

The meaning in his eyes was clear.

Andreas would make no further move on her.

If their marriage was to be more than a piece of paper she would have to be the one to instigate it.

It was a thought that should make her feel safe but didn't. Not in the least.

One thing Carrie did know for certain, required no proof or corroborating evidence for, was that with Andreas her feelings were like kindling.

One touch and she turned into fire.

CHAPTER ELEVEN

ANDREAS'S NEWEST STAFF were true professionals. He'd taken Carrie out shopping in an exclusive enclave in Agon's capital, where an arcade of designer boutiques and chic cafés resided, tiny compared to London and Paris's exclusive areas but with staff who could smile without looking as if their bottoms were being sucked out of their cheeks and who treated their clientele as if it were a pleasure to serve rather than a chore.

When they'd returned to his newest acquisition late afternoon he'd found the garden transformed exactly as he'd asked before they'd left and the scent of charcoal filling the air.

'I thought you said you couldn't cook,' Carrie said accusingly when he'd added the two juicy steaks onto the newly built brick barbecue.

She was sitting at the garden table, lithe legs stretched out, wearing a strapless mint-green summer dress and a cream wrap around her shoulders to stave off the evening chill.

His senses told him she wore no bra under that dress.

'I can burn meat as well as any caveman,' he replied with a grin. 'Why don't you make yourself useful and get a bottle of wine from the fridge?'

'Because I'm not your skivvy any more?' she suggested.

'Do you not feel guilty that I'm doing all the work while you are sitting there doing nothing?'

'Nope.' She looked pointedly at the bowls of salads and rice that had been prepared for them by his new chefs and laid on the beautifully presented table.

The staff had all gone now.

'*Please?*' he asked pointedly.

She pretended to consider then got to her feet. 'Okay, then. Which wine do you want?'

'There's only one variety in the fridge.'

She bounded off into the villa, a spring in her step he'd never seen before.

It occurred to him that her jest about not being his skivvy any more had been the first time she'd alluded to those few days when he'd had her at his beck and call.

They had been on Agon for only three days and the change in her had been incredible. Yesterday they had explored Agon together, admiring the island's rich heritage and what Andreas considered to be the most beautiful palace in the world. They'd eaten out, their conversation light and non-confrontational but the wariness he'd been greeted with at breakfast had still vibrated from her rigid frame. She avoided his gaze. The few times their eyes had met colour had suffused her face and her top lip would pull in. When they'd returned to the villa she had mumbled a goodnight before disappearing—fleeing—to her bedroom.

He hadn't touched her once and he hadn't flirted with her either.

He wanted to make love to her again. He hadn't thought it would be possible to want it more than he had before but that was how it was, a constant ache, a constant fizz in his blood, a constant awareness of her every movement but her virginity had changed everything.

If they were to make love again Carrie had to make the

first move. He needed to know that what they were sharing came from her head as well as her body.

Today, she had greeted him at breakfast with a smile that had been undoubtedly genuine.

That smile had pierced into his chest.

When he had taken her shopping for a dress to wear for his cousin's wedding, he'd prepared himself for a fight. When he'd explained, keeping his tone even, that she was only attending the wedding because of him and therefore it was only right he pay for her dress she had taken him by surprise by actually agreeing.

She hadn't let him buy her anything else though, and he hadn't argued the point. Carrie had a fierce independent streak he admired even if he did find it infuriating. He no longer found it insulting. There was a reason for it and sooner or later he would discover what that was.

She reappeared with the wine at the exact moment he judged the steaks to be cooked.

At the table he put the steaks on their respective plates and sat down, reaching for the wine.

She surprised him again by allowing him to pour her a glass. The only alcohol she had shared with him had been his Scotch the night the truth had come out.

He held his glass out. *'Yamas.'* At her blank expression, he said, 'It means good health.'

She chinked her glass to his and took a sip of her wine. Her eyes widened a touch. 'I'm not a big fan of white wine but this is nice.'

'I should hope so for the price I paid for it,' he said drily. 'I have it imported directly to all my homes. This crate arrived while we were shopping.'

She had another sip. 'This really is lovely. And you have it imported to *all* your homes?'

He shook his head self-mockingly. 'I don't take drugs,

I no longer smoke…good quality wine and Scotch are my only vices.'

'You used to smoke?'

'Something else your investigations into me didn't reveal?'

As he finished the question with a wink, Carrie couldn't help but smile.

She could hardly believe they'd reached a place where they could *joke* about her attempts to investigate him. Both of them.

It was all down to Andreas. He'd rumbled her, had his fun while he punished her, then insisted she marry him to put things right but he wasn't holding a grudge. He wasn't one to hold a grudge but that, she suspected, was because he didn't need to. If a problem arose he fixed it straight away with whatever means he thought necessary.

He was no angel but by no means was he a monster like most of the rich men she'd dealt with through the years. When he wanted something done he expected it to be done immediately, patience was not his strong point, but he wasn't spoilt. Considering the wealth he'd accrued he was surprisingly grounded.

'I smoked when I was a teenager. I was obsessed with everything American and old seventies movies where the cool heroes always smoked and rode motorcycles. I wanted to be Steve McQueen.' He burst into laughter. 'The closest I could afford to a motorcycle was a beaten-up old scooter but cigarettes were easy to come by. I thought I was the coolest kid in Gaios, driving around on that pile of junk without a helmet and a cigarette hanging from my mouth. I turned my poor mother's hair white.'

His self-mockery and evident amusement were infectious and Carrie found herself laughing at the image he'd painted.

When she had set out on this endeavour she hadn't suspected for a minute that Andreas could be such good company. Their one conversation on the phone all those years ago had been short and to the point, his tone what you would expect if speaking to a bank manager. That one time she had seen him outside the headmistress's office he'd oozed menacing power. He'd frightened her.

Yes, Andreas had a dark side but she had come to realise that it only came out when people he loved were threatened.

What would it be like to be loved by this man...?

She would not allow her thoughts to go down that road.

Andreas was rich and powerful. He had charm and looks. He was everything she hated, everything she feared.

But he'd been honest about everything. He wanted his freedom. What they were sharing here, now, was pure circumstance. What she felt for him was a result of the forced proximity she'd been thrown into. When this was all over she would walk away. She wouldn't give this strange chemistry another thought. He would be out of sight and out of mind.

But right here and now he was in her sight and completely filling her mind.

Putting her knife and fork together, she pushed her plate away, put her elbow on the table and rested her chin on her hand. She'd eaten half of the steak he'd cremated for her but had no recollection of it, too caught up in listening to Andreas's staccato voice. 'You sound like you were a right tearaway as a child.'

'I was the bane of my parents' life,' he admitted unrepentantly, 'but also the apple of their eye so I got away with murder.'

'I was a good girl.'

'Really?' He topped their glasses up with more wine.

'Do you have to sound so surprised?'

He studied her as he sipped his wine, his own plate pushed aside too. 'No. I am not surprised.'

'Because I was a virgin?'

There. It had been said. The elephant that had parked itself between them had been acknowledged and the knot in her stomach loosened because of it.

The knot had become like a noose.

'It doesn't suggest a wild past,' he said slowly, his gaze on hers as he put his glass to his lips.

'I never had the chance to be wild,' she admitted. 'My mum was diagnosed with cancer when I was thirteen. I had Violet to look after—she's seven years younger than me—so I guess I supressed any teenage hormones that might have been primed to unleash. I comfort ate a lot. I never felt comfortable in my skin. It's funny because my mum was *beautiful*. Honestly, she was stunning. She'd be hooked up with drips and machines all around her and the doctors would flirt with her. Mind you, she flirted with them too. Men loved her.'

'Were you jealous of her?'

'No.' She shook her head as she thought about it. 'No, I felt sorry for her. She was married twice and had a string of boyfriends. None of them treated her well.'

'And you thought all men were like that?'

'No. I just thought she had terrible taste in men.'

Andreas laughed into his wine but his eyes read something other than amusement. There was compassion there, and something baser, the same something that had been there from the very start.

Carrie hadn't spoken about her mother for a long time and it felt good to do so now, brought her memory alive. Her darling mother had been a princess in Carrie's eyes, a woman who adored her two daughters and never shied from showing her love for them.

'There are some good men out there,' she said softly, staring into the hypnotic gaze that no longer frightened her. The meaning she read in it...it was nothing that she too didn't feel. She wanted Andreas, with a burning yen that had seeped into her soul. 'My grandfather was a good man. He was poor. Humble. Not flashy like the men my mother went for. She was like a magpie, always wanting the shiny pretty things. She could pick a rich man at ten paces and have him eating out of her hand with the flutter of her eyelashes.'

'So your father is a rich man?'

'Actually, he was the only poor one. He didn't even have a job—they were at school when they got together. Mum gave birth to me when she was seventeen.'

'You were an accident?'

'My mum always said I was the best accident in the world.' She would say it while planting kisses all over Carrie's face and tickling her ribs until they were both crying with laughter.

Andreas listened to Carrie open up about her life, watched those plump lips talking, feeling as if he had a fist pushed against his chest, pressing against his heart. Her hazel eyes shone in a way he had never seen before, her love for her mother shining through, dazzling him.

What would it be like to have those eyes shining with love for you...?

'They married when they discovered she was pregnant but split up not long after I was born,' she continued in that same, slow cadence, those shining eyes fixed on him, an openness in them he had never seen before. 'My dad moved away after they split up so I've never seen much of him but he's always remembered my birthday and makes a point of visiting a few times a year. I've always known he loves me.' A look of mischief flittered over her face. 'He's head gardener at the real Hargate Manor.'

He burst into great rumbles of laughter at this unexpected twist. 'It is a real place?'

Her lips puckered with sheepish amusement. 'I've been there a couple of times. It's a beautiful estate.'

Andreas drank some more wine and continued to stare at her. She mesmerised him. She'd mesmerised him from the moment she'd stepped into his office.

'*You're* beautiful,' he said throatily.

She tilted her head and smiled, a smile that stole his breath and made a man feel he could fly to the moon. 'You make me feel beautiful.'

A long, breathless moment passed between them as he gazed into eyes that shone with a hundred emotions.

Then she straightened, put her hands on the table and pushed her chair back.

She stood up, the wrap that had covered her shoulders sliding off and falling into a puddle at her feet. She didn't notice, a whole range of emotions flittering in hazel eyes that burned into him.

Slowly she trod towards him.

The air between them thickened in those few small movements and by the time she stood before him it crackled.

Andreas could no longer breathe.

Two elegant hands cradled his cheeks, delicate fingers rubbing against his skin. She leaned forward and pressed the tip of her nose to his.

Her eyelids closed and she breathed him in then her lips brushed his.

'You make me feel beautiful,' she repeated in a murmur into his mouth. The sweetness of the wine mingled with the sweetness of her breath and seeped right into his airways and through his veins.

Carrie had a taste that had been designed for him.

And it was *all* for him, he thought, the thickening in his loins a weighty ache. No other man had tasted her sweetness. And no other man would…

'You make me feel like a woman,' she whispered before her lips closed around his and she was kissing him, deep scorching kisses, her fingers sliding to cradle his head, everything a mimic of the night she had kissed him in the Seychelles but everything new.

This time there was no restraint. No pretence, no holding back, no hate, no anger.

Just two people with an unquenchable thirst for each other.

In one motion, he gathered her to him, pulling her onto his lap just as he had what seemed a lifetime ago and as he felt her bottom press into his lap, raw hunger slammed into him.

In a flurry of ravenous kisses her soft, pillowy breasts crushed against his chest, Carrie's fingers raked over his neck, over his shoulders, her nails scraping over his shirt, her hot tongue trailing over his cheeks and jaw, tasting him, her teeth biting into his skin, delicious jets of pleasure igniting everywhere.

And he touched her back with equal fervour, roaming his hands over the hot flesh that quivered and burrowed closer into him at his every touch, as if she were trying to burn their clothing off through willpower alone.

Somehow, with her chest crushed so tightly to his, she found the buttons on his shirt and opened them enough to burrow beneath the material to find his bare skin. Her fingers splayed all over his chest, nails raking his skin, scorching a trail of burning heat over him with her touch alone, her mouth devouring his again, her breaths shortening.

His mouth found her neck and he inhaled her earthy yet delicate scent, that erotic, womanly smell that was Carrie's alone.

When she found the waistband of his trousers, she didn't hesitate to tug at the button but when she couldn't undo it, cupped her hand over the tightly compressed erection and squeezed over the material.

He groaned into her neck at the constrained pleasure her touch there unleashed, then licked all the way up to her chin and her mouth.

Her eyes were open yet hooded. If a look ever had the power to make him come without a touch, the look ringing from her eyes would be it.

Holding her tightly, he lifted her in one motion and sat her on the table so he was standing between her parted thighs.

She stared at him, desire vibrating from her, then tugged the top of her dress down to her waist.

She wore no bra.

Her plump golden breasts shone under the rising moon. Spearing her hair as he cradled her head to support her, he lowered her back then dipped his head to take one of the pebbled nipples into his mouth.

The gasp that flew from her mouth turned into a moan as he slavered her with his attention, kissing, nipping, licking.

Her legs hooked around his waist, gyrating herself closer to him, her ankles digging into his buttocks as her back arched, her need for him as beautifully obvious as the emerging stars above them.

When he ran a hand over one of her clinging thighs and slid higher to her buttocks, he was the one to moan when he found her hot and damp. She jerked against him, trying to find whatever relief she could get.

Abandoning her breasts, he kissed her hard on her mouth and she matched it, a violent fever spreading between them as he pinched the sides of her knickers with his fingers and she raised her bottom to allow him to pull them down to her hips.

With one final clash of mouth and tongue, he then tugged her knickers down her legs and past her pretty feet, threw them onto the floor and removed his wallet from his back pocket. As he took the square foil out, Carrie returned to undoing his trousers, this time unbuttoning it with one flick of her fingers and tugging the zip down.

As he took the condom out of its wrapping she tugged his trousers down his hips, freeing his erection.

There was not a moment of hesitation.

Andreas slipped the condom on in one deft movement, hooked an arm around her waist to pull her to him, and thrust himself inside her.

Tight and hot, she welcomed him, pulling him deeper inside her, the look in her eyes as he stared into them sinking him deeper into her spell.

She slipped a hand around his waist and up his shirt, her nails biting into his skin, urging him on, their lovemaking hot and frenzied, tender and hard all at the same time, and then she was grabbing his buttocks to drive him even harder into her, mumbled, sensual words flying incoherently from her lips until her head tilted back. A ragged cry escaped her mouth and then she was thickening around him, clinging to him and Andreas found himself slamming headlong into the ecstasy of his own release, brighter, sharper and more intense than anything he had ever known before.

As he held her protectively, waiting for the shudders vibrating through both their bodies to lessen and the heavy beats of their echoing hearts to subside, a fierce possessiveness grabbed at his chest, words floating in his head he couldn't shake.

Carrie was his.

CHAPTER TWELVE

CARRIE APPLIED HER mascara for the third time and willed her hand to stop shaking and poking the wand in her eye.

The nerves she was feeling were almost as bad as when she'd waited in the reception room to be taken in to Andreas for the first time.

His cousin was getting married in three hours. Andreas had gone to collect his parents and niece from the airport and drop them at the hotel where the evening reception would be held. The whole family was staying at the hotel, Carrie and Andreas included. Apparently it was a Samaras tradition for the bride and groom to have their first breakfast as a married couple with their family all looking at them and knowing exactly what they'd been getting up to in the marital bed.

Thank goodness she and Andreas were marrying in a Chelsea registry office. It would be just them and a couple of witnesses.

She was terrified of meeting his parents but even more scared of seeing Natalia again. It scared her even more than having to pretend to everyone that she and Andreas were in the throes of a whirlwind love affair.

A whirlwind lust affair she could easily fake, mainly because that wouldn't involve any fakery.

She could hardly keep her hands off him.

She didn't know exactly when the shift in her thinking had occurred, just knew that as she'd changed for dinner after their shopping trip, she'd looked in her mirror and asked herself what she was so afraid of. Why fight something so pleasurable? Why deny them both? She'd slipped her dress on and closed her eyes, remembering his touch on her skin.

Carrie had discovered the joys of sex. Twenty-six years of a dormant libido had been unleashed and now her body was making up for lost time on all it had missed out on.

She told herself that on an hourly basis.

The good news was that she had a full six months to get all this making up out of her system because she couldn't quite quell the fear that her body only reacted this way because of Andreas. *For* Andreas.

But as she also continually told herself, if it was only him she reacted this way to, then so what? It was still only sex, glorious, blissful sex.

Ta da. Her make-up was done. Third time lucky.

Her phone rang.

She grinned to remember how Andreas had deliberately kept her incommunicado when she had first infiltrated his life. It was one of the reasons he'd chosen to take her to the Seychelles, because the signal on his peninsular was so dire.

Her grin dropped when she saw her sister's name flash up.

Carrie had left three messages for her in the past week. She'd bitten back the hurt to find herself being ignored again. Violet had always been good at ignoring her if she didn't want to speak.

Taking a deep breath, she answered it. 'Hi, Vee. How are you?'

Silence.

'Are you there?'

'Is it true?'

Carrie's heart sank. 'Is what true?'

'That you're seeing Andreas Samaras.'

She took another deep breath. 'Yes. It's true.'

And it's all because of you and the lies you told.

'You know what he did to me, right?' After only three months in California her sister had picked up an American twang.

'Violet... Are you still seeing the counsellor?'

'Answer my question.'

'I will when you answer mine. Please, tell me you're still seeing him.'

'Her. My counsellor's a her.'

'I'm sorry. I thought you were seeing a man.'

'I was.' The stiff angry tone suddenly changed. Became softer. 'We decided I would find it easier to talk to a woman.'

'And are you finding it easier?'

'Yes.' She sounded surprised. 'I am. She's really nice and non-judgemental.'

Carrie tried not to take that as a dig against herself. 'I'm glad.'

'Now you answer my question. You know what that man did to me?'

'He didn't do anything to you, did he, Vee?' she said gently, her heart thumping, mouth dry. 'He didn't do what you accused him of. He didn't set you up. The drugs were yours. Vee, it doesn't change how I feel about you. I still love you.'

All that played in her ear was silence but she knew her sister was still there.

'I'm sorry you felt you couldn't trust me enough to tell me the truth but please, I beg you, admit the truth to yourself. Talk it through with your counsellor. You were treated terribly by James but Andreas isn't James. He is nothing like him.

'Violet… I love you. I forgive you. Now, please, find a way to forgive yourself.'

This time the silence on the other end was the silence of a disconnected line.

Violet had hung up on her.

'Was that your sister?'

Carrie jumped and spun around.

She hadn't heard Andreas come in. Normally she was very attuned to his movements around the villa but she had been so engrossed with her one-sided conversation with Violet that she hadn't heard him return.

He was standing in the doorway, his black tuxedo on minus the jacket, a sombre expression on his handsome face.

She nodded.

'What you said…you believe me.'

She nodded again.

'Since when?'

'Since you told me,' she whispered before hanging her head in shame. 'I just couldn't admit it. Violet is my Achilles heel. She always has been.'

He paused before asking, 'Why is she seeing a counsellor?'

'Because she's a drug addict.'

Suddenly she could hold it in no longer. She slumped onto her dressing room chair and burst into tears.

The tightness Andreas had experienced when he'd listened to Carrie say she believed him, to hear her defending him, became a tight ball to see her dissolve before his eyes.

These weren't tears, these were racking sobs, each one tearing his soul.

In three strides he was before her, crouching on his haunches to cradle her head on his shoulder, stroking her back, her tears soaking through his shirt.

It was a long time before the sobs lessened and she removed her face from his shoulder and wiped it with her hands.

Red-rimmed hazel eyes fixed on him and she inhaled deeply. 'My sister is a drug addict. She is in recovery in America, living with her father because one of her drug dealers beat her into a coma when she couldn't pay her tab.' The tears filled her eyes again, spilling over to race down her cheeks, shoulders shaking. 'She nearly died. My baby sister nearly died.'

Stunned at this revelation, Andreas took a moment to process it.

'That bastard didn't just seduce her. He fed her drugs. He gave an innocent girl a drug addiction.' She covered her mouth then dropped her hand as she gave a long, ragged exhalation. 'I must have been blind. I had no idea how bad her addiction was until a few months after her expulsion.' Her lips made a little grimace of distaste. 'I found her in bed with a much older man. There were drugs on the floor…she denied it but I knew she'd had sex with him in exchange for the drugs. She had no other money. Her father had cut her allowance off when she got expelled; she'd been able to afford her own until then. I was only a recent graduate and not earning very much. She had no money and absolutely refused to get a job.'

He got to his feet and ran a hand through his hair, kneading his scalp. 'Why wasn't she at school?'

'Because she'd been expelled,' she reminded him.

'I know but she could have gone to another school after she'd taken her exams.'

'She wasn't allowed to take them.'

Anger coiled in his gut. 'The headmistress promised me Violet could sit them.' He had insisted on it.

'Then she lied to you. Violet wasn't allowed to set foot in that school again. I tried to arrange for her to sit the exams somewhere else but she refused. She gave up on life. She'd stay out all hours and never let me know where she was, then turn up steaming drunk and high as a kite, often cut or bruised from fights she'd got into and I'd patch her up and pray it was the last time I had to put ice on her face or sleep on her floor because I was terrified she'd choke on her own vomit, but it never was. She was arrested God knows how many times, hospitalised, had her stomach pumped... I honestly thought she was going to kill herself.'

Andreas sat heavily on the bed facing her, his heart pounding.

Carrie's beautiful golden skin had paled as she'd relayed this tale of horror that no one should ever have to live through, and to think his beautiful Carrie had been the one to live it made his guts coil again in fresh anger and self-loathing at the part he had unwittingly played in it.

After a few moments of silence, her eyes found his and she continued in a voice so low he strained to hear.

'I watched her try and kill herself for three years and there was nothing I could do to save her, and I tried *every-thing*. I locked her in her room; she smashed the window and jumped out. I staged numerous interventions with professionals; she just laughed in our faces. I even flushed a bagful of her cocaine down the toilet and got a punch in the face for it.' She gave a shaky laugh. 'Natalia has my sympathy. I know what a mean right hook Violet has.'

'Carrie...'

'No, please, whatever you want to say, just let me say this first. I believed Violet's lies that you set her up and I listened to her drunken ranting about you in the same way she would drunkenly rage about James and not once did I question them. As a journalist, you would think I would have had the sense to verify it all first, and I want you to know I am sorry for believing that about you and for all the lies I told in some stupid, futile, *dangerous* attempt at revenge. I could have caused your business and reputation untold damage and I am truly ashamed of myself. I think… I think I lost my mind.'

It was all true, Carrie realised bleakly as she spoke her confession.

She didn't need to verify Andreas's version of events. She knew the truth in her heart.

'What you have had to deal with these last three years would cause anyone to lose their mind,' he said quietly.

'It wouldn't cause you to lose yours,' she said with certainty. 'I don't think anything would ever cause you to lose your mind.'

'I came close when my sister and brother-in-law died,' he admitted. 'I couldn't fix that. All the other stuff my family and I had had to deal with before then, it was all fixable, even my parents' health issues. However bad things got, there was always hope. Tanya and Georgios's death… what hope was to be found there? But then you know all about that with your own mother.'

She nodded. 'Death is the one thing that can't be fixed, isn't it?'

'It's the finality,' he agreed. 'One minute they are there the next they are gone and all that's left are the memories. But I had Natalia to care for just as you had Violet after your mother died and…

'Why is Violet living with her father now?' he interrupted himself. 'Why wasn't she living with him before? I always assumed she was an orphan.'

'She might as well have been an orphan for the time

he gave her. Raymond, Violet's father, divorced our mum and moved to America years before Mum died. When she did die he didn't want Violet—he had a nice new nubile wife and was living the childless dream. We agreed that he would continue paying for Violet's education—did I tell you he was also rich?—and that she would become a weekly boarder so I could concentrate on my studies, but that she would live with me at weekends and holidays. He gave us both an allowance for it to work.' Her smile was bitter. 'When it came to money, his generosity was limitless.'

'And that's when you became Violet's guardian?'

'Yes. He handed his twelve-year-old daughter's welfare into my nineteen-year-old hands and washed his own hands of the pair of us.'

'Theos.' He gave a low whistle. That was the same age Natalia was now. He'd been a grown man of thirty-one when he'd become Natalia's guardian. 'I didn't realise you were so young when you became her guardian. And her father didn't want her? No wonder she went off the rails.' He shook his head, unable to comprehend how a man could turn his back on his own child. Natalia wasn't even his and he knew he would lay down his life to protect her. 'Why is she with him now when he didn't want her before?'

'I blackmailed him.'

He found himself smiling. 'Really?'

She met his eye and matched the smile. There was no joy in either of their curved mouths. 'I'd been begging him for years for help and he kept fobbing me off and fobbing me off. She almost died from that beating, Andreas. She was in a coma for three days. Something in me went ping. I didn't even think about what I was going to say, I just phoned him and said if he didn't fly over and see his daughter and finally take responsibility for her then I would publish a photo of Violet's battered body on the Internet and tell the world he'd refused to help her.'

'And that worked?'

'He arrived the next day. A week later he flew her back to America with him. I don't know why I hadn't threatened it before but I'd spent so long just getting through each day, caring for Violet, plotting my revenge on you and James…' She winced. 'Sorry.'

'It is okay.' He slid off the bed and knelt before her. Taking her hand in his, he kissed the palm. 'No more apologies. I'm the one who is sorry. I should have told you, not the school…'

'You did the right thing.' Carrie squeezed the hand holding hers so tenderly. 'You were protecting Natalia. Violet would have been expelled sooner or later. She was using drugs on school property. They would have noticed eventually.' She shrugged then took a deep breath. '*I* should have noticed. I should have seen what was happening to her—I *did* see—but I didn't know what I was seeing. Does that make sense?'

'Carrie…' He raised himself up and put a hand to her neck and pressed his forehead to hers. 'You must not blame yourself. None of what happened to her is your fault. You have put your life on hold to raise her and to save her. She is nineteen now, yes? The same age you were when you became her guardian. You have given her all the support and help you can, you have avenged her against the monster who first steered her on this awful path. You can do no more. I heard you say to Violet that she has to forgive herself. You must do the same and forgive yourself too.' Kissing her forehead, he moved back and rubbed his thumbs under her eyes.

The motion made her remember the make-up she must

have ruined with all her tears and she let out a cry. 'Your cousin's wedding!'

'It doesn't matter.'

'It does. We need to go.'

His brow furrowed and he stared intently into her eyes. 'Do you feel able to? I can make an excuse if you would rather stay.'

'No. They are expecting us.' She blew a long breath out and gave a wobbly smile. 'We have a wedding announcement of our own to make. You would look very strange doing it without your fiancée by your side.'

'Are you sure?'

How could she be anything but sure? She would do whatever was needed to kill the whispers against Andreas's business and his reputation. That was a mess of *her* making, no one else's.

Andreas was a good man who had put his life on hold for his family, just as she had for her family. A good, generous man who didn't deserve to have his reputation smeared by rumours and innuendoes. He deserved to spend the rest of his life living it with the freedom he'd had denied him for so long, and in six months he would be able to do just that. He could hop from country to country as he pleased, for work and pleasure, however he saw fit. He could drink Scotch in a palm-lined bar until the sun came up, he could bed all the women he wanted without worrying about being a bad influence on an impressionable teenager...

A hot red pain pulsed in the centre of her brain at this thought and she slammed her palm to her forehead.

'Are you okay?'

She heard the concern in his voice and quickly forced a smile.

Where had that pain come from?

'Yes, I'm fine. Just imagining how badly my face needs repairing from all those ugly tears.'

He stroked her cheek. 'Your tears are not ugly and your face just needs a clean.'

'Give me five minutes.'

He nodded and got to his feet before helping her to her own. Then he took her head in his hands and kissed her. It was gentle and fleeting but with so much tenderness in it that for one awful moment she thought she might cry again.

CHAPTER THIRTEEN

ANDREAS'S DRIVER JOINED the procession of cars lining up to enter the church's car park. There seemed to be some issue with one of the cars—an engine failure if Andreas was to guess correctly—and nothing was moving.

He could see his parents and niece standing at the front, chatting happily with the dozens of other guests. Both his parents had many siblings so family weddings were always large, noisy affairs.

Carrie was looking out of the window at the exuberant greetings taking place too. 'Why did you buy a holiday home in the Seychelles rather than closer to your family?' she asked, turning to face him with a wrinkle in her forehead. 'The way you speak of them—you clearly adore them.'

He looked down at their entwined fingers then back to her face. She'd cleaned herself up and put on only a little make-up. Her eyes were still a little red but he doubted anyone else would notice. She still looked ravishing in her long, off-the-shoulder cream silk dress with subtle blue leaf prints.

'I wanted a bolt-hole away from them all,' he admitted. 'My parents only like to travel short distances. The Seychelles is too far for them.'

And he'd thought he was done with family.

Not *done* done, just his time for some distance whenever he wanted to escape but...

'I was preparing myself for my freedom. I have been planning it for two years now, since Natalia told me she was going to medical school and I could see my freedom from responsibility waving a flag at me.'

His heart-rate began to accelerate, blood racing to his head, staring from Carrie to his family, his family to Carrie, Carrie to his family.

His father had just whispered something in his mother's ear, lovingly squeezing her seventy-four-year-old waist.

Andreas thought of the longevity of their marriage, and all they had been through, all the ups and downs, all the highs and lows.

Why had he thought having the freedom to see and do whatever he liked was better than having someone he loved to share all the experiences with?

He had a sudden vision of him and Carrie, forty years from now, surrounded by their own grown-up children...

Children?

He had long stopped wanting children. He'd raised a teenager he loved as if she were his own and had been so certain, so damned *adamant* he didn't want to go through it again...

'I can't do it,' he said suddenly.

'Do what?'

'Introduce you to my family as my fiancée when we don't mean it. I cannot marry you knowing it isn't true. I cannot make false vows.' And as he said the words aloud, he knew them to be true, and a weight he hadn't felt on his shoulders lifted.

Somewhere, somehow, he had fallen for his poisonous viper of a journalist.

He could laugh at his old notions about her.

There was nothing poisonous about Carrie. Prise off the shell she carried herself in and there was a kind, loving, independent, fiercely protective woman. When Carrie loved someone, it was with everything she had. She loved with her whole heart.

And he loved her with the whole of his.

'Oh.' She had gone very still beside him.

He tugged the hand he was holding to his mouth and pressed his lips to the knuckles. 'Marry me for real.'

'What?'

'I am serious. Marry me. For real. Not for six months.'

'No.'

'Carrie…'

'The answer is no.' She pulled her hand from his and shifted away so her back was to the door, staring at him warily as if he were a dangerous dog that could bite. 'I agreed to six months. You can't change the terms now.'

'I am not changing the terms. I am telling you I cannot go through with the terms we agreed on. It would not feel right.'

'Why not? Is it because I was a virgin so you feel honour-bound to keep me for ever?' She spoke slowly, not taking her eyes from his face.

'It has nothing to do with you being a virgin. I admit, I like knowing I'm the only man you have been with…'

She gave the briefest of smiles, one that did not reach her wary, watchful eyes. 'Your sexist undertones are coming out.'

'I am being honest with you and I say *this* with all honesty too—you could have slept with a hundred men and I would still be asking you marry me for real.'

In the few, intense weeks they had been together they had seen the worst in each other and the best. She had slipped so effortlessly into his life it was as if she had always been there.

'Okay.' She dragged the last syllable out then nodded her head. 'Well, I am telling *you*, with all honesty, that I will not commit to anything longer than six months.'

'Why not?' he challenged.

'You have to ask? The whole reason I am here is to put right the awful wrong I did to you but that shouldn't mean I have to give up my whole life…'

'Do you not feel anything for me other than a debt you need to pay?' he asked, forcing his voice to stay even, not wanting to jump to conclusions. They had done that enough already…

But if they hadn't jumped to their prior conclusions about each other they wouldn't be sitting there now…

And he wouldn't be feeling as if he'd started swimming only to find the water had turned into treacle. The shell he had so carefully prised open was reforming around her. He could virtually see the seams knitting themselves together.

'Are you telling me I have imagined everything that has happened between us?'

'No, I'm not saying any of those things.' There was an air of desperation in her voice. 'You can't just throw something like this at me and expect me to fall in line with it.'

'I don't want you to fall in line.' He took a deep breath and pinched the bridge of his nose. 'How long do you want to have?'

'Six months.'

'I mean how long do you want to think about it?' he asked through gritted teeth.

'I don't need to think about it.' She pulled her knees up to her chest and hugged them tightly. 'We marry for six months and then we divorce and I move back into my London house and you live the life you've been dreaming of.'

'I don't want that life any more. Being with you…it has…not changed me but made me see I want someone to share it all with.'

'Oh, so you want a constant companion while you live the high life and I'm here and available and you've got to marry me anyway so I'll do? How am I supposed to do that around work? Or am I expected to give up my job?'

'Did I say *any* of that?' he demanded, the anger clawing in his guts finally finding a vent.

He wouldn't say he'd expected her to agree to his proposal on a whim but he'd thought—in as much as he'd thought about it, which he hadn't really considering he'd only just accepted his own feelings for her—she would at least be receptive to the idea.

He acknowledged his own lie to himself.

His feelings for Carrie had been like a runaway train from the minute she'd stepped into his office. He'd thought it had been the same for her.

Had he *really* got it so wrong?

Had the closeness they'd developed really just been a figment of his imagination?

'Six months of marriage where we live in London then you can relocate your headquarters to Athens and I stay put. That's what we agreed,' she said obstinately.

'What if I were to offer to live permanently in London with you? For ever.' He laid his challenge down.

'The answer is still no. I do not want to marry you. Don't you get that? I will pay my debt. I will do six months. And then I will leave.'

'How can you be so cold?' he asked in disbelief. 'I am offering to give everything up for you and you…'

'Cold?' she interrupted. Suddenly she leapt from her perch on the seat and pushed him back so she was on top of him, pinning him down, her little hands holding his wrists above his head, her snarling face above his.

She'd moved so quickly he'd had no time for defence. If the situation were more humorous and less of a feeling that everything was fraying at the seams, he would have admired her ninja skills.

'Don't you call me cold!' she shouted. 'Don't you dare! I have spent my life caring for the people that I love and losing them. I nursed my mother for six years and then she was gone. I have loved and cared for Violet her entire life and what good did that do? She's gone too! She is lost to me. I would give my entire life to have them back so don't you dare call me cold and don't you dare ask me to commit the rest of my life to a man who's been yearning for his freedom and would only break my heart. Yes, Andreas, *you*,' she spat. 'If our marriage was for real you would bore of me in months; that yearning for freedom would still be in you getting stronger and stronger and then what would happen? You'd get your chequebook out and pay me off like all rich men do when something nicer and newer grabs their attention.'

Andreas stared into her spitting eyes and felt the very coldness he'd accused her of creep into his veins.

Everything made sudden gut-aching sense.

He twisted his wrists easily from her hold and snatched her hands, pulling them together to hold her wrists in one hand while he levered himself up with his free hand.

Then they were staring at each other, enough hate and poison swirling between them to choke on.

He had been wrong about her. Prise her shell off and she was still just a poisonous viper of a journalist.

'Oh. I get it,' he said slowly. 'You still think I'm just a rich bastard who is pre-programmed to cheat and treat women like dirt.'

Her eyes widened. Suddenly the fury went from them and she blinked rapidly, shaking her head. 'No. No, sorry, I didn't mean it like that. I know you're not like other…'

'You have said enough,' he cut in icily, then he dropped her wrists and banged on the dividing window. 'I'll get out here. Take Miss Rivers back to the villa to collect her belongings and then take her to the airport.'

He turned back to stare at her now pale face for the last time. 'I will arrange for my jet to take you back to London. Your debt to me is over.'

Then, without a word of goodbye, he got out of the car and strode through the other idle cars to his family.

Carrie watched him walk away, her heart in her mouth, loud drumbeats banging in her head. The scratchy panic that had torn her insides into pieces as Andreas had spoken of marriage had gone and all that was left was a numbness, as if she had been anaesthetised.

She rubbed her wrists, the look in his eyes as he'd let go of them, discarding them as if they were trash, right there in her mind.

Andreas had looked at her as if she were a toxin.

He merged into the merry crowd outside the pretty white church without once looking back.

A separate merry crowd had gathered together to push the broken-down car away. She watched them as if through a filter, seeing but not seeing, Andreas's hateful look the only thing she could picture with clarity, as she sat there too numb to take anything else in.

He had never looked at her like that before. Not even when the truth had first unravelled itself.

She was barely aware of her own car moving until the driver made a slow U-turn in the space that had opened up before them and crunched away from the happy wedding party, just as Andreas had made a U-turn on their plans…

Their plans?

There were no plans now, she realised, her heart hammering more painfully than it had ever done.

Their relationship, such as it was, was over.

They were over.

She was still too numb to do more than swallow back a huge lump that had formed in her throat.

Andreas sipped at his single malt as he read through the emails Debbie had decided were worthy of his attention, keeping one eye on the time. An old friend from his Manhattan days, when he'd been a mere employee, was due any minute. As was their tradition, they'd agreed to meet in their old 'watering hole', as Frank still liked to call it.

'Can I get you another drink, sir?'

He looked up from the screen at the young, pretty waitress who had been paying him extra attention since he'd arrived at the bar and settled himself in an empty corner booth. It was still early but tonight was the opening game of the baseball season and this bar was a firm favourite for Yankee fans. He estimated that he and Frank would have an hour of catching up before the place filled up.

'I'm good for the moment, thank you,' he answered with a quick grin. 'I'll let you know if I need anything else.'

She winked before sashaying away. 'Be sure that you do.'

Focussing his attention back on his smartphone, he rubbed the back of his neck and chided himself for wasting an opportunity for a little flirtation.

This pretty waitress was a perfect example of what he'd been looking forward to all these years: grabbing opportunities for fun when they came along. Andreas was now free to do what he liked with whom he liked when he liked. Natalia had announced at his cousin's wedding that she was moving in with her boyfriend. A boyfriend she had conveniently forgotten to mention to her protective uncle until she was certain things would work out between them.

He'd wished her luck and even managed to inject sincerity in his voice.

Who knew, he thought cynically, taking another sip of his Scotch, maybe it would work for them? And if it didn't he would be there to pick up the pieces. He'd come to accept that when it came to Natalia, he would always be there.

The main thing, he had told himself numerous times, was that his freedom had officially arrived. He didn't even have a fake fiancée to worry about.

Lord knew what he would do if the rumours about him gained traction. It had been six days since he'd shut the door on the viper and their relationship. He'd ordered Debbie to check in frequently with their media contacts and inform him immediately if the rumours started up again. So far, all was quiet.

Maybe their brief relationship had been enough on its own to quell the rumours.

The waitress caught his eye again. She really was incredibly pretty, a true all-American girl with a toothy smile and perfectly blonde hair.

Carrie's hair had been blonde the first time he'd met her, their first oh-so-fleeting glance…

He took a deep breath and downed his Scotch.

Do not think of her. Not by name.

It was easier to depersonalise her. Depersonalise her and forget about her.

Less than a minute after he'd slammed his empty glass on the table, the waitress brought him another over.

'Where are you from?' she asked, lingering at the table.

'Greece.' He returned the smile and willed himself to feel something.

Anything.

'Greece, huh? I've always wanted to go there.'

She'd moved close enough for him to smell her perfume. It was nice. Floral.

It did nothing for him.

Carrie's scent had been evocative. It had hit him in the loins.

His mind suddenly loosened, memories he'd shut tightly away springing free. The heat of her kisses, the movement of her lips when she spoke, the way she smiled sleepily when she looked at him after waking...

The way she had cried on his shoulder, her desolation over her sister, the way she had clung to him, as if he were the lifeline she'd needed when her emotions had thrown her out to sea...

Carrie...

Carrie...

Carrie!

Her name rang loudly in his ears.

'What's your name?'

'Carrie.'

'Sorry?'

He blinked and saw the waitress looking at him with puzzlement.

He'd said her name aloud.

Carrie.

Scared, terrified Carrie who'd spent her life watching her mother and sister being used and sometimes abused by rich men.

Her kisses didn't lie. Her lovemaking didn't lie.

Her scared brain did.

'Her name is Carrie,' he said more clearly. 'The woman I love. She's called Carrie.'

He hadn't told her he loved her. He'd held that back as the strength and vehemence of her rejection had accelerated, protecting his ego.

Why had he not recognised the fear in her eyes for what it was rather than just listened to what she'd said? Why had he not laid his heart truly on the line for her?

The reason for that was simple. As this pretty waitress would no doubt say, the reason was because he was a shmuck.

He got to his feet, pulling a couple of twenty-dollar bills from his wallet, and thrust them into the waitress's hand. 'If a tall bald man called Frank asks for Andreas, tell him I remembered I had to be somewhere else.'

Hurrying out of the bar, he hailed the first cab that came his way and instructed the driver to take him to the airport.

CHAPTER FOURTEEN

CARRIE CLOSED HER laptop after her video chat with her sister feeling slightly lighter.

They had just shared their first real, meaningful conversation since Violet had confessed to her affair with James.

Violet had done as Carrie had beseeched and confessed her lies about Andreas to her counsellor. It had been at the counsellor's behest that Violet had arranged the video chat.

Seeing her sister's face on the screen, in real time, had been almost as good as the conversation itself. She'd put on weight, no longer the gaunt stick-thin figure who could still fit in children's clothes. Her complexion was clearer too, although the effect of that was to highlight the scars that had accumulated on her face over the years. Raymond had promised that he would pay for treatment for the scars once she had been clean for a year.

The man who'd been such a scummy, negligent father had finally come into his own and was doing the right thing by his daughter. He'd even come to the computer and waved at Carrie, which she'd conceded was a big deal for him considering the last time they'd spoken she'd been blackmailing him.

In all, things were looking good. Much more positive.

The only dark cloud had come when Violet had asked how things were going for Carrie with Andreas. When

Carrie had responded with a prepared airy, 'It fizzled out,' Violet had been crestfallen.

'I thought you'd be pleased,' Carrie had said, trying her hardest to keep things light.

Violet had bitten her lips in the exact same way their mother had done. 'I just want you to be happy,' she'd blurted out.

'I *am* happy,' Carrie had promised, her stomach wrenching.

Violet had not looked convinced.

All week Carrie had kept her airy face on, telling curious colleagues that yes, she and Andreas had had a brief romance but that they had decided it wouldn't work between them long term.

Her only real gulp-inducing moment had been when the features editor had asked when she would have the exclusive interview written up. She'd forgotten all about that.

She opened her laptop back up and decided to write the feature now. She had no transcripts of any of their conversations but she knew if she started, they would come back to her.

She would write it, email it to Andreas for his approval—after all, everything they had discussed had been between the two of them and not for public consumption—and if he agreed, she would send it to the features editor. If he refused she would say he'd pulled out. She would take the blame for it. Happily. She would not have his name tarnished.

Even if he did hate her.

She caught sight of the time and saw it was almost one in the morning.

It was Saturday.

This was supposed to be their wedding day.

She took a long breath and opened a new document to write on.

The time didn't matter. She'd hardly slept more than a couple of hours a night since her return to London.

The nights had become her enemy, a time when her brain did nothing but try to think of Andreas.

And now it was time to slay his ghost. Finally allow herself to think about him properly, write the feature and then spend the rest of her life forgetting about him.

Oh, but the pain in her chest. It *hurt*. Really hurt. It was as if someone had punched her right in her heart.

So she started writing.

She soon discovered she didn't need transcripts.

Every minute of their time together had lodged in her brain.

Every shared conversation had committed to memory.

Andreas Samaras's fortune came about almost by accident, she wrote, her fingers almost flying off the keys as she wrote about the terrible time when his parents' business had gone under and how it had been the spur he'd needed to work as hard as he could to save them from financial ruin.

The more she wrote, the clearer it became, the clearer he became, emerging from a picture in her mind so he might as well be standing right there, in front of her. If she stretched out a hand she'd be able to touch him.

His life. His selflessness.

Everything he'd done had been for his family. His great wealth couldn't insulate them from tragedy but it ensured his parents never had to worry and his niece could train as a doctor without the usual student encumbrances. His extended family had benefitted too, aunts, uncles, cousins, all either having their mortgages paid off or new homes bought for them.

No member of the Samaras family would ever struggle financially while Andreas was alive.

Five hours later, her hands cramped, hot pains shooting up her arms, she stopped, exhausted, and burst into tears.

For the first time she admitted to herself what she had thrown away.

She hadn't meant to cast him in the same torrid light as those other rich men who had abused their power. She had been long past that, had long accepted Andreas was nothing like those men.

His proposal, his idea they should marry for keeps, hadn't just taken her by surprise but terrified her. She'd already been feeling raw after spilling her soul to him and had panicked.

He'd never said that one word she'd longed to hear from his lips, the same word that also would probably have made her dive out of the window.

At no point had he mentioned love.

But she had never given him the chance. She had said no without even having to think.

No, I will not marry you properly. No, I will not take the chance of us finding happiness together because I'm a big scared, distrustful baby who requires proof.

What proof could he give her that their marriage would last and that he would never cheat or break her heart? None, because that proof didn't exist! He had no crystal ball or time portal.

And neither did she.

All she could do was trust her instincts and her heart, and both were telling her—*screaming* at her—that she had made the biggest mistake of her life.

Andreas had offered her his world but she'd been too scared to take it from him.

And now it was too late.

Shoving her laptop so hard it fell off her desk, Carrie buried her face in her hands and wept.

It was too late.

Too, too late.

Andreas banged hard on the blue front door for the third time.

Still no response.

Pushing the letterbox open, he crouched down. 'Carrie? Please. Open the door. Please.'

'She's gone out.'

He spun round to find an elderly woman walking a small dog up the neighbouring front path.

'Did she say where she was going?'

The woman shook her head as she rummaged in her pocket for her keys. 'She went out when Trixie and I went for our walk. Half an hour ago or so.'

'Did she say when she was coming back?'

'No. She was all dressed up so I wouldn't think she'll be back soon.' The woman opened her door then looked at him one last time. 'If you're thinking of robbing her place, I'd be very careful. She has a very noisy burglar alarm.'

Despite the situation, he couldn't help but grin. 'Noted.'

The door slammed shut.

With a heavy, defeated sigh, he slumped down onto Carrie's front door step and cradled his head in his hands.

He would just have to wait until she came back from wherever she'd gone *all dressed up*.

Carrie rarely dressed up. She was always, always elegant, but never noticeably dressed up. The only occasion she had properly dressed up for had been his cousin's wedding, the day everything had imploded between them.

That had been a week ago.

He looked at his watch. Half past one. Their wedding was supposed to take place in half an hour...

His brain began to tick.

Had Carrie cancelled the registry office? Because he hadn't…

And just like that, he was on his feet, racing past his idling driver, pounding the ground to the nearest Tube station, racing down the stairs, yanking his bank card out and waving it at the turnstile, pausing only to check which line he needed to take before racing to the platform.

People of all shapes and sizes were clambering onto a train and he joined the throng.

He hadn't used the Tube in years but this was one occasion where speed trumped luxury. He hardly noticed the people jostling into him. He certainly didn't care.

Four minutes later and he was in Chelsea, following his nose to the registry office, checking his watch constantly until, with five minutes to spare, he was there and racing up the stairs to the waiting room outside the room he'd booked for their service.

The waiting room was empty.

He doubled over, partly from exertion but mostly from grief.

The cramp in his stomach spread to his chest and clenched around his heart.

The pain was indescribable.

What a fool he was.

He'd allowed hope to override common sense. What on earth had he been thinking?

Why would Carrie have come here? She'd made her feelings perfectly clear but he, egotistical fool that he was, had been unable to accept the truth and had…

'Andreas?'

He froze.

Slowly he straightened before turning around.

The door to the officiating room had opened. Standing

at the threshold, clearly on her way out, stood Carrie, the registrar hovering behind her.

She stared at him as if she'd seen a ghost.

The neighbour had been right that she'd been dressed up. She wore a knee-length summery cream dress and a soft cream leather jacket. On her feet were cream heels.

The only colour on her were her eyes. They were red raw.

'What are you doing here?' she whispered.

'What are you doing here?' he countered, not trusting what his eyes were telling him.

Silence hung over them as they gazed at each other, Carrie drinking in the tall figure she had resigned herself to never seeing again.

She'd told herself she was running a fool's errand but that hadn't stopped her rifling through her wardrobe for the most bridal-type clothing she could find.

She'd fallen into bed, utterly exhausted, at six in the morning and after three hours' fitful sleep had woken with a cast-iron certainty that she had to get herself to the registry office.

Even now, with what looked and sounded like Andreas standing in front of her, she couldn't say where this certainty had come from. It had been a compulsion that had taken over her.

She'd made it to the registry office well before the appointed time and had watched one happy couple and two dozen happy guests pile into the room, then pile out twenty minutes later.

During those twenty minutes she had waited on her own.

When the last guest had gone and her reality had come crashing back down on her, she had burst into fresh tears. The registrar had been sympathy itself, taking her into the room and making her a cup of tea, giving her the time she needed to gather herself together in privacy rather than have her humiliated should anyone come into the waiting room while she was wailing.

And now, as she looked at the ghost before her, a scent played under her nose, a fresh, tangy cologne that had her bruised heart battering against her ribs.

She gazed into the light brown eyes she loved so much, saw them narrow with the same disbelief that must have been ringing in hers then saw the truth hit him at the exact same moment it hit her.

In seconds, he'd hauled her into his arms and was kissing her fiercely as she clung to him, inhaling his scent, more tears spilling from her eyes and splashing onto his face.

It was *him*! Andreas was there! He had come.

'I'm sorry, I'm sorry, I'm sorry,' she cried, raining kisses all over his face, hungrily inhaling more of his scent, tasting his skin…

It really was *him*.

Eventually he disentangled their clinging bodies to take her face in his hands and stare at her.

There was a wonder in his face. 'You are here. Oh, *matia mou*, you are *here*. I didn't dare believe…'

'I'm so sorry,' she said, tears falling over the fingers cradling her face with such tenderness.

'No, my love, it is I who is sorry. My pride—my ego— never let me say what was in my heart.' His words came in a rush. 'I want to marry you for ever because my heart will not accept anything less. I love you. You are the bravest, most loyal and loving woman I have ever met. You are stubborn and sexy and I love everything about you. The only freedom I want is the freedom to wake next to your face every day for the rest of my life, so please, I beg you, marry me. I love you. I can't be without you.'

Carrie covered his hands with her own feeling as if her heart could burst. If it did, glitter and starlight would explode over them.

'I love *you*, Andreas, and I'm so sorry for...' she raised her shoulders helplessly '...*everything*. You are the best person I know. You're sexy and funny...the way you have taken care of your family... I should never have... I was scared.'

'I know.' He covered her mouth with his. 'I need to learn patience. You know what I'm like. I want something and I want it *now*. You need to think things through. I have to accept our brains work differently.'

She laughed softly into his lips. 'I'll teach you patience if you'll teach me spontaneity.'

'It's a deal.'

Their kiss to seal their deal was broken by a loud cough.

They broke apart to find the registrar looking at his watch, a faint smile on his lips. 'If we're going to marry you we will have to do it now, I'm afraid. We have another wedding party due any minute and my colleagues who are supposed to be acting as your witnesses have other duties to attend to.'

Andreas looked at Carrie. 'Well? Do you want to do it?'

She kissed him. 'I'm here, aren't I?'

The brightest, most dazzling grin she had ever seen broke out on his handsome face. 'Then let's do it.'

So they did.

And neither of them ever regretted it.

EPILOGUE

'YOUR VEIL IS falling off!' Natalia screeched as Carrie attempted to get out of the limousine.

'I don't know why I agreed to wear the stupid thing,' she said in a mock grumble.

'Because you want to make an old woman happy... Violet, can you hold your side still for me?'

Between them, Carrie's two bridesmaids fixed her veil then both inspected her face one last time before the door swung open and her father was there to help them all out, bemused to be wearing a fitted tuxedo, a beaming smile on his craggy, weather-beaten face, delighted to be there, as proud as punch of his only child.

As soon as they were all standing, Agon's glorious spring sun shining on them, the girls fussed with her dress, making sure there were no wrinkles around her protruding bump.

Carrie was six months pregnant. It was a year to the day since she and Andreas had exchanged their vows in the Chelsea registry office with two strangers acting as their witnesses.

When they had gone to visit his parents to share their happy news, his mother had promptly burst into tears. Those tears were only pacified when Andreas had promised they would do it all over again, properly. And by

properly he meant a full church wedding with his entire
family in attendance, everyone congregating to the same
hotel afterwards and everyone then meeting the happy
couple for breakfast.

As Carrie had taken an instant shine to both of his parents she had been happy to go along with the plans for them
but then, as the date neared, found herself excited for hers
and Andreas's own sake.

A big white wedding, surrounded by friends and family,
the people who loved them, everyone wishing them well…

It had been a strange experience, being embraced into
the bosom of the Samaras family, especially as her own
was so small. She hadn't properly appreciated what a close-
knit family they all were, not until she and Andreas had
moved to Agon permanently a few months ago and found
their villa under constant siege from aunts, uncles and
cousins all inviting themselves round for a holiday. Anyone
would think they weren't all scattered on varying Greek islands with their own beautiful beaches a short walk away.
Andreas had since bought the neighbouring villa for his
family to use so they could have some privacy. Their only
real houseguests now were his parents, Violet and Natalia.

Her sister and his niece were tentatively rekindling their
old friendship. Both were doing well. Violet had decided to
stay in California permanently. She was still clean. Every
day was still a battle but, she had assured Carrie, it was
a battle that was getting easier. She *wanted* to stay clean.
She wanted to live a long, healthy life. Her words were
music to Carrie's ears.

As for Carrie, she'd handed her notice in when they
moved to Agon. She had come to love their home there,
loved the life, the sunshine, everything about it. Somewhere along the way she had lost her drive for investigative journalism and, anyway, it wasn't as if she could go

undercover any more when she was half of a famous couple. Her exclusive feature on Andreas—he had *loved* it—had been a huge hit and the features editor had offered her freelance work, interviewing business leaders and politicians. With Andreas's encouragement, Carrie had been delighted to accept.

The church doors swung open, the organ started to play and, her arm securely in her father's hold, her free hand resting on her kicking baby, she began the slow walk to her husband to repeat the vows they had made in private to the rest of the world.

Andreas stood at the top of the aisle next to his father, who was acting as his best man. The two Samaras men had identical beaming grins.

Her heart skipped to see him.

Her heart *always* skipped to see him.

She had never believed heaven existed.

With Andreas she had found it.

* * * * *

ENGAGED TO HER RAVENSDALE ENEMY

MELANIE MILBURNE

To Monique Scott. You left an indelible mark on our family, enriching our lives in so many fabulous ways. You are the daughter I never had. You are the most amazing young woman, a gorgeous mother, and a wonderful friend. Love always. Xxxx

CHAPTER ONE

IT WASN'T GIVING back the engagement ring Jasmine
Connolly was most worried about. She had two
more sitting in her jewellery box in her flat in Mayfair above her bridal-wear shop. It was the feeling
of being rejected. *Again.* What was wrong with her?
Why wasn't she good enough? She hadn't been good
enough for her mother. Why did the people she cared
about always leave her?

But that wasn't all that had her stomach knotting in
panic. It was attending the winter wedding expo next
weekend in the Cotswolds as a singleton. How could
she front up *sans* fiancé? She might as well turn up at
the plush hotel she'd booked months and months ago
with 'loser' written on her forehead. She had so looked
forward to that expo. After a lot of arm-twisting she
had secured a slot in the fashion parade. It was her
first catwalk show and it had the potential to lead to
bigger and more important ones.

But it wasn't just about designing wedding gowns.
She loved everything to do with weddings. The commitment to have someone love you for the rest of your

life, not just while it was convenient or while it suited them. Love was supposed to be for ever. Every time she designed a gown she stitched her own hopes into it. What if she never got to wear one of her own gowns? What sort of cruel irony would that be?

She glanced at her empty ring finger where it was gripping the steering wheel. She wished she'd thought to shove on one of her spares just so she didn't have to explain to everyone that she was—to quote Myles—'taking a break'.

It didn't matter how he termed it, it all meant the same thing as far as Jaz was concerned. She was dumped. Jilted. Cast off. Single.

Forget about three times a bridesmaid, she thought sourly. What did it mean if you were three times a dumped fiancée?

It meant you sucked at relationships. Really sucked.

Jaz parked the car in her usual spot at Ravensdene, the family pile of the theatre-royalty family where she had grown up as the gardener's daughter and surrogate sister to Miranda Ravensdale and her older twin brothers, Julius and Jake.

Miranda had just got herself engaged. Damn. It.

Jaz was thrilled for her best mate. Of course she was. Miranda and Leandro Allegretti were perfect for each other. No one deserved a happy ending more than those two.

But why couldn't she have hers?

Jaz put her head down against the steering wheel and banged it three times. *Argh!*

There was a sound of a car growling as it came up

the long driveway. Jaz straightened and quickly got out of her car and watched as the Italian sports car ate up the gravel with its spinning tyres, spitting out what it didn't want in spraying arcs of flying stones. It felt like a fistful of those stones were clenched between her back molars as the car came to a dusty standstill next to hers.

Jacques, otherwise known as Jake, Ravensdale unfolded his tall, athletic frame from behind the wheel with animal grace. Jaz knew it was Jake and not his identical twin brother Julius because she had always been able to tell them apart. Not everyone could, but she could. She felt the difference in her body. Her body got all tingly and feverish, restless and antsy, whenever Jake was around. It was as if her body picked up a signal from his and it completely scrambled her motherboard.

His black hair was sexily tousled and wind-blown. Another reason to hate him, because she knew if she had just driven with the top down in that chilly October breeze her hair would have looked like a tangled fishing net. He was dressed casually because everything about Jake was casual, including his relationships—if you could call hook-ups and one-night stands relationships.

His dark-blue gaze was hidden behind designer aviator lenses but she could see a deep frown grooved into his forehead. At least it was a change from his stock-standard mocking smile. 'What the hell are you doing here?' he said.

Jaz felt another millimetre go down on her molars.

'Nice to see you too, Jake,' she said with a sugar-sweet smile. 'How's things? Had that personality transplant yet?'

He took off his sunglasses and continued to frown at her. 'You're supposed to be in London.'

Jaz gave him a wide-eyed, innocent look. 'Am I?'

'I checked with Miranda,' he said, clicking shut the driver's door with his foot. 'She said you were going to a party with Tim at his parents' house.'

'It's Myles,' she said. 'Tim was my…erm…other one.'

The corner of his mouth lifted. 'Number one or number two?'

It was extremely annoying how he made her ex-fiancés sound like bodily waste products, Jaz thought. Not that she didn't think of them that way too these days, but still. 'Number two,' she said. 'Lincoln was my first.'

Jake turned to pop open the boot of the car with his remote device. 'So where's lover-boy Myles?' he said. 'Is he planning on joining you?'

Jaz knew she shouldn't be looking at the way Jake's dark-blue denim jeans clung to his taut behind as he bent forward to get his overnight bag but what was a girl to do? He was built like an Olympic athlete. Lean and tanned with muscles in all the right places and in places where her exes didn't have them and never would. He was fantasy fodder. Ever since her hormones had been old enough to take notice, that was exactly what they had done. Which was damned inconvenient, since she absolutely, unreservedly loathed him. 'No…erm…he's staying in town to do some work,' she said. 'After the party, I mean.'

Jake turned back to look at her with a glinting smile. 'You've broken up.'

Jaz hated it that he didn't pose it as a question but as if it were a given. *Another Jasmine Connolly engagement bites the dust.* Not that she was going to admit it to him of all people. 'Don't be ridiculous,' she said. 'What on earth makes you think that? Just because I chose to spend the weekend down here while I work on Holly's dress instead of partying in town doesn't mean I'm—'

'Where's that flashy rock you've been brandishing about?'

Jaz used her left hand to flick her hair back over her shoulder in what she hoped was a casual manner. 'It's in London. I don't like wearing it when I'm working.' Which at least wasn't a complete lie. The ring was in London, safely in Myles' family jewellery vault. It miffed her Myles hadn't let her keep it. Not even for a few days till she got used to the idea of 'taking a break'. So what if it was a family heirloom? He had plenty of money. He could buy any number of rings. But no, he had to have it back, which meant she was walking around with a naked ring finger because she'd been too upset, angry and hurt to grab one of her other rings on her way out of the flat.

How galling if Jake were the first person to find out she had jinxed another relationship. How could she bear it? He wouldn't be sympathetic and consoling. He would roll about the floor laughing, saying, *I told you so.*

Jake hooked his finger through the loop on the collar of his Italian leather jacket and slung it over his shoulder. 'You'd better make yourself scarce if you're not in the mood for a party. I have guests arriving in an hour.'

Jaz's stomach dropped like a lift with snapped cables. 'Guests?'

His shoes crunched over the gravel as he strode towards the grand old Elizabethan mansion's entrance. 'Yep, the ones that eat and drink and don't sleep.'

She followed him into the house feeling like a teacup Chihuahua trying to keep up with an alpha wolf. 'What the hell? How many guests? Are they all female?'

He flashed her a white-toothed smile. 'You know me so well.'

Jaz could feel herself lighting up with lava-hot heat. Most of it burned in her cheeks at the thought of having to listen to him rocking on with a harem of his Hollywood wannabes. Unlike his identical twin brother Julius and his younger sister Miranda, who did everything they could to distance themselves from their parents' fame, Jake cashed in on it. Big-time. He was shameless in how he exploited it for all it was worth—which wasn't much, in Jaz's opinion. She had been the victim of his exploitative tactics when she'd been sixteen on the night of one of his parents' legendary New Year's Eve parties. He had led her on to believe he was serious about…

But she never thought about that night in his bedroom. *Never*.

'You can't have a party,' Jaz said as she followed him into the house. 'Mrs Eggleston's away. She's visiting her sister in Bath.'

'Which is why I've chosen this weekend,' he said. 'Don't worry. I've organised the catering.'

Jaz folded her arms and glowered at him. 'And I bet I know what's on the menu.' *Him*. Being licked and ego-stroked by a bevy of bimbo airheads who drank champagne like it was water and ate nothing in case they put on an ounce. She only hoped they were all of age.

'You want to join us?'

Jaz jerked her chin back against her neck and made a scoffing noise. 'Are you out of your mind? I couldn't think of anything worse than watching a bunch of wannabe starlets get taken in by your particular version of charm. I'd rather chew razor blades.'

He shrugged one of his broad shoulders as if he didn't care either way. 'No skin off my nose.'

Jaz thought she would like to scratch every bit of skin off that arrogant nose. She hadn't been alone with him in years. There had always been other members of his family around whenever they'd come to Ravensdene. Why hadn't Eggles told her he would be here? Mrs Eggleston, the long-time housekeeper, knew how much Jaz hated Jake.

Everyone knew it. The feud between them had gone on for seven years. The air crackled with static electricity when they were in the same room even if there were crowds of other people around. The antagonism she felt towards Jake had grown exponentially every year. He had a habit of looking at her a certain way, as if he was thinking back to that night in his room when she had made the biggest fool of herself. His dark-blue eyes would take on a mocking gleam as if he could remember every inch of her body where it had been lying waiting for him in his bed in nothing but her underwear.

She gave a mental cringe. Yes, her underwear. What had she been thinking? Why had she fallen for it? Why hadn't she realised he'd been playing her for a fool? The humiliation he had subjected her to, the shame, the embarrassment of being hauled out of his bed in front of his... *Grrhh!* She would *not* think about it.

She. Would. Not.

Jaz's father wasn't even here to referee. He was away on a cruise of the Greek Islands with his new wife. Her father didn't belong to Jaz any more—not that he ever had. His work had always been more important than her. How could a garden, even one as big as the one at Ravensdene, be more important than his only child? But no, now he belonged to Angela.

Going back to London was out of the question. Jaz wasn't ready to announce the pause on her engagement. Not yet. Not until she knew for sure it was over. Not even to Miranda. Not while there was a slither of hope. All she had to do was make Myles see what he was missing out on. She was his soul mate. Of course she was. Everybody said so. Well, maybe not everybody, but she didn't need everyone's approval. Not even his parents' approval, which was a good thing, considering they didn't like her. But then, they were horrid toffee-nosed snobs and she didn't like them either.

Jaz did everything for Myles. She cooked, she cleaned, she organised his social calendar. She turned her timetable upside down and inside out so she could be available for him. She even had sex with him when she didn't feel like it. Which was more often than not, for some strange reason. Was that why Myles wanted a break? Because she wasn't sexually assertive enough? Not raunchy enough? She could do raunchy. She could wear dress-up costumes and play games. She would hate it but if it won him back she would do it. Other men found her attractive. Sure they did.

She was fighting off men all the time. She wasn't vain but she knew she had the package: the looks, the figure, the face and the hair. And she was whip-smart. She had her own bridal design company and she was not quite twenty-four.

Sure, she'd had a bit of help from Jake's parents, Richard and Elisabetta Ravensdale, in setting up. In fact, if it hadn't been for them, she wouldn't have had the brilliant education she'd had. They had stepped in when her mother had left her at Ravensdene on an access visit when she was eight and had never returned.

Not that it bothered Jaz that her mother hadn't come back for her. Not really. She was mightily relieved she hadn't had to go back to that cramped and mouldy, rat-infested flat in Brixton where the neighbours fought harder than the feral cats living near the garbage collection point. It was the principle of the thing that was the issue. Being left like a package on a doorstep wasn't exactly how one expected to be treated as a young child. But still, living at the Elizabethan mansion Ravensdene in Buckinghamshire had been much preferable. It was like being at a country spa resort with acres of verdant fields, dark, shady woods and a river meandering through the property like a silver ribbon.

This was home and the Ravensdales were family.

Well, apart from Jake, of course.

Jake tossed the bag on his bed and let out a filthy curse. What the hell was Jasmine Connolly doing here? He had made sure the place was empty for the weekend. He had a plan and Jasmine wasn't part of it. He did everything he could to avoid her. But when he couldn't he did everything he could to annoy her. He got a kick out of seeing her clench her teeth and flash those grey-blue eyes at him like tongues of flame. She was a pain in the backside but he wasn't going to let her dictate what he could and couldn't do. This was his family home, not hers. She might have benefited from being raised with his kid sister Miranda but she was still the gardener's daughter.

Jaz had been intent on marrying up since she'd been a kid. At sixteen she'd had her sights on him. *On him!* What a joke. He was ten years older than her; marriage hadn't been on his radar then and it wasn't on it now. It wasn't even in his vocabulary.

Jaz did nothing but think about marriage. Her whole life revolved around it. She was a good designer, he had to give her that, but it surely wasn't healthy to be so obsessed with the idea of marriage? Forty per cent of marriages ended in divorce—his parents' being a case in point. After his father's love-child scandal broke a month ago, it had looked like they were going to have a second one. The couple had remarried after their first divorce, and if another was on the way he only hoped it wouldn't be as acrimonious and publicly cringe-worthy as their last.

His phone beeped with an incoming message and he swore again when he checked his screen. Twenty-seven text messages and fourteen missed calls from Emma Madden. He had blocked her number but she must have borrowed someone else's phone. He knew if he checked his spam folder there would be just as many emails with photos of the girl's assets. Didn't that silly little teenager go to school? Where were her parents? Why weren't they monitoring her phone and online activity?

He was sick to the back teeth with teenaged girls with crushes. Jasmine had started it with her outrageous little stunt seven years ago. He'd had the last word on that. But this was a new era and Emma Madden wasn't the least put off by his efforts to shake her off. He'd tried being patient. He'd tried being polite. What was he supposed to do? The fifteen-year-old was like a leech, clinging on for all she was worth. He was being stalked. By a teenager! Sending him presents at work. Turning up at his favourite haunts, at the gym, at a business lunch, which was damned embarrass-ing. He'd had his work cut out trying to get his client to believe he wasn't doing a teenager. He might be a playboy but he had some standards and keeping away from underage girls was one of them.

Jake turned his phone to silent and tossed it next to his bag on the bed. He walked over to the window to look at the fields surrounding the country estate. Autumn was one of his favourite times at Ravensdene. The leaves on the deciduous trees in the garden were in their final stages of turning and the air was sharp and fresh with the promise of winter around the cor-ner. As soon as his guests arrived he would light the fire in the sitting room, put on some music, pour the champagne, party on and post heaps of photos on so-cial media so Emma Madden got the message.

Finally.

CHAPTER TWO

THE CARS STARTED arriving just as Jaz got comfortable in the smaller sitting room where she had set up her workstation. She had to hand-sew the French lace on Julius's fiancée Holly's dress, which would take hours. But she was happiest when she was working on one of her designs. She outsourced some of the basic cutting and sewing of fabric but when it came to the details she did it all by hand. It gave her designs that signature Jasmine Connolly touch. Every stitch or every crystal, pearl or bead she sewed on to a gown made her feel proud of what she had achieved. As a child she had sat on the floor in this very sitting room surrounded by butcher's paper or tissue wrap and Miranda as a willing, if not long-suffering, model. Jaz had dreamed of success. Success that would transport her far away from her status as the unwanted daughter of a barmaid who turned tricks to feed her drug and alcohol habit.

The sound of car doors slamming, giggling women and high heels tottering on gravel made Jaz's teeth grind together like tectonic plates. At this rate she was going to be down to her gums. But no way was she going back to town until the weekend was over. Jake could party all he liked. She was not being told what to do. Besides, she knew it would annoy him to have her here. He might have acted all cool and casual about it but she knew him well enough to know he would be spitting chips about it privately.

Jaz put down her sewing and carefully covered it with the satin wrapping sheet she had brought with her. This she had to see. What sort of women had he got to come? He had a thing for busty blondes. Such a cliché but that was Jake. He was shallow. He lived life in the fast lane and didn't stay in one place long enough to put down roots. He surrounded himself with showgirls and starlets who used him as much as he used them.

It was nauseating.

Jake was standing in the great hall surrounded by ten or so young women—all blonde—who were dressed in skimpy cocktail wear and vertiginous heels. Jaz leaned against the doorjamb with her arms folded, watching as each girl kissed him in greeting. One even ruffled his hair and another rubbed her breasts—which Jaz could tell were fake—against his upper arm.

He caught Jaz's eye and his mouth slanted in a mocking smile. 'Ah, here's the fun police. Ladies, this is the gardener's daughter, Jasmine.'

Jaz gave him an 'I'll get you for that later' look before she addressed the young women. 'Do your parents know where you all are?' she said.

Jake's brows shot together in a brooding scowl. 'Knock it off, Jasmine.'

Jaz smiled at him with saccharine sweetness. 'Just checking you haven't sneaked in a minor or two.'

Twin streaks of dull colour rode high along his aristocratic cheekbones and his mouth flattened until it was a bloodless line of white. A frisson of excitement coursed through her to have riled him enough to show a crack in his 'too cool for school' façade. Jaz was the only person who could do that to him. He sailed through life with that easy smile and that 'anything goes' attitude but pitted against her he rippled with latent anger. She wondered how far she could push him. Would he touch her? He hadn't come anywhere near her for seven years. When the family got together for Christmas or birthdays, or whatever, he never greeted her. He never hugged or kissed her on the cheek as he did to Miranda or his mother. He avoided Jaz like she was carrying some deadly disease, which was fine by her. She didn't want to touch him either.

But, instead of responding, Jake moved past her as if she was invisible and directed the women to the formal sitting room. 'In here, ladies,' he said. 'The party's about to begin.'

Jaz wanted to puke as the women followed him as though he were the Pied Piper. Couldn't they see how they were being used to feed his ego? He would ply them with expensive champagne or mix them exotic cocktails and tell them amusing anecdotes about his famous parents and their Hollywood and London theatre friends. Those he wouldn't bother sleeping with he would toss out by two or three in the morning. The one—or two or three, according to the tabloids—he slept with would be sent home once the deed was done. They would never get a follow-up call from him. It was a rare woman who got two nights with Jake Ravensdale. Jaz couldn't remember the last one.

The doorbell sounded behind her. She let out a weary sigh and turned to open it.

'I'll get that,' Jake said, striding back into the great hall from the sitting room.

Jaz stood to one side and curled her lip at him. 'Ten women not enough for you, Jake?'

He gave her a dismissive look and opened the door. But the smile of greeting dropped from his face as if he had been slapped. 'Emma…' His throat moved up and down. 'What? Why? How did you find me?' The words came spilling out in a way Jaz had never seen before. He looked agitated. *Seriously* agitated.

'I had to see you,' the girl said with big, lost waif, shimmering eyes and a trembling bottom lip. 'I just *had* to.'

And she was indeed a girl, Jaz noted. Not yet out of her teens. At that awkward age when one foot was in girlhood and the other in adulthood, a precarious position, and one when lots of silly mistakes that could last a lifetime could be made. Jaz knew it all too well. Hadn't she tried to straddle that great big divide, with devastating consequences?

'How'd you get here?' Jake's voice had switched from shocked to curt.

'I caught a cab.'

His brows locked together. 'All the way from London?'

'No,' Emma said. 'From the station in the village.'

Poor little kid, Jaz thought. She remembered looking at Jake exactly like that, as if he was some demigod and she'd been sent to this earth solely to worship him. It was cruel to watch knowing all the thoughts that were going through that young head. Teenage love could be so intense, so consuming and incredibly irrational. The poor kid was in the throes of a heady infatuation, travelling all this way in the hope of a little bit of attention from a man who clearly didn't want to give her the time of day. Jake was here partying with a bunch of women and Emma thought she could be one of them. What a little innocent.

Jaz couldn't stand by and watch history repeat itself. What if Emma was so upset she did something she would always regret, like *she* had done? There had to be a way to let the kid down in such a way that would ease the hurt of rejection. But brandishing a bunch of party girls in Emma's face was not the way to do it.

'Why don't you come in and I'll—?' Jaz began.

'Stay out of it, Jasmine,' Jake snapped. 'I'll deal with this.' He turned back to the girl. 'You have to leave. Now. I'll call you a cab but you have to go home. Understand?'

Emma's eyes watered some more. 'But I can't go home. My mother thinks I'm staying with a friend. I'll get in heaps of trouble. I'll be grounded for the rest of my life.'

'And so you damn well should be,' Jake growled.

'Maybe I could help,' Jaz said and held out her hand to the girl. 'I'm Jaz. I'm Jake's fiancée.'

There was a stunned silence.

Jake went statue-still beside Jaz. Emma looked at her with a blank stare. But then her cheeks pooled with crimson colour. 'Oh… I—I didn't realise,' she stammered. 'I thought Jake was still single otherwise I would never have—'

'It's fine, sweetie,' Jaz said. 'I totally understand and I'm not the least bit offended. We've been keeping our relationship a secret, haven't we, darling?' She gave Jake a bright smile while surreptitiously jabbing him in the ribs.

He opened and closed his mouth like a fish that had suddenly found itself flapping on the carpet instead of swimming safely in its fishbowl. But then he seemed to come back into himself and stretched his lips into one of his charming smiles. 'Yeah,' he said. 'That's right. A secret. I only just asked her a couple of minutes ago. That's why we're…er…celebrating.'

'Are you coming, Jakey?' A clearly tipsy blonde came tottering out into the hall carrying a bottle of champagne in one hand and a glass in the other.

Jaz took Emma by the arm and led her away to the kitchen, jerking her head towards Jake in a non-verbal signal to get control of his guest. 'That's one of the bridesmaids,' she said. 'Can't handle her drink. I'm seriously thinking of dumping her for someone else. I don't want her to spoil the wedding photos. Can you imagine?'

Emma chewed at her bottom lip. 'I guess it kind of makes sense...'

'What does?'

'You and Jake.'

Jaz pulled out a kitchen stool and patted it. 'Here,' she said. 'Have a seat while I make you a hot chocolate—or would you prefer tea or coffee?'

'Um...hot chocolate would be lovely.'

Jaz got the feeling Emma had been about to ask for coffee in order to appear more sophisticated. It reminded her of all the times when she'd drunk vile-tasting cocktails in order to fit in. She made the frothiest hot chocolate she could and handed it to the young girl. 'Here you go.'

Emma cupped her hands around the mug like a child. 'Are you sure you're not angry at me turning up like this? I had no idea Jake was serious about anyone. There's been nothing in the press or anything.'

'No, of course not,' Jaz said. 'You weren't to know.' *I didn't know myself until five minutes ago.* 'We haven't officially announced it yet. We wanted to have some time to ourselves before the media circus begins.' And it would once the news got out. Whoopee doo! If this didn't get Myles' attention, nothing would.

'You're the gardener's daughter,' Emma said. 'I read about you in one of the magazines at the hair-dresser's. There was an article about Jake's father's love-child Katherine Winwood and there were pictures of you. You've known Jake all your life.'

'Yes, since I was eight,' Jaz said. 'I've been in love with him since I was sixteen.' *It didn't hurt to tell her one more little white lie, did it?* It was all in a good cause. 'How old are you?'

'Fifteen and a half,' Emma said.

'Tough age.'

Emma's big brown eyes lowered to study the contents of her mug. 'I met Jake at a function a couple of months ago,' she said. 'It was at my stepfather's restaurant. He sometimes lets me work for him as a waitress. Jake was the only person who was nice to me that night. He even gave me a tip.'

'Understandable you'd fancy yourself in love with him,' Jaz said. 'He breaks hearts just by breathing.'

Emma's mouth lifted at the corners in a vestige of a smile. 'I should hate you but I don't. You're too nice. Kind of natural and normal, you know? But then, I guess I would hate you if I didn't think you were perfect for him.'

Jaz smiled over clenched teeth. 'How about we give your mum a call and let her know where you are? Then I'll drive you to the station and wait with you until you get on the train, okay? Have you got a mobile?'

Silly question. What teenager didn't? It was probably a better model than hers.

When Jaz got back from sending Emma on her way home, Jake was in the main sitting room clearing away the detritus of his short-lived party. Apparently he had sent his guests on their merry way as well. 'Need some help with that?' she said.

He sent her a black look. 'I think you've done more than enough for one night.'

'I thought it was a stroke of genius, actually,' Jaz said, calmly inspecting her nails.

'Engaged?' he said. '*Us?* Don't make me laugh.'

He didn't look anywhere near laughing, Jaz thought. His jaw was locked like a stiff hinge. His mouth was flat. His eyes were blazing with fury. 'What else was I supposed to do?' she said. 'That poor kid was so love-struck nothing short of an engagement would've convinced her to leave.'

'I had it under control,' he said through tight lips.

Jaz rolled her eyes. 'How? By having a big bimbo bash? Like that was ever going to work. You're going about this all wrong, Jake—or should I call you Jakey?'

His eyes flashed another round of sparks at her. 'That silly little kid has been stalking me for weeks. She gate-crashed an important business lunch last week. I lost a valuable client because of her.'

'She's young and fancies herself in love,' Jaz said. 'You were probably the first man to ever speak to her as if she was a real person instead of a geeky kid. But throwing a wild party with heaps of women isn't going to convince her you're not interested in her. The only way was to convince her you're off the market. Permanently.'

He snatched up a half-empty bottle of champagne and stabbed the neck of it in her direction. 'You're the last woman on this planet I would ever ask to marry me.'

Jaz smiled. 'I know. Isn't it ironic?'

His jaw audibly ground together. 'What's your fiancé going to say about this?'

Here's the payoff. She would have to tell Jake about the break-up. But it would be worth it if it achieved the desired end. 'Myles and I are having a little break for a month,' she said.

'You conniving little cow,' he said. 'You're using me to make him jealous.'

'We're using each other,' Jaz corrected. 'It's a win-win. We'll only have to pretend for a week or two. Once the hue and cry is over we can go back to being frenemies.'

His frown was so deep it closed the gap between his eyes. 'You're thinking of making an...*an announcement*?'

Jaz held up her phone. 'Already done. Twitter is running hot with it. Any minute now I expect your family to start calling.' As if on cue, both of their phones starting ringing.

'Don't answer that.' He quickly muted his phone. 'We need to think this through. We need a plan.'

Jaz switched her phone to silent but not before she saw Myles' number come up. Good. All going swimmingly so far. 'We can let your family in on the secret if you think they'll play ball.'

'It's too risky.' Jake scraped a hand through his hair. 'If anyone lets slip we're not the real deal, it could blow up in our faces. You know what the press are like. Do you think Emma bought it? Really?'

'Yes, but she'll know something's up if you don't follow through.'

He frowned again. 'Follow through how? You're not expecting me to marry you, are you?'

Jaz gave him a look that would have withered a plastic flower. 'I'm marrying Myles, remember?'

'If he takes you back after this.'

She heightened her chin. 'He will.'

One side of his mouth lifted in a cynical arc. 'What's Miranda going to say? You think she'll accept you're in love with me?'

Miranda was going to be a hard sell, but Jaz knew she didn't like Myles, so perhaps it would work. For a time. 'I don't like lying to Miranda, but she's never been…'

'You should've thought of that when you cooked up this stupid farce,' Jake said. 'No. We'll run with it.'

'What did you tell your party girls?' Jaz said. 'I hope I didn't make things too awkward for you.' Ha ha. She *loved* making things awkward for him. The more awkward, the better. What a hoot it was to see him squirm under the shackles of a commitment.

'I'm not in the habit of explaining myself to anyone,' he said. 'But no doubt they'll hear the news like everyone else.'

Jaz glanced at her bare ring finger. Who would take their engagement seriously unless she had evidence? 'I haven't got a ring.'

His dark eyes gleamed with malice. 'No spares hanging around at home?'

She sent him a beady look. 'Do you really want me to wear some other man's ring?'

His mouth flattened again. 'Right. I'll get you a ring.'

'No fake diamonds,' she said. 'I want the real thing. The sort of clients I attract can tell the difference, you know.'

'This is what this is all about, isn't it?' he said. 'You don't want your clients to think you can't hold a man long enough to get him to marry you.'

Jaz could feel her anger building like a catastrophic storm inside her. This wasn't about what her clients thought. It was about what *she* felt. No one in their right mind wanted to be rejected. Abandoned. To be told they weren't loved in the way she desperately dreamed of being loved. Not after she had invested so much in her relationship with Myles.

What did Jake know of investing in a relationship? He moved from one woman to the next without a thought of staying long enough to get to know someone beyond what they liked to do in bed. Only Jake could make her this angry—angry enough to throw something. It infuriated her that he alone could reduce her to such a state. 'I can hold a man,' she said. 'I can hold him just fine. Myles has cold feet, that's all. It's perfectly normal for the groom to get a little stressed before the big day.'

'If he loved you he wouldn't ask for a break,' Jake said. 'He wouldn't risk you finding someone else.'

That thought had occurred to Jaz but she didn't want to think about it. She was good at not thinking about things she didn't want to think about. 'Listen to you,' she said with a scornful snort. 'Jake Ravensdale, playboy extraordinaire, talking like a world expert on love.'

'Where did you take Emma?'

'I put her on the train once I'd talked to her mother and made sure everything was cool,' Jaz said. 'I didn't want her to get into trouble or do anything she might regret.' *Like I did.* She pushed the thought aside. She wouldn't think about the rest of that night after she had left Jake's bedroom.

Jake picked up a glass, filled it with champagne and knocked it back in one gulp. He shook his head like a dog coming out of water and then poured another glass. With his features cast in such serious lines, he looked more like his twin Julius than ever.

'We need a photo,' Jaz said. 'Hand me a glass.'

He looked at her as if she had just asked him to poke a knitting needle in his eye. 'A photo?' he said. 'What for?'

She helped herself to a glass of champagne and came to stand beside him but he backed away as if she was carrying dynamite. Or knitting needles. 'Get away from me,' he said.

'We have to do this, Jake,' she said. 'Who's going to believe it if we don't do an engagement photo?'

'You don't have a ring,' he said. 'Yet.' The way he said 'yet' made it sound as though he considered the task on the same level as having root canal therapy.

'Doesn't matter,' Jaz said. 'Just a shot with us with a glass of champers and grinning like Cheshire cats will be enough.'

'You're a sadist,' he said, shooting her a hooded

look as she came to stand beside him with her camera phone poised. 'You know that, don't you? A totally sick sadist.'

It was impossible for Jaz not to notice how hard and warm his arm was against hers as she leaned in to get the shot. Impossible not to think of those strongly muscled arms gathering her even closer. Was he as aware of her as she was of him? Was that why he was standing so still? He hadn't been this close to her in years. When family photographs had been taken—even though strictly speaking she wasn't family—she had always been up the other end of the shot close to Miranda or one of Jake's parents. She had never stood right next to Jake. Not so close she could practically feel the blood pumping through his veins. She checked the photo and groaned. 'Oh, come on,' she said. 'Surely you can do better than that. You look like someone's got a broomstick up your—'

'Okay, we'll try again.' He put an arm around her shoulders and leaned his head against hers. She could feel the strands of his tousled hair tickling her skin. Her senses were going haywire when his stubbly jaw grazed her face. He smelt amazing—lime and lemongrass with a hint of ginger or some other spice. 'Go on,' he said. 'Take the goddamn shot.'

'Oh...right,' Jaz said and clicked the button. She checked the photo but this time it looked like she was the one being tortured. Plus it was blurred. 'Not my best angle.' She deleted it and held up the phone. 'One more take. Say cheese.'

'That's enough,' he said, stepping away from her

once she'd taken the shot. 'You have to promise me you'll delete that when this is all over, okay?'

Jaz criss-crossed her chest with her hand. 'Cross my heart and hope to die.'

He grunted as if her demise was something he was dearly praying for.

She sent the tweet and then quickly sent a text to Miranda:

I know you never liked Myles. You approve of fiancé # 4?

Miranda's text came back within seconds.

OMG! Definitely!!! Congrats. Always knew you were hot for each other. J Will call later xxxxx

'Who are you texting?' Jake asked.

'Miranda,' Jaz said, putting her phone down. 'She's thrilled for us. We'll finally be sisters. Yay.'

He muttered a curse and prowled around the room like a shark in a fishbowl. 'Julius is never going to fall for this. Not for a moment.'

'He'll have to if you want Emma to go away,' Jaz said. 'If you don't play along I'll tell her the truth.'

He threw her a filthy look. 'You're enjoying this, aren't you?'

She smiled a victor's smile. 'What's that saying about revenge is a dish best eaten cold?'

He glowered at her. 'Isn't it a little childish to be harking on about that night all these years later? I did you a favour back then. I could've done you that night but how would that have worked out? Ever thought about that? No. You want to paint me as the big, bad guy who made you feel a little embarrassed about that schoolgirl crush. But, believe me, I could have done a whole lot worse.'

Jaz stepped out of his way as he stormed past her to leave the room. *You did do a whole lot worse*, she wanted to throw after him. But instead she clamped her lips together and turned back to look at the discarded bottles and glasses.

Typical. Jake had a habit of leaving his mess for other people to clean up.

CHAPTER THREE

JAKE WAS SO mad he could see red spots in front of his eyes. Or maybe he was having a brain aneurysm from anger build-up. Seven years of it. He paced the floor of his room, raking his hair, grinding his teeth, swearing like a Brooklyn rapper at what Jasmine had done to him. Engaged! What a freaking farce. No one would believe it. Not him. Not the playboy prince of the pick-ups.

His stomach turned at the thought. Committed. Tied down. Trapped. He was the last person who would ever tie himself down to one woman and certainly not someone like Jasmine Connolly. She was a manipulative little witch. She was using him. Using him to lure back her third fiancé. Who on earth got engaged three times? Someone who was obsessed with getting married, that was who. Jasmine didn't seem to care who she got engaged to as long as they had money and status.

But through the red mist of anger he could see her solution had some merit. Emma Madden had taken the news of their 'engagement' rather well. He had been poleaxed to see that kid standing on the doorstep. He could count on half a hand how many times he'd been caught off guard but seeing that kid there was right up there. If anyone had seen her—anyone being the press, that was—he would have been toast. He didn't want to be cruel to the girl but how else could he get rid of her? Jasmine's solution seemed to have worked. So far. But how long would he have to stay 'engaged'?

Then there was his family to deal with. He could probably pull off the lie with his parents and Miranda but not his twin. Julius knew him too well. Julius knew how much he hated the thought of being confined in a relationship. Jake was more like his father in that way. His father wasn't good at marriage. Richard and Elisabetta fought as passionately as they made up. It was a war zone one minute and a love fest the next. As a child Jake had found it deeply unsettling—not that he'd ever showed it. His role in the family was the court jester. It was his way of coping with the turbulent emotions that flew around like missiles. He'd never known what he was coming home to.

Then eventually it had happened. The divorce had been bitter and public and the intrusion of the press terrifying to a child of eight. He and Julius had been packed off to boarding school but, while Julius had relished the routine, structure and discipline, Jake had not. Julius had excelled academically while Jake had scraped through, not because he wasn't intellectually capable but because in an immature and mostly subconscious way he hadn't wanted his parents to think their divorce had had a positive effect on him.

But he had more than made up for it in his business analysis company. He was successful and wealthy and had the sort of life most people envied. The fly-in, fly-out nature of his work suited his personality. He didn't hang around long. He just got in there, sorted out the problems and left. Which was how he liked to conduct his relationships.

Being tied to Jasmine, even if it was only a game of charades, was nothing less than torture. He had spent the last seven years avoiding her. Distancing himself from all physical contact. He had even failed to show up for some family functions in an effort to avoid the tension of being in the same room as her. He'd had plenty of lectures from Julius and Miranda about fixing things with Jasmine but why should *he* apologise? He hadn't done anything wrong. He had done the opposite. He had solved the problem, not made it worse. It was her that was still in a snit over something she should have got over years ago.

She had been a cute little kid but once she'd hit her teens she'd changed into a flirty little vamp. It had driven him nuts. She had followed him around like a loyal puppy, trying to sneak time with him, touching him 'by accident' and batting those impossibly long eyelashes at him. He had gone along with it for a while, flirting back in a playful manner, but in the end that had backfired, as she'd seemed to think he was serious about her. He wasn't serious about anyone. But on the night of his parents New Year's Eve party, when she'd been sixteen and he twenty-six, he had drawn the line. He'd activated a plan to give her the message loud and clear: He was a player, not the soppy, romantic happy-ever-after beau she imagined him to be.

That night she had dressed in a revealing outfit that was far too old for her and had worn make-up far too heavy. To Jake she had looked like a kid who had rummaged around in her mother's wardrobe. In the dark. He had gone along with her flirtation all evening, agreeing to meet with her in his room just after midnight. But instead of turning up alone as she'd expected he'd brought a couple of girls with him, intending to shock Jasmine into thinking he was expecting an orgy. It had certainly done the trick. She had left him alone ever since. He couldn't remember the last time she had spoken to him other than to make some cutting remark and the only time she looked at him was to spear him with a death-adder glare. Which had suited him just fine.

Until now.

Now he had to work out a way of hanging around with her without wanting to... Well, he didn't want to admit to what he wanted to do with her. But he was only human and a full-blooded male, after all. She was the stuff of male fantasies. He would never admit it to anyone but over the years he'd enjoyed a few fantasies of her in his morning shower. She was sultry and sulky, yet she had a razor-sharp wit and intelligence to match. She had done well for herself, building her business up from scratch, although he thought she was heading for a burnout by trying to do everything herself. Not that she would ever ask his advice. She was too proud. She would rather go bankrupt than admit she might have made a mistake.

Jake dragged a hand down his face. This was going to be the longest week or two of his life. What did Jasmine expect of him? How far did she want this act to go? She surely wouldn't want to sleep with him if she was still hankering after her ex? Not that she showed any sign of being attracted to him, although she did have a habit of looking at his mouth now and again. But everyone knew how much she hated him. Not that a bit of hate got in the way of good sex.

Sheesh. He had to stop thinking about sex and Jasmine in the same sentence. He had never seen her as a sister, even though she had been brought up as one at Ravensdene. Or at least not since she'd hit her teens. She'd grown from being a gangly, awkward teenager into an unusual but no less stunning beauty. Her features were not what one could describe as classically beautiful, but there was some indefinable element to the prominence of her brows and the ice-blue and storm-grey of her eyes that made her unforgettable. She had a model-slim figure and lustrous, wavy honey-brown hair that fell midway down her back. Her skin was creamy and smooth and looked fabulous with or without make-up, although she used make-up superbly these days.

Her mouth… How could he describe it? It was perfect. Simply perfect. He had never seen a more beautiful mouth. The lower lip was full and shapely, the top one a perfect arc above it. The vermillion borders of her lips were so neatly aligned it was as if a master had drawn them. She had a way of slightly elevating her chin, giving her a haughty air that belied her humble beginnings. Her nose, too, had the look of an aristocrat about it with its ski-slope contour. When she smiled—which she rarely did when he was around— it lit up the room. He had seen grown men buckle at the knees at that smile.

Jake's phone vibrated where he'd left it on the bedside table. He glanced at the screen and saw it was Julius. His twin had called six times now. *Better get it over with*, he thought, and answered.

'Is this some kind of prank?' Julius said without preamble.

'No, it's—'

'Jaz and you?' Julius cut him off. 'Come on, man. You hate her guts. You can't stand being in the same room as her. What happened?'

'It was time to bury the hatchet,' Jake said.

'You think I came down in the last shower?' Julius said. 'I know wedding fever has hit with Holly and me, and now Miranda and Leandro, but you and Jaz? I don't buy it for a New York picosecond. What's she got on you? Is she holding a AK-47 to your head?'

Jake let out a rough-edged sigh. He could lie to anyone else but not his identical twin. All that time in the womb had given them a connection beyond what normal siblings felt. They even felt each other's pain. When Julius had had his appendix out when he was fifteen Jake had felt like someone was ripping his guts out. 'I've been having a little problem with a girl,' he said. 'A teenager.'

'I'm not sure I want to hear this.'

'It's not what you think,' Jake said and explained the situation before adding, 'Jasmine intercepted Emma at the door and told her we were engaged.'

'How did this girl Emma take it?'

'Surprisingly well,' Jake said.

'What about Jaz's fiancé?'

'I have no idea,' Jake said. 'He's either relieved she's off his hands or he's going to turn up at my place and shoot out my kneecaps.'

'Always a possibility.'

'Don't remind me.'

There was a beat of silence.

'You're not going to sleep with her, are you?' Julius said.

'God, no,' Jake said. 'I wouldn't touch her with a barge pole.'

'Yes, well, I suggest you keep your barge pole zipped in your pants,' Julius said dryly. 'What actually happened with you guys that night at the party? I know she came to your room but you've never said what went on other than you didn't touch her.'

'I didn't do anything except send her on her way,' Jake said. 'You know what she was like, always following me about, giving me sheep's eyes. I taught her a lesson by offering her a foursome but she declined.'

'A novel approach.'

'It worked.'

'Maybe, but don't you think her anger is a little out of proportion?' Julius said.

'That's just Jasmine,' Jake said. 'She's always had a rotten temper.'

'I don't know… I sometimes wonder if something else happened that night.'

'Like what?'

'She'd been drinking and was obviously upset after leaving your room,' Julius said. 'Not a good combination in a teenage girl.'

Jake hung up a short time later once they'd switched topics but he couldn't get rid of the seed of unease Julius had planted in his mind. Had something happened that night after Jasmine had left his room? Was that why she had been so protective of young Emma, making sure she got home safely with an adult at the other end to meet her? The rest of that night was a bit of blur for him. Most of his parents' parties ended up that way. Even some of his parties were a little full-on too. There was always a lot of alcohol, loud music blaring and people coming and going. He had been feeling too pleased with himself for solving the Jasmine problem to give much thought to where she'd gone after leaving his room. At twenty-six what he had done had seemed the perfect solution. The only solution.

Now, at thirty-three, he wasn't quite so sure.

Jaz was making herself a nightcap in the kitchen when Jake strolled in. 'Finding it hard to sleep without a playgirl bunny or three in your bed to keep you warm?'

'What happened after you left my room that night?'

Jaz lowered her gaze to her chocolate drink rather

than meet his piercing blue eyes. The chocolate swirled as she stirred it with the teaspoon, creating a whirlpool not unlike the one she could feel in the pit of her stomach. She never thought about that night. That night had happened to another person. It had happened to a foolish, gauche kid who'd had too much to drink and had been too emotionally unstable to know what she was doing or what she was getting into.

'Jasmine. Answer me.'

Jaz lifted her gaze to his and frowned. 'Why do you always call me Jasmine instead of Jaz? You're the only one in your family who insists on doing that. Why?'

'It's your name.'

'So? Yours is Jacques but you don't like being called that,' Jaz pointed out. 'Maybe I'll start to.'

'Julius knows.'

Her heart gave a little stumble. 'Knows what?'

'About us,' he said. 'About this not being real.'

Jaz took a moment to get her head sorted. She'd thought he meant Julius knew about *that night*… But how could he? He would have said something if he did. He was the sort of man who would have got her to press charges. He wouldn't have stood by and let someone get away with it. 'Oh…right; well, I guess he's your twin and all.'

'He won't tell anyone apart from Holly.'

'Good,' Jaz said. 'The less people who know, the better.'

Jake pulled out a kitchen stool and sat opposite her at the island bench. 'You want to make me one of those?'

She lifted her chin. 'Make it yourself.'

A slow smile came to his mouth. 'I guess I'd better in case you put cyanide in it.'

Jaz forced her gaze away from the tempting curve of his mouth. It wasn't fair that one man had so much darn sex appeal. It came off him in waves. She felt it brush against her skin, making her body tingle at the thought of him touching her for real. Ever since his arm had brushed against hers, ever since he'd slung his arm around her shoulders and leaned in against her, she had longed for him to do it again. It was like every nerve under her skin was sitting bolt upright and wide awake, waiting with bated breath for him to touch her again.

She was aware of him in other parts of her body. The secret parts. Her breasts and inner core tingled from the moment he'd stepped into the same room. It was like he could turn a switch in her body simply by being present. She watched covertly as he moved about the kitchen, fetching a cup and the tin of chocolate powder and stirring it into the milk before he turned to put it in the microwave.

She couldn't tear her eyes away from his back and shoulders. He was wearing a cotton T-shirt that showcased every sculpted muscle on his frame. How would it feel to slide her hands down his tautly muscled back? To slip one of her hands past the waistband of his jeans and cup his trim buttocks, or what was on the other side of his testosterone-rich groin?

Jaz gave herself a mental shake. She was on a mission to win back Myles. Getting involved with Jake was out of the question. Not that he would ever want *her*. He loathed her just as much as she loathed him. But men could separate their emotions from sex. She of all people knew that. Maybe he would want to make the most of their situation—a little fling to pass the time until he could get back to his simpering starlets and Hollywood hopefuls. Her mind started to drift... What would it feel like to have Jake make love to her? To have his hands stroke every inch of her flesh, to have his mouth plunder hers?

Jake turned from the microwave. 'Is something wrong?'

Jaz blinked to reset her vision. 'That was weird. I thought I saw you actually lift a finger in the kitchen. I must be hallucinating.'

He laughed and pulled out one of the stools opposite hers at the kitchen bench. 'I can find my way around a kitchen when I need to.'

Jaz's top lip lifted in a cynical arc. 'Like when no slavishly devoted woman is there to cater to your every whim?'

His eyes held hers in a penetrating lock. She felt the power of it go through her like a current of electricity. 'How much did you have to drink that night?' he asked.

She pushed her untouched chocolate away and slipped off the stool. 'Clean up your mess when you're done in here. Eggles won't be back till Sunday night.'

Jaz almost got to the door, but then Jake's hand came out of nowhere and turned her to face him. His warm, strong fingers curling around her arm sent a shockwave through her body, making her feel as if someone inside her stomach had shuffled a deck of cards. Quickly. Vegas-quick. She moistened her lips with her tongue as she brought her gaze to his dark-blue one. His ink-black lashes were at half-mast, giving him a sexily hooded look. She looked at his mouth and felt that shuffle in her heart valves this time. She could look at his twin's mouth any time without this crazy reaction. What was it about Jake's mouth that turned her into a quivering mess of female hormones? Was it because, try as she might, she couldn't stop thinking about how it would feel pressed to hers? 'I don't remember giving you permission to touch me,' she said.

Instead of releasing her he slid his fingers down to the bones of her wrist and encircled it like a pair of gentle handcuffs. 'Talk to me,' he said in a deep, gravel-rough voice that made the entire length of her spine soften like candle wax in a steam room.

Jaz tested his hold but all it did was take him with her to the doorframe, which was just an inch or so behind her. She pressed her back against it for stability because right then her legs weren't doing such a great job of holding her upright. He was now so close she could see the individual pinpricks of stubble along his jaw and around his nose and mouth. She could feel their breath intermingling. His muscle-packed thighs were within a hair's breadth of hers, his booted feet toe-to-toe with her bare ones. 'Wh-what are you doing?' she said in a voice she barely recognised as her own.

His eyes went to her mouth, lingering there for endless, heart-stopping seconds. 'Ever wondered what would happen if we kissed?'

Like just about every day for the last seven years. 'You'd get your face slapped, that's what.'

A smile hitched up one side of his mouth. 'Yeah, that's what I thought.'

Jaz felt like her heart rate was trying to get into the *Guinness Book of Records*. She could smell those lime and lemongrass notes of his aftershave and something else that was one part musk and three parts male. 'But you're not going to do it, right?'

He moved around her mouth like a metal detector just above the ground where something valuable was hidden. He didn't touch down but he might as well have because she felt the tingling in her lips as if he was transmitting raw sexual energy from his body to hers. 'You think about it, don't you? About us getting down to business.'

Oh, dear God in heaven, where is my willpower? Jaz thought as her senses went haywire. She had never wanted to be kissed more in her life than right then. She had never wanted to feel a man's arms go around her and pull her into his hard body. Desire moved through her like a prowling, hungry beast looking for satiation. She felt it in her blood, the tick of arousal. She felt it in her breasts, the prickly sensation of them shifting against the lace of her bra as if they couldn't wait for him to get his hands or mouth on them. She felt it in her core, the pulse and contraction of her inner muscles in anticipatory excitement. 'No, I don't. I never think about it.'

He gave a soft chuckle as he stepped back from her. 'No, nor do I.'

Jaz stood in numb silence as he went back to the island bench to pick up his hot chocolate. She watched as he lifted the mug to his lips and took a sip. He put the mug down and cocked a brow at her. 'Something wrong?'

She pushed herself away from the doorframe, tucking her hair back over one shoulder with a hand that wasn't as steady as she would have liked. 'We haven't discussed the rules about our engagement.'

'Rules?'

Jaz gave him a look. 'Yes, rules. Not your favourite word, is it?'

His eyes glinted. 'Far as I'm concerned, they're only there to be broken.'

She steeled her spine. 'Not this time.'

'Is that a dare?'

Jaz could feel every cell in her body being pulled and tugged by the animal attraction he evoked in her. She couldn't understand why someone she hated so much could have such a monumental effect on her. She wanted to throw herself at him, tear at his clothes and crawl all over his body. She wanted to lock her mouth on his and tangle her tongue with his in an erotic salsa. She wanted him *inside* her body. She could feel the hollow vault of her womanhood pulsating with need. She could even feel the dew of her intimate moisture gathering. She wanted him like a drug she knew she shouldn't have. He was contraband. Dangerous. 'Is the thought of being celibate for a week or two really that difficult for you?'

He gave a lip shrug. 'Never done it before, so I wouldn't know.'

Jaz mentally rolled her eyes. 'Do you have shares in a condom manufacturer or something?'

His dark eyes gleamed with amusement. 'Now there's an idea.'

She picked up her mug of chocolate, not to drink, but to give her hands something to do in case they took it upon themselves to touch him. 'I find your shallow approach to relationships deeply offensive. It's like you only see women as objects you can use to satisfy a bodily need. You don't see them as real people who have feelings.'

'I have the greatest respect for women. That's why I'm always honest with them about what I want from them.'

Jaz eyeballed him. 'I think it's because you're scared of commitment. You can't handle the thought of someone leaving you so you don't let yourself bond with them in the first place.'

He gave a mocking laugh. 'You got a printout of that psychology degree you bought online?'

'That's another thing you do,' Jaz said. 'You joke your way through life because being serious about stuff terrifies you.'

His mouth was smiling but his eyes were not. They had become as hard as flint. 'Ever wondered why

your three fiancés have dumped you before you could
march them up the aisle?'

Jaz ground her teeth together until her jaw ached.
'Myles hasn't dumped me. We're on a break. It's not
the same as being…breaking up.'

'You're a ballbreaker. You don't want a man. You
want a puppet. Someone you can wind around your
little finger to do what you want when you want. No
man worth his testosterone will stand for that.'

Jaz could feel her anger straining at the leash of her
control like a feral dog tied up with a piece of cotton.
Her fingers around the mug of chocolate twitched.
How she would love to spray it over Jake's arrogant
face. 'You enjoy humiliating me, don't you? It gives
you such a big, fat hard-on, doesn't it?'

His jaw worked as if her words had hit a raw nerve.
'While we're playing Ten Things I Hate About You,
here's another one for my list. You need to get over
yourself. You've held onto this ridiculous grudge for
far too long.'

Jaz saw the hot chocolate fly through the air before she fully registered she'd thrown it. It splashed
over the front of his T-shirt like brown paint thrown
at a wall.

Jake barely moved a muscle. He was as still as a
statue on a plinth. Too still.

The silence was breathing, heaving with menace.

But then he calmly reached over the back of his
head, hauled the T-shirt off, bunched it up into a rough
ball and handed it to her. 'Wash it.'

Jaz swallowed as she looked at the T-shirt. She had

lost control. A thing she had sworn she would never do. Crazy people like her mother lost control. They shouted and screamed and threw things. Not her. She never let anyone do that to her. A tight knot of self-disgust began to choke her. Tears welled up behind her eyes, escaping from a place she had thought she had locked and bolted for good. Tears she hadn't cried since that night when she had finally made it back to her bedroom with shame clinging to her like filth. No amount of showering had removed it. If she thought about that night she would feel it clogging every pore of her skin like engine grease. She took the T-shirt from him with an unsteady hand. 'I'm sorry…'

'Forget about it.'

I only wish I could, Jaz thought. But when she finally worked up the courage to look up he had already turned on his heel and gone.

CHAPTER FOUR

JAKE WAS VAINLY trying to sleep when he heard the sound of the plumbing going in the other wing of the house where Jasmine's room was situated next to Miranda's. He lay there for a while, listening as the pipes pumped water. Had Jasmine left on a tap? He glanced at the bedside clock. It was late to be having a shower, although he had to admit for him a cold one wouldn't have gone astray. He rarely lost his temper. He preferred to laugh his way out of trouble but something about Jasmine's mood had got to him tonight. He was sick of dragging their history around like a dead carcass. It was time to put it behind them. He didn't want Julius and Holly's or Miranda and Leandro's wedding ruined by a ridiculous feud that had gone on way too long.

He shoved off the bed covers and reached for a bathrobe. He seemed to remember Jasmine had a tendency for long showers but he still thought he'd better check to make sure nothing was amiss. He made his way to the bathroom closest to her room and rapped his knuckles on the door. 'You okay in there?' he said.

No answer. He tapped again, louder this time, and called out but the water continued. He tried the door but it was locked. He frowned. Why did she think she had to lock the door? They were alone in the house. Didn't she trust him? The thought sat uncomfortably on him. He might be casual about sex but not *that* casual. He always ensured he had consent first.

Not that he was going to sleep with Jasmine. That would be crazy. Crazy but tempting. Way too tempting, if he was honest with himself. He had spent many an erotic daydream with her body pinned under his or over his, or with her mouth on him, sucking him until he blew like a bomb. She had that effect on men. She didn't do it on purpose; her natural sensuality made men fall over like ninepins. Her beauty, her regal manner, her haughty 'I'm too good for the likes of you' air made men go weak at the knees, himself included. Just thinking about her naked body under that spray of water in the shower was enough to make him rock-hard.

He waited outside her door until the water finally stopped. 'Jasmine?'

It was a while before she opened the door. She was wearing a bathrobe and her hair was wrapped turban-like with a towel. Her skin was rosy from the hot water and completely make-up free, giving her a youthful appearance that took him back a decade. 'What?' She frowned at him irritably. 'Is something wrong with your bathroom?'

He frowned when he saw her red-rimmed eyes and pink nose. 'Have you been crying?'

Her hand clutching the front of her bathrobe clenched a little tighter but her tone was full of derision. 'Why would I be crying? Oh, yes, I remember now. My fiancé wanted a month's break. Pardon me for being a little upset.'

Jake felt a stab of remorse for not having factored in her feelings. He had such an easy come, easy go attitude to his relationships he sometimes forgot other people invested much more emotionally. But did she really love the guy or was she in love with the idea of love and marriage? Three engagements in three years. That must be some sort of record, surely? Had she been in love each time? 'You want to talk about it?'

Her eyes narrowed in scorn. 'What—with *you*?'

'Why not?'

She pushed past him and he got a whiff of honeysuckle body wash. 'I'm going to bed. Good night.'

'Jasmine, wait,' Jake said, capturing her arm on the way past. His fingers sank into the soft velour of her bathrobe as he turned her to face him. He could feel the slenderness of her arm in spite of the pillowy softness of the thick fabric, reminding him of how feminine she was. A hot coil of lust burned in his groin, winding tighter and tighter. 'I might've been a little rough on you downstairs earlier.'

Her brows lifted and she pulled out of his light hold. 'Might've been?'

He let out a whooshing breath. 'Okay, I *was* rough on you. I didn't think about how you'd be feeling about the break-up.'

'It's not a break-up. It's a *break*.'

Jake wasn't following the semantics. 'You don't think it's permanent?'

Her chin came up. 'No. Myles just needs a bit of space.'

He frowned. 'But what about us? Don't you think he's going to get a little pissed you found someone else so soon?'

She looked at him as if he were wearing a dunce's cap. 'Yes, but that's the whole point. Sometimes people don't know what they've got until it's gone.'

'Has he called you since the news of our—' Jake couldn't help grimacing over the word '—engagement was announced?'

'Heaps of times but I'm not answering,' Jaz said. 'I'm letting him stew for a bit.'

'Do you think he believes it's true?'

'Why wouldn't he? Everyone else bought it. Apart from Julius, of course.'

'I'm surprised Miranda fell for it, to tell you the truth,' Jake said.

Jaz frowned. 'Why do you say that? Have you spoken to her?'

'She sent me a congratulatory text but I haven't spoken to her. I've been dodging her calls. But you're her closest friend. She'll suss something's amiss once she sees us together.'

Her lips compressed for a moment. 'I don't think it will be a problem. Anyway, she's busy with her own engagement and wedding plans.'

Jake studied her for a beat. 'Are you in love with this Myles guy?'

Her brow wrinkled. 'What sort of question is that? Of course I am.'

'Were you in love with Tim and Linton?'

'*Lincoln*,' she said with a scowl. 'Yes, I was.'

'You're pretty free and easy with your affection, aren't you?'

Jaz gave him a gelid look. 'That's rich coming from the man who changes partners faster than tyres are changed in a Formula One pit lane.'

Jake couldn't help smiling. 'You flatter me. I'm fast but not that fast.'

'Have you heard from Emma?'

'No.'

'So my plan is working.'

'So far.' He didn't like to admit it but there was no denying it. From being bombarded with texts, emails and calls there had been zilch from Emma since Jasmine had delivered her bombshell announcement. Another thing he didn't like to acknowledge was how he'd had nothing but congratulations from all his friends and colleagues. Even his parents had stopped slinging insults at each other via the press long enough to congratulate him. He had even had an email from a client he'd thought he'd lost, promising not just his business but that of several high-profile contacts.

This little charade was turning out to be much more of a win-win than Jake had expected.

'What we need is to be seen out in public,' Jaz said. 'That will make it even more believable.'

'In public?'

'Yes, like on a date or dinner or something.'

'You reckon we could get through a whole meal together without you throwing something at me?'

Her gaze moved out of reach of his. 'I'll do my best.'

Jaz woke the next morning to a call from Miranda. 'I know it's early but I can't get Jake on his phone to congratulate him,' Miranda said. 'I figured he'd be in bed with you. Can you hand me to him? That is, if it's not inconvenient?' The way she said 'inconvenient' was playful and teasing.

Jaz swallowed back a gulp. 'Erm…he's having a shower right now. I'll get him to call you, okay?'

'Okay,' Miranda said. 'So how's it going? Does it seem real? I mean, for all this time you've been at each other's throats. Is it good to be making love instead of war?'

Jaz got out of bed but on her way to the window caught sight of her reflection in the mirror. How could she lie to her best friend? Lying by text was one thing. Lying in conversation was another. It didn't seem right. Not when they had been friends for so long. 'Miranda, listen, things aren't quite what they seem… I'm not really engaged to Jake. We're pretending.'

'Pretending?' Miranda sounded bitterly disappointed. 'But why?'

'I'm trying to win Myles back,' Jaz said. 'He wanted to take a break and I thought I'd try and make him jealous.'

'But why did Jake agree to it?' Miranda said.

'I didn't give him a choice.' Jaz explained the situation about Emma briefly.

'Gosh,' Miranda said. 'I was so excited for you. Now I feel like someone's punched me in the belly.'

'I'm sorry for lying but—'

'Are you sure about Myles?' Miranda said. 'I mean, *absolutely* sure he's the one?'

'Of course I'm sure. Why else would I be going to so much trouble to win him back?'

'Pride?'

Jaz pressed her lips together. 'It's not a matter of pride. It's a matter of love.'

'But you fall in and out of love all the time,' Miranda said. 'How do you know he's the right one for you when you could just as easily fall in love with someone else tomorrow?'

'I'm not going to fall in love with anyone else,' Jaz said. 'How can I when I'm in love with Myles?'

'What do you love about him?'

'We've had this conversation before and I—'

'Let's have it again,' Miranda said. 'Refresh my memory. List three things you love about him.'

'He's…'

'See?' Miranda said. 'You're hesitating!'

'Look, I know you don't like him, so it wouldn't matter what I said about him; you'd find some reason to discount it.'

'It's not that he's not nice and polite, handsome and well-educated and all that,' Miranda said. 'But I worry you only like him because you can control him. You've got a strong personality, Jaz. You need someone who'll stand up to you. Someone who'll be your equal, not your puppet.'

Jaz swung back from the window and paced the carpet. 'I don't like controlling men. I hate them. I always have and I always will. I could never fall in love with someone like that.'

'We'll see.'

She frowned. 'What do you mean, "we'll see"? I hope you're not thinking what I think you're thinking because it's not going to happen. No way.'

'Come on, Jaz,' Miranda said. 'You've had a thing for Jake since you were sixteen.'

'I was a kid back then!' Jaz said. 'It was just a stupid crush. I got over it, okay?'

'If you got over it then why have you avoided him like the black plague ever since?'

Jaz was close to Miranda but not close enough to tell her what had happened that night after she'd left Jake's room. She wasn't close enough to anyone to tell them that. Sharing that shame with someone else wouldn't make it go away. The only way she could make it go away was not to think about it. If she told anyone about it they would look at her differently. They might judge her. Blame her. She didn't want to take the risk. Her tough-girl façade was exactly that—a façade.

Underneath all the bravado she was still that terrified sixteen-year-old who had got herself sexually assaulted by a drunken guest at the party. It hadn't been rape but it had come scarily close to it. The irony was the person who did it had been so drunk they hadn't remembered a thing about it the following morning. The only way Jaz could deal with it was to pretend it hadn't happened. There was no other way. 'Look, I'm not avoiding Jake now, so you should be happy,' she said. 'Who knows? We might even end up friends after this charade is over.'

'I certainly hope so because I don't want Julius and Holly's wedding, or mine and Leandro's, spoilt by you two looking daggers at each other,' Miranda said. 'It's bad enough with Mum and Dad carrying on World War Three.'

'That reminds me. Have you met Kat Winwood yet?' Jaz asked.

'No.' Miranda gave a sigh. 'She won't have anything to do with any of us. I guess if I were in her shoes I might feel the same. What Dad did to her mother was pretty unforgiveable.'

'Yes, well, paying someone to have an abortion isn't exactly how to win friends and influence people, I'll grant you that,' Jaz said.

'What about you?' Miranda said. 'You mentioned a couple of weeks back you were thinking about meeting her. Any luck?'

'Nope,' Jaz said. 'I might not be a Ravensdale but I'm considered close enough to your family to be on the black list as well.'

'Maybe Flynn can get her to change her mind,' Miranda said, referring to the family lawyer, Flynn Carlyon, who had been a year ahead of Jake and Julius at school. 'If anyone can do it he can. He's unlikely to give up until he gets what he wants.'

'But I thought the whole idea was to get her to go away,' Jaz said. 'Wasn't that what Flynn was supposed to do? Pay her to keep from speaking to the press?'

'Yes, but she wouldn't take a penny off him. She hasn't said a word to the media anyway and it's been over a month,' Miranda said. 'Dad's agent called him last night about putting on a party to celebrate his sixty years in showbiz in January. Dad wants Kat there. He says he won't go ahead with it unless she comes.'

'Sixty years?' Jaz said. 'Gosh. What age did he start?'

'Five. He had a walk-on part in some musical way back. Hasn't he shown you the photos?'

'Nope,' Jaz said. 'I must've missed that bragging session.'

'Ha ha,' Miranda said. 'But what are we going to do about Kat? She has to come to Dad's party otherwise he'll be devastated.'

'Well, at least Flynn will have a few weeks to change her mind.'

'I can't work her out,' Miranda said. 'She's a struggling actor who's only had bit parts till now. You'd think she'd be jumping at the chance to cash in on her biological father's fame.'

'Maybe she needs time to get her head around who her father is,' Jaz said. 'It must've come as a huge shock finding out like that just before her mother died.'

'Yes, I guess so.' Miranda sighed again and then added, 'Are you sure you know what you're doing,

Jaz—I mean with Jake? I can't help worrying this could backfire.'

'I know exactly what I'm doing,' Jaz said. 'I'm using Jake and he's using me.'

There was a telling little silence.

'You're not going to sleep with him, are you?' Miranda said.

Jaz laughed. 'I know he's your brother and all that but there are some women on this planet who can actually resist him, you know.'

And I had better keep on doing it.

Jake was coming back in from a morning run around the property when he saw Jaz coming down the stairs, presumably for breakfast. She was wearing light-grey yoga pants and a baby-girl pink slouch top that revealed the cap of a creamy shoulder and the thin black strap of her bra. Her slender feet were bare apart from liquorice-black toenail polish and her hair was in a messy knot on the top of her head that somehow managed to look casual and elegant at the same time. She wasn't wearing a skerrick of make-up but if anything it made her look all the more breath-snatchingly beautiful. But then, since when had her stunning grey-blue eyes with their thick, spider-leg long lashes and prominent eyebrows needed any enhancement?

He caught a whiff of her bergamot-and-geranium essential oil as she came to stand on the last step, making her almost eye-to-eye with him. The urge to touch her lissom young body was overpowering. He had to curl his hands into fists to prevent himself from running a hand down the creamy silk of her cheek or tracing that gorgeous mouth with his finger.

Her eyes met his and a punch of lust slammed him in the groin. The fire and ice in that stormy sea of grey and blue had a potent impact on him. It happened every time their eyes collided. It was like a bolt of electricity zapping him, making everything that was male in him stand to attention. 'I told Miranda the truth about us,' she said with a touch of defiance.

Jake decided to wind her up a bit. 'That we have the hots for each other and are about to indulge in a passionate fling that's been seven years in the making?'

She folded her arms like a schoolmistress who was dealing with a particularly cheeky pupil, but he noticed her cheeks had gone a faint shade of pink. 'No,' she said as tartly as if she had just bitten into a lemon. 'I told her we aren't engaged and we still hate each other.'

He picked up a stray strand of hair that had escaped her makeshift knot and tucked it safely back behind the neat shell of her ear. He felt her give a tiny shiver as his fingers brushed the skin behind her ear and her mouth opened and closed as if she was trying to disguise her little involuntary gasp. 'You don't hate me, sweetheart. You *want* me.'

The twin pools of colour in her cheeks darkened another shade and her eyes flashed with livid blue-tipped flames. 'Do you get charged extra on flights for carrying your ego on board?'

Jake smiled crookedly as he trailed his fingertip from the crimson tide on her cheekbone to the neat hinge of her jaw. 'I see it every time you look at me. I feel it when I'm near you. You feel it too, don't you?'

The point of her tongue sneaked out over her lips in a darting movement. 'All I feel when I'm near you is the uncontrollable urge to scratch my nails down your face.'

He unpeeled one of her hands from where it was tucked in around her middle and laid it flat against his jaw. 'Go on,' he said, challenging her with his gaze. 'I won't stop you.'

Her hand was like cool silk against his skin. A shiver scooted down his spine as he felt the slight scrape of her nails against his morning stubble but then, instead of scoring his face, she began to stroke it. The sound of her soft skin moving over his raspy jaw had an unmistakably erotic element to it. Her touch sent a rocket blast through his pelvis and he put a hand at the base of her spine to draw her closer to his restless, urgent heat. The contact of her body so intimately against his was like fireworks exploding. His mouth came down in search of hers but he didn't have to go far as she met him more than halfway. Her soft lips were parted in anticipation, her vanilla-milkshake breath mingling with his for a spine-tingling microsecond before her mouth fused with his.

She gave a low moan of approval as he moved his mouth against hers, seeking her moist warmth with the stroke and glide of his tongue. She melted against him, her arms winding around his neck, her fingers delving through his hair, holding his head in place as if she was terrified he would pull back from her.

Jake had no intention of pulling back. He was enjoying the taste of her too much, the heat and unbridled passion that blossomed with every stroke and flicker of his tongue against hers. She pressed herself against him, her supple body fitting along his harder contours as if she had been fashioned just for him. He cupped her neat behind, holding her against the throbbing urgency of his arousal as his mouth fed hungrily off the sweet and drugging temptation of hers.

He lifted his mouth only far enough to change position but she grabbed at him, clamping her lips to his, her tongue darting into his mouth to mate wantonly with his. His blood pounded with excitement. His heart rate sped. His thighs fizzed with the need to take charge, to possess the hot, tight, wet vault of her body until this clawing, desperate need was finally satisfied.

Hadn't he always known she would be dynamite in his arms? Hadn't he always wanted to do this? Even that night when she'd been too young to know what she was doing. He had ached and burned to possess her then and he ached and burned now. One kiss wasn't going to be enough. It wasn't enough to satisfy the raging lust rippling through his body. He wanted to feel her convulsing around him as he took her to heaven and back. He knew they would be good together. He had always known it on some level. He felt it whenever their eyes met—the electric jolt of awareness that triggered something primitive in him.

Nothing would please him more than to see her gasping out his name as she came. Nothing would give him more pleasure than to have her admit she wanted him as much as he wanted her. To prove to her it wasn't her 'taking a break' fiancé she was hankering after but *him* she wanted. The man she had wanted since she was a teenager. The man she said she hated but lusted after like a forbidden drug. *That* was what he saw in her eyes—the desire she didn't want to feel but was there, simmering and smouldering with latent heat.

Jake slipped a hand under her loose top in search of the tempting globe of her breast. She hummed her pleasure against his lips as he moved her bra aside to make skin-on-skin contact. For years he had wanted to touch her like this—to feel her soft, creamy skin against his palm and hear her throatily express her need. He passed his thumb over her tightly budded nipple and then circled it before he bent his head and took it into his mouth. She gave another primal moan as he suckled on her breast, using the gentle scrape of his teeth and the sweep and salve of his tongue to tantalise her.

He slipped a hand down between their hard-pressed bodies, cupping her mound, his own body so worked up he wondered if he was going to jump the gun for the first time since he'd been a clumsy teenager.

But suddenly Jaz pulled back, pushing against his chest with the heels of her hands. 'Stop,' she said in a breathless-sounding voice. 'Please…stop.'

Jake held his hands up to show he was cool with her calling a halt. 'Your call, sweetheart.'

She pressed her lips together as she straightened

her top, her hands fumbling and uncoordinated. 'You had no right to do that,' she said, shooting him a hard look.

He gave a lazy smile. 'Well, look who's talking. I wonder what lover boy would say if he'd been a fly on the wall just now? His devoted little "having a break" fiancée getting all hot and bothered with just a friendly kiss.'

Her eyes went to hairpin-thin slits. 'There was nothing friendly about it. You don't even like me. You just wanted to prove a point.'

'What point would that be?'

She tossed her head in an uppity manner as she turned to go back upstairs. 'I'm not having this conversation. You had no right to touch me and that's the end of it. Don't do it again.'

Jake waited until she was almost to the top of the stairs before he said, 'What about when we're out in public? Am I allowed to touch you then?'

A circle of ice rimmed her flattened mouth as she turned to glare at him. 'Only if it's absolutely necessary.'

He smiled a devilish smile. 'I'll look forward to it.'

CHAPTER FIVE

JAZ STORMED INTO her room and shut the door. She would have slammed it except she had already shown Jake how much he had rattled her. She didn't want to give his over-blown ego any more of a boost. She was furious with him for kissing her. How dared he take such liberties? A little voice reminded her that she hadn't exactly resisted but, on the contrary, had given him every indication she was enjoying every pulse-racing second of it.

Which she had been. Damn it.

His kiss had made her face what she didn't want to face. What she hadn't wanted to face for seven years. She wanted him. It was like it was programmed into her genes or something. He triggered something in her that no other man ever had. Her body sizzled when he was around. His touch created an earthquake of longing. How could a kiss make her feel so...so alive? It was crazy. Madness. Lunacy.

It was just like him to make a big joke about everything. This was nothing but a game to him. He enjoyed baiting her. Goading her. *Tempting* her. Why had she allowed him to get that close to her? She should have stepped back while she'd had the chance. Or maybe she hadn't had the chance because her body had other ideas. Wicked ideas that involved him touching her and pleasuring her in a way she had never quite felt before. Why had *his* touch made her flesh tingle and quake with delight? Why had *his* kiss made her heart race and her pulse thrum with longing?

It was just a kiss. It wasn't as if she hadn't been kissed before. She'd had plenty of kisses. Heaps. Dozens. Maybe hundreds… Well, maybe things had been a bit light on that just lately. She couldn't quite recall the last time Myles had kissed her. Not properly. Not passionately, as if he couldn't get enough of her taste and touch. Over the last few weeks their kisses had turned into a rather perfunctory peck on the cheek at hello and goodbye. And as to touching her breasts, well, Myles wasn't good at breasts. He didn't seem to understand she didn't like being pinched or squeezed, like he was someone checking a piece of fruit for ripeness.

Jaz let out a frustrated breath. Why did Jake have to be the expert on kissing her and handling her breasts? It wasn't fair. She didn't want him to have such sensual power over her. He could turn her on by just looking at her with that glinting dark gaze.

Of course it would be *so* much worse now. Now he had actually kissed her and touched her breasts and her lady land. God, she'd almost come on the spot when he'd cupped her down there. How could one man's touch have such an effect on her? She didn't even like him. She loathed him. He was her arch-enemy. He wasn't just a thorn in her side. He was the whole damn rose bush. Unpruned. He was everything she avoided in a partner.

But he sure could kiss. Jaz had to give him that. His lips had done things to hers no man had ever done before. His tongue had lit a blazing fire in her core and it hadn't gone out. The hot coals were smouldering there even now. Her body felt restless. Feverish. Hungry. Starving for more of his electrifying caresses. What would it feel like to have him deep inside her? Moving in her body in that hectic rush for release?

Sex had always been a complicated issue for her. She put it down to the fact her first experience of it had been so twisted and tangled up with shame. She had taken a drink from a young man at the party, more to get back at Jake for rejecting her. She had flirted with the man, hoping Jake would see that not all men found her repulsive. But she hadn't factored in the amount of alcohol she had already consumed or her overwrought emotional state. She couldn't quite remember how she had ended up in one of the down-stairs bathrooms with the man, sweaty and smelling of wine as he tore at her clothes and groped and slob-bered all over her until she'd finally got away. All she could remember was the shame—the sickening shame of not being in control.

Now whenever she had sex that same shame lurked at the back of her mind. Although she enjoyed some aspects of making love—the touching and being needed—she hadn't always been able to relax enough to orgasm. Not that any of her partners had seemed to notice. She might not be a proper Ravensdale but she sure could act when she needed to. Pretending to orgasm every time hadn't been her intention. But once had turned into twice and then it had been far easier than explaining.

How could she explain her behaviour that night? The rational part of her knew the man at the party had some responsibility to acquire proper consent before he touched her, but how did she know if she'd given it or not? It would be his word against hers, that was, if he'd actually remembered. She'd seen him the next morning as the overnight guests were leaving but he had looked right through her as if he had never seen her before. Had she agreed to kiss him in the bathroom or had he come in on her and seized the opportunity to assault her? She didn't know and it was the not knowing that was the most shameful thing for her.

Jaz wasn't into victim blaming but when it came to herself she struggled to forgive herself for allowing something like that to happen. She had buried her shame behind a 'don't mess with me' façade and a sharp tongue but deep inside she was still that shocked and terrified girl.

And she had a scary feeling if she spent too much time alone with Jake Ravensdale he would begin to see it.

Jaz was doing some work on Holly's dress in her room and when her phone rang she picked it up without thinking. 'Jasmine Connolly.'

'Jaz. Finally you answered,' Myles said. 'Why on earth haven't you returned my calls?'

'Oh, hi, Myles,' she said breezily. 'How are you?'

He released a whooshing breath. 'How do you think I am? I turn my back for a moment and my fiancée is suddenly engaged to someone else.'

Jaz smiled as she put her needle and thread down. It was working. It was actually working. Myles was insanely jealous. She had never heard him speak so possessively before. 'You were the one who suggested we take a break.'

'Yes, but dating other people is not the same as getting engaged to them. We'd only been apart twenty-four hours and you hooked up with him. No one falls in love that quickly. No one, and especially not Jake bloody Ravensdale.'

Jaz hadn't really taken in that bit. The bit where Myles had said they were free to date other people. She'd thought he was just having some breathing space. Her 'engagement' to Jake wouldn't have the same power if Myles was seeing someone else. What if he fell in love? What if *he* got engaged to someone else? 'Are you seeing other people?'

There was a short silence.

'I had a drink with an old friend but I haven't got myself bloody engaged to them,' he said in a sulky tone.

Jaz twirled a tendril of her hair around her finger as she walked about the room with the phone pressed to her ear. How cool was this, hearing Myles sound all wounded and affronted by her moving on so quickly?

Didn't that prove he still loved her? The irony was he'd been the first to say those three magical little words. But he hadn't said it for weeks. Months, even. But a couple more weeks of having Jake Ravensdale brandished in his face would do the trick. Myles would soon be begging her to take him back. 'I have to go,' she said. 'Jake is taking me out to dinner.'

'I give it a week,' Myles said. 'Two at the most. He won't stick around any longer than that. You mark my words.'

Two is all I need. The winter wedding expo in the Cotswolds was the coming weekend. It was her stepping stone to the big time. She hoped to expand her business and what better way than to attend with a heart-stopping, handsome fiancé in tow? There was no way she wanted to go alone. She would look tragic if she went without a fiancé. She couldn't bear to be considered a fraud, making 'happy ever after' dresses but failing to find love herself. But if she took Jake Ravensdale as her fiancé —the poster boy for pick-ups—it would give her serious street cred. Besides, it would be the perfect payback to him for humiliating her. It would be unmitigated torture for commitment-phobe Jake to be dragged around a ballroom full of wedding finery.

She smiled a secret smile. Yes, staying 'engaged' to Jake suited her just fine.

Jake was scrolling through his emails in the library— thankfully none were from Emma Madden—when Jaz came sashaying in, bringing with her the scent of flowers and temptation. His body sprang to attention when she approached the desk where he was sitting. She had changed out of her yoga pants and top and was now wearing skin-tight jeans, knee-length leather boots and a baby-blue cashmere sweater with a patterned scarf artfully gathered around her slim neck. Her honey-brown hair was loose about her shoulders and her beautiful mouth was glistening with lip-gloss, drawing his gaze like a magnet. He could still taste her. Could still feel the way her tongue had danced with his in sensual heat. He saw her gaze drift to his mouth as if she were recalling that erotic interlude. 'Forgiven me yet?' he said.

She tossed her hair back over her shoulders in a haughty manner, giving him an ice-cool glare. 'For?'

'You know exactly what for.'

She shifted her gaze, picked a pen off the desk and turned it over in her slender hands as if it was something of enormous interest to her. 'I was wondering what you're up to next weekend.'

He leaned back in the leather chair and balanced one ankle over his thigh. 'My calendar is pretty heavily booked. What did you have in mind?'

Her grey-blue eyes came back to his. 'I have a function I need to attend in Gloucester. I was hoping you'd come with me—you know, to keep up appearances.'

'What sort of function?'

'Just a drinks thing.'

Jake steepled his fingers against his nose and mouth. The little minx was up to something but he would play along. He might even get another kiss or two out of her. 'Sure, why not?'

She put the pen down. 'I'm going to head back to London now.'

He felt a swooping sensation of disappointment in his gut. It would be deadly boring staying here without her to spar with. They hadn't had any time together without anyone else around for years. He hadn't realised how much he was enjoying it until the prospect of it ending now loomed. But there would be other opportunities as long as this charade continued. And he was going to make the most of them. 'You're not staying till morning?'

'No, I have stuff to do at the boutique first thing and I don't want to get caught up in traffic.'

Jake suspected she was wary of spending any more time with him in case she betrayed her desire for him. He wasn't being overly smug about it. He could see it as plain as day. It mirrored his raging lust for her. Not that he was going to act on it but it sure was a heap of fun making her think he was. 'Are you going to see Myles?'

Her gaze slipped out of reach of his. 'Not yet. We agreed on a month's break.'

'A lot can happen in a month.'

Her lips tightened as if she was trying to remove the sensation of his on them. 'I know what I'm doing.'

'Do you?'

Her eyes clashed with his. 'I know you think relationships are a complete waste of time but commitment is important to me.'

'He's not the right man for you,' Jake said.

Her hands went to her slim hips in a combative

pose. 'And I suppose you think you're an expert on who exactly would be?'

He pushed back his chair to come around to her side of the desk. She took half a step backwards but the antique globe was in the way. Her eyes drifted to his mouth and her darting tongue took a layer of lip-gloss off her lips. 'If Myles was the right man for you he'd be down here right now with his hands at my throat.'

Her eyes glittered with enmity. 'Not all men resort to Neanderthal tactics to claim a partner.'

He took a fistful of her silky hair and gently anchored her. 'If I was in love with you I would do whatever it took to get you back.'

Her eyelids went to half-mast as her gaze zeroed in on his mouth for a moment. 'Men like you don't know the meaning of the word love. Lust is the only currency you deal in.'

Jake glided his hand down from her hair to cup her cheek, his thumb moving over the creamy perfection of her skin like the slow arm of a metronome. He watched as her pupils enlarged like widening pools of black ink, her mouth parting, her soft, milky breath coming out in a soundless gasp. 'There's nothing wrong with a bit of lust. It's the litmus test of a good relationship.'

'You don't have relationships,' she said, still looking at his mouth. 'You have encounters that don't last longer than it takes to change a light bulb.'

He gave a slanted smile. 'Who needs a light bulb when we've got this sort of electricity going on?'

She pursed her lips. 'Don't even think about it.'

He brushed his thumb across her bunched up lips. 'I think about it all the time. How it would feel to have you scraping your nails down my back as I make you come.'

She gave a tiny shudder. Blinked. Swallowed. 'I'd much rather scrape them down your arrogant face.'

Jake smiled. 'Liar. You're thinking about it now, aren't you? You're thinking about how hot I make you feel. How turned on. I bet if I slipped my fingers into you now you'd be dripping wet for me.'

Twin pools of pink flagged her cheekbones. 'It's not going to happen, Jake,' she said through tight lips. 'I'm engaged to another man.'

'Maybe you'll feel different once you're wearing my ring. I'll pick you up at lunchtime tomorrow at the boutique. Be ready at two p.m.'

Her eyes flashed with venom. 'I have an appointment with a client.'

'Cancel it.'

She looked as if she was going to argue the point but then she blew out a hiss of a breath and stormed out of the room, slamming the door behind her for good measure.

Barely a minute later he heard her car start with a roar and then the scream of her tyres as she flew down the driveway.

He smiled and turned back to his laptop. *Yep. A heap of fun.*

CHAPTER SIX

JAZ HAD JUST finished with a customer who had purchased one of her hand-embroidered veils for her daughter when Jake came into the boutique. The woman smiled up at him as he politely held the door open for her. 'Thank you,' she said. 'I hear congratulations are in order. You've got yourself a keeper there.' She nodded towards Jaz. 'She'll make a gorgeous bride. When's the big day?'

Jake smiled one of his laidback smiles. 'We haven't set a date yet, have we, sweetheart?'

'No, not yet,' Jaz said.

'I can't wait to see the ring,' the woman said. 'I bet you'll give her a big one.'

Jake's dark-blue eyes glinted as they glanced at Jaz. 'You bet I will.'

Jaz felt a tremor go through her private parts at his innuendo. Did the man have no shame? She was trying to act as cool and professional as she could and one look at her from those glittering midnight-blue eyes and she felt like she was going to melt into a sizzling pool at his feet. She wouldn't have mentioned anything about their 'engagement' to the customer but it seemed there wasn't a person in the whole of London who hadn't heard fast-living playboy Jake Ravensdale was getting himself hitched.

The woman left with a little wave, and the door with its tinkling bell closed. Jake came towards the counter where Jaz had barricaded herself. 'So this is your stamping ground,' he said, glancing around at the dresses hanging on the free-standing rack. 'How much of a profit are you turning over?'

She gave him a flinty look. 'I don't need you to pull apart my business.'

His one-shoulder shrug was nonchalant. 'Just asking.'

'You're not just asking,' Jaz said. 'You're looking for an opportunity to tell me I'm rubbish at running my business, just like you keep pointing out how rubbish I am at running my personal life.'

'You have to admit three engagements—four, if you count ours—is a lot of bad decisions.'

She gripped the edge of the counter. 'And I suppose you've never made a bad decision in the whole of your charmed life, have you?'

'I've made a few.'

'Such as?'

He looked at her for a long moment, his customary smile fading and a slight frown taking its place. 'It was crass of me to bring those girls to my room that night. There were other ways I could've handled the situation.'

Jaz refused to be taken in by an admission of regret seven years too late. 'Did you sleep with them?'

'No.'

There was a pregnant pause.

'Where did you go after that?' he said. 'I didn't see you for the rest of the night.'

Jaz looked down at the glass-topped counter where all the garters were arranged. 'I went back to my room.'

He reached across the counter to take one of her hands in his. 'Look at me, Jasmine.'

She slowly brought her gaze up to his, affecting the expression of a bored teenager preparing for a stern lecture from a parent. 'What?'

His eyes moved between each of hers as if he was searching for something hidden behind the cool screen of her gaze. She could feel the warm press of his hand against hers, his long, strong, masculine fingers entwining with hers, making her insides slip and shift. She could smell the sharp citrus of his aftershave. She could see the dark shadow of his regrowth peppered along his jaw. She could see every fine line on his mouth, the way his lips were set in a serious line—such a change from his usual teasing slant. He began to move the pad of his thumb in a stroking fashion over the back of her hand, the movements drugging her senses.

'It wasn't that I wasn't attracted to you,' he said. 'I just didn't want to make things awkward with you being such a part of the family. That and the fact you were too young to know what you were doing.'

Jaz pulled her hand away. 'Then why lead me on as if you were serious about me? That was just plain cruel.'

He let out a deep sigh. 'Yeah, I guess it was.'

She studied his features for a moment, wondering if this too was an act. How could she believe he was sorry for how he'd made her think he was falling in love with her? He had been so charming towards her, telling her how beautiful she was and how he couldn't wait to get her alone. She had fallen for every lie, waiting in his room, undressing down to her underwear for him in her haste to do anything she could to please him. She had been too emotionally immature to realise he had been winding her up. She had been too enamoured with him to see his charm offensive for what it was. He had pulled her strings like a puppet master. Hating him was dead easy when he wasn't sorry for how he'd treated her. For the last seven years she had stoked that hatred with every look or cynical lip curl he aimed her way. But if this apology were genuine she would have to let her anger and hatred go.

That was scary.

Her anger was a barrier. A big, fat barricade around her heart because falling in love with Jake would be nothing less than an exercise in self-annihilation. She only fell in love with men she knew for certain would love her back. Her ex-fiancés were alike in that they had each been comfortable with commitment. They'd wanted the same things she wanted…or so they had said.

Jake glanced at his watch. 'We'd better get a move

on. I made an appointment with the jeweller for two-fifteen. Have you got an assistant to hold the fort for you till you get back?'

'No, my last girl was rude to the clients,' Jaz said. 'I had to let her go. I haven't got around to replacing her. I'll just put a "back in ten minutes" sign on the door.'

He frowned. 'You mean you run this show all by yourself?'

She picked up her purse and jacket from underneath the counter. 'I outsource some of the cutting and sewing but I do most of everything else because that's what my customers expect.'

'But none of the top designers do all the hack work,' Jake said as they walked out of the boutique into the chilly autumn air. 'You'll burn yourself out trying to do everything yourself.'

'Yes, well, I'm not quite pulling in the same profit as some of those houses,' Jaz said. 'But watch this space. I have a career plan.'

'What about a business plan? I could have a look at your company structure and—'

'No thanks,' Jaz said and closed and locked the boutique door.

'If you're worried about my fee, I could do mate's rates.'

She gave him a sideways look. 'I can afford you, Jake. I just choose not to use your…erm…services.'

He shrugged one of his broad shoulders. 'Your loss.'

The jeweller was a private designer who had a studio above an interior design shop. Jaz was acutely con-

scious of Jake's arm at her elbow as he led her into
the viewing area. After brief introductions were made
a variety of designs was brought forward for her to
peruse. But there was one ring that was a stand out.
It was a mosaic collection of diamonds in an art deco
design that was both simple yet elegant. She slipped
it on her finger and was pleased to find it was a perfect fit. 'This one,' she said, holding it up to see the
way the light bounced off the diamonds.

'Good choice,' the designer said. 'It suits your
hand.'

Jaz didn't see the price. It wasn't the sort of jeweller
where price tags were on show. But she didn't care if
it was expensive or not. Jake could afford it. She did
wonder, however, if he would want her to give it back
when their 'engagement' was over.

Jake took her hand as they left the studio. 'Fancy
a quick coffee?'

Jaz would have said no except she hadn't had lunch
and her stomach was gurgling like a drain. 'Sure,
why not?'

He took her to a café a couple of blocks from her
boutique but they had barely sat down before someone from a neighbouring table took a photo of them
with a camera phone. Then a murmur went around the
café and other people started aiming their phones at
them. Jaz tried to keep her smile natural but her jaw
was aching from the effort. Jake seemed to take it all
in his stride, however.

One customer came over with a napkin and a pen.
'Can I have your autograph, Jake?'

Jake slashed his signature across the napkin and handed back the pen with an easy smile. 'There you go.'

'Is it true you and Miss Connolly are engaged?' the customer asked.

Jaz held up her ring hand. 'Yes. We just picked up the ring.'

More cameras went off and the Twitter whistle sounded so often it was as if a flock of small birds had been let loose in the café.

'Nice work,' Jake said when the fuss had finally died down a little.

'You were the one who suggested a coffee,' Jaz said, shooting him a look from beneath her lashes.

'I heard your stomach rumbling at the jeweller's. Don't you make time for lunch?'

She stirred her latte with a teaspoon rather than lose herself in his sapphire-blue gaze. 'I've got a lot on just now.'

He reached across the table and took her left hand in his, running his fingertip over the crest of the mosaic ring. 'You can keep it after this is over.'

Jaz brought her gaze back to his. 'You don't want to recycle it for when you eventually settle down?'

He released her hand and sat back as he gave a light laugh. 'Can you see me doing the school run?'

'You don't ever want kids?'

'Nope,' he said, reaching for the sugar and tipping two teaspoons in. 'I don't want the responsibility. If I'm going to screw anyone's life up, it'll be my own. *That* I can live with.'

'Why do you think you'd screw up your children's lives?' Jaz said.

He stirred his coffee before he answered. 'I'm too much like my father.'

'I don't think you're anything like your father,' she said. 'Maybe in looks but not in temperament. Your father is weak. Sorry if I'm speaking out of turn but he is. The way he handled his affair with Kat Winwood's mother is proof of it. I can't see you paying someone to have an abortion if you got a girl pregnant.'

He shifted his lips from side to side. 'I wouldn't offer to marry her, though.'

'Maybe not, but you'd support her and your child,' Jaz said. 'And you'd be involved in your child's life.'

He gave her one of his slow smiles that did so much damage to her resolve to keep him at a distance. 'I didn't realise you had such a high opinion of me.'

She pursed her lips. 'Don't get too excited. I still think you'd make a terrible husband.'

'In general or for you?'

Jaz looked at him for a beat or two of silence. She had a sudden vision of him at the end of the aisle waiting for her with that twinkling smile on his handsome face. Of his tall and toned body dressed in a sharply tailored suit instead of the casual clothes he preferred. Of his dark-blue eyes focused on her, as if she were the only woman he ever wanted to gaze at, with complete love and adoration.

She blinked and refocused. 'Good Lord, not for me,' she said with a laugh. 'We'd be at each other's throats before we left the church.'

Something moved at the back of his gaze as it held hers, a flicker like a faulty light bulb. But then he picked up his coffee cup and drained it before putting it down on the table with a decisive clunk. 'Ready?'

Jake walked Jaz back to the boutique holding her hand for the sake of appearances. Or so he told himself. The truth was he loved the feel of her small, neat hand encased in his. He couldn't stop himself from thinking about those soft, clever little fingers on other parts of his body. Stroking him, teasing him with her touch. Why shouldn't he make the most of their situation? He had a business deal to secure and being engaged to Jasmine Connolly was going to win him some serious brownie points with his conservative client Bruce Parnell. It wasn't as if it was for ever. A week or two and it would be over. Life would go back to normal.

'I have a work function on Wednesday night,' he said when Jaz had unlocked the door of the boutique. 'Dinner with a client. Would you like to come?'

She looked at him with a slight frown. 'Why?'

He tugged a tendril of her hair in a teasing manner. 'Because we're madly in love and we can't bear to be apart for a second.'

Her frown deepened and a flash of irritation arced in her gaze. 'What's the dress code?'

'Lounge suit and cocktail.'

'I'll have to check my calendar.'

Jake put his hand beneath her chin and tipped up her face so her eyes couldn't escape his. 'I'm giving you the weekend for the wedding expo. The least you could do is give me one week night.'

Her cheeks swarmed with sheepish colour. 'How did you know it was a wedding expo?'

He gave her a teasing grin. 'I knew there had to be a catch. Why else would you want me for a whole weekend?'

Her mouth took on that disapproving schoolmarm, pursed look that made him want to kiss it back into pliable softness. 'I don't want *you*, Jake. You'll only be there for show.'

He bent down and pressed a brief kiss to her mouth. 'I'll pick you up from here at seven.'

Jaz was still doing her hair when the doorbell sounded on Wednesday evening. She had run late with a client who had taken hours to choose a design for a gown. She gave her hair one last blast with the dryer and shook her head to let the waves fall loosely about her shoulders. She smoothed her hands down her hips, turning to one side to check her appearance in the full-length mirror. The black cocktail dress had double shoestring straps that criss-crossed over her shoulders, the silky fabric skimming her figure in all the right places. She was wearing her highest heels because she hadn't been able to wear them when going out with Myles, as he was only an inch taller than her. A quick spray of perfume and a smear of lip-gloss and she was ready.

Why she was going to so much trouble for Jake was not something she wanted to examine too closely. But when she opened the door and she saw the way his eyes ran over her appreciatively she was pleased she had chosen to go with the wow factor.

But then, so had he. He was dressed in a beautifully tailored suit that made his shoulders seem all the broader and, while he wasn't wearing a tie, the white open-necked shirt combined with the dark blue of his suit intensified the navy-blue of his eyes.

Jaz opened the door a little wider. 'I'll just get my wrap.'

Jake stepped into her flat and closed the door. She turned to face him as she draped her wrap over her shoulders, a little shiver coursing over her flesh as she saw the way his gaze went to her mouth as if pulled there by a powerful magnet.

The air quickened the way it always did when they were alone.

'Is something wrong?' she said.

He closed the small distance between their bodies so that they were almost touching. 'I have something for you,' he said, reaching into the inside pocket of his jacket.

Jaz swallowed as he took out a narrow velvet jewellery case the same colour as his eyes. She took it from him and opened it with fingers that were suddenly as useless as a glove without a hand. Jake took it from her and deftly opened it to reveal a stunning diamond pendant on a white-gold chain that was as fine as a gossamer thread.

Jaz glanced up at him but his face was unreadable. She looked back at the diamond. She had jewellery. Lots of it. Most of it she had bought herself because jewellery was so personal, a bit like perfume and make-up. She hadn't had a partner yet who had ever got her taste in jewellery right. But this was… perfect. She would have chosen it herself if she could have afforded it. She knew it was expensive. Hideously so. Why had Jake spent so much money on her when he didn't even like her? 'I'll give it back once we're done,' she said. 'And the ring.'

'I chose it specifically for you,' he said, taking it out of the box. 'Turn around. Move your hair out of the way.'

Jaz did as he commanded and tried not to shudder in pleasure as his long strong fingers moved against the sensitive skin on the back of her neck as he secured the pendant in place. She could feel the tall, hard frame of his body against her shoulder blades, his strongly muscled thighs against her trembling ones. She knew if she leaned back even half an inch she could come into contact with the hot, hard heat of him. She felt his hands come down on the tops of her shoulders, his fingers giving her a light squeeze as he turned her to face him. She looked into the midnight blue of his inscrutable gaze and wondered if her teenage crush was dead and buried after all. It felt like it was coming to life under the warm press of his hands on her body.

He trailed a lazy fingertip from beneath her ear to her mouth, circling it without touching it. But it felt like he had. Her lips buzzed, fizzed and ached for the pressure of his. 'You look beautiful.'

'Amazing what a flashy bit of jewellery can do.'

He frowned as if her flippant comment annoyed him. 'You don't suit flashy jewellery and I wouldn't insult you by insisting on you wearing it.'

'All the same, I don't expect you to spend so much money on me. I don't feel comfortable about it, given our relationship.'

His eyes went to her mouth for a moment before meshing with hers. 'Why do you hate me so much?'

Jaz couldn't hold his gaze and looked at the open neck of his shirt instead. But that just made it worse because she could see the long, strong, tanned column of his throat and smell the light but intoxicating lemony scent of his aftershave. She didn't know if it was the diamond olive branch he had offered her, his physical closeness or both that made her decide to tell him the truth about that night. Or maybe it was because she was tired of the negative emotion weighing her down. 'That night after I left your room... I... Something happened...'

Jaz felt rather than saw his frown. She was still looking at his neck but she noticed the way he had swallowed thickly. 'What?' he said.

'I accepted a drink off one of the guests. I'm not sure who it was. One of the casual seasonal theatre staff, I think. I hadn't seen him before or since. I was upset after leaving you. I didn't care if I got drunk. But then... I, well, you've probably heard it dozens of times before. Girls who get drunk and then end up regretting what happened next.'

'What happened next?' Jake's voice sounded raw,

as if something had been scraped across his vocal chords.

Jaz still couldn't meet his gaze. She couldn't bear to see his judgement, his criticism of her reckless behaviour. 'I had a non-consensual encounter. Or at least I think it was non-consensual.'

'You were...*raped*?'

She looked at him then. 'No, but it was close to it. Somehow I managed to fight him off, but I was too ashamed to tell anyone what happened. I didn't even tell Miranda. I haven't told anyone before now.'

Jake's expression was full of outrage, shock and horror. 'The man should've been charged. Do you think you'd recognise him if you saw him again? We could arrange a police line-up. We could check the guest list of that night. Track down everyone who attended...'

Jaz pulled out from under his hold and crossed her arms over her body. 'No. I don't want to even think about that night. I don't even know if I gave the guy the okay to mess around. I was the one who started flirting with him in the first place. But then things got a little hazy. It would be his word against mine and you know what the defence lawyers would make of that. I was too drunk to know what I was doing.'

'But he might've spiked your drink or something,' Jake said. 'He committed a crime. A crime for which he should be punished.'

'That only happens in the movies,' Jaz said. 'I've moved on. It would make things so much harder for me if I had to revisit that night in a courtroom.'

His frown made a road map of lines on his forehead. 'I can see why you hate me so much. I'm as guilty as that lowlife.'

'No,' she said. 'That's not true.'

'Isn't it?'

Jaz bit her lip. 'I know it looks like I've blamed you all this time but that's just the projection of negative emotion. I guess I used you as a punching bag because I felt so ashamed.'

Jake came over to her and took her hands from where they were wrapped around her body, holding them gently in his. 'You have no need to be ashamed, Jaz. You were just a kid. I was the adult and I acted appallingly. I shouldn't have given you any encouragement. Leading you on like that only to throw those girls in your face was wrong. I should've been straight with you right from the get-go.'

Jaz gave him a wobbly smile. 'You just called me Jaz. You haven't done that in years.'

His hands gave hers a gentle squeeze. 'We'd better get a move on. My client isn't the most patient of men. That is if you're still okay with going? I can always tell him you had something on and go by myself.'

'I'm fine,' she said. And she was surprised to find it was true. Having Jake of all people being so understanding, caring and protective made something hard and tight inside her chest loosen like a knotted rope suddenly being released.

He gently grazed her cheek with the backs of his knuckles. 'Thank you for telling me.'

'I'd rather you didn't tell anyone else,' Jaz said. 'I don't want people to look at me differently.'

'Not even Miranda?'

She pulled at her lip with her teeth. 'Miranda would be hurt if I told her now. She'd blame herself for not watching out for me. You know what a little mother hen she is.'

Jake's frown was back. 'But surely—?'

'No,' Jaz said, sending him a determined look. 'Don't make me regret telling you. Promise me you won't betray my trust.'

He let out a frustrated sigh. 'I promise. But I swear to God, if I find out who hurt you I'll tear him apart with my bare hands.'

CHAPTER SEVEN

Later, in the car going back to Jaz's place, Jake wondered how on earth he'd swung the deal with his client. His mind hadn't been on the game the whole way through dinner. All he'd been able to think about was what Jaz had told him about that wretched night after she had left his room. He was so churned up with a toxic cocktail of anger, guilt and an unnerving desire for revenge that he'd given his client, Bruce Parnell, the impression he was a distracted, lovesick fool rather than a savvy businessman. But that didn't seem to matter because at the end of the dinner his client had signed on the dotted line and wished Jake and Jaz all the best for their future.

Their future.

What *was* their future?

Jake was so used to bickering with her that he wasn't sure how he was going to navigate being friends with her instead. While it had been pistols and pissy looks at dawn, he'd been able to keep his distance. But now she'd shared her painful secret with him he couldn't carry on as if nothing had changed.

Everything had changed. The whole dynamic of their relationship was different. He wanted to protect her. To fix it for her. To give her back her innocence so she didn't have to carry around the shame she felt. A shame she had no need to feel because the jerk who had assaulted her was the one who should be ashamed.

But Jake too felt shame. Deep, gut-clawing shame. Shame that he hadn't handled her infatuation with him more sensitively. His actions had propelled her into danger—danger that could have been avoided if he had been a little more understanding. He could see now why Jaz had stepped in with the engagement charade when Emma Madden had turned up at the door. She had been sensitive to the girl's need for dignity, offering her a safe way home with someone at the other end to make sure she was all right.

What had *he* done? He had sent Jaz from his room in an acute state of public humiliation only to fall into the hands of some creep who'd plied her with drink and drugs and God knew what else. Had that been her first experience of sex—being groped and man-handled by a drunken idiot? He couldn't remember if she'd had a boyfriend back then. Miranda had been going out with Mark Redbank from a young age but Jaz had never seemed all that interested in boys. Not until she'd developed that crush on him.

He couldn't bear the thought of her being touched in such a despicable way. Was that why she only ever dated men she could control? None of her ex-fiancés were what one would even loosely consider as alpha men. Was that deliberate or unconscious on her part?

Jake glanced at her sitting quietly in the passenger seat beside him. She was looking out at the rain-lashed street, her hands absently fiddling with the clasp on her evening bag. 'You okay?' he said.

She turned her head to look at him, a vacant smile on her face. 'Sorry. I think I used up all my scintillating conversation at dinner.'

'You did a great job,' Jake said. 'Bruce Parnell was quite taken with you. He was being cagey about signing up with me but you had him at hello.'

'Did you know he fell in love with his late wife the very first time they met? And they married three months later and never spent more than two nights apart for the whole of their marriage? He would fly back by private jet if he had to just to be with her.'

He glanced at her again between gear changes. 'He told you all that?'

'And he's still grieving her loss even though it's been ten years. It reminded me of Miranda after Mark died.'

'Luckily Leandro got her to change her mind,' Jake said. 'I was sure she was going to end up a spinster living with a hundred cats.'

Jaz gave a tinkling laugh. 'I was worried too, but they're perfect for each other. I've known it for ages. It was the way Leandro looked at her. He got this really soft look in his eyes.'

Jake grunted. 'Another one bites the dust.'

'What have you got against marriage? It doesn't always end badly. Look at Mr Parnell.'

'That sort of marriage is the exception,' Jake said.

'Look at my parents. They're heading for another show-stopping divorce as far as I can tell. It was bad enough the first time.'

'Clearly Julius doesn't hold the same view as you,' she said. 'And yet he went through the same experience of your parents' divorce.'

'It was different for Julius,' Jake said. 'He found solace in studying and working hard. I found it hard to adjust to boarding school. I pushed against the boundaries. Rubbed the teachers up the wrong way. Wasted their time and my own.'

'But you've done so well for yourself. Aren't you happy with your achievements?'

Was he happy? Up until a few days ago he had been perfectly happy. But now there was a niggling doubt chewing at the edge of his conscience. He moved around so much it was hard to know where was home. He had a base in London but most of the time he lived out of hotel rooms. He never cooked at home. He ate out. He didn't spend the night with anyone because he hated morning-after scenes. He didn't do reruns. One night was enough to scratch the itch. But how long could he keep on moving? The fast lane was a lonely place at times. Not that he was going to admit that to Jaz—or to anyone, when it came to that.

But this recent drama with Emma Madden had got him thinking. Everyone saw him as shallow and self-serving. He hadn't given a toss for anyone's opinion before now but now it sat uncomfortably on him like an ill-fitting jacket. What if people thought he was like the man who had groped Jaz? That he was taking advantage of young women who were a little star-struck. It had never concerned him before. He had always enjoyed exploiting his parents' fame. He had used it to open doors in business and in pleasure. But how long could he go on doing it? He was turning into a cliché. The busty blondes he attracted only wanted him because he was good looking and had famous parents. They didn't know him as a person.

Jake pulled up outside Jaz's flat above her boutique. 'How long have you been living above the shop?' he asked as he walked her to the door.

She gave him a wary look. 'Is this another "how to run your business" lecture?'

'It's a nice place but pretty small. And the whole living and working in the same place can be a drag after a while.'

'Yes, well, I was planning to move in with Myles but he put the brakes on that,' she said, scowling. 'His parents don't like me. They think I'm too pushy and controlling. I think that's the main reason he wanted a break.'

What's not to like? What parents wouldn't be proud to have her as their daughter-in-law? She was smart and funny, and sweet when she let her guard down. His parents were delighted with their 'engagement'. He hadn't figured out yet how he was going to tell them when it was over. They would probably never speak to him again. 'Do you really want to take Myles back?'

Her chin came up. 'Of course.'

'What if he doesn't want to come back?'

She averted her gaze. 'I deal with that *if* it happens.'

Jake looked at her for a long beat. 'You're not in love with him.'

Her eyes flashed back to his. 'And you know this how?'

'Because you're more concerned about what other people think of you than what he does. That's what this thing between us is all about. You're trying to save face, not your relationship.'

She flattened her lips so much they disappeared inside her mouth. 'I know what I'm doing. I know Myles better than anyone.'

'If you know him so well why haven't you told him about that night?'

She flinched as if he had struck her. But then she pulled herself upright as if her spinal column were filling with concrete. 'Thank you for dinner,' she said. 'Good night.'

'Jaz, wait—'

But the only response he got was the door being slammed in his face.

Jaz was at the boutique the next morning when Miranda came in carrying coffee and muffins. 'I thought I'd drop in to start the ball rolling on my wed—' Miranda said, but stopped short when her gaze went to Jaz's ring hand. 'Oh, my God. Did Jake buy that for you?'

'Yes, but it's just for show.'

Miranda snatched up Jaz's hand and turned it every which way to see how the light danced off the diamonds. 'Wow. I didn't realise he had such good taste in rings *and* in women.'

Jaz gave her a speaking look. 'You do realise none of this is for real?'

Miranda's eyes twinkled. 'So you both say, but I was just at Jake's office and he's like a bear with a sore paw. Did you guys have a tiff?'

'That's nothing out of the normal,' Jaz said, taking her coffee out of the cardboard holder.

Miranda cocked her head like an inquisitive bird. 'What's wrong?'

'Nothing. We just argued…about stuff.'

'All couples argue,' Miranda said. 'It's normal and healthy.'

'We're *not* a couple,' Jaz said. 'We're an act.'

Miranda frowned. 'You're not seriously still thinking of going back to Myles?'

Jaz pushed back from her work table. 'That's the plan.'

'It's a dumb plan,' Miranda said. 'A stupid plan that's totally wrong for you and for Myles. Can't you see that? You're not in love with him. You're in love with Jake.'

Jaz laughed. 'No, I'm not. I'm not that much of a fool.'

'I think he's in love with you.'

Jaz frowned. 'What makes you think that?'

'He bought you that ring for one thing,' Miranda said. 'Look at it. It's the most beautiful ring I've ever seen—apart from my own, of course.'

'It's just a prop.'

'A jolly expensive one.' Miranda leaned over the counter and lifted the scarf Jaz had tied around her neck. 'Aha! I knew it. More diamonds. That brother of mine has got it *so* bad.'

'It's a goodwill gesture,' Jaz said. 'I helped him nail an important business deal last night.'

Miranda stood back with a grin. 'Has he sent you flowers?'

Just then the bell at the back of the door pinged and in came a deliveryman with an armful of long-stemmed snow-white roses tied with a black satin ribbon. 'Delivery for Miss Jasmine Connolly.'

'I'll take that as a yes,' Miranda said once the deliveryman had left.

'They might be from Myles,' Jaz said. Not that Myles had ever bought flowers in the past. He thought they were a waste of money—ironic, given he had more money than most people ever dreamed of having.

'Read the card.'

Jaz gave her a brooding look as she unpinned the velum envelope from the arrangement. She took out the card and read the message: *I'm sorry. Jake.*

'They're from Jake, aren't they?' Miranda said.

'Yes, but—'

Miranda snatched the card out of Jaz's hand. 'Oh, how sweet! He's saying sorry. Gosh, only a man in love does that.'

'Or a man in the wrong.'

Miranda's smooth brow furrowed in a frown. 'What did he do?'

Jaz shifted her lips from side to side. Why was everything suddenly so darn complicated? 'Haven't you got heaps of dusty old paintings to restore?' she said.

Miranda chewed at her lower lip. 'Is it about that night? I know that's always been a sore point between you two. Is that what he was apologising for?'

Jaz let out a long breath. 'In a way.'

'But he didn't do anything. He didn't sleep with you. He's always flatly denied it. He would never have done anything like that. He thought you were just a kid.' Miranda swallowed. 'He didn't sleep with you... did he?'

'No, but someone else tried to,' Jaz said.

Miranda's eyes went wide in horror. 'What do you mean?'

'I stupidly flirted with this guy at the party after I left Jake's room,' Jaz explained. 'I only did it as a payback to Jake. I don't know how it happened but I suddenly found myself fighting off this drunken guy in one of the downstairs bathrooms. I thought he was going to rape me. I was so shocked and frightened but somehow I managed to get away.'

Miranda's hands were clasped against her mouth in shock. 'Oh, my God! That's awful! Why didn't you tell me?'

'I wanted to tell you,' Jaz said. 'Many times. But I just couldn't bring myself to do it. You were dealing with Mark's cancer and I didn't want to add to your misery. I felt so ashamed and dirty.'

'Oh, you poor darling,' Miranda said, flinging her arms around Jaz and hugging her. 'I wish I'd known so I could have done something to help you. I feel like I've let you down.'

'You didn't,' Jaz said. 'You've always been there for me.'

Miranda pulled back to look at her. 'So that's why you only ever dated vanilla men, isn't it?'

She scrunched up her nose. 'What do you mean?'

'You know exactly what I mean,' Miranda said. 'Bland men. Men you can control. You've never gone for the alpha type.'

Jaz gave a little lip shrug. 'Maybe…'

Miranda was still looking at her thoughtfully. 'So Jake was the first person you've ever told?'

Jaz nodded. 'Weird, huh?'

'Not so weird,' Miranda said. 'You respect him. You always have. That's why he annoys you so much. He sees the you no one else sees.'

Jaz fingered the velvet-soft petals of the roses once Miranda had left. Why had Jake sent her white roses? They were a symbol of purity, virtue and innocence. Was that how he saw her?

Miranda was full of romantic notions because she was madly in love herself. Of course she would like to think her brother was in love with her best friend. But Jake wasn't the type to fall in love. He was too much of a free agent.

Not that Jaz had any right to be thinking along those lines. She was on a mission to win back Myles. Myles was the man she planned to settle down with. Not a man like Jake who would pull against the restraints of commitment like a wild stallion on a leading rein.

Myles was safe and predictable.

Jake was danger personified.

But that didn't mean she couldn't flirt with danger just a wee bit longer.

Jake had never been so fed up with work. He couldn't get his mind to focus on the spreadsheets he was supposed to be analysing. All he wanted to do was go to Jaz's boutique and see if she was still speaking to him. She hadn't called or texted since they had parted last night. The absence of communication would have delighted him a week ago. Now it was like a dragging ache inside his chest. She was a stubborn little thing. She would get on her high horse and not come down even if it collapsed beneath her. That was why she was still hung up on Myles. She wasn't in love with her ex. It was her pride that had taken a hit. She hadn't even told the guy the most devastating thing that had happened to her.

Jake couldn't think about that night without feeling sick. He blamed himself. He had brought that on her by being so insensitive. Why hadn't he gone and checked on her later? He could at least have made an effort to see she was okay. But no, he had partied on as if nothing was wrong, leaving her open to exploitation at the hands of some lowlife creep who had tried to take advantage of her in the worst way imaginable.

Jake's phone buzzed with an incoming message. He picked it up to read it:

Thanks for the roses. Jaz.

He smiled and texted back:

Free for dinner tonight?

Her message came back:

Busy.

He frowned, his gut tensing when he thought of whom she might be busy with. Was it Myles? Was she meeting her ex to try and convince him to come back to her? He waited a minute or two before texting back:

We still on for the w/end?

She texted back.

If u r free?

Jake grimaced as he thought of wandering around a wedding expo all weekend but he figured a man had to do what a man had to do.
He texted back.

I'm all yours.

CHAPTER EIGHT

JAZ WAS READY and waiting for Jake to come to her flat on Friday after work to pick her up. They had only communicated via text messages since yesterday. He had called a couple of times but she hadn't answered or returned the calls. Not that he had left a voice mail message. She hadn't realised how much she had been looking forward to hearing his voice until she checked her voice mail and found it annoyingly silent. Myles, on the other hand, had left several messages asking to meet with her to talk. They were each a variation on his earlier call where he'd told her Jake would never stick around long enough to cast a shadow.

The funny thing was Jake had cast a very long shadow. It was cast all over her life. She could barely recall a time when he hadn't been in it. Ever since she was eight years old she had been a part of his life and he of hers. Even once their charade was over he would still be a part of her life. There would be no avoiding him, not with Julius and Holly's wedding coming up, not to mention Miranda and Leandro's a few months after. Jaz was going to be a bridesmaid at both. There would be other family gatherings to navigate: Christmas, Easter and birthdays. His mother Elisabetta was turning sixty next month in late November and there was no way either Jake or Jaz could ever do a no-show without causing hurt and the sort of drama everyone could do without.

The doorbell sounded and her heart gave a little flutter. Jake was fifteen minutes early. Did that mean he was looking forward to the weekend? Looking forward to being with her? She opened the door to find Myles standing there with a sheepish look on his face. 'Myles…' Jaz faltered. 'Erm… I'm kind of busy right now.'

'I have to talk to you,' he said. 'It's important you hear it from me before you hear it from someone else.'

'Hear what?'

'I'm seeing someone else. It's…serious.'

Jaz blinked. 'How serious?'

'I know it seems sudden but I've known her for ages. We were childhood friends. Do you remember me telling you about Sally Coombes?'

'Yes, but—'

'I wasn't unfaithful to you, if that's what you're thinking,' Myles said. 'Not while we were officially together.'

Jaz hadn't been thinking it, which was kind of weird, as she knew she probably should have been. All she could think was that she had to get rid of Myles before Jake got here, as she didn't want Jake to end their 'engagement' before she attended the wedding expo. She couldn't bear to go to it alone.

Everyone would be taking photos and posting messages about her being so unlucky in love. Not a good look for a wedding designer. What would that do to her credibility? To her pride? People would find out eventually. She couldn't hope to keep Jake acting as her fiancé indefinitely. But one weekend—maybe another couple of weeks—was surely not too much to ask? 'But you've been calling and leaving all those messages,' she said. 'Why didn't you say something then?'

'I wanted to tell you in person,' Myles said. 'I'm sorry if I've hurt you, Jaz. But I've had my doubts about us for a while now. I guess that's why I instigated the break. It was only when I caught up with Sally I realised why I was baulking. As soon as we started talking, I realised she was the one. We dated when we were younger. She was my first girlfriend and I was her first boyfriend. It's like it's meant to be. I hope you can understand and find it in yourself to forgive me for messing you around.'

'I don't know what to say…' Jaz said. 'Congratulations?'

Myles looked a little pained. 'I want you to be happy. I really do. You're a great girl. I care about you. That's why I'm so concerned about your involvement with Jake Ravensdale. I don't want him to break your heart.'

Jaz stretched her lips into a rictus smile. 'I'm a big girl. I can handle Jake.'

Myles looked doubtful. 'Sally and I aren't making a formal announcement for a week or two. We thought it would be more appropriate to wait for a bit. I just wanted you to be one of the first to know.'

'Thanks for dropping by,' Jaz said. 'I appreciate it. Now, I'm sure you have heaps to do. I won't keep you. Say hi to Sally for me. Tell her if she wants a good deal on a wedding dress I'm the person she needs to see.'

'No hard feelings?' Myles said.

'No hard feelings,' Jaz said, and was surprised and more than a little shocked to find it was true.

Myles had not long disappeared around the corner when Jake's sports car prowled to the kerb. Jaz watched as he unfolded himself from behind the wheel with athletic grace. He was wearing dark-blue jeans and a round-neck white T-shirt with a charcoal-grey cashmere sweater over the top. His hair was still damp from a recent shower as she could see the deep grooves where either his fingers or a wide-toothed comb had been. His jaw was freshly shaven and as he came up to where she was standing on the doorstep she could smell the clean, sharp citrus tang of his aftershave.

Funny, but she hadn't even noticed what Myles had been wearing, the scent of his aftershave or even if he had been wearing any.

'Am I late?' Jake asked with the hint of a frown between his brows.

'No,' Jaz said. 'Perfect timing.'

He leaned down to press a light-as-air kiss to her mouth. 'That's for the neighbours.' Then he put his arms around her and pulled her close. 'And this one's for me.'

Jaz closed her eyes as his lips met hers in a drugging kiss that made her toes curl in her shoes. His tongue mated with hers in a sexy tangle that mimicked the driving need rushing through her body, and his, if the hard ridge of his erection was any indication.

Her hands went around his waist and her pelvis jammed against the temptation of his, her heart skipping all over the place as he made a deep, growly sound of male pleasure as she gave herself up to the kiss. His hands pressed against her bottom to pull her closer, his touch so intimate, so possessive, she could feel her body preparing itself for him. The ache of need pulsed between her legs, her thighs tingling with nerves activated by the anticipation of pleasure.

Only the fact they were on a busy public street was enough to break the spell as a car went past tooting its horn.

Jake released her with a teasing smile. 'Nice to know you've missed me.'

Jaz gave a dismissive shrug. 'You're a good kisser. But then, you've had plenty of practice.'

'Ah, but there are kisses and there are kisses. And yours, baby girl, are right up there.'

Don't fall for his charm. Don't fall for him, she thought as she followed him to the car.

The drive to Gloucester took just over two hours but the time passed easily with Jake's superb driving and easy conversation. He told her about Bruce Parnell, who was so impressed with Jake's choice of

fiancée he had recommended several other big-name
clients. 'It's the sort of windfall I'd been hanging
out for,' he said. 'Word travels fast in the corporate
sector.'

'What are you going to say to him when we're no
longer a couple?'

He didn't answer for a moment and when he flashed
her a quick smile she noticed it didn't quite make the
distance to his eyes. 'I'll think of something.'

It was only as Jaz entered the hotel where the wedding expo was being held that she remembered she
had only booked one room. It would look suspicious
if she asked for another room or even a twin. She and
Jake were supposed to be engaged. Everyone would
automatically assume they would share a suite. People had already taken out their camera phones and
taken snapshots as they came in. She would look a
fool if she asked for separate rooms. What woman in
her right mind would pass on the chance to spend the
night with Jake Ravensdale? Herself included.

Hadn't she always wanted him? It had been there
ever since she'd been old enough to understand sexual
attraction. It had gone from a teenage crush to a full-
blown adult attraction. It simmered in the air when
they were together. How long could she ignore it or
pretend it wasn't there? Hadn't she already betrayed
herself by responding so enthusiastically to his kiss?
Had her overlooking of the hotel reservation been her
subconscious telling her what she didn't want to face?

As if Jake sensed her dilemma he leaned down
close to her ear and whispered, 'I'll sleep on the sofa.'

Jaz was so distracted by the sensation of his warm breath tickling the sensitive skin around her ear she didn't hear the attendant call her to the counter. Jake put a gentle hand at her back and pressed her forward. She painted a smile on her face and said, 'I have a booking for Connolly.'

'Welcome, Miss Connolly,' the attendant said. 'We have your king deluxe suite all ready for you.'

King deluxe. At least there would be enough room in the bed to put a bank of pillows up as a barricade, Jaz thought as she took the swipe key.

The hotel was going to town on the wedding theme. The suite, on the thirteenth floor, was decked out like a honeymoon suite. French champagne was sitting chilled and frosted in a silver ice bucket with a white satin ribbon tied in a big bow around it. There were two crystal champagne flutes and a cheese-and-fruit plate with chocolate-dipped strawberries on the table. The bed was covered in fresh rose petals and there were heart-shaped chocolates placed on the pillows.

'Hmm,' Jake said, rubbing thoughtfully at his chin. 'No sofa.'

Something in Jaz's belly slipped like a Bentley on black ice. There were two gorgeous wing chairs in the bay window, and a plush velvet-covered love seat, but no sofa. 'Right; well, then, we'll have to use pillows,' she said.

'Pillows?'

'As a barricade.'

He gave a soft laugh. 'Your virtue is safe, sweetheart. I won't touch you.'

Jaz rolled her lips together. Shifted her weight from foot to foot. Knotted her hands in front of her body where they were clutching her tote bag straps. Of course she didn't want to sleep with him. He was her enemy. She didn't even like him… Well, maybe a little. More like a lot. Why the heck didn't he want to sleep with her? She hadn't cracked any mirrors lately. She might not be his usual type but she was female and breathing, wasn't she? Why was he being so fussy all of a sudden? He'd kissed her and she'd felt his re-action to her. He wanted her. She knew it as surely as she knew he was standing there. 'What?' she said. 'You don't find me attractive?'

He frowned. 'Listen, a kiss or two or three is fine, but doing the deed? Not going to happen. Not us.'

'Why not us?'

'You're not my type.'

Jaz bristled. 'I was your type when you kissed me outside my flat. Half of flipping Mayfair was wit-ness to it.'

His frown carved a little deeper. 'You're not seri-ous about taking this to that extreme, are you? This is supposed to be an act. When actors do a love scene they don't actually have sex, you know.'

She moved to the other side of the room to stand in front of the window, folding her arms across her body. 'Fine. I get the message. I'd better tape up all the mirrors. The last thing I need is another seven years of bad luck.'

Jake came up behind her, placed his hands on the tops of her shoulders and gently turned her to face him. He searched her face for endless seconds. 'What about Myles?'

Jaz pressed her lips together and lowered her gaze. 'He's engaged to someone else.'

'God, that was quick.'

'He's known her since childhood. I'm happy for him. I really am. It's just I can't bear the thought of everyone knowing I've been dumped,' she said. 'Especially this weekend.'

His fingers massaged her shoulders. 'What's so important about this weekend?'

Jaz rolled her eyes. 'Duh! Look around you, Jake. This is a winter wedding expo. One of my designs is in the fashion parade tomorrow. Next year I want ten. This is my chance to expand my business. To network and get my name out there.'

'But your personal life should have nothing to do with your talent as a designer.'

'Yes, but you told me on the way down how Mr Parnell looks at you differently now you're—' she put her fingers up in air-quotation marks '—"engaged". It's the same for me. I design wedding gowns for everyone else but I'm totally rubbish at relationships. What sort of advertising for my brand is that?'

He drew in a breath and dropped his hands from her shoulders, using one hand to push through his hair. 'So…what do you want me to do?'

'Just play along a little longer,' she said. 'I know it's probably killing you but please can you do this one thing for me? Just pretend to be my fiancé until… well, a few more days.'

His brow was furrowed as deep as a trench. 'How many days?'

Jaz blew out an exasperated breath. 'Is it such torture to be tied to me for a week or two? *Is* it? Am I so hideous you can't bear the thought of people thinking you've sunk so low as to do it with—?'

Jake's hands came back to hold her by the upper arms. 'Stop it. Stop berating yourself like that.'

She looked into his midnight-blue gaze, trying to control her spiralling emotions that were like a twisted knot inside her stomach. 'Do you know what it's like to be the one no one wants?' she said. 'No, of course you don't, because everyone wants you. Even my mother didn't want me. She made that perfectly clear by dumping me on my dad. Not that he wanted me either.'

'Your dad loves you,' Jake said.

Jaz gave him a jaded look. 'Then why did he let me move into the big house instead of staying with him at the gardener's cottage? He was relieved when your parents offered to take me in and pay for my education. He didn't know what to do with an eight-year-old kid. I was an inconvenience he couldn't wait to pass off.'

Jake's expression was clenched so tightly in a frown his eyebrows met over his eyes. 'Did he actually say that to you?'

'He didn't need to,' she said on an expelled breath. 'I'm the one no one wants. It should be tattooed across my forehead—*Unwanted*.'

Jake's hands tightened on her arms. 'That's not true. I want you. I've wanted you for years.'

Jaz moistened her tombstone-dry lips. 'You do? You're not just saying that to make me feel better?'

He brought her close against his body. 'Do you think I could fake that?'

She felt the thickened ridge of him swelling against her body. 'Oh…'

'I've always kept my distance because I don't want the same things you want,' he said. 'I'm not interested in marriage—it's not my gig at all. But a fling is something else. I don't even do those normally. My longest relationship was four days when I was nineteen.'

She pulled at her lower lip with her teeth. 'So you'd agree to a fling with me? Just for a week or two?'

He brushed his thumb over her savaged lip. 'As long as you're absolutely clear on the terms. I'm not going to be that guy waiting at the altar of a church aisle for the bride to show up. I'm the guy working his way through the bridesmaids.'

'I happen to be one of the bridesmaids,' Jaz said. 'At two weddings.'

He gave her a sinful smile as his mouth came down to hers. 'Perfect.'

It was a smouldering kiss with an erotic promise that made Jaz's body quake and shudder with want. Every time his tongue touched hers a dart of lust speared her between the legs. Her body wanted him with a desperation she had never felt with such intensity before. It moved through her flesh in tingling waves, making her aware of her erogenous zones as if it was the first time they had been activated. Her breasts were pressed up against his chest, her nipples already puckered from the friction of his hard body. Her hands fisted in his sweater, holding him in case he changed his mind and pulled back.

His mouth continued its passionate exploration of hers, his tongue making love with hers until she was making whimpering sounds of encouragement and delight.

His light stubble grazed her face as he changed position, his hands splaying through her hair as he held her in an achingly tender embrace. He lifted his mouth off hers, resting his forehead against hers. 'Let's not rush this,' he said.

'I thought you lived in the fast lane?' Jaz said, tracing his top lip with her fingertip.

His expression was gravely serious as he caught her hand and held it in the warmth of his against his chest. 'You deserve more than a quick tumble, Jaz. Way more.'

She looked into the sapphire density of his gaze and felt a fracture form in the carapace around her heart like a fissure running through a glacier. 'Are you worried about what happened in the past? Then don't be. I'm fine with sex. I've had it heaps of times.'

'But do you enjoy it?'

'Of course I do,' she said then added when he gave her a probing look, 'Well, mostly.'

He threaded his fingers through her hair like a parent finger-combing a child's hair. 'Are you sure you want to go through with this? It's fine if you've changed your mind. No man's ever died from having an erection, you know.'

Jaz couldn't help smiling. 'Perhaps not, but I think I might if you don't finish what you started.'

He brought his mouth back down to hers, giving her a lingering kiss that was hot, sexy, sweet and tender at the same time. His hands gently moved over her, skimming her breasts at first before coming back to explore them in exquisite detail. He peeled away her top but left her bra in place, allowing her time to get used to being naked with him. He kissed his way down the slope of her breast, drawing on her nipple through the lace of her bra, which added a whole new dimension of feeling. Then, when he had removed his sweater and shirt, he unhooked her bra and gently cradled her breasts in his hands.

Jaz wasn't generously endowed but the way he held her made her feel as if she could be on a high street billboard advertising lingerie. His thumbs brushed over each of her nipples and the sensitive area surrounding them. He lowered his mouth to her puckered flesh and subjected her to the most delicious assault on her senses. The nerves beneath her skin went into a frenzy of excitement, her blood thrumming with the escalation of her desire.

She ran her hands over his muscled chest, delighting in the lean, hard contours of his body. He hadn't followed the trend of being completely hairless. The masculine roughness of his light chest hair tickled her fingers and then her satin-smooth breasts as he drew her closer. It made her feel more feminine than she had ever felt before.

His hands settled on her hips, holding her against his erection, letting her get the feel of him; not rushing her, not pressuring her. Just holding her. But Jaz's body had urgent needs it wanted assuaged and she moved against him in a silent plea for satiation. She had rarely taken the initiative with a partner before. But with Jake she wanted to express her desire for him, to let him know her body ached to be joined to his.

Jaz went for the waistband of his jeans, unsnapping the metal stud and then sliding down his zip. He sucked in air but let her take control. She traced her fingertips over the tented fabric of his underwear, her belly doing a cartwheel when she thought of how potent he was, of how gorgeously turned on he was for her, yet controlling it to make her feel safe. She peeled back his underwear, stroking him skin to skin, flicking her gaze up to his to see how he was reacting to her touch. 'You like that?'

'This is getting a little one sided,' he said, pushing her hand away. 'Ladies come first according to my rules.'

'I think I like your rules,' Jaz said as he carried her to the bed as if she weighed no more than one of the feather pillows.

He placed her down amongst the scented rose petals and then, shucking off his jeans but leaving his underwear in place, he joined her. He helped her out of her trousers but left her knickers on. Not that they hid much from his view. Had that been another sub-conscious thing on her part, to wear her sexiest un-derwear?

He traced the seam of her body through the gossamer-sheer lace. 'Do you have any idea of how long I've wanted to do this?'

Jaz shivered as his touch triggered her most secret nerves into a leaping dance of expectation. 'Me too,' she said but it was more a gasp of sound as he brought his mouth to her and pressed a kiss to her abdomen just above the line of her knickers.

He slowly peeled the lace down to reveal her wom-anhood. For once she didn't feel that twinge of shame at being naked and exposed in front of a man. It was like he was worshiping her body, treating it with the utmost respect with every stroke and glide of his hands.

He put his mouth to her, separating her folds so he could pleasure the most sensitive part of all. She had never been entirely comfortable with being pleasured this way. Occasionally she had been tipsy enough to get through it. But this time she didn't need the buf-fer of alcohol. Nor did she need to pretend. The sen-sations took her by surprise, every nerve pulling tight before exploding in a cascade of sparks that rippled through her body in pulsating waves.

When it was over she let out a breath of pure bliss. 'Wow. I think that might've measured on the Rich-ter scale.'

He stroked a hand down the flank of her thigh in a smooth-as-silk caress. 'Want to try for a ten?'

Jaz reached for him, surrounding his taut thickness with her fingers. 'I'd like to see you have some fun first, in the interests of being fair and all.'

He smiled a glinting smile. 'I can't argue with that.'

He reached across her to where he'd left his wallet when he'd removed his jeans and took out a condom, dealing with the business of applying it before he came back to her. He moved over her so she was settled in the cradle of his thighs, one of his legs hitched over her hip so she wasn't taking his whole weight. 'Not too heavy for you?' he said. 'Or would you like to go on top?'

Jaz welcomed the press of his body against hers, the sexy tangle of their limbs sending a frisson of anticipation through her female flesh. 'No, I like it like this. I don't like feeling like I'm riding a horse.'

He gave a deep chuckle. 'I wouldn't throw you off.'

No, but you'll cast me off when you're ready to move on. Jaz pushed the thought aside and ran her hands up his body from his pelvis to his chest and back again. This was for now. A fling she'd wanted since she was a teenager. This was her chance to have what she had always wanted from him: his sole attention, his searing touch, his mind-blowing caresses, and his gorgeously hot body. She knew and understood the rules. There were no promises being made. There was no hope of 'happy ever after'. It was a mutual lust fest to settle the ache of longing that had started so long ago and had never been sated. It was a way—she rationalised it—to rewrite that night seven years ago. This was what she had wanted from

Jake way back then—not to be pawed over by some drunk but to be treated with respect, to be pleasured as well as give it. This was the healing she needed to move on with her life, to reclaim her self-respect and her sexual confidence. 'I want you,' she said. 'I don't think I've ever wanted to have sex more than right now.'

He brushed a wayward strand of hair off her face, his dark gaze lustrous with desire. 'I'm pretty turned on myself.'

She stroked him again, watching as his breathing rate increased with every glide of her hand. 'So I can tell.'

He moved her hand so he could access her body, taking his time to caress her until she was swollen and wet. Her need for him was a consuming ache that intensified with every movement of his fingers. She writhed beneath him, restless to feel the ultimate fulfilment, wanting him to possess her so they both experienced the rapture of physical union.

Finally he entered her, but only a short distance, holding back, allowing her to get used to him. His tenderness made her feel strangely emotional. She couldn't imagine him being so tender with his other lovers. She knew it didn't necessarily mean he was falling in love with her. She wasn't that naïve. But it made her feel special all the same. Wasn't this how her teenaged self had imagined it would be? Jake being so tender and thoughtful as he made beautiful, magical love to her?

He thrust a little deeper, his low, deep groan of

pleasure making her skin come up in a spray of goose bumps. He began to move, setting a slow rhythm that sent her senses reeling with delight. Each movement of his body within hers caused a delicious friction that triggered all her nerve endings, making them tingle with feeling. She lifted her hips to meet each downward thrust, aching for the release that was just out of reach. Her body was searching for it, every muscle contracting, straining, swelling and quivering with the need to fly free.

He slipped his hand down between their rocking bodies, giving her that little bit of extra coaxing that sent her flying into blessed oblivion. Her body shook with the power of it as each ripple turned into an earthquake. It was like her body had split into thousands of tiny pieces, each one spinning off into the stratosphere. She lost all sense of thought. Her mind had switched off and allowed her body free rein.

He didn't take his own pleasure until hers was over. She held him to her as his whole body tensed before he finally let go, but he did so without any increase in pace, without sound. Had he done that for her sake? Held back? Restrained his response so she hadn't felt overwhelmed or threatened? He hadn't rushed to the end. He hadn't breathed heavily or gripped her too hard, as if he had forgotten she was there.

He didn't roll away but continued to hold her as if he was reluctant to break the intimate union of their bodies.

Or was she deluding herself?

Had he been disappointed? Had she not measured

up to his other lovers? She was hardly in the same league. She might have had multiple partners but still nowhere near the number he'd had. Compared to him, she was practically a novice.

One of his hands glided up and down the length of her forearm in a soft caress that made her skin tingle as if champagne bubbles were moving through her blood. 'You were amazing,' he said.

Jaz couldn't ignore the doubts that were winding their way through her mind like a rampant vine. Hadn't she been exciting enough for him? Hadn't her body delighted his the way his had delighted hers? Was that why his response had been so toned down? Maybe he hadn't toned it down. Maybe she hadn't quite 'done it' for him. The chemistry he had talked about hadn't delivered on its promise.

It was *her* fault. Of course it was. Wasn't that why she had been engaged three times and summarily dumped?

She was rubbish at sex.

Jaz eased out of his embrace, reached for one of the hotel bathrobes and slipped it on, tying the waist ties securely. 'You don't have to lie to me, Jake,' she said. 'I know I'm not crash-hot in bed. There's no point pretending I am.'

He frowned as if she was speaking Swahili instead of English. 'Why on earth do you think that?'

She folded her arms, shooting him a flinty look. 'It's probably my fault for talking you into it. If you didn't want to do it then you should've said.'

He swung his legs over the edge of the bed and

came over to stand in front of her. He was still completely naked while Jaz was wrapped as tightly as an Egyptian mummy. He put one of his hands on her shoulder and used the other to edge up her chin so her eyes meshed with his. 'You didn't talk me into anything, Jaz,' he said. 'I just didn't want you to feel uncomfortable. Not our first time together.'

She rolled her lips together before releasing a little puff of air. 'Oh…'

He gently brushed back her hair, his eyes searching hers for a moment or two. 'Was that night at the party your first experience of kissing and touching?' he finally asked.

Jaz chewed one corner of her mouth. 'I wanted it to be you. That was my stupid teenage fantasy—that you would be the first person to make love to me.'

He gave her a pained look, his eyes dark and sombre with regret. 'I'm sorry.'

She twisted her lips in self-deprecating manner. 'I guess that's why sex has always been a bit awkward for me. I never felt comfortable unless I was in a committed relationship. But even then I often felt I wasn't up to the mark.'

'You have no need to feel inadequate,' he said. 'No need at all.'

She rested her hands on the wall of his naked chest, her lower body gravitating towards his arousal as if of its own volition. 'You said "our first time together". Does that mean there's going to be a second or a third?'

He put a hand in the small of her back and drew

her flush against him, his eyes kindling with sensual promise. 'Start counting,' he said and lowered his mouth to hers.

CHAPTER NINE

JAKE HAD NEVER made love with such care and concern for a partner. Not that he'd been unduly rough or selfish with any of his past lovers, but being with Jaz made him realise what he had been missing in his other encounters. The level of intimacy was different, more focused, more concentrated. The slow burn of desire intensified and prolonged the pleasure. Each stroke of her soft hands made his blood pound until he could feel it in every cell of his body. Her lips flowered open beneath his, her tongue tangling with his in an erotic duel that sent a current of electricity through his pelvis. He held her to his hardness, delighting in the feel of her lithe body moulded against his.

He slipped a hand through the V-neck of her bathrobe to cup her small but perfect breasts; her skin was as smooth as satin, her nipples pert with arousal. He lowered his mouth to her right breast, teasing her areola with his tongue, skating over her tightly budded nipple, before drawing it into his mouth as she gave a breathless moan of approval. He moved to her left breast, taking his time to explore and caress it with the same attention to detail.

He worked his way up from her breasts to linger over the delicate framework of her collarbone, dipping his tongue into the shallow dish below her neck. Her skin was perfumed with grace notes of honeysuckle and lilac with a base note of vanilla. He spread his fingers through her hair, cradling her head as he kissed her deeply. Her soft little sounds of longing made his heart race and his blood run at fever pitch. Her tongue danced with his in flicks, darts and sweeps that made him draw her even closer to his body.

He eased her bathrobe off her shoulders, letting it fall in a puddle at her feet. He slid his hands down her body to grasp her by the hips, letting her feel the fullness of his erection against her mound. She moved against him, silently urging him on. He left her only long enough to get another condom, quickly applying it before he led her back to the bed. She held her arms out to him as he joined her on the mattress, wrapping them around his neck as he brought his mouth back down to hers.

When he entered her tight, wet heat he felt every ripple of her body welcoming him, massaging him, thrilling him. He began to move in slow thrusts, each one going deeper than the first, letting her catch his rhythm. She whimpered against his mouth, soft little cries of need that made the hairs on his scalp tingle. He continued to rock against her, with her, each movement of their bodies building to a crescendo. He could feel the build-up of tension in her body, the way she strained, gasped and urged him on by gripping his shoulders, as if anchoring herself.

He reached down to touch her intimately, stroking her slick wetness, feeling her swell and bud under his touch, the musky scent of her arousal intermingled with his, intoxicating his senses like the shot of an illicit drug. Her orgasm was so powerful he could feel it contracting against his length, triggering his own release until he was flying as high and free as she.

This time he didn't hold back. He couldn't. He gave a deep groan and pumped and spilled. The rush of pleasure swept through him, spinning him away from everything but what was happening in his body.

Jake had never been big on pillow talk or cuddling in the afterglow. He'd never been good at closeness and contact once the deed had been done.

But with Jaz it was different.

He felt different.

He wasn't sure why. Maybe it was because she wasn't just another girl he had picked up hardly long enough to catch her name. She was someone he knew. Had known for years. She was someone who mattered to him. She was a part of his life—always had been and probably always would be.

He felt protective of her, especially knowing his role in what had happened to her. He wanted her to feel safe and respected. To be an equal partner in sex, not a vessel to be used and cast aside.

But isn't that what you usually do? Use them and lose them?

The thought came from the back of his conscience like a lone heckler pushing through a crowd.

He used women, yes, but they used him back. They knew the rules and played by them. If he thought a woman wasn't going to stick to the programme, he wouldn't allow things to progress past a drink and a flirty chat. He was a dab hand at picking the picket-fence-and-puppies type. But the women that pursued him were mostly out for a good time, not a long time, which suited him perfectly.

He didn't want the responsibility of a relationship. He found the notion of a committed relationship suffocating. Having to answer to someone, having to take care of their emotional needs, being blamed when things didn't work out, seemed to him to nothing short of torture. He didn't need that sort of drama. He had seen enough during his childhood. Watching his parents fight and tear each other down only to make up as if nothing was wrong had deeply unsettled him. He never knew what was real, what was dependable and what wasn't. Life with his parents had been so unpredictable and tempestuous he had decided the only way he could tolerate a connection with someone would be to keep it focused solely on the physical. Emotion had no place in his flings with women.

But for some reason it felt right to hold Jaz in his arms: to idly stroke his fingers up and down her silky skin, her slender back, her neat bottom, her slim thighs. He liked the feel of her lying up against him, her legs still entangled with his. He liked the soft waft of her breath tickling the skin against his neck where her head was buried against him.

He liked the thought that she trusted him enough to share her body with him without fear or shame.

Or maybe it was a pathetic attempt on his part to right the wrongs of the past. To absolve himself from the yoke of guilt about what had happened to her.

As if that's ever going to happen.

Jaz lifted her head out from against his neck and shoulder to look at him. 'Thank you,' she said softly.

Jake tucked a strand of her hair back behind her ear. 'For what? Giving you a ten on the Richter scale?'

'It was a twelve,' she said with a crooked little smile, then added, 'But no. For being so…considerate.'

He picked up one of her hands and kissed the ends of her fingers. 'I'm not sure anyone I know would ever describe me as considerate.'

'You like people to think you're selfish and shallow but deep down I know you're not. You're actually really sensitive. The rest is all an act. A ruse. A defence mechanism.'

He released her hand as he moved away to get off the bed. He shrugged on the other fluffy bathrobe, watching as her teeth started pulling at her lower lip as if she sensed what was coming. *Good*, he thought. *Because I'm not going to pull any punches.* There was no way he was going to play at happy families. No way. Sure, the sex was good. Better than good, when it came to that. But that was all it was: sex. If she was starting to envisage him dressed in a tux standing at the end of the aisle then she had better think again.

Freaking hell. Next she would be talking about kids and kindergarten bookings.

'Here's what a selfish bastard I am, Jasmine,' he said. 'If you don't stop doing that doe-eyed thing to me, I'm going to head back to London and leave you to face that bunch of wedding-obsessed wackos downstairs all on your own.'

She sat up and pulled the sheet up, hugging her knees close to her chest, her misty eyes entreating. 'Please don't leave… This weekend is important to me. I have everything riding on it. I don't want anything to go wrong.'

He wanted to leave. Bolting when things got serious was his way of dealing with things. But there was young Emma Madden to consider. If Jaz took it upon herself to let that particular cat out of the bag as payback if he left then he could say goodbye to his business deal. Bruce Parnell would withdraw from the contract for sure. That sort of mud had a habit of sticking and making a hell of a mess while it did. Jake's reputation would be shot. He wouldn't be seen in the public eye as just a fun-loving playboy. He would be seen as a lecherous cradle snatcher with all its ghastly connotations.

'I signed up for two weeks.' He held up two fingers for emphasis. 'That's all. After that, we go our separate ways. Those are the rules.'

'Fine,' she said. 'Two weeks is all I want from you.'

He sent her a narrow look. 'Is it?'

Her expression was cool and composed but he noticed how her teeth kept pulling at her lip. 'I'm not falling in love with you, Jake. I was merely making an observation about your character. Your prickliness proves my point. You don't like people seeing your softer, more sensitive side.'

What softer side? She had romantic goggles on. A couple of good orgasms and she was seeing him as some sort of white knight. 'Don't confuse good physical chemistry with anything else, okay? I'm not interested in anything else. And nor should you be until you've sorted out why you keep attracting the sort of guys who won't stick around long enough to put a ring on your finger and keep it there.'

She gave him a pert look. 'Maybe you could tell me what I'm doing wrong, since you're the big relationships expert.'

Jake watched as she took her sweet ass time getting off the bed to slip on a bathrobe. She didn't bother doing up the waist ties but left the sides hanging open, leaving her beautiful body partially on show. For some reason it was more titillating than if she had been standing there stark naked. His blood headed south until he was painfully erect.

Everything about her turned him on. The way she moved like a sleek and graceful cat. The way she tossed her hair back behind her shoulders like some haughty aristocrat. The way she looked at him with artic eyes while her body radiated such sensual heat. It was good to see her act more confident sexually but he couldn't help feeling she was driving home a point. But he was beyond fighting her over it. He wanted her and he only had two weeks to make the most of it. 'What time do you have to be downstairs?' he asked.

She pushed back her left sleeve to check the watch on her slender wrist. It was one his parents had bought for her for her twenty-first birthday. Another reminder of how entwined with his life she was and always would be. 'An hour,' she said. 'I have to check my dress is properly steamed and pressed for the fashion parade tomorrow.'

He held out his hand. 'Have a shower with me.'

She looked at his hand. Returned her gaze to his with a little flicker of defiance in hers. 'Won't you be quicker on your own?'

'Yeah, but it won't be half as much fun.'

CHAPTER TEN

JAZ'S BODY WAS still tingling when she went down-stairs with Jake for the welcome-to-the-expo drinks party. He kept giving her smouldering glances as they mingled amongst the other designers and expo staff. She wondered if people knew what they had been up to in the shower only minutes earlier. She had hardly had time to get her hair dry and put on some make-up after he had pleasured every inch of her body.

Of course people knew. He was Jake Ravensdale. What he didn't know about sex wasn't worth knowing. Wasn't her thrumming body proof of that? He only had to look at her with that dark-as-midnight gaze and her inner core would leap in excitement. She saw the effect he had on every woman in the room. Hers wasn't the only pulse racing, the only breath catch-ing in her throat, the only mind conjuring up what she would like to do with him when she got him alone.

Congratulations came thick and fast from the peo-ple Jaz knew, as well as many she didn't. It made her feel a little less conflicted about continuing the cha-rade. It was only for two weeks. Two weeks to enjoy the sensual magnificence of a man she had hated for years.

Just shows how easy it is to separate emotion from sex.

One of the models came over with a glass of champagne in one hand. 'Hi, Jake, remember me? We met at a company party last year.'

Jake gave one of his charming smiles. 'Sure I do. How are you?'

The young woman gave a little pout. 'I was fine until I heard you got yourself engaged. No one saw *that* coming.'

Jaz was getting a little tired of being ignored like she was a piece of furniture. 'Hi,' she said holding out her hand to the model. 'I'm Jake's fiancée, Jasmine Connolly. And you are…?'

'Saskiaa with two "a"s,' the girl said with a smile that lasted only as long as her handshake. 'When's the big day?'

'December,' Jaz said. 'Boxing Day, actually.' Why shouldn't she make Jake squirm a bit while she had the chance? 'We're hoping for a white wedding in every sense of the word.'

Jake waited until the model had moved on before he leaned down close to Jaz's ear. 'Boxing Day?'

Jaz looked up at him with a winsome smile. 'I quite fancy the idea of a Christmas wedding. The family will already be gathered so it would be awfully convenient for everyone, don't you think?'

He smiled but it got only as far as his mouth, and that was probably only for the benefit of others who were looking at them. 'Don't overplay it,' he said in an undertone only she could hear.

Jaz kept her smile in place. 'You didn't remember that girl, did you?'

A frown pulled at his brow. 'Why's that an issue for you?'

'It's not,' she said. 'I don't expect you even ask their name before you sleep with them.'

'I ask their permission, which is far more important in my opinion.'

Jaz held his look for as long as she dared. 'I know it comes as naturally to you as breathing, but I would greatly appreciate it if you wouldn't flirt with any of the women, in particular the models. Half of them look as if they should still be in school.'

His mouth curved upward in a sardonic smile. 'My parents would be enormously proud of you. You're doing a perfect jealous fiancée impersonation.'

She snatched a glass of champagne off a passing waiter for something to do with her hands. 'Don't screw this up for me, Jake,' she said through tight lips in case anyone nearby could lip-read. 'I need to secure the booking for next year's expo. Once that's in the bag, you can go back to your "single and loving it" life.'

He trailed a lazy fingertip down her arm from the top of her bare shoulder to her wrist. 'Just wait until I get you alone.'

Jaz shivered as his eyes challenged hers in a sexy duel. His touch was like a match to her tinderbox senses. Every nerve was screaming for more. 'Now who's overplaying it?'

He slipped a hand to the nape of her neck and drew her closer, bending down to press a lingering kiss on her lips. Even though Jaz's eyes were closed in bliss she could see the bright flashes of cameras going off around them. After a moment he eased back and winked at her devilishly. 'Did I tell you how gorgeous you look tonight?'

Jaz knew he was probably only saying it for the benefit of others but a part of her wanted to believe it was true. She placed a hand on the lapel of his suit jacket, smoothing away an imaginary fleck of lint. 'You've scrubbed up pretty well yourself,' she said. 'Even without a tie.'

He screwed up his face. 'I hate the things. They always feel like they're choking me.'

Typical Jake. Hating anything that confined or restrained him. 'I suppose that's why you got all those detentions for breaking the uniform code at that posh school you went to?'

He grinned. 'I still hold the record for the most detentions in one term. Apparently I'm considered a bit of a legend.'

Jaz shook her head at him, following it up with a roll of her eyes. 'Come on.' She looped her arm through his. 'I want to have a look at the displays.'

Oh, joy, Jake thought as Jaz led him to where the wedding finery was displayed in one of the staterooms. The sight of all those meringue-like wedding gowns and voluminous veils was enough to make him break out in hives. Or maybe it was the flowers. There were arrangements of every size and shape: centrepieces, towers of flowers, bouquets, bunches and buttonholes. There were displays of food, wine and French champagne, a honeymoon destination stand and a bespoke jeweller in situ. There were a few men there partnering their fiancées or girlfriends but they were pretty thin on the ground. Jake understood Jaz wanted to secure her signing for next year but he couldn't help feeling she had insisted he accompany her as a punishment.

But that was one of the things he secretly admired in her. She was feisty and stood her ground with him. She was the only woman he knew who didn't simper at him or adapt to suit him. He felt the electric buzz of her will tussling with his every time she locked gazes with him. For years they had done their little stand-off thing. What would they do once they parted company? Would they go back to their old ways or find a new way of relating? With two family weddings coming up, it would be tasteless to be at loggerheads. There was enough of that going around with his parents' carry-on. The dignified thing would be to be mature and civil about it and be friends.

But would he ever be able to look at her as a friend without thinking of how she came apart in his arms? How it felt when he held her close? How her mouth tasted of heat, passion and sweetness mixed in a combustible cocktail that made his senses whirl out of control? Would he ever be able to stand beside her and not want to pull her into his arms?

He'd slept with a lot of women but none of them had had that effect on him. He barely gave his lovers another thought once he moved on to the next. Was it because Jaz was someone who had always been on the periphery of his life? Sometimes even at the centre, at the very heart, of his family?

Had that familiarity added something to their love-making?

It wasn't just physical sex with her. There were feelings there…feelings he couldn't describe. He cared about her. But then everyone in his family cared about her.

Every time he looked at her he felt the stirring in his groin. He couldn't look at her mouth without thinking of how it felt fused to his own. How her tongue felt as it played with his, how her body felt as she pushed herself, as if she wanted to crawl into his skin and never leave. Even now with her arm looped through his he could feel the brush of her beautiful body against his side. He couldn't wait to get her back to their suite and get her naked.

They walked past a photographer's stand but then Jaz suddenly swivelled and, pulling Jake by the hand, led him back to where the photographer had set up a romantic set with love-hearts, red roses and a velvet-covered sofa in the shape of a pair of lips. 'Can you take our picture?' she asked the photographer.

'Sure,' the photographer said. 'Just sit together on the sofa there for a sec while I frame the shot.'

Jake looked down at Jaz sitting snuggled up by his side as if butter wouldn't melt in her hot little mouth.

'I'm keeping a score,' he said in an undertone. 'Just thought I'd put that out there.'

She gave him a sly smile. 'So am I.'

Jaz thought she might have overdone it with the champagne, or maybe it was being with Jake all evening. Being with him made her tipsy, giddy with excitement. He never left her side; his arm was either around her waist or he held hands with her as she worked the room. It was a torturously slow form of foreplay. Every look, every touch, every brush of his body against hers was a prelude to what was to come. She could see the intention in his dark-blue gaze. It was blatantly, spine-tinglingly sexual. It made every inch of her flesh shiver behind the shield of her clothes, every cell of her body contracting in feverish anticipation.

'Time for bed?' Jake said, his fingers warm and firm around hers.

Jaz felt something in her belly slip sideways. When he touched her like that she couldn't stop thinking of where else he was going to touch her when he got her alone. Her entire body tingled in anticipation. Even the hairs on the nape of her neck shivered at the roots. 'I wonder if we'll win the "most loved-up couple" photo competition?' she said. 'Or the all-expenses-paid wedding and honeymoon package? That would be awesome.'

His eyes sent her a teasing warning. 'Don't push it, baby girl.'

She laughed as he led her to the lift. 'I can't remember a time when I've enjoyed myself more. You should have seen your face when that florist threw you that bouquet. You looked like you'd caught a detonated bomb.'

The lift doors sprang open and Jake pulled her in, barely waiting long enough for the doors to close to bring his mouth down to hers in a scorching kiss. Jaz linked her arms around his neck, pressing as close to him as she could to feel the hardened length of him against her tingling pelvis. He put a hand on one of her thighs and hooked it over his hip, bringing her into closer contact with the heat and potency of him. She could see out of the corner of her eye their reflection in the mirrored walls. It was shockingly arousing to see the way their bodies strained to be together, the flush on both of their faces as desire rode hard and fast in their blood.

Jake put his hand on the stop button and the lift came to a halt. Jaz looked at the erotic intent in his eyes and a wave of lust coursed through her so forcefully she thought she would come on the spot. He nudged her knickers to one side while she unzipped his trousers with fingers that shook with excitement. How he got a condom on so quickly was a testament to how adept he was at sex, she thought. He entered her with a slick, deep thrust that made her head bang against the wall of the elevator. He checked himself at her gasp, asking, 'Are you okay?'

Jaz was almost beyond speech, her breath coming out in fractured, pleading bursts. 'Yes…oh, yes… Don't stop. *Please* don't stop.'

He started moving again, each thrust making her wild with need. He put one of his hands on the wall beside her head to anchor himself as he drove into her with a frantic urgency that made the blood spin, sizzle and sing in her veins. He brought his hand down between their joined bodies, his fingers expertly caressing her until her senses exploded. She clung to him as the storm broke in her, through her, over her.

He followed close behind, three or four hard pumps; a couple of deep, primal grunts and it was over.

Jaz wriggled her knickers back in place and smoothed her dress down as the lift continued up to their floor. 'I reckon you must hold some sort of record for getting a condom on,' she said into the silence. 'It's like a sleight of hand thing. Amazing.'

He gave her a glinting look as he zipped his trousers. 'Always pays to be prepared.'

A shiver danced its way down her spine as he escorted her out of the lift to their suite, his hand resting in the small of her back. Once they were inside their suite he closed the door and pulled her to him until she was in the circle of his arms. 'Happy with how tonight went?' he said.

Was he talking about her business or their lovemaking? 'I've got a meeting with the expo organisers next week,' Jaz said. 'It's an exciting opportunity. I'm hoping it will lead to bigger events, maybe even internationally.'

He smoothed a wisp of her hair back off her face. 'Why did you choose to design wedding gear? Why not evening, or fashion in general?'

Jaz slipped out of his hold, feeling a lecture coming on. Of course he would think weddings were a waste of time and money. He was a playboy. A wedding was the last thing on earth that would interest him. But to her they signified everything she had dreamed about as a child. Her parents hadn't married. They hadn't even made a formal commitment to each other. They had just hooked up one night and look how that had turned out. She had been passed between them like a parcel no one wanted until finally her mother had dumped her with her dad without even saying goodbye or 'see you later'.

'Jaz?'

She turned to look at him, her mouth set. 'Do you know what it's like to grow up without a sense of family? To have to *borrow* someone else's family in order to feel normal?'

Jake frowned. 'I'm not sure what that has to do with your choice of career but—'

'It has *everything* to do with it,' Jaz said. 'For as long as I can remember, I wanted to be normal. To have normal parents, not one who's off her face most of the time and the other who hadn't wanted a kid in the first place. I didn't have anything from either of my parents that made me feel a part of a unit. I was a mistake, an accident, an inconvenience.' She folded her arms and continued. 'But when a couple marries, it's different. It's a public declaration of love and commitment and mostly—not always, but mostly—one expressing a desire to have children.'

Jaz looked at him as the silence swelled. Had she said too much? Revealed too much? What did it matter? She was tired of him criticising her choices. 'A wedding dress is something most brides keep for the rest of their lives,' she said. 'It can be passed down from a mother to a daughter. General fashion isn't the same. It's seasonal, transient. Some pieces might be passed on but they don't have the emotional resonance a wedding dress has. That's why I design wedding gowns. Every woman deserves to be a princess for a day. I like being able to make that wish come true.'

Even if I can't make it come true for myself.

Jake gave a slow nod. 'Sounds reasonable.'

'But you think I'm crazy.'

'I didn't say that.'

Jaz went to the drinks fridge and poured a glass of mineral water, taking a sip before she turned to face him again. He was looking at her with a contemplative look on his face, his brows drawn together, his mouth set in a serious line, his gaze centred on hers. 'I'm sorry if tonight's been absolute torture for you but this weekend's really important to me.'

His mouth tilted in a wry smile. 'You're not one bit sorry. You've enjoyed every minute, watching me squirm down there.'

Jaz smiled back. 'It was rather fun, I have to admit. I can't wait to see what press photos show up. I wonder if they got the one of you with the bouquet. Or maybe I should text it or post it online?'

He closed the distance between them and pulled her down to the bed in a tangle of limbs. 'Cheeky minx,' he said, eyes twinkling with amusement.

Jaz stroked the sexy stubble on his face, her belly fluttering with excitement as his hard body pressed against hers. His hooded gaze went to her mouth, his thumb coming up to brush over her lower lip until it tingled, as if teased by electrodes. 'What are you thinking?'

'You mean you can't tell?' he said with a wicked sparkle in his eyes.

She snatched in a breath as his body moved against her, triggering a tide of want that flooded her body, pooling hotly in her core. 'When you hook up with someone, how many times do you have sex with them in one night?'

A frown creased his forehead. 'Why do you want to know?'

Jaz traced the trench of his frown with her finger. 'Just wondering.'

He caught her hand and pinned it on the bed beside her head, searching her gaze for a pulsing moment. 'Wondering what?'

'If you've done it more with me than with anyone else.'

'And if I have?'

She looked at his mouth. 'Is it…different…? With me, I mean?'

He nudged up her chin with a blunt fingertip, locking his gaze with hers. 'Different in what way?'

Jaz wasn't sure why she was fishing so hard for compliments. He had made it clear how long their fling was going to last. Just because he had made love to her several times tonight didn't mean anything other than he had a high sex drive. He was, after all, a man in his sexual prime. But their love-making was so different from anything she had experienced with other partners. It was more exciting, more satisfying, more addictive, which was a problem because she couldn't afford to get too used to having him. 'I don't know…more intense?'

He slid his hand along the side of her face to splay his fingers through her hair. It was an achingly tender hold that made Jaz's heart squeeze as if someone had crushed it in a vice. Could it be possible he was coming to care for her? *Really* care for her? Was that why their intimacy was so satisfying? Did their physical connection reflect a much deeper one that had been simmering in the background for years?

But she didn't love him.

Not the slavish way she had as a teenager. She was an adult now. Her feelings for him were mature and sensible. She knew his faults and limitations. She didn't whitewash his personality to make him out to be anything he was not. She was too sensible to hanker after a future with him because he wasn't the future type. He was the 'for now' type.

Falling in love with Jake Ravensdale once had been bad enough. To do it twice would be emotional suicide.

'It is different,' Jake said. 'But that doesn't mean I want it to continue longer than we agreed.'

'I'm not asking for an extension,' Jaz said. 'I can't afford to waste my time having a long-term fling with someone who doesn't want the same things I want. I want to get on with my life and find my soul mate. I want to start a family before I'm thirty.'

His frown hadn't quite gone away but now it was deeper than ever. 'You shouldn't rush into your next relationship. Take your time getting to know them. And what's the big rush on having kids? You're only twenty-three. You've got heaps of time.'

'I don't want to miss out on having kids,' Jaz said. 'I know so many women who've left it too late or circumstances have worked against them. I can't imagine not having a family. It's what I've wanted since I was a little girl.'

He moved away from her and got off the bed, scraping a hand through his hair before dropping it back by his side.

Jaz chewed at her lower lip. 'Did I just kill the mood?'

He turned around with a smile that didn't involve his eyes. 'It's been a long day. I'm going to have a shower and hit the sack. Don't wait up.'

When Jake came out of the bathroom after his shower half an hour later, Jaz wasn't in the bed. In fact, she wasn't in the suite. He frowned as he searched the room, even going so far as to check under the bed. Where the hell was she? He glanced at her bag on the luggage rack. She obviously hadn't checked out of the hotel as her things were still here. Although, come to think of it, he wouldn't put it past her to flounce off, leaving him to pack her things. What was she up to? Their conversation earlier had cut a little close to the bone…for him, that was. Why did she have to carry on about marriage and kids all the time? She was a baby herself. Most twenty-three-year-olds were still out partying and having a good time.

But no, Jaz wanted the white picket fence and a bunch of wailing brats. What would happen to her stellar career as a wedding designer then? She would be doing more juggling than a circus act.

And as to finding her soul mate... Did she really believe such a thing existed? There was no such thing as a perfect partner. She was deluding herself with romantic notions of what her life could be like.

Well, he had news for her. It would be just like everyone else's life—boring and predictable.

Jake called her number but it went straight through to voice mail. He paced about the suite, feeling more and more agitated. The weird thing was he spent hours of his life in hotel rooms, mostly alone. He rarely spent the whole night with anyone. It was less complicated when it came to the 'morning after the night before' routine.

But every time he looked at that bed he thought of how it had felt with Jaz, her arms and legs wrapped around him and her hot little mouth clamped to his. He couldn't stop thinking about the lift either. He probably wouldn't be able to get into one ever again without thinking of taking Jaz up against that mirrored wall. His blood pounded at the memory of it. He had been close to doing it without a condom. He still didn't know how he'd got it on in time. He had been as worked up as a teenager on his first 'sure thing' date.

What was it about Jaz that made him so intensely attracted to her? It wasn't like this with his other flings. Once or twice was usually enough before he was ready for more excitement. But with Jaz he was mad with lust. Crazy with it. Buzzing with it. Making love with her eased it for a heartbeat before he was aching for her again. It had to blow out eventually. It *had* to. He wasn't putting down tent pegs just because the sex was good. Just as well they'd agreed on an end date. Two weeks was pushing it. He didn't take that long for holidays because he always got bored. There was no way this was going to continue indefinitely.

No. Freaking. Way.

Jake threw on some clothes and finger-combed his damp hair on his way to the lift. She had to be in the hotel somewhere. He jabbed at the call button. Why the hell was it so slow? Was some other couple holed up in there, doing it? His gut tightened. Surely Jaz wouldn't pick up someone and…? No. He slammed his foot down on the thought like someone stomping on a noxious spider.

The lift was empty.

So was his stomach as he searched the bar for the glimpse of that gorgeous honey-brown head. He went to the restaurant, and then looked through the foyer, but there was no sign of her anywhere. He hadn't re-alised until then what had fuelled his heart-stopping panic. It hit him like a felling blow right in the middle of his chest. He couldn't draw breath for a moment. His throat closed. He could feel his thudding pulse right down to his fingertips.

He had dismissed her. Rejected her. What if she had been upset and gone downstairs to God knew what? What if some unscrupulous guy had intercepted her? Shoved her into a back room and done the unthinkable?

The stateroom where the displays were set up was closed with a burly security guard posted outside.

The security guard gave Jake the eye as he tried the doorknob. 'Sorry, buddy,' the guard said with a smirk. 'You'll have to wait till morning to try a dress on.'

Jake wanted to punch him.

He retraced his steps; his growing dread making his skin break out in a clammy sweat until his shirt was sticking to his back like cling-film. Where could she have gone? He couldn't get the image of her trapped in some room—*some locked bathroom*—with an opportunist creep mauling her. He would never be able to live with himself if she got hurt under his watch. She was with him. He was supposed to be her partner. Her 'fiancé'. What sort of fiancé would let her wander off alone to be taken advantage of by some stranger? She was gullible with men. Look at the way she'd got engaged three times. He hadn't liked one of them. They were nice enough men but not one of them was worthy of her.

Jake strode past the restrooms. Could she be in there? Locked inside one of the cubicles with someone? He did a quick whip round and checked that no one was watching before he pushed open the outer door. 'Jaz? Are you in there?' There was no answer so he went in through to where the cubicles were.

A middle-aged woman turned from the basins with

her eyes blazing in indignation. 'This is the ladies' room!'

'I—I know,' Jake said, quickly back-pedalling with the woman following him like an army sergeant. 'I'm looking for my…er…fiancée.'

The woman blasted him with a look that was as icy as the wind off the North Sea in winter. 'I've met men like you before. Lurking around female toilets to get your sick thrills. I've a good mind to call security.'

Jake looked at her in open-mouthed shock, which didn't seem to help his cause one little bit, because it looked like he'd been sprung doing exactly what the woman accused him of. 'No, no, no,' he said, trying to placate her as she took out her phone. If she took a snapshot of him in the female restrooms and it went viral he could forget about his reputation and his career. Both would be totally screwed. 'My fiancée is this high…' He put his hand up to demonstrate. 'Really pretty with light-brown hair and grey-blue eyes and—'

'Is there a problem?' The security guard from outside the display room spoke from behind Jake.

Jake rolled his eyes. This was turning into such a freaking farce. And meanwhile Jaz was still missing. He turned to face the guard. 'I'm looking for my fiancée. She's not answering her phone. I thought she might be in the ladies' room.'

The security guard's mouth curled up on one side. 'You seem to have a thing for what belongs to the ladies, don't you, buddy?'

Jake clenched his hands in case he was tempted

to use them to knock that sneer off the guard's face. *Time to play the famous card.* 'Look, I'm Jake Ravensdale,' he said. 'I'm—'

'I don't care if you're Jack the bloody Ripper,' the guard said. 'I want you out of here before I call the cops.'

'You can check with Reception,' Jake said. 'Get them to check the bookings. I'm here with Jasmine Connolly, the bridal designer.' *Dear God, had Jaz put him on the booking information?* he thought in panic as the guard took out his intercom device and called the front desk.

The guard spoke to someone at Reception and then put his device back on his belt, his expression now as nice as pie. 'Nice to meet you, Mr Ravensdale,' he said. 'Enjoy your stay. Oh, and by the way...' He put on a big, cheesy grin. 'Congratulations.'

Jake went back to the suite with his whole body coiled as tight as a spring. He pushed open the door to see Jaz getting ready for bed. 'Where the bloody hell have you been?' he said. 'I've been scouring the hotel from top to bottom for the last hour looking for you.'

'I went down to check on my dress before the room was locked.'

'Did you not think to leave a note or a send me a text?'

A spark of defiance shone in her grey-blue gaze as it collided with his. 'I assumed you were finished with me for the evening. You told me not to wait up.'

Jake smothered a filthy curse under his breath. 'Do you have any idea of how damned worried I was?'

She looked at him blankly. 'Why would you be worried?'

He pushed his hand back through his hair. 'I was worried, that's all.'

She came over to him to lay a hand on his arm. Her soft fingers warmed his flesh, making every one of his taut muscles unwind and others south of the border tighten. 'Are you okay?'

Was he okay? No. He felt like he would never be okay again. *Ever.* His head was pounding with the mother of all headaches. His heart rate felt like someone had given him an overdose of adrenalin. Two overdoses. His legs were shaking. His guts had turned to gravy. 'I'm fine.' Even to his own ears he knew he sounded unnecessarily curt.

'You don't sound it,' Jaz said, frowning at him in concern. 'Are you unwell? Have you caught food poisoning or something? You look so pale and sweaty and—'

'I almost got myself arrested.'

Her eyes rounded. 'What on earth for?'

'Long story.'

'Tell me what happened, Jake,' she said. 'I need to know, since we're here at this expo together, because it could reflect badly on me.'

Should he tell her it all or just a cut-down version? 'I panicked when you weren't in the suite. I didn't know where you'd gone.'

She began to stroke his arm, her eyes as clear, still

and lustrous as a mountain tarn as she looked into his. 'Were you worried I wasn't coming back?'

His hands came down on her shoulders in a grip that was unapologetically possessive. 'I was out of my mind with worry,' he said. 'I tried to check the display room but the security guard gave me a hard time. And then he found me coming out of the ladies' toilets—'

Her brow puckered. 'Why'd you go in there?'

Jake swallowed. 'I was worried someone might have cornered you in there and…' He couldn't even say what he'd thought. It was too sickening to be vocalised.

Her eyes softened. 'Oh, you big goose,' she said. 'I'm a big girl now. I can fend for myself, but thanks anyway.'

He brought her closer so her hips were against his, watching the way her tongue came out to moisten her lips; it made every one of those muscles in his groin go rock-hard. 'I swear to God I've aged a decade in the last hour.'

'Doesn't feel like it to me.'

He pressed her even closer. 'I want you.'

A little light danced like a sprite in her gaze. 'Again?'

He walked her backwards toward the bed, thigh to thigh, hip to hip, need to need. 'How much sleep do you need?' he said as he nibbled at her mouth, their breaths intermingling.

'Seven hours—five in an emergency—otherwise I get ratty.'

Jake helped her out of her clothes with more haste than finesse. 'I can handle ratty.'

She gave a tinkling laugh. 'Don't say I didn't warn you.'

He put his mouth on her naked breast, drawing her tight nipple into his mouth. It was music to his ears to hear her breathless moan of pleasure. It made his blood pump all the more frantically. He pushed her gently down on the bed, shoving pillows, petals and clothes out of the way as he came down beside her. He wanted to go slow but his earlier panic did something to his self-control. He needed to be inside her. He needed to be fused with her, to have her writhing and shuddering as he took her to paradise. He needed to quell this feverish madness racing in his blood. Her body gripped him like a fist as he surged into her velvet heat. The ripples of her inner core massaged him inexorably closer to a mind-blowing lift-off. He held on only long enough to make sure she was with him all the way. When she came around him he gave a part-growl, part-groan as he lost himself to physical bliss...

CHAPTER ELEVEN

JAZ WAS TRYING not to show how nervous she was the next morning but Jake must have sensed it because he kept looking at her with a watchful gaze. She picked at the breakfast he had had delivered to their suite but barely any made it to her mouth.

'At least have a glass of juice,' he said, pushing a glass of freshly squeezed orange juice towards her.

'I think I'm going to be sick.'

He took her hand from across the table and gave it an encouraging squeeze. 'Sweetheart, you're going to knock them for six down there.'

She bit down on her lip, panic and nerves clawing at her insides like razor blades whirled in a blender. 'Who am I fooling? I'm just a gardener's daughter from the wrong side of the tracks. What am I doing here pretending I'm a high street designer?'

'Imposter syndrome,' Jake said, leisurely pouring a cup of brewed coffee. 'That's what all this fuss is about. You don't believe in yourself. You think you've fluked it, that someone is going to come up behind you and tap you on the shoulder and tell you to get the hell out of here because you're not up to standard.'

That was exactly what Jaz was thinking. She had been thinking it most of her life. Being abandoned by her mother had always made her feel as if she wasn't good enough. She tried so hard to be the best she could be so people wouldn't leave her. But invariably they eventually did. Three times she had got engaged and each time it had ended. Her fiancés had ended it, not her. She was ashamed to admit she might well have married each and every one of them if they hadn't pulled the plug first. She was so terrified of failing, she over-controlled everything: her work, her relationships, her life. Her business was breaking even…just. But she'd had a lot of help. If it hadn't been for Jake's parents, she might never have got to where she was.

How long could she go on doing everything herself? She was constantly juggling. Sometimes she felt like a circus clown on stilts with twenty plates in the air. She couldn't remember the last time she'd taken a holiday. She took her work everywhere. She had Holly's dress with her in case there was a spare minute to work on the embroidery. She hadn't had a chance to draw a single sketch for Miranda. How long could she go on like that? Something had to give. She was going to get an ulcer at this rate. Maybe she already had one.

'You're right,' she said on a sigh. 'Every time I get myself to a certain place, I make myself sick worrying it's going to be ripped out from under me.'

'That's perfectly understandable given what happened with your mother.'

Jaz lowered her gaze as she smoothed out a tiny crease in the tablecloth. 'For years I waited for her to come back. I used to watch from the window whenever a car came up the drive. I would get all excited thinking she was coming back, that she had got herself sorted out and was coming back to take me to the new life she'd always promised me. But it never happened. I haven't heard from her since. I don't even know if she's still alive.'

Jake covered her hand with the warm solidness of his. 'You've made your own new life all by yourself. You didn't need her to come back and screw it up.'

'Not *all* by myself,' Jaz said. 'I'm not sure where I'd be if it hadn't been for your parents.' She waited a beat before adding, 'Do you think you could have a look over my books some time? I'm happy to pay you.'

'Sure, but you don't have to pay me.'

'I insist,' Jaz said. 'Your family has helped me enough. I don't want to be seen as a charity case.'

Jake lightly buttered some toast and handed it to her. 'One mouthful. It'll help to settle your stomach.'

Jaz took the toast and bit, chewed and swallowed but it felt like she was swallowing a cotton ball. 'Do you have it?'

'Have what?'

'Imposter syndrome?'

He smiled crookedly, as if the thought was highly amusing. 'No.'

'I suppose it was a silly question,' she conceded. 'Mr Confidence in all situations and with all people.'

A shadow passed over his features like a hand moving across a beam of light. 'There have been times when I've doubted myself.'

'Like when?'

'At boarding school, especially in my senior year,' he said, frowning slightly as he stirred his coffee. 'I played the class clown card so often I lost sight of who I really was. It wasn't until I left school and went to university that I finally found my feet and became my own person instead of being Julius's badly behaved twin brother.'

Jaz had always seen Jake as a supremely confident person. He seemed to waltz through life with nary a care of what others thought of him. She was the total opposite. Her desperate desire to fit in had made her compromise herself more times than she cared to admit. Weren't her three engagements proof of that? She had wanted to be normal. To belong to someone. To be wanted. 'I guess it must be hard, being an identical twin and all,' she said. 'Everyone is always making comparisons between you and Julius.'

There was a small silence.

'Yeah. We look the same but we're not the same,' Jake said. 'Julius is much more grounded and focused than I am.'

'I don't know about that,' Jaz said. 'You seem pretty grounded to me. You know what you want and go for it without letting anyone get in your way.'

He was frowning again as if a thought was wan

dering around in his head and he wasn't quite sure where to park it. 'But I don't stick at stuff,' he finally said. 'Not for the long haul.'

'But you're happy living your life that way, aren't you?'

After another moment of silence he gave her an absent smile. 'Yeah, it works for me. Now, have a bit more toast. It'd be embarrassing if you were to faint just when it's your chance to shine.'

Jaz did a last-minute check with the model for the gown she had prepared for the show. It was the first time any of her work would be worn by a professional model on a catwalk. The advertising she had done in the past had been still shots with models from an agency and a photographer who was a friend of a friend.

But this was different. This was her dream coming to life in front of her. Hundreds, possibly thousands or even millions, would see her design if the images went global. It would be the start of the expansion of her business she had planned since she had left design college.

Why then did she still feel like a fraud?

Because she was a fraud.

A fake.

Not because she didn't know how to design and sew a beautiful wedding gown. But because she wasn't in a committed relationship and the ring she was wearing on her finger was going to be handed back in two weeks' time. She was like the blank-faced models wearing the wedding gowns. They weren't really brides. They were acting a role.

Like *she* was acting a role.

She was pretending to be engaged to Jake when all she wanted was to be engaged to him for real. How had she not realised it until now? Or had she been shying away from it because it was a truth she hadn't wanted to face?

She was in love with Jake.

Hadn't she always been in love with him? As a child she had looked up to him as a fun older brother. He had been the playful twin, the one she could have a laugh with. Then when her female hormones had switched on she had wanted him as a woman wanted a man. But she hadn't been a woman back then—she had been a child. He had respected that and kept his distance. Wasn't that another reason why she loved him? He hadn't exploited her youthful innocence. Yes, he hadn't handled her crush with the greatest sensitivity, but at least he hadn't taken advantage of her.

Jaz was done with acting. Done with pretending. How could she stretch this out another week or two? Jake wasn't in love with her. Didn't their conversation over breakfast confirm it? He was happy with the way his life was a single man. He would go back to that life as soon as their 'engagement' ended.

Jake said she could keep the ring but why would she do that? It was little more than a consolation prize. A parting gift. Every time she looked at it she would be reminded of what she wanted and couldn't have. It might be enormous fun being with Jake. It might be wonderful to be his lover and feel the thrill of his desire and hers for him.

But what was she *doing*?

She was living a lie. That was what she was doing. Fooling people that she was in a real relationship with real hopes and dreams for the future. What future? Two weeks of fantastic, mind-blowing sex and then what? Jake would pull the plug on their relationship just like her three exes had done. She would be abandoned. Rejected. Left hanging. Alone.

Not this time. Not again.

This time she would take control. Do the right thing by herself and set the boundaries. Two weeks more of this and she would want it to be for ever. Good grief! She wanted it to be for ever now. That was how dangerous their fling had become. One night of amazing sex and she was posting the wedding invitations.

It was ridiculous.

She was ridiculous.

Jake wasn't a 'for ever' type of guy. He wanted her but only for as long as it took to burn out their mutual attraction. How long would it take? He had set the limit at two weeks. Most of his relationships didn't last two days. Why should she think *she* was so special? Sure they knew each other. They had a history of sorts. They would always be in each other's lives in some way or another.

It would be best to end it now.

On *her* terms.

Before things got crazy. Crazier…because what was crazier than falling in love with a man just because you couldn't have him? That was what she had done. It was pathological. She was in love with a man who didn't—*couldn't*—love her.

It was time to rewrite the script of her life. No longer would she fall for the wrong men. No longer would she settle for second best…even though there was no way she would ever describe Jake as second best. He was first best. *The* best. The most fabulous man she had ever known—but he wasn't hers.

He wasn't anyone's.

It would break her heart to end their affair. Weird to think she'd thought her heart had been broken by her three failed engagements; none of them, even all of them put together, had made her feel anywhere near as sad as ending her fling with Jake.

It wasn't just the sex. It was the way he made her feel as a person. He valued her. He understood her. He knew her doubts and insecurities. He had taught her to put the dark shadow of the past behind her. He protected her. He made her feel safe. He had helped her heal. His touch, his kisses, his glorious love-making, had made her fully embrace her femininity.

He had given her the gift of self-acceptance, but with that gift had come realisation. The realisation she could no longer pretend to be something she was not. She had to stop hiding behind social norms in order to feel accepted. If she never found love with a man who loved her equally, unreservedly and for ever, then she would be better off alone. Settling for anything less was settling for second best. It was compromising and self-limiting and would only bring further heartbreak in the end.

But it would be hard to be around Jake as just a friend. She would go back to being the gardener's daughter—the little ring-in who didn't really belong in the big house.

The girl who didn't belong to anyone.

Jake watched from the front row beside Jaz as her design came down the catwalk. She had only just got to her seat in time to see her moment in the spotlight. The dress was amazing. He found his mind picturing her wearing it. It had a hand-sewn beaded bodice and a frothy tulle skirt that was just like a princess's dress. The veil was set back from the model's head and flowed out behind her like a floating cloud.

If anyone had told him a week ago he'd be sitting at a wedding expo oohing and aahing at wedding gowns he would have said they were nuts. The atmosphere was electric. The ballroom was abuzz with expectation. The music was upbeat and stirring, hardly bridal or churchy at all. The applause was thunderous when Jaz's design was announced and continued even after the model had left the catwalk. He clapped as loudly as anyone, probably louder. 'Told you they'd love your work,' he said. 'You'll have orders coming out of your ears after this.'

She looked at him with a tremulous smile. 'You think?'

She still doubted herself. Amazing, he thought. What would it take for her to believe she was as good if not better than any of the other designers here? He tapped her on the end of her retroussé nose. 'Sure of it.'

Jake took her hand while the press did their interviews after the show. He was getting quite used to the role of devoted fiancé. Who said he couldn't act? Maybe some of that Ravensdale talent hadn't skipped a generation after all. Or maybe he was getting used to being part of a couple. There was certainly something to be said about knowing who he was going to sleep with that night—earlier, if he could wangle it. Instead of wondering how the sex would be, he knew for certain it would be fantastic. He had never had a more satisfying lover.

Jaz's body was a constant turn-on as it brushed against his as the crowd jostled them. He drew her closer as a photographer zoomed in on them. Her cheek was against his; the fresh, flowery scent of her made his sinuses tingle. She turned her head and he swooped down and stole a kiss from her soft-as-a-pillow mouth, wishing he could get her alone right here and now.

But instead of continuing the kiss she eased back, giving him a distracted-looking smile. Her hands went back to her lap where she was gripping the programme as if she had plans to shred it.

'You okay?' Jake said.

Her gaze was trained on the next set of models strutting their stuff. 'We need to talk,' she said. 'But not here.'

Here it comes. The talk. The talk where she would say she wanted the whole shebang: the promises of for ever, the kids, the dog and the house. The things he didn't want. Had never wanted. Would never want. Why had he thought she would be any different? He had broken his own rules for what? For a fling that should never have started in the first place.

Might as well get it over with. Once the show was over, he took her by the elbow and led her back to their suite. *Their suite.* How cosy that sounded. Like they were a couple. But they weren't a couple. A couple of idiots, if anything. They had no right to be messing around. *He* had no right. She was a part of his family. By getting involved with her he had jeopardised every single relationship she had with his family. Would everyone treat her differently now they knew she had been his lover? Would they look at her differently? Would he be harangued for the next decade for not doing the right thing by her and leaving her alone?

'I know what you're going to say,' Jake said even before he had closed the door of the suite.

She pressed her lips together for a moment. Turned and put the programme and her bag on the bed, then turned back to him and handed him her engagement ring. 'I think it's best if we end things now,' she said. 'Before we head back to London.'

Jake stared at the ring and then at her. She wanted to end it? *Now?* Before the two weeks were up? That wasn't how 'the talk' usually went. Didn't she want more? Didn't she want them to continue their affair? Wasn't she going to cry, beg and plead with him to fall in love with her and marry her? She looked so composed, so determined, as if she had made up her mind hours ago.

'But I thought you said two weeks?'

'I know but I can't do it any more, Jake,' she said, putting the ring in the top pocket of his jacket and patting it as if for safekeeping. 'It was fun while it lasted but I want to move on with my life.'

'This seems rather...sudden.'

She stepped back and looked up at him with those beautiful storm, sea and mountain-lake eyes. 'Remember when we talked at breakfast?' she said. 'I've been thinking since... I can't pretend to be someone I'm not. It's not right for me or for you. You're not the settling down type and it was wrong of me to shackle you to me in this stupid game of pretend. I should've just accepted Myles's break-up with dignity instead of doing this crazy charade. It will hurt too many people if we let it continue. It has to stop.'

Jake wanted it to stop. Sure he did. But not yet. Not until he was satisfied his attraction to her had burned itself out. It was nowhere near burning out. It had only just started. They'd been lovers two days. *Two freaking days!* That wasn't long enough. He was only just starting to understand her. To know her. How could she want to end it? They were good together. Brilliant. The best. Why end it when they could have two more weeks, maybe even longer, of fantastic sex?

But how *much* longer?

The thought stood up from a sofa in the back of his mind where it had been lounging and stretched. Started walking toward his conscience...

Jake knew she was right. They had to end it some time. It was just he was usually the one to end flings. He was the one in the control seat. It felt a little weird to be on the receiving end of rejection. 'What about Emma Madden?' he said. 'Aren't you worried she might make a comeback when she hears we've broken up?'

'I think Emma is sensible enough to know you're not the right person for her. It will hurt her more if we tell even more lies.'

'What about Bruce Parnell?' *God, how pathetic was he getting? Using his clients as a lever to get her to rethink her decision?*

'Tell him the truth,' she said. 'That you're not in love with me and have no intention of marrying me or anyone.'

The truth always hurt, or so people said. But it didn't look like it hurt Jaz. She didn't seem to be the least bit worried he wasn't in love with her. She hadn't even asked him to declare his feelings, which was just as well, because they were stuffed under the cushions on that sofa in his mind and he wasn't going looking for them any time soon.

'You're right,' he said. 'Best to end it now before my parents start sending out invitations.'

She bit her lip for a moment. 'Will you tell them or will I?'

'I'll tell them I pulled the plug,' Jake said. 'That's what they'll think in any case.'

Her forehead puckered in a frown. 'But I don't want them to be angry with you or anything. I can say I got cold feet.'

'Leave it to me. Do you still want me to have a look over your business?'

'You wouldn't mind?'

'Why would I?' he said with a smile that was harder work than it had any right to be. 'We're friends, aren't we?'

Her smile was a little on the wobbly side but he could see relief in every nuance of her expression. 'Yes. Of course we are.'

It was on the tip of his tongue to ask for one more night but before he could get the words out she had turned and started packing her things. He watched her fold her clothes and pack them neatly into her bag. Every trace of her was being removed from the suite.

'I'm getting a lift back to London with one of the photographers,' she said once she was done. 'I thought it would be easier all round.'

'Is the photographer male?' The question jumped out before Jake could stop it and it had the big, green-eyed monster written all over it.

His question dangled in the silence for a long beat.

'Yes,' she said. 'But I've known him for years.'

Jaz had known *him* for years and look what had happened, Jake thought with a sickening churning in his gut.

She stepped up on tiptoe to kiss his cheek. 'Good-bye, Jake. See you at Julius's wedding.'

Wedding.

Jake clenched his jaw as the door closed on her exit. That word should be damned well banned.

CHAPTER TWELVE

JAZ WAS WORKING on Miranda's dress a few days later when the bell on the back of her shop door tinkled. She looked up and saw Emma Madden coming in, dressed in her school uniform. 'Hi, Emma,' she said, smiling as she put down the bodice she was sewing freshwater pearls on. 'How lovely to see you. How are you?'

Emma savaged her bottom lip with her teeth. 'Is it because of me?'

Jaz frowned. 'Is what because of you?'

'Your break-up with Jake,' she said. 'It's because of me, isn't it? I made such a stupid nuisance of myself and now you've broken up and it's all my fault.'

Jaz came out from behind the work counter and took the young girl's hands in hers. 'Nothing's your fault, sweetie. Jake and I decided we weren't ready to settle down. We've gone back to being friends.'

Emma's big, soulful eyes were misty. 'But you're so perfect for each other. I can't bear the thought of him having anyone else. You bring out the best in him. My stepdad says so too.'

Jaz gave Emma's hands a little squeeze before she

released them. 'It's sweet of you to say so but some things are not meant to be.'

'But aren't you...*devastated*?' Emma asked, scrunching up her face in a frown.

Jaz didn't want to distress the girl unnecessarily. No point telling Emma she cried every night when she got into her cold bed. *On. Her. Own.* No point saying how she couldn't get into a lift without her insides quivering in erotic memory. No point saying how every time she ate a piece of toast or drank orange juice she thought of Jake helping her through her fashion show nerves at the expo. 'I'm fine about it,' she said. 'Really. It's for the best.'

Emma sighed and then started looking at the dresses on display. She touched one reverently. 'Did you really make this from scratch?'

'Yup,' Jaz said. 'What do you think? Not too OTT?'

'No, it's beautiful,' Emma said. 'I would love to be able to design stuff like this.'

'Have you ever done any sewing?'

'I did some cross-stitch at school but I'd love to be able to make my own clothes,' Emma said. 'I sometimes get ideas for stuff... Does that happen to you?'

'All the time,' Jaz said. 'See that dress over there with the hoop skirt? I got the idea from the garden at Ravensdene. There's this gorgeous old weeping birch down there that looks exactly like a ball gown.'

Emma traced the leaf-like pattern of the lace. 'Wow... You're amazing. So talented. So smart and beautiful. So everything.'

So single, Jaz thought with a sharp pang. 'Hey, do

you fancy a part-time job after school or at weekends? I could do with a little help and I can give you some tips on pattern-making and stuff.'

Emma's face brightened as if someone had turned a bright light on inside her. 'Do you mean it? *Really?*'

'Sure,' Jaz said. 'Who wants to work for a fast-food chain when you can work for one of London's up-and-coming bridal designers?'

Take that, Imposter Syndrome.

Three weeks later...

'Jake, can I get you another beer?' Flynn Carlyon asked on his way to the bar at Julius's stag night. 'Hey, you haven't finished that one—you've barely taken a mouthful. You not feeling well or something?'

Jake forced a quick smile. 'No, I'm good.'

He wasn't good. He was sick. Not physically but emotionally. He hadn't eaten a proper meal in days. He couldn't remember the last time he'd had a decent sleep. Well, he could, but remembering the last time he'd made love with Jaz caused him even more emotional distress.

Yes, *emotional* distress.

The dreaded E-word—the word he'd been trying to escape from for the last few weeks. Maybe he'd been trying to escape it for the last seven years. He couldn't stop thinking about Jaz. He couldn't get the taste of her out of his mouth. He couldn't get the feel of her out of his body. It had been nothing short of torture to drop in the business plan for her last week and not touch her. She had seemed a little distracted, but when she told him she'd employed Emma Madden to help in the shop after school he'd put it down to that—Jaz was worried he would have a problem with it. He didn't. He thought it was a stroke of genius, actually. He wished he'd thought of it himself.

Julius came over with a basket of crisps. 'He's off his food, his drink and his game,' he said to Flynn. 'He hasn't looked twice at any of the waitresses, even the blonde one with the big boobs.'

Flynn grinned. 'No kidding?'

'I reckon it's because he's in love with Jaz,' Julius said. 'But he's too stubborn to admit it.'

Jake glowered at his twin. 'Just because you're getting married tomorrow doesn't mean everyone else wants to do the same.'

'Mum's still not speaking to him,' Julius said to Flynn. 'She quite fancied having Jaz as a daughter-in-law.'

'Pity she isn't so keen on having Kat Winwood as a daughter,' Flynn said wryly.

'So, how's all that going with you and Kat?' Jake said, desperate for a subject change. 'You convinced her to come to Dad's Sixty Years in Showbiz party yet?'

'Not so far but I'm working on it,' Flynn said with an enigmatic smile.

'Better get your skates on, mate,' Julius said. 'You've only got a month and a bit. The party's in January.'

'Leave Kat Winwood to me,' Flynn said. 'I know how to handle a feisty Scotswoman.'

'I bet you've handled a few in your time,' Jake said.

'You can talk,' Flynn said with another grin. 'How come you haven't handled anyone since Jaz?'

Good question. Why hadn't he? Because he couldn't bear to wipe out the memory of her touch with someone else. He didn't want anyone else. But Jaz wanted marriage and kids. He had never seen himself as a dad. He had always found it so...terrifying to be responsible for someone else. He was better off alone. Single and loving it, that was his credo.

Jake put his untouched beer bottle down. 'Excuse me,' he said. 'I'm going to have an early night. See you lot in church.'

'You look amazing, Holly,' Jaz said outside the church just before they were to enter for Julius and Holly's wedding. 'Doesn't she, Miranda?'

Miranda was wiping at her eyes with a tissue. 'Capital A amazing. Gosh, I've got to get control of myself. My make-up is running. If I'm like this as a bridesmaid, what I am going to be like as a bride?'

Holly smiled at both of them. She was a radiant bride, no two ways about that. But happiness did that to you, Jaz thought. There could be no happier couple than Julius and Holly... Well, there was Miranda and Leandro, who were also nauseatingly happy. It was downright painful to be surrounded by so many blissfully happy people.

But Jaz was resolved. She wasn't settling for anything but the real deal. Love without limits. That was what she wanted. Love that would last a lifetime.

Love that was authentic and real, not pretend.

As Jaz led the way down the aisle she saw Jake standing next to Julius. It was surreal to see them both dressed in tuxedos looking exactly the same. No one could tell them apart, except for the way Julius was looking at Holly coming behind Miranda. Had a man ever looked at a woman with such love? *Yes*, Jaz thought when she caught a glimpse of Leandro, who was standing next to Jake looking at Miranda as if she was the most adorable girl in the world. Which she was, but that was beside the point. It was so *hard* not to be jealous.

Why couldn't Jake look at her like that?

Jaz caught his eye. He was looking a little green about the gills. Her own stomach lurched. Her heart contracted. Had he hooked up with someone last night after Julius's stag night? Had he had a one-nighter with someone? Several someones? She hadn't heard anything much in the press about him since they had announced they'd ended their 'engagement'. But then she had been far too busy with getting Holly's dress done on time to be reading gossip columns.

Miranda had let slip that Jake had left the stag night early. Did that mean he had hooked up with someone? One of the barmaids at the wine bar the boys had gone to? Why else would he leave early? He was the party boy who was usually the last man standing. It didn't bear thinking about. It would only make the knot of jealousy tighten even more in the pit of her stomach. She had to put a brave face on. She couldn't let her feelings about Jake interfere with Julius and Holly's big day.

Jaz smiled at Elisabetta and Richard Ravensdale, who were sitting together and giving every appearance of being a solid couple, but that just showed what excellent actors they both were. Elisabetta had dressed the part, as she always did. She would have outshone the bride but Jaz had made sure Holly's dress was a show-stopper. Holly looked like a fairy-tale princess. Which was how it should be, as she'd had a pretty ghastly life up until she'd met Julius, which kind of made Jaz feel hopeful that dreams did come true… at least sometimes.

The service began and Jaz tried not to look at Jake too much. She didn't want people speculating or commenting on her single status. Or worse—pitying her. Would she ever be seen as anything other than the charity case? The gardener's daughter who'd made good only by the wonderful largesse of the Ravensdales?

Even the business plan Jake had drawn up for her was another example of how much she owed them. He wouldn't take a penny for his time. He hadn't stayed for a coffee or anything once he'd talked her through the plan. He hadn't even kissed her on the cheek or touched her in any way.

But looking at him now brought it all back. How much she missed him. How much she loved him. Why couldn't he love her?

Young Emma was right—they were perfect together. Jake made her feel safe. He watched out for her the way she longed for a partner to do. He stood up *to* her and stood up *for* her. How could she settle for anyone else? She would never be happy with anyone else. It wouldn't matter how many times she got engaged, no one would ever replace Jake. Nor would she want them to.

Jake was her soul mate because only with him could she truly be herself.

The vows were exchanged and for the first time in her life Jaz saw Julius blinking away tears. He was always so strong, steady and in charge of his emotions. He was the dependable twin. The one everyone went to when things were dire. Seeing him so happy made her chest feel tight. She wanted that same happiness for herself. She wanted it so badly it took her breath away to see others experiencing it.

Jake was still looking a little worse for wear. What was *wrong* with him? Didn't he have the decency to pull himself together for his brother's wedding? Or maybe it was the actual wedding that was making him look so white and pinched. He hated commitment. It had been bad enough at the wedding expo, although she had to admit he'd put on a good front. Maybe some of that Ravensdale acting talent had turned up in his genes after all. He could certainly do with some of it now. The very least he could do was look happy for his twin brother. He fumbled over handing Julius the wedding rings. He had to search in his pocket three times. But at least he had remembered to bring them.

Jaz decided to have a word with him while they were out with the bride and groom for the signing of the register. If she could put on a brave front, then so could he. He would spoil the wedding photos if he didn't get his act together. She wasn't going to let anyone ruin Julius and Holly's big day. No way.

Jake couldn't take his eyes off Jaz. She looked amazing in her bridesmaid dress. It was robin's-egg blue and the colour made her eyes pop and her creamy skin glow. How he wanted to touch that skin, to feel it against his own. His fingers ached; his whole body ached to pull her into his arms and kiss her, to show her how much he missed her. Missed what they'd had together.

Seeing his identical twin standing at the altar as his bride came towards him made Jake feel like he was seeing another version of himself. It was like seeing what he might have been. What he could *have* if he were a better man. A more settled man—a man who could be relied on; a man who could love, not just physically, but emotionally. A man who could commit to a woman because he could see no future without her by his side. A man who could be mature enough to raise a family and support them and his wife through everything that life threw at them.

That was the sort of man his twin was.

Why wasn't *he* like that?

Or was he like that in the part of his soul he didn't let anyone see? Apart from Jaz, of course. She had seen it. And commented on it.

Jake gave himself a mental shake. No wonder he hated weddings. They made him antsy. Restless.

Frightened.

For once he didn't shove the thought back where it came from. It wasn't going back in any case. It was front and centre in his brain. He *was* frightened. Frightened he wouldn't be good enough. Frightened he would love and not be loved in return. Frightened of feeling so deeply for someone, allowing someone to have control over him, of making himself vulnerable in case they took it upon themselves to leave.

He loved Jaz.

Hadn't he always loved her? Firstly as a surrogate sister and then, when she'd morphed into the gorgeous teenager with those bedroom eyes, he had been knocked sideways. But she had been too young and he hadn't been ready to admit he needed someone the way he needed her.

But he was an adult now. He'd had a taste of what they could be together—a solid team who complemented each other perfectly. She was his equal. He admired her tenacity, her drive, her passion, her talent. She was everything he wanted in a partner.

Wasn't that why he'd been carrying the engagement ring she had given back to him everywhere he went? It was like a talisman. The ring of truth. He loved Jaz and always would.

How could he have thought he could be happy without her? He had been nothing short of morose since they'd ended their fling. He was the physical embodiment of a wet weekend: gloomy, miserable, boring as hell. He had been dragging himself through each day. He hadn't dated. He hadn't even looked at anyone. He couldn't bear the thought of going through the old routine of chatting some woman up only so he could have sex with her. He was tired of no-strings sex. No-strings sex was boring. He wanted emotional sex, the sort of sex that spoke to his soul, the kind of sex that made him feel alive and fulfilled as a man.

He had to talk to Jaz. He had to get her alone. How long was this wretched service going to take? Oh, they were going to sign the wedding register. Great. He might be able to nudge Jaz to one side so he could tell her the words he had told no one before.

Jaz wasted no time in sidling up to Jake when Julius and Holly were occupied with signing the register. 'What is *wrong* with you?' she said in an undertone.

'I have to talk to you,' he said, pulling at his bow tie as if it were choking him.

She rolled her eyes. 'Look, I know this is torture for you, but can you just allow your brother his big day without drawing attention to yourself? It's just a bow tie, for pity's sake.'

He took her by the hand, his eyes looking suspiciously moist. Did he have an allergy? There were certainly a lot of flowers about. But then the service had been pretty emotional. Maybe it was a twin thing. If Julius cried, Jake would too, although she had never seen it before.

'I love you,' he said.

Jaz's eyelashes flickered at him in shock. *'What?'*

His midnight-blue eyes looked so amazingly soft she had to remind herself it was actually Jake looking at her, not Julius looking at Holly. 'Not just as a friend,' he said. 'And not just as a lover, but as a life partner. Marry me, Jaz. Please?'

Jaz's heart bumped against her breastbone. 'You can't ask me to marry you in the middle of your brother's wedding!'

He grinned. 'I just did. What do you say?'

She gazed at him, wondering if wedding fever had got to her so bad she was hallucinating. Was he really telling her he loved her and wanted to marry her? Was he really looking at her as if she was the only woman in the world who could ever make him completely happy? 'You're not doing this as some sort of joke, are you?' she asked, narrowing her eyes in suspicion. It would be just like him to want to have a laugh to counter all the emotion, to tone down all the seriousness, responsibility and formality.

He gripped her by the hands, almost crushing her bridesmaid's bouquet in the process. 'It's no joke,' he said. 'I love you and want to spend the rest of my life proving it to you. The last three weeks have been awful without you. You're all I think about. I'm like a lovesick teenager. I can't get you out of my head. As soon as I saw you walking down the aisle, I realised I couldn't let another day—another minute—go by without telling you how I feel. I want to be with you. Only you. Marry me, my darling girl.'

Jaz was still not sure she could believe what she was hearing. And nor, apparently, could the bridal party as they had stalled in the process of signing the register to watch on with beaming faces. 'But what about kids?' she said.

'I love kids. I'm a big kid myself. Remember how great I was with you and Miranda when you were kids? I reckon I'll be a great dad. How many do you want?'

Jaz remembered all too well. He had been fantastic with her and Miranda, making them laugh until their sides had ached. It was her dream coming to life in front of her eyes. Jake wanted to marry her and he wanted to have babies with her. 'Two at least,' she said.

He pulled her closer, smiling at her with twinkling eyes. 'I should warn you that twins run in my family.'

Jaz smiled back. 'I'll take the risk.'

'So you'll marry me?'

Could a heart burst with happiness? Jaz wondered. It certainly felt like hers was going to. But, even better, it looked like Jake was feeling exactly the same way. 'Yes.'

Jake bent his head to kiss her mouth with such heart-warming tenderness it made Jaz's eyes tear up. When he finally lifted his head, she saw similar moisture in his eyes. 'I was making myself sick with worry you might say no,' he said.

She stroked his jaw with a gentle hand, her heart now feeling so full it was making it hard for her to breathe. 'You're not an easy person to say no to.'

He brushed her cheek with his fingers as if to test she was real and not a figment of his imagination. 'How quickly can you whip up a wedding dress?'

She looked at him in delighted surprise. 'You want to get married sooner rather than later?'

He pressed a kiss to her forehead, each of her eyelids, both of her cheeks and the tip of her nose. 'Yes,' he said. 'As soon as it can be arranged. I don't even mind if it's in church or a garden, on the top of Big Ben or twenty leagues under the sea. I won't be happy until I can officially call you my wife.'

'Ahem.' Julius spoke from behind them. 'We're the ones trying to get married here.'

Jake turned to grin at his brother. 'We should've made it a double wedding.'

Julius smiled from ear to ear. 'Congratulations to both of you. Nothing could have made my and Holly's day more special than this.'

Miranda was dabbing at her eyes as she came rushing over to give Jaz a bone- and bouquet-crushing hug. 'I'm so happy for you. We're finally going to be sisters. Yay!'

Jaz blinked back tears as she saw Leandro looking at Miranda just the way Jake was looking at her—with love that knew no bounds. With love that would last a lifetime.

She turned back to Jake. 'Do you still have that engagement ring?'

Jake reached into his inside jacket pocket, his eyes gleaming. 'I almost gave it to Julius instead of the wedding rings.' He took it out and slipped it on her finger. 'There. That's got to stay there now. No taking it off. Ever. Understood?'

Jaz wrapped her arms around his waist and smiled up at him in blissful joy. 'I'm going to keep it on for ever.'

* * * * *

LET'S TALK
Romance

For exclusive extracts, competitions
and special offers, find us online:

- facebook.com/millsandboon
- @MillsandBoon
- @MillsandBoonUK

Get in touch on 01413 063232

For all the latest titles coming soon, visit
millsandboon.co.uk/nextmonth